THE FACE OF TERROR

He had hoisted himself up on the pillows as if he had been drawing himself up to ward off something—something in his sleep. He was on his side, with one arm under him and the other stretched out and hanging down toward the floor. And his face—his face—his face had a look of fright, of terror, of rage—so many things. He looked—and this is exactly how he looked—like a man looking at something he couldn't bear to see . . . like a man who had been frightened to death. . . .

"No one writes medical mystery better than Livingston. . . . If he were a drink, he'd be Jack Daniels."

—S.F.X. Dean

THE
NIGHTMARE
FILE

by
Jack Livingston

AN ONYX BOOK

NEW AMERICAN LIBRARY

To my wife, Juno Myers

1

I could make out that Edna was putting down the phone as I came into the office, but I couldn't see what she was saying to me because my eyes were filled with tears. They weren't tears of rage, grief, joy, or indignation. They were tears that are generally deemed inexcusable in the male—tears of pain. Of course, they may have been a straightforward reaction of the nerves around the tear ducts, and the pain might have been incidental. I was not in shape to analyze why I was crying, nearly blinded. The tendrils of useless nerve ends in my right ear were inflamed, and were sending white hot lancets into the depths of my skull, slicing across the backs of my eyeballs and shooting down the line of my manly jaw.

I blotted my eyes with a handkerchief and was able to see Edna repeat, "Do you know a lady named . . . ?"

She stopped when she saw my face. "Call Dr. Beaman," I croaked, "and tell him it's an emergency. My ear is killing me." I stumbled through the door to my office and sank into the chair behind my desk, where I held my fragmenting head in my hands.

Edna was back in what was probably five minutes, but which seemed like a century. She was carrying a steaming mug of black coffee. I surprised her by not drinking it. Instead, I held it up against my ear. It burned, but it felt good. I looked up to watch Edna say, "Eleven o'clock at Dr. Beaman's office. Is that

quick enough? If not, he says you can go down to the
emergency room. . . ."

"No, no," I interrupted. "I can hang on." I looked
at my watch and realized that my eyes had cleared. It
was nine-twenty in the morning. The heat of the coffee had seeped into the zones of my tormented ear.
The aspirins I had taken earlier rattled against the pit
of my stomach, like marbles tossed on a dance floor.

Edna said, "Joe—can you talk at all?"

I nodded reluctantly. "We can try."

"There is this woman called up just before you
came in. Do you know some woman named Evalina?"

I thought about it while the coffee cooled next to
my ear. When it seemed no longer to penetrate, I
drank it and held out the cup to Edna for more. "No,"
I said.

She disappeared with the cup while I tried not to
grind my teeth. When she came back with the next
cup of heat, she was saying, "Well, this woman, Evalina,
seemed to know who you were and all. But she was
hysterical and very hard to understand. She said her
husband had died—just died."

"She wants the morgue," I said uncharitably.

Edna's pretty face expressed dismay and bewilder-
ment. Her green eyes clouded up under the white,
unwrinkled brow framed by honey-gold hair. "This
woman, this Evalina, didn't even leave a number to
call back. She kept saying, 'He knows the number.' I
got the idea it was some kind of list of yours, some
kind of listing she was talking about. But she was
sobbing and choking, and I could hardly understand
anything."

"I don't have a list of ladies," I told Edna. "I
certainly don't have a list of married ladies, and particularly a list of married ladies whose husbands have
just died." This didn't come out as trippingly as it
sounds. It was grumbled haltingly. The heat from the
coffee mug continued to dissolve the lancinating focus
of pain. I asked sullenly, "How did he die, this husband of hers?"

"She didn't say. She just kept repeating, sobbing,
'He's dead. He's dead. He can't be dead.' "

Again, I considered putting the heat inside me, where it could warm the soft tissue up alongside my eustachian tube, or what is left of it. I took a sip and tilted my head to the right, something like the way a canary drinks. After I'd swallowed the coffee, I said to Edna, "It sounds like a case of rooty-toot-toot to me." When she looked blank, I added with a simpering expression, *"I didn't know the gun was loaded! There was this little old gun he brought home from the war and I was just waving it at him, kidding like!"*

Edna began, "I don't think . . ."

"Or maybe it was," I rode over her expression, *"I really don't understand it! I was just cutting some chops off the loin of pork and when hubby came up behind me and put his hands on me I just whirled around with the cleaver that came with the nice carving set Uncle Henry gave us and let him have it right between the baby blues!"*

"I didn't get," Edna began again, dismayed, "the impression that she had . . . uh . . . murdered him."

"Housewives can be deceptive," I observed.

As Edna began to remonstrate, a flaming poniard stabbed through my ear again and filled my eyes with more unmanly tears. Edna took the cup from my blind hand and left to refill it. I went through the routine once more of warming the outside, and then the inside. This time I used the coffee to bounce a few more aspirin off my belly. I also took out my trusty Zippo lighter and torched off a cigarette, not only to calm my screeching nerves, but in the hope that the cigarette smoke would anesthetize the nerve ends in my throat.

When I could speak again, I said, "All right. Obviously you don't think it was a case of premenstrual tension."

Edna expostulated, "God but you're nasty—uncaring and unfeeling."

"I am also unmarried and unmurdered."

"She didn't say he was murdered," Edna declared. And then doubt entered those gorgeous green eyes.

"Well, did she or didn't she?" I asked with a rare show of patience.

"She was hysterical," Edna repeated hesitantly. "She

started by saying, 'My name is Evalina,' and then she'd begin crying and sobbing and saying, 'He's dead. He's dead. He can't be dead. Tell Joe to come right away. We need him. I need him. Evalina.' And then she started to cry so I couldn't tell if she was crying or babbling. She was saying, 'In his sleep. In his sleep. I can't believe it. I don't believe it.' And then she cried some more and said, I thought she said, something about being on a list or a listing."

The penny dropped.

"Listing," I repeated. "But he calls her Evie, not Evvie. The corners of his mouth go back like this." I demonstrated the lip difference between Evie and Evvie. "But her name could be Evalina, and the last name is Listing, if it's who I think it is."

Edna's lovely bosom heaved with satisfaction. "Then you do know—you know—her husband?"

"Gene Listing, yeah." I was feeling the odd, incompatible assortment of sensations following the news of an acquaintance dying. "Gene Listing," I said again, staring over Edna's head and into a screen of memories. My voice, then, must have sounded rough and violent, because Edna jumped. "How did she say he died?"

"In his sleep?" Edna's expression was more question than statement.

"Impossible," I answered, slapping the desk. "I don't believe it."

2

I believed it even less sitting in Dr. Beaman's waiting room. I kept glancing up at the receptionist (a new one—there was always a new one), who would mouth reassuringly, "The doctor will be with you soon." I let my gaze wander over the other patients scattered about the room, some with dark glasses to hide the black eyes of nose operations, some nervously stretching their necks and feeling their throats, two with huge wads of cotton sticking out of their ears. And then there was the empty chair directly across from mine. It was the chair Gene Listing had been sitting in the first time I saw him.

It was a bit much that the chair should be empty. At times while I was regarding it suspiciously the pain would shoot through my face and fill my eyes with tears again, so that the chair shimmered with a silvery halo in the antiseptic light. This, too, was suspiciously coincidental, because my first impression of Gene had been one of diffused silveriness, the kind of diffusion you see on the patina of old, worn silver. It was his blond hair, shot with gray, that started the impression. It picked up the light and scattered it over his head. His face was very pale; I didn't know at the time that this was not his natural complexion. He wore a gray pinstripe suit that was beautifully cut but so old that it glittered. His black oxfords were ancient and creased with wear, but they shone with a dazzling polish. He kept stretching his neck, as if his shirt collar was uncomfortable, but the old, well-fitting broadcloth collar didn't look tight around his throat to me. The stretching was a tic.

He reached into his shirt pocket, stayed his hand, and then glanced up at the big domineering sign—NO SMOKING—and grimaced. He took a pack of Pall Malls from his pocket and was instantly speared by an outraged glance from the receptionist (an old dragon, she was, I remembered). He examined the scarlet package and found it empty. His eyes widened in frustration.

Because smoking is such a suggestive, contagious thing, I had immediately reached for *my* cigarettes and brought forth a full pack of Lucky Strikes. The silvery man eyed me hungrily. His eyebrows rose in a tacit question, and I nodded. We both got up. "We're going out into the hall for a smoke," I told the dragon. She looked as if I had made an obscene proposition. "You'll let us know when Dr. Beaman's ready, won't you?" She was about to object, but we both turned sharply away and headed for the hallway door.

In the hallway I offered him a cigarette, and we both lit up with a small gold lighter he produced. It, too, looked very old, but serviceable for another century. He said to me, "You having trouble with your throat too?"

"No," I answered, rather stupidly surprised—Dr. Beaman is, after all, an otolaryngologist—"I'm just here for my regular checkup. I get ear problems."

"Oh," he said. We were both nervous strangers, made more nervous by the aura of the waiting room. He seemed to feel the need to explain himself. "It was just that when you spoke to the receptionist . . ."

"My voice, you mean. It always sounds like that—whatever that is. I can't hear it and so I really can't control it. I'm deaf."

He absorbed this over a long drag on the cigarette. "So you read lips?"

"That's right." He nodded his appreciation of the fact, but there didn't really seem to be anything more for either of us to say. We smoked in silence, his thoughtful and mine perpetual. My silence, however, is broken by the clanks and bangs of the machinery noise that goes on more or less continually in my head. We finished our cigarettes, dumped them in the sandpit by the door, and returned to our chairs inside. The nicotine, I noticed, had put some color in his cheeks.

He looked even better departing the doctor's office. His color was normal, his eyes were bright and his step sprightly as he strode past me and dropped a courteous nod in my direction. I forgot all about him as I went into Dr. Beaman for an inspection of the roaring wilderness that lies on the nether side of my skull.

I felt a tap on my shoulder and realized that the scene was going to be repeated, except for the empty chair. I had been staring at it so intently that the receptionist hadn't been able to attract my attention.

Beaman came into the examining room, where I had been placed, and was full of detestable health and heartiness. I watched him warily while he decided to bawl me out. "I thought I told you to come in at the first sign of a cold," he said. "If you wait until it's in full bloom, there's always hell to pay."

"Nobody sent me a telegram," I answered bitterly. "I woke up this way this morning. I'm sorry to trouble you."

"Don't get smart with me, Binney," he appeared to growl. He glanced at the jottings the nurse had made, blood pressure, etc., and delicately held my wrist. "Low-grade fever," he muttered, "and pulse to go with it. And you haven't had any symptoms?"

"So help me," I swore. "I just woke up this morning with this crowbar going through my head." Beaman prepared an otoscope and took a perfunctory look at my ear. I knew it was preliminary, perhaps only to see if he could discern light at the other end.

"Take off your shirt," he demanded, and when I began to comply, he noticed my shirt pocket and sneered, "Still smoking, eh? Afraid the undertakers will starve?" I ground my teeth, took off my shirt, and let him play with his stethoscope. He satisfied himself that my heart was not on vacation and that my lungs were reasonably clear. "No worse than they ever sound," he grumbled, "although I wish you'd quit those Goddamned cigarettes." I had no wisecrack to defend me from this, and clenched my jaw.

Beaman had me lie on my side while he looked in my ear again. Then he picked up a swab and began taking samples of gook from inside my ear. He was very tender, cautious, and delicate, as always. One of the swabs he put in a small plastic box, the other he put into a complicated-looking bottle. He got me sitting upright again and asked me, "You having any trouble with your eyes?"

"They're tearing a lot," I admitted.

"With your vision?" I shook my head. "How many fingers?" he demanded, holding up his index finger. When I gave him the appropriate answer, he held up three fingers. I said, "Three fingers," and inquired irritably, "Is this an IQ test?"

"On your side, Binney," he ordered me. I obliged him and waited there until I could feel the warm drops he dispensed into my ear, which he then plugged up with cotton. He tugged me upright and said, "Put your shirt back on and come into my office."

When I went in he was seated at his desk, writing something on the record he keeps in my permanent folder. I watched him scribble contentedly away for a while and asked him, "Do you remember a patient of yours named Gene Listing?" He shook his head without looking up. Scribble, scribble. I added hopefully, "A blond-gray middle-aged guy. Had some trouble with his throat. A cancer scare. Talked like a diplomat. Worked for a magazine. Old but expensive clothes. Smoked a lot until he quit."

Beaman finished whatever he was writing and closed the folder. "Listing," he said to me. "Pharyngeal leukoplakia. Tonsillar node, benign. No problem. Quit smoking because I told him he had to."

The fact that my ear had quit stabbing my brains permitted me a superior smile. "Right man, wrong conclusion," I told Beaman. "That isn't why he quit."

If there's one thing a doctor can't stand, it's a superior smile. Beaman scowled at me and said, "What's the story?"

"I heard this morning that he's dead."

"He started smoking again?"

"No. As far as anybody could tell, he was the picture of health. But he died in his sleep."

"That's always possible."

"Sure. But do you believe it?"

"What's to believe?" He pursed his lips. "An MI—a myocardial infarction can happen any time. You walk out of the cardiologist's office with a clean bill of health and, bingo, over you go. Always embarrassing for the cardiologist, of course, but they've gotten used to it."

"Is it really all that common?"

"No. Of course not. Doctors like to talk about it because it's dramatic. But like most dramatic things, it's quite rare. Any opinion on what happened? Death certificate?"

"Not that I know of. His wife called me this morning and asked me to come over and see her."

"Really? Were you that good friends with him?"

"I think she wants me in a professional capacity. I'd only met her twice. I can't see any other reason."

"Well," he advised me, "try to gentle her down. These things are hard to accept. There're always a lot of crazy theories, guilt, paranoia, accusations." He looked at me with a glint of compassion. "You're in for a rough afternoon."

I offered, "Maybe she thinks it was suicide."

Beaman nodded. "She might have something there. The last time Listing was here he was the most miserable, nastiest son of a bitch who ever sat in that chair."

"Any idea why?" I asked him. There might have been a cutting edge to my voice. Beaman came near to blushing. He pursed his lips and pulled his prescription pad in front of him. "Something to do with quitting smoking, I guess," he seemed to mumble.

"You guess?"

Beaman completed two prescriptions. Then he sat back in his chair and looked at me, "I'm an otolaryngologist," he declared. "And that's where my competence ends. I told Listing the last time I saw him that I thought he needed counseling. He told me that he was already getting counseling, although the way he described it did no credit to the procedure." Beaman reflected on this for a moment and then looked up questioningly. He said, "You mentioned something about a wrong conclusion."

"Yes," I explained. "He didn't quit smoking because you told him to. He quit because he thought he would lose his job if he didn't. As it turned out, quitting itself almost made him lose his job, or, maybe, finally, it actually did."

"His job was more important than his health?"

"Isn't it always?"

Beaman said, "If he talked to his boss the way he talked to me, I'm not surprised that he lost his job. Of course, I'm only a poor schlemiel of a physician . . ."

"I didn't say he actually lost it," I interrupted.

But Beaman was unheeding. "Came in here, sneering at me—'Any more little spots, Doc?'—I hate being called doc—'Any more scare symptoms to swell the old pocketbook?'—I asked him, 'If you're feeling so Goddamned healthy, how come you're here?' And he said, 'Got to go by the numbers, now, Doc. Get everything certified and accounted for—color of urine, number of bowel movements, quality of erections, brightness of eye. Got to have the medical records on tap if you want to get ahead these days. Need a clean bill of health.' "

"And did he get one?"

"Sure. He was as clear as a bell. Cleared up the minute he stopped smoking. There was no real problem, anyway."

"Then why did you tell him to quit?"

"Everybody should quit smoking," said Beaman with a pious expression on his dark, intelligent face. "And a lot of them need a kick in the ass to do it. Scare tactics. Any physician worth his salt would do it."

I began to huff up to start an argument, but he said, "I haven't got time to sit around arguing preventive medicine with you." He handed me the first prescription. "These are the eardrops, part analgesic, part antibiotic. A few drops every three or four hours. Warm them up, a little above body temperature, but not too much or you'll ruin the antibiotic. Be sure to put the cotton back in your ear."

He handed me another prescription. "This is a straight course of antibiotics. See if we can get the bug systemically if we don't get it locally. Be sure you take 'em on schedule, and be sure you take every one of them—the full course, understand?—because if you don't take the full course, you change the bugs, and then nobody knows what in the hell he's doing."

I nodded, although it was hard to see the end of his admonition. The dagger had entered the side of my skull again, and the tears flowed. Hazily, I saw him reach for his prescription pad. I blotted my eyes. When I could see again, he was handing me a prescription and saying, "This is codeine. You'd better have some around in case the drops don't do the trick."

I said, "I hate codeine."

He looked exasperated. "Get it anyway. It's all we can do short of hospitalization. Just hang on to it. You don't have to take it." He picked up another pad. "Hand this appointment slip to the receptionist on the way out. I'm putting this culture on rush, so I want you back here Friday at noon." He handed me the slip. "Be here," he threatened me, "no matter what. If it's all cleared up by then, fine. I'll check it out. But be here."

I stood up, preparatory to leaving, but Beaman stopped me. "Joe," he said, "what was all that crap Listing was giving me about medical records and all that malarkey?"

"The outfit he worked for," I told Beaman, "went on a health kick. No smoking in the office—any office. All the upper echelon were signed up to a cardiac clinic. It was supposed to be a benefit. Exercise was prescribed and monitored—you know, exercycles, handball, what have you. Gene's promotion, ultimately, I think, his job, depended on entering this program. He hated it. It wasn't what he'd signed on for when he took the job. It put him in a bind. He hated exercise. He hated gyms. He hated locker rooms and all the bullshit that goes on in locker rooms. He hated jock sniffing. Smoking cigarettes was the one bad habit he had. He drank, but he wasn't a lush, at least not until he quit smoking. He didn't chase the girls or go out for nooners with a typist. He didn't toot coke, and he didn't take tranks. He did his work and expected to succeed on his merits. They threw him a curve. He was a decent, reasonably healthy, intelligent, good-natured man—right up until the day he quit smoking. They kicked that crutch out from under him and he went on his ass. What did they expect?"

"I see," said Dr. Beaman, "I see." He looked down at the top of his desk as if it were a screen that would show him the whole flickering scenario.

I was about to depart with my appointment slip when he looked up from the desk. "The last time Listing was here," he said, "he called me a 'nigger taster.' He said to me, 'Just write it up for me, Doc, so it shows I'm clean, and I'll put it in with the records of all the other nigger tasters.'" Beaman's face was paler. "I don't know what he meant. Do you?"

"The last time I saw him," I answered, "which was probably later the same day you saw him, I ran into him at Henry's—you know the place. He was almost unrecognizable"—Beaman nodded a sad assent—"crazy as hell, fat and drunk. They finally threw us out of the place, and I had to take him home.

"He had been roaring and babbling about doctors and 'nigger tasters.' I didn't know what they were, either, but it turns out they were bright-eyed little guys who went around to the slave auctions through the South. They had the knack of telling which of the slaves would be a steady, valuable worker, and which had some kind of chronic disease that would make him fall down on the job.

"They made the decision by tasting the sweat of the slave while he was up on the block. They'd come up and taste his sweat—lick the skin—and smell him. Sick people smell differently, I guess, and I suppose they taste different too." Beaman nodded. "So the nigger taster would tell the bidder whether the slave was a good buy or not. It was a kind of personal way of kicking the tires."

Beaman, still leaning on the edge of his desk, looked

up at me. His face was just a bit paler. "Wonderful," he said. "That's just wonderful." His eyes, looking a bit trapped, bored into mine. He roused himself. "Be here on Friday," he said. "Noon." He stared over my shoulder.

I left him that way and took my appointment slip out to the woman in the waiting room.

3

After picking up my prescriptions, I headed, as if by autopilot, for Henry's East Side Restaurant, my habitual stop after seeing the doctor. Henry's is a spacious establishment designed to absorb and expel the lunchtime crowd with speed and dispatch. The restaurant section is a large dining room adjacent to the bar with a curving stairway leading to an even larger dining room below. No restaurant ever got the benefit of an overflow from Henry's. The bar room, itself, is well equipped with padded booths that range along the wall and then march in a separate island down the center of the room.

There aren't many places left like Henry's, a remnant of the forties, when *cocktail lounge* meant deeply padded leather, soft lights, thick carpets, and intimate conversation. The atmosphere is an echo of the fabulous nightclubs whose names now ring like species from a text on paleontology—Reubens, The Stork Club, The Copacabana. Henry had put a lot of money into the place and had never seen any reason to change. The motif is vaguely African in black and silver, shaded just this side of Art Deco. The bar itself, designed to hold a large and busy crowd, is a long serpentine affair that tends to divide the barflies into separate groups. It is heavily padded on the edge to save overenthusiastic imbibers from fracturing their skulls on the way down.

As in Beaman's office, I was assailed again by the

ghost of Gene Listing. There weren't many other patrons at this hour to crowd him out or obscure the
specter of him as he had been, at our first encounter
here, standing down near the end of the wavy bar. I
hadn't noticed him immediately, then, stepping up, as
I was this instant, to the center of the bar and ordering
a bourbon and soda. It was after I had finished that
drink and found another appearing in front of me that
I'd become aware of him. Looking inquiringly down
toward the end of the bar, I'd seen the stranger from
Beaman's office, who smiled and lifted his glass. I
saluted back, and then went down to join him and
thank him.

"What's the occasion?" I'd asked him.

It was pretty obvious that he'd taken a few aboard
by the time I'd arrived. "Two things," he said. "Your
cigarette saved my life, or at least my sanity. The
second is that I've been given a reprieve. The office
will see no more of me this day."

That wasn't as drastic as it sounds. The hour was
deep into the afternoon that day, and the lunchtime
crowd had all departed, save two drunks down at the
other end of the bar. They were separate, silent, and
sodden. "Reprieve?" I asked him gently.

"Cancer scare," he said, and finished off his drink,
a martini. "The middle-aged driver's license, without
which no one is truly a citizen." He waved the bartender down. "I am going to get hugely and satisfactorily blotto," he told me. "Care to come along?"

I put my hand over my glass. "Even when I was a
kid," I told him, "I learned not to try to play catch-up."

"Perfectly right," he said. He tossed down the olive
and stuck out his hand. "My name's Gene Listing."

"Joe Binney."

I waited for the story. "I went in for a sore throat,"
he said, "and they found a wart on my tonsils. Well,
you know the routine. It's the end of the world. They're
going to rip out your throat and teach you to talk
through your rectum. The biopsy. The waiting. And
then—the big favor. You don't have cancer—as if
they've personally done you a favor. And then the
finger shaking—you know? *We've let you off this time,*

not that you deserve it.' You deserve to have cancer, it seems, because you've been a naughty boy and smoked cigarettes behind the barn. Dare I say it? They seem almost regretful that you don't have cancer. They're reluctant to let you go. Have you noticed? There's the implied threat, *'We'll get you yet, you bastard.'* "

It made me grin. "You're shook," I told him.

"You're Goddamned right I'm shook."

Now, I tried to reconstitute the image of him as he had taken a sip of the fresh martini, set it down, and headed for the men's room at the bottom of the curving staircase. Walking away from me, I saw a fairly tall middle-aged man who had the roundness and softness apparent in most fifty-year-old men who are anchored to a sedentary job. When he returned I took a good look at his face. It was fleshy and deeply carved, without being gross. His eyes, peering out from almost invisible blond eyebrows, were a pale, faded blue that disguised their sharpness until they were quite near. Looking at him close up was something of a shock, because the pale blue eyes had sharp black pupils that bored into what they were looking at. They betrayed the smiling geniality.

The bartender handed me my first drink of this day—an early one to be sure—and with the first cooling sip I became aware that the pain in my ear had diminished. It was replaced with a dull ache and the sensation of swelling, pressing inward. I knew that it was foolish to drink with a fever and an infection, but the doctor's office, with its associations of pain, anxiety, and, sometimes, despair, had always served as a launching pad for my flight to the security of a peaceful, reassuring bar. I decided that I would have just one more before going off to deal with Evie Listing.

When Gene had come back from the men's room, he'd polished off his martini and ordered another. This time I accepted a refill. That led to my quite properly buying a round, and then his buying back, after which I had insisted on buying another round. The celebration of his reprieve was irresistible. Guarded against the dangers of the outside world by the dark, padded depths of the bar, we drank and talked and smoked. To a passerby, I suppose, we appeared to be just what we were, two middle-aged men well sunk in the vices and follies of the world, embarked on an endless round of reminiscence.

The yield of all this reminiscence was that Gene Listing was a senior editor on a business magazine, a large and important one that supplied international coverage as well as domestic. He held down the foreign affairs desk, a position that put him in line for the political affairs desk, which covered both national and international politics. He felt that he was fully qualified for it, had earned it, and should succeed to it when the present political editor, whom he liked, retired.

For my part, the yield was brutally simple. Gene was delighted to learn that I was a private investigator, declaring that he had never met one before, and that he had suspected we were a legend, like trolls. He listened with a deceptively offhand intelligence in those pale blue eyes while I described my loss of hearing in underwater demolition when I was a kid in the navy, my subsequent drift into free-lance bookkeeping, and finally, the PI dodge. We were ordering up my fifth bourbon by then, and looking at him over the rim of it, I realized that he could, despite the formidable number of martinis he had downed, quite probably quote the whole story back to me days later. I mentioned this to him and supposed aloud that this was what journalistic training meant.

"Training?" he repeated, smiling. "I never had any journalistic training beyond what I picked up on the job. I drifted into this the same way you drifted into investigating. As a matter of fact, it's not all that different—putting bits and pieces together."

Not quite. It developed that he had been an all-but-thesis candidate for a Ph.D. in Asian Studies out of Johns Hopkins, but had inherited some money and so lurched off on a grand tour to see a world he had heretofore only read about. (I, on the other hand, had felt lucky to secure my high-school diploma one week before I joined the navy.) That, at least, was Gene's story as it came across the bar. "Money was my ruination," he said, laughing. But behind the sharp blue eyes I sensed a distancing from something, some phantom, some event that was extremely painful to him.

I probed gently. "What were you going to do with the doctorate, teach?"

"No, no." He shook his big blond head. "Government was our game. My family went into government the way the Chinese used to go into laundries. I was slated for the foreign service, a career officer in the foreign service, ultimately, what you would call a diplomat. That all went to hell in the *wanderjahre.*"

"Just like that?"

He seemed on the verge of opening up about it, but it was a demonstration of his ability to hold his liquor that he did not. He had begun to speak, but turned it into a chuckle and then a laugh. "Maybe it was just as well," he said. "You can become a statesman, but on the other hand, there's always the possibility of turning into what Napoleon called Talleyrand: a silk stocking—"

I interrupted inadvertently, as I often do, because I can't hear the concluding drop of a sentence. "A silk stocking," I said. "Is that so bad?"

"Wait for it," Listing admonished me. "What Napoleon called Talleyrand was 'a silk stocking—full of shit.' "

Listing's *wanderjahre* had taken him all over the world until—"I slapped up in Stuttgart, of all places, broke, failed, and essentially futureless. That's when I met the Brat."

"The brat?"

Listing was downing what I recognized would be his last martini at Henry's on this day. The intake of alcohol on both sides was beginning to make my lip reading a hazardous affair.

"Evie, my wife, an Army brat in Stuttgart. Her old man was a chicken colonel bucking for a star in NATO. He turned out to be reasonably human later on, but I've seen stray dogs treated with more courtesy than he showed to me at that time and in that place. Nonetheless, we got married, Evie and I, and beyond having me summarily executed, which I'm sure he thought of, there was very little he could do about it."

Just speaking the name, Evie, seemed to charge him with a mission. He looked at me and said, "I trust you don't have any miscreants to track down this evening?" When I signified a blank assent, he excused himself and went to the pay telephone downstairs.

If only he hadn't stumbled on the top step coming back, precariously wavering there as if to plunge down the long curving staircase, but righting himself finally, I wouldn't have accepted his invitation to dinner. I want no part of irate wives presented with drunken husbands. But Gene Listing was suddenly of that special drunkenness that has been supercharged with emotion (his reprieve). I didn't think it would be fair to turn him loose on the town. So, with dread, I accompanied him to a cab, got us both accepted, and headed for the Upper West Side.

Meeting Mrs. Listing, Evie, the Brat, at the door to their fifth-floor apartment, with Gene Listing more or less hanging on my shoulder, was not at all what I had expected. She was experienced, gentle, wryly amused, and nice. It wasn't until we were both inside and seated that I realized he must, of course, have told her the good news over the phone. It was a reprieve for both of them.

I was to see Evie once more after that, I reflected, emptying my drink and setting it back on the bar, under much uglier circumstances. I shuddered to think how I would find her now. I toyed with the idea of one more drink, but it simply didn't seem right to get bombed on this occasion—at least, not at Henry's.

I squared myself away, touched the cotton tuft in my ear, and headed for the Listing apartment.

4

I took the elevator up to Evie's apartment and shared the small space with the two ghosts of Gene Listing. Both ghosts were drunk, but one was smiling and the other was scowling.

Evie opened the door almost instantly at my ring and laid her hand on my arm. "Oh, Joe," she said. "Thank you. Thank you for coming." She pulled me inside.

Evie was a small, trim woman in her early forties, whose brown hair showed streaks of gray. She had the elegant bones of a good figure, and the outline had not deserted her. The structure was not discernible in her face now, however, because it was puffy with weeping. Her mouth was a thin slash, although I remembered it as full and breaking easily into laughter. She was wearing brown, shapeless cotton slacks and a blue jersey. Her feet were shod in carpet slippers. There was no makeup on her face.

Still holding my arm, she towed me toward the couch, but then she suddenly stopped and changed her course to head for the easy chair. She stopped there, too, and finally led me to a comfortable occasional chair. She put both hands on my shoulders as if to press me down into it. I sat. "Let me get you something," she said. "What would you like? A drink? Coffee?"

"Coffee would be fine," I answered warily. Evie

made very good coffee. Further, it would give her something to do. She was ticking like a bomb. I did not want to get us involved in drinking. She went out of the room toward the kitchen, nearly running.

The big, comfortable living room was in disarray. She had evidently been unable to touch anything after Gene had been removed. I wondered where the children were—whether they had been kept home from school, sent to relatives or friends, or whether they were sitting, stunned, in their bedrooms. The six-room apartment sat on the Upper West Side—as rare as a black pearl fished from the Hudson—accommodating the family of a salaried man at a rent that he could afford. Like most jewels of its kind, it was an heirloom. It had been occupied by an aunt of Evie's and then passed on to her, rent-control intact. The furniture was big and comfortable, a hodgepodge of hand-me-downs. The other times I had been here, however, it had all been neat. Now it was not. A heavy red rug with an Aztec design had been used as a blanket on the couch. It was kicked down to the end in a disorderly pile. The commodious desk of the big secretary had been pulled down, and papers lay scattered across it, some of them only half drawn from the mahogany pigeonholes. Small tables and knickknacks had been moved from their accustomed places—I suppose to clear a path for the removal of Gene through the entrance door of the apartment. The whole room suggested a house that had been hit by a severe tremor. There was also the unmistakable odor that accompanies catastrophe—of physical distress and death. This odor was now being penetrated by the sharp smell of fresh coffee brewing.

She brought the coffeepot in on a tray, handed me a cup of coffee, set the tray down on one of the displaced tables, and took a cup for herself. She remained standing with hers, as if she could not bear to be stationary in this room. "This is delicious," I told her, tasting the very hot brew. I glanced about, as if trying to penetrate the walls. "Where are the children?" I asked her. "In their rooms?"

"I sent them down to the Gaylords'," she answered. "They're old friends of ours. They knew my aunt."

"I would have thought," I ventured, "that you'd want the kids around you right now."

"Oh, I do. I do," she said. Moisture appeared very suddenly in her eyes, and her face struggled visibly against it. The cup trembled on its saucer. "But I'm afraid if we were all together, we'd all dissolve. And I have to think. I have to control myself."

"You're doing very well," I offered.

"Please don't be nice," she said with a sharp, almost terrified slash of her hand. "I can't stand that. It's one of the reasons I sent the kids away." She turned from me then and said something, apparently distractedly because she threw out her right hand, fingers outstretched. She remembered then that I have to see in order to understand and turned back to me saying, "This place is a wreck. I've got to straighten it up. Give me a few minutes and then we'll talk. OK?" She pointed to the secretary. "I had to practically tear that thing apart to find Gene's papers before they—before they could—never mind." She went over to the secretary and began carefully to put papers back in their pigeonholes.

I sat sipping my coffee and thinking about the children in the apartment down below, particularly of the boy, Nick, who was sixteen when I first met him, and now must be seventeen. I had met Nick first on the evening I had brought home the smiling ghost of Gene, him and his thirteen-year-old sister, Claire, now fourteen. The children had joined us at dinner, a huge casserole of Spanish rice, surprised with tender chunks of ham and thick, crisp, fleshy slices of green pepper. Dessert had been a sharp-tasting apple pie, followed by a nice wedge of Stilton.

Gene had been very drunk right up until the moment his apartment door opened, revealing the small, resilient figure of Evie. He had reeled back just a bit, and I saw him say, "Hiya, Brat," after which he had leaned forward to drape two arms around her shoulders and place a huge, wet, martini-filled kiss on her face. She had put both hands up on his face and kissed him back. I had remained loitering in embarrassed isolation, eager to depart, but Evie had seized me by the hand and pulled me into the apartment.

When Gene stepped into his home his footing became more secure. He instantly demanded another martini, which Evie fixed, along with one for herself, and then provided a bourbon and soda for me. The homemade martini had the paradoxical effect of sobering Gene. He recounted to Evie the good news of the doctor's findings while the children set the table. We went into the dining room to eat.

The meal sobered him further. We sat back and lighted cigarettes over our coffee while the children cleared the table. Their chores finished, the children reappeared in the dining room. Claire seated herself at the table, but Nick was headed for the street. "Hold on, Nick," Gene said to him. "Have you got a minute?" Nick seemed impatient to depart, but something, evidently, in Gene's voice held him back. "Your mother told me last night," Gene said to him, "that the people you're going around with are dipping into coke."

Nick threw a furious glance at his mother, whose face remained completely untroubled. He looked back somewhat defiantly at his father.

"I wish you wouldn't fool around with crap like that," Gene said to him. "One of the lesser dangers is that it will rot your skull."

The boy decided to take a mature stance. He folded his arms across his chest, planted one foot behind the other, and looked directly at his father. Gene stared benignly back at him. Nick said, "Oh, boy. It's all right for you to stagger home with a bag on. I mean drugs are drugs, right?"

"No," Gene said smiling. "Not right. Drugs are not drugs. Pop-psych has addled your wits."

"What's the difference?" the boy challenged him.

Gene stared at him. "Do you really and truly not see the difference?"

"No," said Nick, with a stubborn, outthrust lower lip. "I don't."

"One way is legal, the other isn't."

"Legal, schmegal," said the boy.

Gene laughed. He said, "Can you subtract three minutes from your inviolable schedule to hear my opinion on the difference between legal and schmegal?"

A smile touched the corners of Nick's mouth. "Shoot," he said.

"Legal," Gene held up one finger. "I cannot be arrested for drinking in a licensed establishment, and, as long as I don't drive home or create a disturbance, no cop under ordinary circumstances can lay a glove on me. I remain a free man."

Gene held up two fingers. "Schmegal," he announced. "The minute you dip your shell-tipped fingers into coke, you become the potential victim of every petty shit heel connected either legitimately or illegitimately to the United States Government, not to mention a number of even shabbier governments.

"If you think you are displeasing the government and its minions by indulging in coke, disabuse yourself," he instructed the boy. "Coke supplies the government with a wide net to cast over the population, something deeply desirable to all governments, all of whom are paranoid, voracious, and forever seeking a method to consolidate power—to earn fear, respect, and tribute. Coke provides an excellent bargaining point for them. If you are busted, your fate is in the hands of any cheap political hack of a judge who happens to have been stuck up on the bench in the absence of intelligent and honorable applicants for that position. You can become a pushbutton. The end result may be that you have put yourself in the hands of a community more vicious, more crooked, more brutal than the criminal element itself. The fate of the schmegal is to become a pisspot into which any branch of the government may leak at will. I had always hoped that you would be less accommodating."

He held up both hands to forestall Nick's departure. "One more thing," he said. "I am not blind to the fact that it's difficult not to join your crowd on a lark. But coke is not a lark. I suggest that the graceful way out of it is to tell them that you're allergic to the stuff. Tell them that your face puffed up and you couldn't breathe. It's a lie, of course, a white lie, a snow-white lie, if you will. But it will give you a chance for a couple of things. For one, it gives you a chance to see how coke heads act when you're sober. Secondly, you can find out whether you're truly in the company of friends. Friends don't care whether you snort coke or not. Pushers do. If they urge you strenuously, decide whether you want to be regarded as an outlet, OK?"

Nick zipped up his jacket while Gene was saying, "If you are busted, say absolutely nothing until you talk to me. Understand? I'll be down there in a flash. Count on it." Nick had been running the zipper up and down. Now he pulled it all the way to his chin and turned to leave. But before he left, I thought that I had seen something change in his eyes.

Suddenly before me there was a field of red on which an Aztec pattern danced. It moved to one side so that I could see Evie's tortured face saying, "What can I do? How can I put it back?"

"I'm sorry," I told her. "I hadn't caught what you were saying."

"The rug," said Evie. "Gene tore it off the wall and used it for a blanket out here on the couch. He said that he wouldn't sleep with me anymore." Her face was so stricken that I withdrew from the sight. "Can I hang it back up where it used to be?" she asked me. "I can't do it by myself. Will you help me?"

There was a large pale rectangle on the wall of the bedroom. I stood on the bed and held up the heavy rug, while Evie secured the fastenings. When we left the room, she gave the rug one last regretful glance.

Back in the big front room she began to wander through the space, touching the couch, the easy chair, the secretary, and the small tables that had all been put back in place. I stood by the chair she had put me in when I arrived. Evie turned around and looked at me. Her face was rigid, white. "Now everything is back in place," she said. "It's all neat and just the way it used to be. And I can't stand it. I can't stand it." She began to cry.

I sat down in my appointed chair. "Evie," I said. "Bring me another cup of coffee, and then sit down and tell me what happened."

5

"You know what he's been like—what he was like,"
said Evie. "After all, you did bring him home that
night—I mean the last time you were here."

She had got hold of a cup of coffee for herself and
was sitting in the straight-backed chair by the secretary. She had provided me with another, which I sipped
while regarding her warily. I did not at that moment
want to get submerged in what Gene had been like. I
remembered that well enough. I said to her, "First of
all, tell me about this morning. I know it will be hard,
but let's get it out of the way. Tell me exactly what
happened."

"I heard him yell—scream, sort of—a kind of a
strangled sound. It wasn't quite like any other sound
I'd ever heard. And I said to myself, 'Another nightmare.' I didn't know what to do. I've felt so helpless
all this time.

"So I turned over and tried to go back to sleep. But
I couldn't sleep. Finally, I crept into the front room,
here. I didn't want to disturb him, so I tried to look at
him over the back of the couch. I saw him lying there,
very, very still. He'd kicked the covers, that rug—you
know, he'd ripped that right off the bedroom wall
when he said he was never going to sleep with me
again—" She blushed a red so fiery that it seemed a
flame illuminating her face. "And he used that for his
bed clothes. Anyway, he was lying there very still—

something about it disturbed me, but everything has been so strange that I put it out of my mind. I haven't been able to think or do anything rational about Gene these last few months. So I went into the kitchen and made some coffee. I sat in the kitchen drinking coffee and wondering for about the thousandth time what I was going to do about Gene. Living with him had become impossible. I guess that's all solved, now." Her chin began to tremble. She put her cup on the floor and began to cry again. She put her hands over her face. I did not try to comfort her. I waited her out.

She bent down, dried her eyes with the bottom of her jersey, and gathered herself together. "At seven-thirty," she said at last, "I was supposed to wake him anyway, so he could go to work. I poured a cup of coffee and took it in to him. It was light in the room by then. I could see things clearly. He hadn't moved. He still had that odd way of lying there. When I saw that he hadn't moved, I almost dropped the coffee. Without really looking at him, I knew he was dead. It was like a presence in the room. You understand"—she made a little pleading gesture—"I knew he was dead, but I didn't believe it. I mean, I had these two thoughts—sensations—'He's dead! I don't believe it!' So the part 'I don't believe it' won, and I went around the couch to give him his cup of coffee, even though I knew he was dead. Can you understand that? What I was doing?"

I nodded.

"So I went around the couch to wake him. It was very strange. I felt that if I went around the couch and gave him his coffee he would come alive. Do you know what I mean? And that's when I saw his face. And I did drop the coffee.

"He had hoisted himself up on the pillows as if he had been drawing himself up to ward off something—something in his sleep. He was on his side, with one arm under him and the other stretched out and hanging down toward the floor. And his face—his face—his face had a look of fright, of terror, of rage—so many things. His eyes were wide—wide open, staring, bulging, seeing something, looking at something, horror-struck. I threw myself on him and shook him, like waking him up from a nightmare, but he just rolled back and collapsed on the couch. I had only pushed him on his back, and he was staring at the ceiling."

I halted her. "Stop there," I said. "Stop for a few minutes. You asked me here as a professional, and I have to ask you some professional questions. The expression on Gene's face—you said it was horrified, but can I ask you something? Are you sure it was horror, terror? Are you sure it wasn't a kind of smiling?"

Her face worked as she stared at me, but before she could make up her mind as to what I was suggesting, I said, "I don't mean a smiling of any normal kind. I mean the lips pulled back in a kind of a grin"—I demonstrated with a forefinger at each corner of my lips, pulling them back—"more of a mockery, a caricature of a smile."

"No," she said. "No."

"Think about it," I urged her. "If his expression was like that, it could explain a lot."

"No," she repeated, staring at me.

"And when you say his posture was odd," I pursued, "was it taut? Rigid? As if he had been pulled back by a bowstring?"

"No," she said. "No."

"My reasons for asking this," I said, "are that the smile I was trying to describe, the *risus sardonicus*, the sardonic smile, comes from a constriction of the facial muscles. The bowstring rigidity also comes from a constriction of the muscles—the back muscles being more powerful than the belly muscles. When people are found like that, the doctor looks for two things in particular. One of them is tetanus, and the other is strychnine."

"No," she said. She was being reasonable, but her eyes said that she hated me. I was making things much more real, much more final than she was prepared for. I didn't see how it could be helped.

"If it turns out that he did have the *risus sardonicus* or the opisthotonous, the bowstring rigidity, there are two things we can consider." I hoped it was working. I hoped that drawing the whole subject of Gene's death from the real experience into the abstract would help blunt the image. There was still hatred in her eyes and a kind of defiance, but there was also an awakened interest. "The first thing," I plodded on in what I hoped was a level voice, "is tetanus. Tetanus is something you can pick up anywhere. You can scratch yourself on a rose thorn and get it. You can nick yourself on an old tin can, you can accidentally scrape the skin of your hand on an iron fence, you can—and this is how most people get it—step on a rusty nail, a penetrating wound . . ."

"Nothing like that happened to Gene," she interrupted. Her mouth snapped shut around the words.

"Pardon me for mentioning it," I tried to say softly, "but would he have told you if he had?"

"There weren't," she began with a defiant, uncertain air, "there weren't any symptoms."

"Would he have mentioned them? Were you close enough to him to know? It all could have been accelerated. It could have happened overnight. So that is one possibility."

Her mouth hardened into a line of denial. She stared at me.

I rolled on. "The next thing to consider is poison. Poison self-administered, accidentally ingested, or administered deliberately by someone else. In this case, the poison could be strychnine, which is painful and deadly. However, a rapid death means a large amount. A smaller amount would cause a lengthy agony. There would have been more than just one outcry. You wouldn't have been able to ignore it. You would have called for help. Very probably he would have been saved. So if it was strychnine, it was administered by a knowing hand." She began to object, but I closed her down with a gesture. "So that leaves us with these questions: Did Gene have a knowing hand? Was he, in fact, suicidal? Had he ever mentioned suicide to you in these last few months?" She shook her head in vigorous denial. "If not that, had he made any serious enemies in these past few months? Christ knows," I added warmly, "he seems to have made plenty of casual enemies."

Evie burst out with, "It wasn't like that! I mean the smile, the grimace you're talking about, or stiffening his body. His lips weren't drawn back like that. His mouth looked as if he were crying, or screaming or gaping. And his eyes were staring, bulging, as if he were looking at something he couldn't bear to see. He looked—and this is exactly how he looked—like a man who had been frightened to death. It wasn't a look I hadn't seen before. I'd seen him wake up from nightmares before—looking like—that."

"Evie," I stopped her. "You see what I'm doing, don't you? I know that you think Gene's simply dying in his sleep is impossible, but it happens all the time, all over the world. What I'm trying to do is show you some of the alternatives and rule them out."

"No," she insisted stubbornly. "It wasn't like that. Maybe it happens all over the world, but it didn't happen to Gene."

"Go ahead and talk," I said patiently. "I'm here to help as much as I can."

"In the first place," said Evie, with that air of demented certainty that goes with obsessions, "if he had any heart trouble, we certainly would have known. Since he's been going to that damned health clinic, he's been monitored like an astronaut, and his heart was perfectly sound for a man his age. Otherwise they wouldn't have let him do those stupid exercises, which he hated. Heart trouble is the last thing Gene could have had."

"Look," I contradicted her gently, "all those places can give you is a reasonable degree of physical fitness. They don't guarantee immortality—particularly not for fifty-year-old men who are hitting the jug like there's no tomorrow and undergoing terrific emotional stress. I don't care if Gene was in shape to buck for the Olympics. He was an emotional wreck and his life was being shot to hell. And what's more," I overrode her objections, "I don't care what the health clinic said about Gene, he sure as hell didn't look like a man in good shape to me. He was overweight—those martinis were going right to his belly. In fact, he wasn't getting anywhere with those exercises. All he was doing was torturing himself. And he wasn't getting proper rest or sleep. You said yourself he was having nightmares. He didn't always have nightmares, did he?"

"Oh, God," said Evie. "He hated it. He hated it so much." She put her hands up to her face and began to rock back and forth in the hard chair. I saw her small chin move beneath her hands and said sharply, "Evie, I don't know what you're saying unless I can see your face."

She took her hands away. Her eyes were filled with tears. "Why couldn't they let him alone?" she said. "Why couldn't they just let him the hell alone?" She put her hands back up and began to rock again.

I knew who *they* were. *They* had been described to me with some vehemence by Gene himself. That had been the second time I brought Gene home, the second ghost, the scowling ghost.

"These bastards," Gene had told me, "have bought the company as an investment stratagem—the way a kid buys a new section of track for his toy train. What do they know about publishing or journalism? Zero. Have they hired anyone who does? No."

I had run into him again at Henry's, late in the afternoon. I realize now that he had just come from Dr. Beaman's, to whom he referred lengthily and bitterly as a "nigger taster." I had just emerged from a long struggle with a client over the expenses I had put on my bill. I was feeling sour, but had nothing on me like the black mood that enveloped Gene.

"You are looking," Gene told me, "at the latest victim of the hygiene fad. The first thing this new outfit did was to ban smoking in the office—anywhere on the premises. The second thing they did was to offer the services of a cardiac fitness company, free of charge, with the implied threat, 'Go or else.' They have managed to fuck up my life very possibly beyond repair." He hammered on the bar for another martini.

While his attention was focused on the bartender, I

took a good look at Gene. His complexion had changed. His face was red. He stood a little back from the bar with both hands on the edge in the attitude of a serious drinker, and his posture revealed the sag of a belly hanging down over his belt. He smelled bad. His suit was unkempt. He needed a haircut. His light blue eyes were fuzzy and despairing. I was on his left. To my left were two exquisite young men sipping Perrier. When the martini was served, Gene took a brain-chilling draft of it. I took out my pack of cigarettes and offered him one. It was the only merciful act I could think of at the time.

"No, thank you," said Gene. "I've quit smoking."

"Just like that?" I was astounded. "Jesus Christ. That's marvelous."

"Jesus Christ has absolutely nothing to do with it," said Gene, a solemn expression on his blotched face. "It is a simple act of willpower. If I am told that I must quit smoking in order to keep my job, then I will quit smoking in order to keep my job. It is a simple economic necessity. I am not of an age where I can flit from one job to another, unlike some lucky youngsters who are simply walking out of the place. I have ten years of hard work invested there, and I have a serious promotion coming up. I want the promotion and I deserve it—otherwise the whole thing is pointless, and I might as well have spent my time as a street cleaner."

He finished the martini and ordered another. He did not offer to buy a drink for me. I reached for my cigarettes again, but paused. Gene caught my hesitation and greeted it with a soft, watery smile. "Go ahead and smoke," he advised me. "My misfortune is not yours. I'm not so stupid or hysterical as to be influenced by someone else's smoking." He returned to his martini while I gratefully lighted up. He sipped at it and relapsed into misery:

"Gene," I said timidly, "don't you think in a little while you'll feel better about this?"

He turned around and glared at me. "I haven't got a little while," he said, and the glare turned into a look of savage desperation. "I work for a weekly publication. I have got deadlines that are absolutely ironclad.

Work must be done. I have to produce things day in and day out—words on paper that can be read with pleasure and comprehension. I am not meeting deadlines. The work I turn in is sent back because it is Christ-awful. I don't smoke, but neither do I think or perform. These cocksuckers have reached into my head and turned out the light."

He must have been speaking loudly, because I felt a stir to my left. I looked into the bar mirror and saw the two exquisites share the kind of supercilious smiles that will get you killed in certain saloons, though probably not in Henry's. "So I can't work," Gene went on, oblivious. "My lungs are clear, but my brains have turned to oatmeal."

"Gene," I tried as best I knew how to keep my voice low and gentle, "do you think a shrink might do you any good to get over it?"

I don't remember seeing before this a man about to laugh and cry at the same time. "I'm going to one right now," said Gene, "provided courtesy of the cardiac clinic, thank you. I'm getting nowhere. All he does is irritate me. I don't know whether he's willfully obtuse or a congenital half-wit. I keep going to him because I have to make a demonstration of willingness to comply with the company's policy. Otherwise, I'm out on my ass—along with my pension, my life insurance, my medical insurance—all the reasons I took the fucking job in the first place.

"Behind it all, I've had the feeling that they've wanted to fire me all along. I'm not going to give them the excuse. Except"—and he looked at me with absolute desperation—"if I can't work, they will fire me. It will all have been for nothing. All that work. All these years. What am I going to do?"

I said, a little more boldly this time, "Look, for Christ's sake, Gene, look at what you've done. You quit smoking—bang—like that, on the money. There isn't one man in a million can do it. They've got all kinds of programs to help with this and that, but you just did it. Sheer willpower. Doesn't that make you proud?"

"No, it does not." He drained his martini and ordered another. I had hardly touched my drink. "I was proud before I quit. That's what gave me the will-power to quit in the first place. Self-respect. Now I have lost my self-respect because it appears that I cannot hold a job without the aid of cigarettes. Cigarettes were an enormous psychological prop to me. I feel as if an old friend had died. Fundamentally, I am in mourning."

"But your health," I began.

"My health!" He rounded on me with that look of savage desperation that was now becoming familiar. "Let me tell you about my health. I quit smoking and suddenly became a balloon.

"Look at me," he demanded, standing clear of the bar and raising his arms. "Did I look like this the last time you saw me?"

I looked at the swelling pear of his belly and shook my head. He returned to his drink. "Yes. Well, my weight shot up. I tried to control that with dieting. So instead of eating, I drink. And the drink puts on weight; I know that. And then my blood pressure. My blood pressure had always been perfectly fine, thank you. But now my blood pressure has shot up. How should it not? I'm worried sick every minute of the day. I have to produce, and yet I cannot produce. And, no doubt, my liver is manufacturing cholesterol by the bucketful, because stress produces cholesterol. Even I know that." He put his face close to mine. His eyes had a beggary in them. "I am no longer myself." He seemed to plead. "I am not me. I have lost my autonomy, my authority. I am a cipher, no different from those two cunts standing behind you."

It must have got to them, because I noticed the flash of one stiffening abruptly in the mirror. More importantly, I caught the glint of battle in Gene's pale eyes. It was the first sign of animation I'd seen in him that afternoon. So, I thought, even in the depths of his misery and drunkenness he had noticed the supercilious smiles and smug enjoyment of his predicament. I thought I had better head things off. I turned to the worthies behind me.

"Tell your friend," said the foremost, "to watch his rotten mouth."

"He's loaded," I said. "We didn't mean to keep you up."

"Smoking," the youngster sniffed, looking over my shoulder toward Gene, "would appear to be the least of his troubles."

Now, apparently, Gene had said something I couldn't see, because the young man said, "Smoking is a slow form of suicide."

I stepped back, so that I could see what Gene was saying, and also to give myself room for maneuvering. I am not the world's champion saloon fighter, but I didn't think I'd have any trouble here. Gene was saying, "When have I heard that before?" He rolled up his eyes in mock recollection. He tried to focus his eyes on his elegant antagonist. "Do you actually believe that?" he demanded.

"Yes, I do."

"That all the people all over the world who are smoking merrily away are actually trying to kill themselves?"

"Everyone knows it," said the young man, his mouth grim.

"Then everyone, as usual, is full of shit," said Gene. "Suicide is an act of will, like murder. You think I've been deliberately trying to kill myself since I was fifteen years old, is that it?"

"Well . . ." began the young man uncertainly.

"Leading to the inevitable question of *why*? Why should I have been trying to commit suicide all these years?"

"I'm sure I don't know."

"Well, if you're sure you don't know," asked Gene with a reasonable and honest expression on his red face, "why don't you just keep your fucking mouth shut?"

The young man tensed, taking all the time of a transcontinental flight to telegraph his intentions. I looked at him. "Don't start anything," I told him, "unless you want your suit spoiled."

He flushed and made the wise decision. He swept

the change off the bar and he and his friend rolled out of the place. They had not succeeded in departing, however, without hearing Gene bellow, "Go home and suck on a titty, you fucking milksop."

The bartender appeared in front of me. "Get him out of here," he said. He took our glasses off the bar.

6

Getting Gene home from there was not the work of a moment. Cabs accelerated past us. Finally, one old-timer took us aboard on the strength of my solemn promise that Gene would not puke all over the backseat.

I tugged Gene into the apartment elevator, where he slumped in a corner and scowled at me. When I presented him at the apartment door, the greeting was nothing like the first time around. Evie's face was filled with apprehension and dread as she let us in. Young Nick was standing in the center of the room, apparently, like most adolescents, in transit. Gene staggered over to the corner of the couch, where he stood and swayed and fixed the kid with a malevolent grin. "And how is my little snowbird this evening?" he asked the boy. "Out for a few lines with his moronic friends?"

The boy's face went white, then rigid. He sped toward the door and slammed it behind him. Evie said to Gene, "You dirty disgusting bastard. Nick hasn't had a thing to do with any of that and you know it."

"Don't tell me," Gene said with a drunken leer at her. He waved his arm dramatically. "And my darling daughter," he inquired, "where is she? Out in the back of somebody's automobile?" He reeled a bit so that he was turned away from me and I could no longer see what either he or Evie were saying. I was grateful. I began a crablike regression toward the door.

"Good-bye," I croaked to Evie. She barely glanced up as I let myself out.

Now, Evie appeared to have collected herself again. She had stopped rocking and was staring grimly into the depths of the room. "Evie," I said, breaking in as softly as I could, "can we take this back a little further? I mean, can you tell me why Gene should have had such a terrible reaction to all this? You know, it's happening all over the country—the health kick. Why did Gene get blown away like this? It's not a normal reaction."

"Nobody ever accused Gene of being normal." She smiled wanly. "Gene was different, and it was the difference that he thought gave a certain value to his work. He had the education and the experience to have certain insights—to make certain connections that nobody else could see. That's what made him valuable in his job, or so we thought. They didn't ask him if he smoked when they hired him."

"And when he quit smoking," I pursued, "from day one he changed completely. Is that it?"

"No, not really," she answered slowly, thoughtfully. "He came home and announced that he had quit smoking, that he was forced to quit smoking. It was the new law down at the office. They told him he had to quit, so he quit on the spot. He looked pretty grim, but he allowed that he'd manage. I offered to quit, too, but he said"—she smiled a little ghost of a smile—" 'For Christ's sake don't you quit too, Brat. One of us has got to stay sane for a while.'

"So for the first two or three days he was worried because he couldn't do his work, but he was quiet. Then he had to go down to that cardiology place and take a stress test, whatever they call it, on a treadmill with a heart machine. When he came home from that he was furious and depressed. He'd been trotting on this treadmill, looking at some electric squiggle on the monitor, and he didn't know what the squiggles meant, although he knew they were his heartbeat. When they told him to stop, he didn't know if that was good or bad, or what was happening. It was not the kind of situation Gene likes. I don't suppose anyone does. He said he felt like an animal. The whole thing depressed him, and he was already depressed from having quit smoking. But when he really blew up was when he got the reading or diagnosis or whatever from the heart mill. It was a form letter explaining that the test had revealed a cardiac irregularity, which Gene interpreted as meaning that he had a bad heart. The letter had a lot of gobbledygook in it, and then a list of things Gene had to do, or not do—no smoking, no coffee, no alcohol, low-fat diet, mild exercise . . . to be provided by the cardiac mill and carefully monitored, of course— etcetera and blah, blah."

"There's your answer, of course," I said. "Gene had a bad heart, right?"

"No," she said violently, jerking upright in the chair. "Gene did not have a bad heart."

"Evie," I began, "they wouldn't send out a notice like that unless they had something to go on . . ."

"Oh, but they did and they do," she interrupted. "Gene told me that at the time he had a little viral infection—just beginning, no real symptoms. And what they finally found was that he'd had a subclinical viral infection that made his heart act up under stress. Unfortunately for Gene, they didn't find that out until two weeks later. By that time, Gene was just about out of control."

"He overreacted?" I asked her. "He thought he was going to die because of a few squiggles?"

"Gene wasn't afraid that he was going to die," she answered with a scornful expression. "Who is, except neurotics? What those squiggles meant to Gene was that he might very well not get the promotion he was slated for . . ."

"But that doesn't sound like Gene," I objected. "I mean he never struck me as the apple-biting, nickel-grabbing gung-ho executive."

"Of course he wasn't," said Evie. "But these days either you go up or you go out. Not getting a promotion is pretty much the same as being asked to leave, and Gene was not of an age where he could simply step into another job. He was stuck. And let's face it," she added, "he wanted that promotion. He'd earned it. It was coming to him."

"And he was going to lose it because of a squiggle?"

"Gene's point was very simple. When he got that letter, he asked me, 'What company is going to promote a man into a policy-making job if that man has a bad heart? Who's going to promote a man who might drop dead tomorrow?'

"I tried to argue with him, but I was frightened too. I didn't know what the damned diagnosis meant. It said the same thing to me that it said to Gene, that he had a bad heart, that he had to live a special way now, like an invalid. That maybe he was going to die. And remember, this came right after the cancer scare, which was also a phony."

"But this," I suggested, "was perhaps not a phony?"

"But it was! It was!" she insisted, clenching her hands. "Two weeks later he took another test that he said came out more or less normal. But, oh, what a two weeks! He'd quit smoking. He stopped drinking coffee. He wouldn't touch liquor. He ate practically nothing. He was like a ghost, a crazy ghost. He stopped talking to me. He couldn't work. He'd sit all day in front of his typewriter at work, but nothing happened. He couldn't put ideas together. The stuff that he finally ground out was almost gibberish. He was frightened. He was crazy."

"But the second test—" I returned to it. "Didn't that fix him up. Didn't that solve everything?"

"He was already out of control by then," said Evie. "He was a changed person. He was no longer my husband, my Gene.

"And the other thing is that while the second stress test was supposed to be normal, his blood pressure had gone way up, and they found out that his cholesterol had gone up. It was obvious, even to them, that he was crazy as hell. So they prescribed stuff for his blood pressure—Gene had never needed any kind of medicine before—and they scheduled him for a psychotherapist to help him get over smoking, they said. And they also assigned a physiotherapist to help him with his exercises, what have you. So suddenly here's

Gene, who'd hardly ever gone to a doctor, loaded
down with a shrink, a trainer, and a lot of mysterious
mumbo jumbo about his heart."

She began to cry again. "No wonder he went crazy,"
she said. "They got together and decided that Gene
Listing should be somebody else. So he became somebody else, but not the person they had in mind."

I asked her, "What about these nightmares? Did
Gene always have them? Or did they start up right
after he quit smoking?"

"No, no," she said. "It was very curious. They
started almost a month after he quit smoking, after
he'd had the second heart test and they found out
about his blood pressure and gave him this stuff to
take. The nightmares began—I hadn't really thought
about this—after he started working on this new story
on his own hook. I mean, it was a story that he was
developing by himself."

She pursed her lips and thought. "I see what was
happening, now . . ." she said. "He couldn't really
work, so he went haring off into this wild, hopeless,
silly story about Southeast Asia tribesmen that nobody
was ever going to be able to print. But I kept my
mouth shut." She paused, recollecting the facts. "The
story was about these tribesmen, refugees, who were
having nightmares and would—" She looked at me
with alarm widening her eyes—"die in their sleep during a nightmare."

"Die in their sleep?" I repeated stupidly. "What
tribesmen are you talking about?"

"Well," she began, troubled, "I don't really know.
These people were called the *Hmuong,* except it's
spelled differently—aitch, em, you, oh, en, gee—but
the aitch is silent.

"Anyway, these people are refugees, in the United
States, and for the last five years they've been having
nightmares and dying in their sleep. Nobody was ever
able to explain really how they died, what killed them.
But Gene thought he saw something in the story that
had been overlooked. He started building a file. It was
crazy and useless. It had nothing to do with his job.
There's no place in the book for a story like that. It's

all very hard-nosed down there—'Just the facts, ma'am.' Even more so now, with Basket, the editor—"

"Basket," I repeated cautiously, "really?"

"No, not really. His real name is Basswell, but he wears these tight slacks that seem to outline his genitals. And so they took to calling him Basket, behind his back, of course."

"I see," I said, almost sadly, "I see."

"Yes, well, this story was just sort of a relief valve for Gene. Something on his own initiative."

She paused, and her face seemed to close up with sadness and disappointment. "I really can't tell you too much about it," she admitted. "Gene and I weren't really speaking to each other very much by then."

"The psychotherapist," I said, trying to pull her back from the grim memories, "do you suppose Gene told him anything about the nightmares?"

"I really wouldn't know," said Evie. "Anything I ever heard from Gene about the therapist was unprintable."

I said, "Gene might have told him things that he kept from you, from everybody. I mean, he might have told the therapist whether he was having heart symptoms, you know, flutterings, blackouts, that kind of thing. I wonder if we could get a transcript?"

"Oh, hell," said Evie. "I can get you transcripts, if that's what you want."

"The therapist sent them to you?"

"No, no. It's all just as crazy as everything else connected with this mess. Gene came back after the first session in an absolute rage. He mimicked the therapist—he was a savage mimic, you know. So there was this very prissy voice saying, 'If only you could hear yourself, Mr. Listing'—they hadn't got on to a first-name basis—'If you could only hear yourself.' And Gene said to me, 'All right. If that son of a bitch wants me to hear myself I'll take along the tape recorder and let's see how he likes that.'

"You know, the office supplies everyone with a little portable tape recorder for interviews. As a point of honor, Gene would never take one with him because he said most journalists push the button and put their minds to sleep. He said he never wanted to be one of those horrible little men who were shoving microphones into people's faces. Anyway, he got the tape recorder out of the secretary, there, and I had to show him how to operate it, because he was absolutely helpless. It's a wonder he was able to work the elevator in this building. And he took it along with him for the next session.

"Of course, he never listened to the tapes. He'd simply sling them into the secretary and put a fresh tape in the machine for the next time. He only did it to irritate the therapist, I'm sure."

"But you do have them," I said. "The tapes, I mean."

"Oh, yes," she said, rising. "They're right here." She went over to the secretary and took out a stack of cassettes. There were six of them. I stared at them. They were, of course, a closed world to me.

"Have you listened to any of them?" I asked her.

Evie was shocked. "I'd never do a thing like that," she said. "They belong to Gene. They're as private as anything could be."

"Would you be willing to listen to them now?"

She regarded me suspiciously, as if I had suggested something mildly obscene. "Why would I want to do that?"

"Well, I certainly can't listen to them." I smiled. "And yet they give us a starting point if you truly want to find out what happened to Gene. Which brings us to a sort of crucial question: Are you still sure you want to? Seriously?"

She sat very still for about ten seconds. "I know what you're thinking," she said slowly. "You think I've been hysterical. All right. Maybe I was. But now the hysteria is gone. The suspicions are still there."

"All right," I said. "Then we have several points we can start from. We have these tapes, where Gene might have let something slip to the therapist, whether he was suicidally depressed, or the content of the nightmares he'd been having, or other things we know nothing about.

"Another point we can start from is purely physical.

We can get copies of the electrocardiogram and get a second opinion on them. What clinic did Gene go to?"

"I've got it on a reminder card, wait," she said, and went once more to the secretary.

"While you're there," I told her, "you'd better dig out the other names, and I'll run them down."

She began sorting things out of the pigeonholes, and I continued, "By the way, I hope you're a good typist."

"A good typist?" She had turned toward me with a few papers in her hand. "It so happens that I'm an excellent typist, but why?"

"Because," I said, "I want you to make a transcript of all those tapes."

She sat down suddenly, holding the assorted bunch of papers. "Oh, my God," she said. "I don't really think I could do that. I mean . . ." and her face tightened defensively. "Can't I just hire a typist to have it done? I'm not sure I could listen . . ."

"I don't know how much money you've got to spend," I said briskly, "but you're talking about a lot. Transcripts are expensive. But the real reason I want you to do it is this: I can't hear Gene's voice. I can't hear anybody's voice. If I'm reading a transcript there's no way I can read any expression into the words. Now, you know Gene's voice and his mannerisms. You know when he's kidding, when he's mocking, when he's angry, when he's serious. If you do the transcript, you can insert these expressions parenthetically. No other typist could do it. We're going to be searching the transcript for clues, tiny clues. These can come out of Gene's attitude, the tone of voice that goes with the words. There is really no one who can catch that but you."

Wordlessly, she handed me the few papers. I looked away from the struggle in her face. Looking at the papers, I saw the name of the cardiologist at the heart mill, the physiotherapist who had given Gene a list of exercises to do at home, the psychotherapist who had scheduled a list of appointments, and even poor old Dr. Beaman, who had sent him a bill. Quite a team, I thought, to preside over the death of a previously healthy man. I folded up the papers and put them in my inside pocket. Evie touched my knee. "I'll do it," she said. But her eyes told me what it would cost her.

I stood up, preparing to go. "One thing," I said. "I'm not hungry, but I can't work for free. Have you got any money? I mean, if you're busted, I'll do what I can as a friend, but that's not the same thing as professional service. Understand what I'm saying?"

She nodded comprehendingly. "There was a pretty good insurance policy with the company," she said. "I don't think there'll be any problem."

"OK," I said, moving toward the door. "My secretary will call you to talk about the fee, which won't be anything startling. And I'll start checking around." I stopped and confronted her. "Are you sure that this is what you wanted?"

Both of us knew that this wasn't really what she wanted. But what she wanted was impossible. She wanted the world to reverse in its orbit. She wanted Gene to have been left alone. She wanted the world to have stopped moving. Worst of all, she wanted a solution, and I was, at that moment, quite certain that there was no solution outside the terrible, immutable grinding of events against human frailty.

"One thing more," I added, my hand on the doorknob. "The last time I was here, Gene came down hard on Nick. Was there any basis to that? Has Nick been fooling around with coke?"

She shook her head. She was close to tears again. "No," she said. "No. Nick did walk away from it. He loved Gene and listened to him. My God, he was hurt, he was crushed when Gene turned on him like that, utterly without reason."

"And Claire?" I asked. "How is she?"

"Gene never came down on her like that—personally, I mean. She was just never around when he was here. Yet I get the feeling that she understood what was happening better than Nick or I did. But she also saw that she couldn't help him. No one could."

I sighed. "All right," I said. "Get on those transcripts. If I can help in any way, call my office. You call me as soon as you have a reasonable amount of the transcripts done, and we'll take it from there."

But riding the elevator down, I wondered . . . take it where? There was nothing there—the death of a middle-aged man with a bum ticker who died in his sleep. There was nothing there, and there was no place to go.

The soft bump of the elevator at the ground floor made me aware of three things simultaneously. The machinery noises in my head had begun to shriek and groan. I had developed a savage headache in the middle of my skull, the kind that are advertised as "tension headaches." Just inside my right ear a force had gathered like a clenched fist pushing into the side of my brain.

"Step right up and see him, folks," I thought bitterly. "The amazing Joe Binney. A man with three headaches, and only one head."

7

That next morning Edna was also divided into three parts, part nurse, part nag, and part avenging angel. I had spent a very bad night, awakened frequently by the pain, and had glanced yearningly at the codeine, as the aspirin bounced uselessly off my belly. I held off on the codeine, however, because I hate the side effects, the constipated stupidity that wipes out effectiveness the following day.

Edna administered to my ruin of a head with more aspirin and hot compresses. I was properly grateful. But she also nagged. "Have you taken your pills?" she asked for the fiftieth time, revealing the core of the nurse who awakens you at three A.M. to take a sleeping pill.

"Look," I told her. "I'm supposed to take four of these a day. No more, no less. I'm doing it faithfully, religiously. Stop nagging me or you'll drive me nuts."

On the subject of Evie Listing, however, she was pure avenging angel. "And that was all you could do for her?" she demanded. "Sit her down to six hours of listening to her dead husband's voice bitching and complaining to a shrink? Very likely bitching and complaining about his wife? Fob her off with some kind of vague promise to look around, and you're still going to charge her the full going rate?"

"I'm a businessman," I said peremptorily. "Not a charity or Lord Peter Wim-wams. I have to eat and pay the rent. So do you. I asked Evie if she was broke and she said no, she wasn't."

"The widow's mite," pronounced Edna scornfully.

"Yes, ma'am," I agreed. "And when my daily rates start eating into it, maybe she'll see the folly of her ways."

"Folly!" Edna exclaimed. Her green eyes flashed, and then, quite suddenly, they softened. She put a cool hand on my wrist. "Joe," she said. "You wouldn't be this cruel, this nasty, if your ear wasn't killing you. Why don't you wait a few days until this has cleared up before you decide anything?"

I withdrew my wrist and stared at her. "My ear has absolutely nothing to do with it," I informed her coldly. "Evie Listing is in big emotional trouble for a lot of reasons, and the kindest thing I can do for her right now is help her defend herself against a lot of very self-destructive feelings. There are some very simple answers to Gene's dying, and the sooner she confronts them the better it will be for her." The pomposity seemed to make my head swell. Edna sat back and looked at me unbelievingly.

"Simple answers such as what?" she inquired with a flat sullen look.

But the pain was too much. "Get me another hot compress," I told her, "and I'll talk. I'll tell you everything."

Nurse and nag took over while Edna applied the hot compress to the side of my head. However, it was five minutes before I could return to battling with the avenging angel.

"The simple answers are these," I told her. "Gene was forced, or thought he was forced, into taking an exercise test on a treadmill. They hooked him up to a heart machine and they got funny answers. It was all down there on the electrocardiogram. There was something the matter with Gene's heart. Gene, through a very human, very typical maneuver of self-defense, told himself that this was all bullshit, that he had some kind of a little cold, or what-have-you, any excuse so that he didn't have to face the fact that he had a bum ticker. It was not only the sign of undeniable mortal-

ity, but spelled a definite limit to his career as well.
When you take a fright like that, coupled with the
need to quit smoking and the blank wall of an end to
your professional career, you're going to get some
very nasty emotional reactions. Gene turned into a
son of a bitch."

"People don't turn into sons of bitches just like
that," Edna objected.

I regarded her tolerantly. "Only a few minutes ago,"
I pointed out, "you told me that I was turning from
Dr. Jekyll to Mr. Hyde before your very eyes. Of
course people turn into sons of bitches. Pain, fear, and
deprivation can turn lots of people into sons of bitches.
The ones who don't turn into sons of bitches just
usually collapse. They turn into meatballs."

She really hated this. "Some people," said Edna,
with a sickeningly pious expression on her ordinarily
pretty face, "are able to accept things as they come
with courage and decency."

"Ah, yes," I answered. "Grace under pressure. The
courage of the matador. If you want to measure the
average man's courage against a matador's, you might
as well measure his intelligence against a nuclear phys-
icist. Matadors and nuclear physicists are exceptions,"
I said. "It's unrealistic to measure other people against
them. Most people turn into sons of bitches or meatballs.

"All right." I made a box of the situation with my
hands. "Here's Evie Listing sitting up in the apartment by herself trying to make sense of things. She is
a decent, sweet, reasonable person, and like all the
other decent, sweet, reasonable people in this world
she is saying to herself, 'It's all my fault.' " I put my
hand up flatly to stem Edna's protest. "Of course it's
not all her fault," I said. "But that's how she feels. I'm
sure of it. She's got a case of the if onlys. 'If only I'd
quit smoking when Gene did. If only I'd fed Gene
differently. If only I had been nicer, more tolerant. If
only this, if only that.' "

"That's part of grief," said Edna.

"Part of normal grief," I amended. "But my feeling
about Evie is that she can't stand it. She can't stand

the guilt she's been feeding herself. She thinks Gene's death was abnormal and her reaction is abnormal grief.

"So," I admitted to Edna, "I'm going to be something of a son of a bitch. I'm going to force her to sit down and listen to six hours of Gene having it all out with his therapist. I'm counting on the idea that no man is a hero to his therapist. I'm hoping to topple the idol and somehow make the whole thing more bearable to Evie. I may be wrong, but I hope it will make her see Gene more realistically and deal with his dying more realistically. I want to save her time and money wasted on a more or less hopeless idea."

"And this," asked Edna, her green eyes narrowing, "is what you're charging her full rates for?"

"No," I answered with more irritation than I thought I had left in me. "That is not what I'm charging her full rates for. I'm going to run down the entire case for her. Get all the evidence I can and lay it out in front of her. Along with the tapes, it ought to convince her that what happened happened inevitably."

"The whole case?" Edna asked again with a look of suspicion. "And how long is that going to take at your well-thought-out, full-bore daily rates?"

"About three days. You think that will ruin her financially?"

"Three days doing what?"

I pulled out the sheaf of bills and receipts I had taken from Evie and had switched to the inside pocket of my other suit (yes, yes, I really do change suits from day to day). "I have here in my hand," I told Edna, waving them at her, "the names and numbers of all those people involved with the alleged rehabilitation of Gene Listing. I'm going to go and see them and get the whole story of what Gene's actual physical status was. Evie was only seeing a tiny part of it—the backlash." I fanned out the various-sized slips on the desk. "We'll make a schedule," I announced, "and I'll start seeing people tomorrow after I've seen Dr. Beaman. And I am not," I threw up my hands for emphasis, "charging Evie anything for yesterday or today."

"I should hope not," said Edna.

"So get out your notebook," I ordered her in a gruff sort of revenge, "and we'll set up the case."

But while she was getting her notebook, the pain stabbed at my ear again. I didn't really want another hot compress, which was beginning to give me a cauliflower ear, so I took the small vial of drops from my other inside pocket. I thought I might hold it in my hands to warm it, but my hands were cold. When Edna returned with the notebook, she found me with my head bent to one side, like a hanged man, squirting drops into my ear. I finished, capped the bottle, plugged my ear with cotton, and stared at her.

"Does that help or hurt?" she asked sympathetically.

"I don't know," I answered honestly. "My trouble is that I've gotten demoralized. I'm worn out. Earaches aren't supposed to last this long." But the drops were working. "Screw it," I said. "Let's draw up the schedule."

I gestured to the sheaf of papers. "These are the people who were supposed to be helping Gene," I said. "But not all the names are here. Also, there are people who weren't really in the business of helping Gene that I want to see. I want to list all the people by function first, and then we'll put names to them. First of all, I want to talk to the head of the exercise outfit he was going to—the heart mill, he called it. I want to see what the setup is, but most of all I want to get copies of the electrocardiograms they took of Gene on the treadmill." Edna looked up inquiringly.

"Gene told Evie he'd checked out on the second time around, and that there was nothing wrong with him. But I wonder if he was telling the truth. Sure as hell, Evie doesn't know. To this day, she doesn't really know if anything was wrong with Gene's heart. It is exactly because of this that she believes he died unexpectedly, that there was no reason for his death. I want to get hold of those graphs and get an independent opinion.

"Now, there's another guy at this place I want to see, the physiotherapist who monitored Gene's exercise program. There's something screwy about the idea that anybody who exercises regularly would wind up looking like Gene. I've got a suspicion that his heart was bad and he wasn't really allowed to exercise, and that's how he managed to lay on all that gut before he died."

"Physiotherapist," muttered Edna. Grimly she worked it out and put it down in God knows what form. I maintained a polite silence.

"From there I go to another fellow whose name is on one of those tickets," I continued. "The psychotherapist." I waited while she wrote it down. "Now, Evie and I are both going to be able to read the transcripts of Gene's sessions with this guy, but that doesn't signify we'll know what they mean. I want to talk to this guy and find out if he thought Gene was suicidal. There could be a lot of tricky, hidden meanings in the transcripts that could go right over our heads. It could be that Gene was so depressed, so agonized over the way things were going, that he knocked himself off. Personally, I don't believe it, but I think Evie has a sneaking suspicion that this was the case. And, of course, that lays another load of guilt on her—an intolerable load, really. If I can knock that idea out of the park, I'm going to do it.

"Finally," I said, "we come to the people who Gene thought were the real root of all his problems, the company he worked for. I want to talk to the new editor, who was supposed to be driving Gene up the wall. But most importantly, if they're cleaning out Gene's desk, I want to get hold of the stuff before they send it on to Evie."

"That's sneaky," opined Edna.

"Edna." I looked at her. "Dear," I said. "Employment, the office, the job, is for many men a compartment for a secret life that their families know nothing about. Their desks, in offices that are secure, are often the repositories of all the information about this secret life. Now, I have no reason to suspect that Gene had a secret life. But on the other hand, he was acting very screwy before he died, and it may have had nothing to do with exercise, smoking, or physical fitness. He may—I say *may*—have been living a double life. It's more common than most people think. The most ordinary guy in the world is more complex than most people think. And Gene was far from ordinary. There is no telling what may be found in his desk. But whatever is found, I don't want it shipped straight back to Evie and the kids.

"Look," I said to her puzzled expression. "I'm hoping that you can see by now that I'm trying to protect Evie. As far as I can see she has led a pretty decent life. Before Gene blew up, I got the impression that they had a very solid marriage. I don't want all that to get destroyed for her because of some stupid accident. She's got to get back to remembering what Gene was like before he went into his tailspin. It's very complicated. She's got to recognize the tailspin, but she's also got to remember the other Gene and what made their lives worthwhile over all those years. You see what I mean?"

"You mean that if you come across something that isn't kosher, you're going to lie to this woman who is paying you."

"Precisely."

"So she would never really know the truth."

"Exactly."

Edna's lips became a thin hard line as she weighed her feelings on this point. Suddenly they curved into a triumphant smile. "It won't work," she said victoriously, "because if he's got a secret life, it will all come out in the transcripts."

"It's a risk," I admitted, "but I don't think it will happen. Gene was seeing this shrink for one reason only—to get back into gear without smoking. From Gene's description of the whole thing, I'd be surprised if he told the guy his right name. I don't think any secret life will be revealed there, if, indeed, there is such a thing."

"But you think there really might be?"

"Yes," I confessed, "for one very strong reason. Why was Gene having those nightmares? He had no history of them, and yet they kept recurring. It might have been just the strain of problems at work, but, somehow, I've always felt that Gene was a little stronger than that. The problems at work were all being expressed right up front, drinking, raising hell, being a general son of a bitch. The nightmares point to something else, something secret and hidden. If there is something like that, I don't want it to blow up in Evie's face."

I was about to speak again, but a sudden pain flashed through my head and gripped the right side of my face in a spasm. "Jesus Christ," I said to Edna, "maybe I've got *tic douloureux.*"

"Joe," she said. "Go home and lie down. Take your codeine. Take morphine. Take heroin. Take something. Don't sit around like this."

I went back home, but I did not take the codeine. Instead, I took the world's most popular narcotic. I watched television on my little ten-inch set. My set is not equipped for the "hearing impaired," but that has never mattered to me. I have always been content with the small, hypnotic square of gray, phlegmatic light.

8

I told the dragon I was stepping out into the hall for a cigarette and got the usual outraged look. I was getting very used to this, and also very sick of it. I had arrived at Dr. Beaman's on this Friday noon, as per schedule. He was jammed up, and I was asked to wait. Since time spent in the doctor's waiting room is among life's least entertaining intervals, I soon felt the need for a cigarette.

I was hoping that the wait would not be unusually long because I had an appointment with another doctor at two-thirty. This appointment was not for my benefit, however, but for Evie's. As I requested, Edna had called the head of Execu-Trim, one Ralph C. Milgrim, M.D., and had set up the meeting. She had told him, wise girl that she is, that I was acting in the interest of Mrs. Eugene Listing, the widow of a former client (this doctor had clients instead of patients), and so he had assumed that I was a lawyer. I had no intention of disabusing him of this notion until absolutely necessary.

I doubted that I would be able to maintain the illusion for very long. I had spent a very bad night, alternately sitting in my easy chair and staring at the stupid screen and lying on the couch to try to sleep. The earache had not stabbed me so much as exerting a steady distracting pressure in my skull. When I had shown up in the office at ten o'clock, Edna had kindly informed me: "Joe, you look like hell." Thanks, Edna.

"I put my cigarette out and went back into the waiting room, where I startled and disappointed the dragon. I was exactly on the point of the prior patient's leaving, and so I was told with great disapproval, "The doctor will see you now."

I handed myself over to the nurse, who put me through the familiar rigmarole and jotted temperature, pulse, and blood pressure on the chart. Beaman came in, glanced at the figures, and took my wrist. How are you feeling?" he asked me.

"Terrible."

He felt my pulse and maintained a discreet silence. He examined my ears with the otoscope and felt around my sick ear with sensitive fingers. He went through the routine again of taking samples of gook. He also looked carefully down my throat.

"What's the verdict?" I asked him.

He stared at me with that peculiar anger doctors show when they're puzzled or frustrated. "The laboratory reports came in on time, but they're inconclusive," he said. He looked at me gravely and pursed his lips. It was all my fault.

"You still have an infection," he told me. Thanks, Doc. "But on the other hand, you haven't finished the course of antibiotics I gave you. You have been taking them, haven't you?" His eyes bulged a little with a threat.

"Yes, sir," I answered. "Faithfully. Religiously."

"And the drops?"

"I am never without them." I reached into my coat on the chair and took the small vial from the inside pocket. I held it up to the light and was surprised to see it was almost empty. Beaman advised me to get it renewed. He continued to stare at me. I grew uneasy. Finally, he made up his mind.

"I'm going to take a couple of X rays," he announced. "Come on into the back here."

I plodded obediently after him, and we were joined by the nurse. Together, they positioned me under the machine (an old dinosaur from prehistoric times, it looked to me), stepped out of the line of fire to protect their gonads, and filled my head with Roentgen rays. I followed Beaman back to the examining room, retrieved my coat, and joined him at his desk in the office.

"I'm sending today's samples to the lab on rush too," he said. "So I want you back here at Monday noon, sharp." He looked at me again after jotting down the appointment. "Those drops are renewable," he reaffirmed, "but the codeine isn't. Do you need another prescription for that?"

"Christ, no," I said. "I haven't touched the stuff."

"Tough guy, eh?"

"Reasonably," I replied. "I guess I'm reasonably tough." I've always been puzzled by this attitude in doctors. Sure as hell, they want you to be tough (fewer complaints) and yet they always seem to resent it. I don't think I will ever figure out why this is so.

He handed me a slip. "Give this to the receptionist on the way out," he said. "And be here Monday noon, without fail." He looked at me again. "You have my emergency number, don't you?"

"My secretary has it," I told him, forbearing to add that there was little chance of my using the telephone.

"If you think you need me, don't hesitate to call," said Beaman. "If there's any trouble getting me, go directly to the emergency room at Lenox, and have them call me. Understand?"

I answered that I understood, but did not mention that I was frightened.

I was frightened enough to avoid my customary groove from Beaman's office to Henry's elaborate saloon. After I had picked up my refill of eardrops, some of which I applied immediately, I began to search for a place to eat. I was hungry, but solid food was not appealing, since the hinge of my jaw, which nestles right under the earlobe, had turned sensitive. I opted for soup, knowing full well that eating soup in a restaurant is a risk secondary only to undertaking a Himalayan expedition barefoot in a breechclout. That soup simmers for days, my friend, and who knows what drops into the pot as the golden hours pass by? I finally found a drugstore counter where soup is decanted from a little can and heated before your very eyes. I had two cans. The waitress regarded me with suspicion. A possible madman.

I was still hungry and still hurting as I entered the reception area of Execu-Trim. Execu-Trim had been one of the first health emporiums to open just as America had appeared to give up on sex. It was established in the cavernous basement of one of the big old hotels on Seventh Avenue, and while the lobby of the hotel spoke of remodeling glitz, the atmosphere one found on descending to the basement was pure high tech. The whole basement had been infected by the transatlantic germ of the Beaubourg Pompidou Center (which I had observed only in garish color from the pages of my dentist's magazines). Here, stony areas of wall that had once collected garbage cans were painted in deep, impressive mauve. Huge overhead pipes that had once been highways for hotel rats were sparkling clean and painted in passionate reds and yellows. Chrome and glass glittered everywhere. Indeed, they hurt my eyes, which I resented. I suppose that the receptionist was a great advertisement for cardiac regularity, but my interest in a lady's heartbeat is seldom rooted in her cholesterol count. When her heart beats faster, it is my hope that this occurs from sexual excitement, not from aerobic dancing.

After I explained my mission, she led me down a plasterboard corridor disguised by brilliant shades of orange. The door at the end announced that this was the office of Ralph C. Milgrim, M.D. She knocked, waited for an answer, opened the door, and introduced me.

Dr. Milgrim, a small pale man in a white coat, was standing next to his desk and talking to a large blond man in gray sweat clothes. The doctor's face had been turned away, so I couldn't get a clue to what he was saying. However, he turned courteously to me to say, "I'll be with you in a moment, Mr. Binney." The young man's eyes barely flicked over me. The receptionist stepped back into the corridor and shut the door. The office had no hint of Beaubourg about it. The walls were gas-chamber green and thickly hung with diplomas.

Dr. Milgrim concluded his conversation. He turned to me and said, "Mr. Binney, this is Don Heemstra, our physiotherapist."

I smiled with real gratification and answered, "I'm delighted to see you here." They were both startled—possibly at the sound of my voice. I added, "I wanted very much to talk to you too. So it saves me a trip." The young Mr. Heemstra smiled uncertainly.

I was invited to sit down and did so. Milgrim sat down behind his desk, losing two thirds of his presence thereby, but emphasizing the sharpness of his nose, the wariness of his eyes, and the glitter of his gold-rimmed spectacles. He smiled at me, but he had one of those politicians' everything's-going-to-be-all-right smiles that I have learned to distrust. He was certainly no advertisement for strength through joy. He was in his late fifties, I judged, with a white, soft face topped by thinning gray hair. The white hands he folded on the blotter in front of him were small and ineffectual-looking. He said to Heemstra, "Mr. Binney is here to inquire about Gene Listing." Heemstra's face showed sympathy and interest.

Heemstra's face was bigger and fleshier than I would have expected in a man performing hours of daily exercise, but I also realized that we go by stereotypes and carry a cardboard cutout image of "gym instructor." The most striking thing about his face was its complexion. I suppose it had often been called "ruddy," but, in fact, it was more of an orange color, as if something had gone wrong with the effect of a sun lamp on his type of skin. Except for his fine blond hair and almost invisible eyebrows, he gave the impression of hairlessness. There was certainly no hair on the thick orange hands he laid in his lap. He had startlingly white teeth and expressive blue eyes, which, again, appeared lashless. Although the sweat clothes covered his body completely, I noticed in the way he moved to the chair and sat in it a smooth flow of controlled power. I guessed that he had under those gray clothes the kind of rubbery, massive, nonbulging muscles you can see in certain Mexican Indians and a few boxers, like Joe Louis and Muhammad Ali. I regarded him with respect.

"Poor Gene," he said, and repeated, "poor Gene," shaking his head. "It's a damned shame." His eyes expressed a concern that was almost motherly.

"Yes . . . well," I began, "his death was certainly unexpected, and very naturally Mrs. Listing is extremely upset." The pompous words tasted like cardboard in my mouth, but I was aiming for a kind of hyperrectitude. "What I'm trying to do for her, really, is reconcile her to the fact that these things do happen. Middle-aged men can keel over suddenly even though they are exercising regularly and undergoing medical supervision."

Both tensed up a bit at the words *medical supervision*, sniffing the air for a possible lawsuit. Heemstra asked me, with a rather wary expression on his broad face, "What else does she think could have happened?"

"I suspect that underneath it all she's afraid he might have managed to commit suicide."

The little doctor nodded sympathetically. "Of course," he said, "of course. The insurance . . ."

"I don't think she's concerned with the insurance," I protested mildly. "I think she's concerned with her own responsibility, her own guilt, if this were the case. Relations between Mr. and Mrs. Listing had been very strained ever since the crisis had occurred."

"Crisis?" asked Dr. Milgrim. "What crisis?"

I was nonplussed. "Correct me if I'm wrong," I said, "but you did refer him to a psychotherapist, didn't you?"

The doctor's little white hand waved it all away. "That's nothing," he said. "That's not a crisis. We do that with anyone who has a little problem quitting smoking."

"He didn't have a problem quitting smoking," I told them. "He quit the moment he was coerced into doing it."

The doctor sat upright, looking grave. "Coerced?" he repeated. "How was he coerced?"

"At his job," I replied. "By the people who hired you to check him out and train him—the obedience school, all that."

Now they were definitely not liking what they heard. "You can hardly call it coercion," the doctor maintained. "His company offered him a beneficial health service, absolutely free of charge."

"And," I returned, "if I offered you an electric blue velvet Buster Brown suit with a flowing collar absolutely free of charge, would you be happy to wear it to work every day?"

"It's not at all the same . . ."

"If you had trouble adjusting to the new life-style," I added, "I'd be happy to recommend a psychotherapist to help you over the bumps."

"It's not at all the same thing," the doctor insisted, with a sharp little tremor of his head. "And you still haven't explained why you think he was coerced."

"He was told by his employer that he would have to quit smoking or lose his livelihood. If that isn't coercion, I don't know what is. Furthermore—" I held my hand up to stay the interruption, "those were not the conditions laid down when he took the job, or he wouldn't have taken it. It was only after he'd invested ten years of his life in the place that they switched the signals on him, when it was very nearly impossible for him to find equivalent work and go on meeting his responsibilities.

"Then," I continued, "they offered," I held my fingers up as quote marks, "absolutely free of charge, a health benefit, making it widely known that the whole company was on a health kick. Supposing he had refused the benefit? He was up for promotion and a new regime was in place. Was he in a position to refuse?

"After that," I would not let them interrupt, "he got a letter from you telling him there was something wrong with his heart. Is he going to get promoted if there is something wrong with his heart? So he tries to get that straightened out, and all the while his work is going to hell because it requires an extreme kind of concentration and he can't concentrate because he was forced to quit smoking. Is it any wonder his marriage went to hell? That he turned into a monster with his kids? Is it any wonder that his wife thinks he may have committed suicide?"

I had noticed from the corner of my eye that Heemstra had been enjoying this confrontation with the doctor. But now he moved forward and said with a little smile, "People don't commit suicide because they quit smoking. I guarantee it."

"I'm glad you've got the suicide problem solved," I told him. "Maybe you can go out to the suburbs and tell the parents why their teenage kids are hanging themselves in the garage."

But I saw that I had gone too far. I attempted reconciliation with a broad gesture of my hands. "Look," I said. "I don't believe Gene committed suicide. I believe he was under tremendous stress with all the problems that had been dumped on him all at once and he just keeled over. That's really all that I'm up here about. I just want to reassure his wife and get her out of the bind she's in. It's more a mission of mercy than anything else."

They were both unhappy with the picture, but they didn't seem to want to pursue it much further. "Very well," said Dr. Milgrim. "What do you want from us?"

"What I would like," I said, attempting to return to my high plane of rectitude from which I had badly slipped, "is all the medical records you have of Gene here. The treadmill electrocardiograms, all of it."

Dr. Milgrim smiled, a wintry scene. "And do you know how to read an electrocardiogram, Mr. Binney?"

"Of course not." I smiled at him, ignoramus that I am. "But I would like to take them to a cardiologist for consultation and have him explain to Mrs. Listing how all this could have happened."

The wintry smile changed back to the politician's now-everything-is-going-to-be-all-right.

"If you will bring Mrs. Listing here," said Dr.

Milgrim, "I will be happy to explain the whole thing to her. Naturally, I feel great sympathy for Mrs. Listing's problem, and anything I can do to help . . ."

"I'm afraid she wouldn't accept an opinion from you," I told him. "As a matter of fact, she regards you as the root of all Gene's problems. What she needs is an independent opinion."

He put his fingertips on the edge of the desk. "Mr. Binney, we can't turn over medical records to just anyone who asks for them."

I assumed my blandest expression. "Why not?" I asked him. "You turn them over to the company that hired you, don't you?"

"Absolutely not!" The thin, pale lips snapped shut. "Medical records are absolutely confidential."

"Well, that's just not true," I argued. "Any third-party payer wants to know what the score is. Gene's little outfit had just become part of a conglomerate. I'm sure they get what they pay for."

"They do get what they pay for," said Dr. Milgrim. "Health benefits for their employees. And that's all they get."

"I can't really believe that," I answered doubtfully. "For instance, very often when a guy is hired he has to pass a physical before he's taken aboard. Right? And the results of that physical go into the personnel records. The company pays for the physical, and the company gets the results. That's one instance of medical records being shared. Personally, I don't think these big companies would pay you a dime if they couldn't get a peek now and then. I don't think they'd promote a guy into a responsible executive position if they didn't think he was pretty healthy and not ready to conk out on them. I think Gene was right; they wouldn't promote a fifty-year-old man with a bad heart."

"They simply would not know," Dr. Milgrim insisted. "Personnel directors can't read electrocardiograms any more than you can."

"Then let me approach this from another tack," I said. "If a man is sent here and it is revealed that his heart is too bad for the exercise program, he is turned down, right? I mean, you wouldn't put a cardiac cripple on one of your bicycles, would you?" Milgrim pursed his lips. "If the man has been turned down," I continued, "surely the company must know, because the company is paying the bills, and you can hardly charge them for someone who doesn't show up, can you?" The lips were now definitely compressed. "So," I concluded, "no matter what you tell the company, they very definitely have a device for measuring the fitness or the attitude of their candidate for promotion. Yet very few middle-aged men in the executive echelon ever thought they were going to be judged by their performance on a stationary bicycle. Most of them thought they were hired for their brains."

"Exercise very definitely increases mental acuity," said Dr. Milgrim.

"Makes you wonder how Einstein or Steinmetz ever got out of the gate, doesn't it?"

This exasperated him. "Mr. Binney," he said, "I can't sit around arguing with you. I am certainly not going to release Mr. Listing's records to you, and that's that."

"Will you release them to another doctor if they're requested?"

"If there's a good reason, which I doubt."

"A subpoena is a very good reason," I began. But suddenly a spear drove into the right side of my head with a blinding flash of pain. I bent over in my chair. Perhaps a cry had escaped me. I don't know what any deaf man's cry would sound like, much less my own— like the tearing of fabric, do you suppose? Perhaps they thought I was having an epileptic seizure. At any rate, it activated Heemstra.

It could only have been Heemstra. Blinded by tears as I was, I couldn't see, but those thick strong hands that clasped me on either side of my shoulders could have belonged only to the big orange man in the sweat clothes. I was eased gently back into the chair, and felt the gentle blotting of Kleenex on my eyes. When my vision cleared, I made out the fleshy, compassionate face. Beyond him was the small white figure of Milgrim, who had come around the desk. He looked shocked and unhappy, and, much, much worse, totally unprepared as to what to do.

"I'm sorry," I said. "It's nothing serious. I've got an ear infection that won't really clear up, and now and then it takes me. It caught me by surprise. I didn't mean to be so dramatic."

Heemstra's blue eyes searched my face. "Are you taking anything for it?"

I took the little bottle of eardrops out of my coat pocket and smiled sheepishly. "This is supposed to do the trick, I'm told." To demonstrate, I took the cotton out of my ear and applied a few drops.

The blue eyes never left my face. "You haven't been given anything stronger than that?"

"I've got some codeine at home," I answered, feeling foolish. "But the ear never hit me quite this hard before." I tried to restore myself, putting the cotton back in. "Besides, I wouldn't want to go around doped up just to avoid a few flashes."

The eyes changed their expression without losing the compassion that seemed built into the blue.

My game was pretty well shot to hell now, and I decided to put a quick end to the misery. I said to Dr. Milgrim, "What I'll do is this. I'm going to retain a physician as a consultant, and I'm going to ask him to request all available records. It will all go through professional courtesy. If you're not willing to extend that courtesy we'll have to go to court, although that is so time-consuming that it would essentially wreck the whole idea of this project, which is simply to get Mrs. Listing off the hook. I sincerely hope we won't have to go into anything like that; but if we have to, we will."

At this point, I ordinarily would have given him one of my cards. Instead, I took out a piece of notepaper and wrote my name and address on it. I still had faint hopes that they thought of me as a lawyer.

I was astounded at how weak and shaky I felt when I stood up. I staggered for a step, but the thick orange hand swept up to steady me. "Are you sure you're all right?"

"I'm OK," I lied. "Thank you for your time and trouble. I'm sure everything is going to be all right."

And with these brave words, I forged my way out of the trained-flea circus and into the street, more frightened than I have been in many years.

9

It seemed to me at the moment that whatever was pressing inward from the right side of my skull had bitten at last into the brain itself. This was three days later, mind you, the Monday afternoon following the Friday afternoon on which I had been assaulted by that disabling stab of pain. On this Monday afternoon I thought that very possibly I was experiencing a hallucination as I stood at the door of Evie's apartment.

The weekend hours had been a gray pool of misery. I had sat in my blind-enshrouded front room staring, when I could bear to look, at the gray-blue flicker of the TV screen. The pressure increased and obsessed me. I almost welcomed the occasional lance of pain that shot through my head.

So I had been grateful for the necessity of forcing myself to the office at ten on this Monday morning, and abjectly grateful for the appointment with Dr. Beaman at twelve.

But now I was looking at something so unexpected I was doubting my senses—as I had every right to do. I had expected the apartment door to be opened by Evie or one of the kids. The appointment had been made for two-thirty on the strength of a phone call to Edna. Evie had told her that some of the transcripts had been typed up, and would I come over and get them, please? I groaned, but I was willing. Now, when the apartment door swung open following my ring, I was confronted with a total stranger. The young woman who opened the door was simply one of the most beautiful women I had ever seen in my life. There was, I am sure, a look of utter amazement on my face as I drank her in, because I saw her face accept it all—I suppose it was not all that unusual to her—and reflect it in a smile. There was also a flash of response in her eyes, a flash without which, in my estimation at least, beauty cannot live.

So I was in shock. Have you ever met someone unexpectedly so beautiful it shocks you? The perfume drifting over the doorsill gave me the courage to test reality. I asked, "Is Mrs. Listing in?" I felt like an idiot. This was not the maid.

She smiled—breathtaking—and replied, "Mrs. Listing is away right now. Is she expecting you?" There are moments when I regret my deafness more poignantly than others. I regretted desperately not being able to hear that voice.

"Yes," I answered, suddenly a schoolboy. "We have an appointment for two-thirty. My name is Joe Binney. Mrs. Listing wanted to give me some papers."

Her eyes were dark brown, fathomless, and nearly matched in texture the dark brown hair that rained onto her shoulders. The eyes flashed with the barest flicker of a suddenly vital interest. She swung the door farther back and stepped aside, saying, "Come in. Come in." Her smile widened with the invitation. And when I say that she stepped aside, I hope I haven't given the impression that this was the one-two-three-click sort of movement we've gotten accustomed to in the business world. When she stepped aside her dress shimmered like a breeze-ruffled pool and reflected all of the soft, intricate joinery of her small, round, beautiful body.

For she was quite small, five-two or -three, unusual in today's vitamin-fed spurt toward the ideal giantess. She was small enough and vivacious-looking enough, in fact, to wear colors so brilliant that they might have been a joke on another woman. The dress she was wearing was Thai silk, apparently simple in design, but imbued with swirls of blood crimson and jungle green on a white ground. It would have overwhelmed most women, and those who were not overwhelmed would have looked like whores. The dress, however, was a designer dress, and the body inside it was so taut, so full to bursting and yet controlled, that any notion of comparison was put aside. She was supremely herself.

I watched her close the door. She turned to me and said, "My name is Celia Listing. I'm Gene Listing's niece, and I've come down to help Evalina sort things out."

Very often when I speak with people, particularly those I've just met, there is an uncomfortable pause in the conversation while I work out what they have said and get accustomed to their lip movements. With Celia Listing, however, this pause became an absurdity. I was stricken. I stood and stared. She smiled at me again, waiting for some kind of reasonable civilized response. Instead of interpreting, I was thinking of how red her lips appeared to be, how white and even her teeth were, and how perfectly in proportion to her adorable mouth. I absorbed the soft white light of her complexion, which obviously bore makeup but gave no hint of how or where it had been applied. Finally, I put her words together and stammered out, "Well, I'm sort of helping Evie too. I'm—I was—a casual friend of Gene's."

She had already made out that I am deaf. There was to be no awkward explanation. It was all very clear in the direct way she addressed me. She gestured to a chair. "Please sit down," she said with marvelous enunciation. "Evie ought to be"—she glanced at a small diamond-studded wristwatch—"right back."

As I sat down I managed to divert my eyes and look around the room. Evie's careful restoration seemed to have been taken apart again. Books had been moved, and a few of them lay open on the floor in front of the bookcase. The secretary, which had been so laboriously tidied up, was open again, and a lot of papers lay on the desk leaf with the disorderly air of having been examined and discarded. The young lady noticed my wandering attention and stepped in front of me.

"Can I get you something?" She smiled. "I happen to make a marvelous martini, and it's not all that early, is it?"

I pondered the notion of having a drink. My instincts of health were against it, but having a drink and joining this lovely creature in a drink were two totally separate categories. "If you're having one," I said honestly, "I'd be glad to."

She did indeed make an interesting martini. It was concocted with incredible swiftness, her absence into the kitchen being startlingly brief, and the result was as powerful as a mountain locomotive. After my first sip, I stared at her with awe and reassured myself that she had poured her own out of the same pitcher.

She had sat down on the sofa, opposite me, and had crossed her white, white, stockingless legs, a simple maneuver that tripled the proof of my cocktail. There was a fluidity of flesh underneath that silk that set off gongs inside my poor sore head. She smiled brilliantly over the rim of her martini glass. "Cheers," she said.

"Cheers," I echoed hopefully.

I made a rather panicky effort to take stock of things after the first icy wave of gin. I was certainly in no shape to drink anything this powerful, however inviting insensibility might be, because I had—had—*responsibilities*. The sparkling glass was held only a few inches under her chin. She said, "What is it you're helping Evie with?"

Well, yes. *That* was the primary responsibility. I said carefully, "Evie's upset, of course. And she's uncertain as to how Gene died. I'm sort of helping to pick up the loose ends. Running errands, and so forth."

"Uncertain?" Her smile had a rueful corner to it. "I thought that was all cleared up."

"Not to Evie's satisfaction."

"Ah," said Celia. "I think that's called denial."

"Maybe," I agreed. "But she does have a right to know."

"But she does know, doesn't she, that it was a heart attack?"

"But she doesn't know what kind, or why."

"Are you a doctor?"

Was she kidding me? I took a deeper sip of the martini than I had meant to in order to cover my embarrassment. It made me cough, and the effect was that of a mild interior explosion. "Oh, no," I assured her. "I'm just a private investigator. And even then, I'm hardly acting professionally. Much more as a friend of the family. Even then, I'm not all that much of a friend. I'd known Gene less than a year. I'm more of an aquaintance." And obviously a clown, I thought to myself.

"But she called you?"

"Well, yes. I guess I was the only private investigator she could think of."

"And what is it you are doing?"

"Just trying to get all the records in one place so we can make some sense out of how he died."

"But if you're not a doctor . . ."

"Oh, we're going to take them to a doctor—a disinterested party."

She had a very pretty way of looking owlish. She took a deep, paralyzing sip of her martini with no obviously ill effects and said with a gleam of suspicion, "And all this is in aid of a lawsuit, is it?"

"I don't think that's what Evie has in mind."

Celia Listing finished her drink, stood up, and commanded me to do the same. I obeyed automatically. She picked up the frosted silver pitcher and filled both our glasses. I hadn't even had a chance to eat my olive, which I wanted desperately for nutritional balance. Celia sat down and looked at me gravely. "You think Evie's undergoing some kind of quiet hysteria, then, do you?"

"No," I answered honestly. "I just think she wants to know how Gene died."

"There must be more to it than that," Celia said, owlish again. "People usually believe what their doctors tell them."

"Gene never really had his own physician," I said stiffly. By this I mean that my lips were becoming stiff. Apparently what I was drinking were nearly straight triple hookers of one hundred proof icy gin. "So I guess he and Evie never had anybody they could really trust."

She said, "I get the impression that you yourself are of two minds about the whole thing."

Her language now had too much the air of case-making about it. I answered guardedly, "I'm just trying to help in any way I can." I didn't really care if this sounded stupid. Sometimes a rocklike stupidity carries its own defense.

"But surely . . ." she began, smiling enchantingly again. Then her smile changed to one of unmistakable greeting, and I turned in my chair to see Evie struggling through the door, bowed down with shopping bags of groceries. I got out of my chair quickly and went over to help her, but I was dismayed at my slight stagger and stumble. I tried to cover it while I went into the kitchen to help Evie with the bags.

In the kitchen, Evie's face was a thundercloud as she vehemently stowed the goods. It was slam here and bang there as the refrigerator door was punished and kitchen cabinet doors were hurled shut. I stood ineffectually by, useless in trying to help her, and, I suppose, I looked as guilty as I felt. I had not made the appointment with her, after all, to sit around and get crocked. Indeed, I had not meant to get crocked. It was a very black mark on the old escutcheon. Evie, after all, was depending on me.

But there was something more to all this, my gin-chilled brain informed me. There had been something in Evie's eyes as she swept the room just before heading into the kitchen. Had she said anything to Celia? If so, I hadn't seen it. Evie had seemed to absorb the entire scene at once and reacted with an ill-contained fury. Was it only me? She had seen me juiced up before. There was something more going on here.

She got the last of the groceries put away, and, with the last can of beans, appeared to have spent her rage. She turned to me, gathering herself, controlling herself, and forced a smile through the lines of fatigue. "I'm glad you're here, Joe," she said. I smiled foolishly, guiltily.

She took my arm and marched us both back into the

front room where Celia stood waiting. She said to Celia, "I take it that introductions are unnecessary." Even Celia's brilliant smile seemed a bit sheepish. She said nothing. Evie then fixed her eyes on the bestrewn desk of the secretary. She said to Celia, "Have you found what you were looking for?"

Celia's smile was a bit uncertain. "Not really. No."

"Is there any place else you'd like to search?" inquired Evie.

Now there was very definitely electricity humming between the two of them. Even my befuddled mind, enclosed in silence, could feel the current. The slight shock of it made everything much clearer. I had assumed that the secretary had been gutted by the two of them before I had arrived. Apparently, this was not so. However, Evie's straight attitude of displeasure gave Celia a footing with which to reply. She said, "Oh, Brat. Search. Really. I was only looking to see if Gene had left something we could use."

It was the moment for me to reestablish myself and appear as something less of a Goddamned fool. I may have spoken more harshly than I intended, because when I asked, "Looking for what kind of thing you could use?" Celia jumped slightly and stared at me with rather widening eyes.

"This is all very silly and rather embarrassing," she said. But if she was embarrassed, it did not reveal itself in a blush. "We, in the family, keep up one of those huge, portentous, and very foolish yearbook family histories. Births and deaths, of course, are written about. *Everything,*" she emphasized this with a gesture, "is written about. And when someone dies, his professional career is described, and described in many instances, I might add, quite fulsomely. The whole effect is to make the family look quite grander than it is. Father has simply asked me to pick up anything showing what Gene was doing in his last days—any scrap of manuscript, notes, what have you. Don't be offended if I tell you this will be embroidered to make it appear as if he had been writing something on the scale of Braudel." Celia's face softened, and she smiled at Evie. "I wasn't prying, Brat, really."

But Evie was having none of it. She stood in a posture of wary defiance, one hip thrust out at an angle. I sensed now what hadn't been evident before, that Evie had put up with a long history of condescension from Gene's family and was calling a halt. She said with a slight nod, "I thought we had agreed to go over the papers together."

Celia turned away abruptly and picked up the empty pitcher. She held it up in front of her. "Brat," she said, "you are exhausted and justifiably irritated with me. Let me make amends by way of a drink. All right? I really am sorry, and I really do apologize. I was hasty and thoughtless, that's all." Evie's guarded response was no more than a slackening of the muscles in her cheeks. Celia fled with the pitcher, and I groaned inwardly at my forthcoming doom.

Evie suddenly focused my attention and said to me directly, and I think silently (I am never too sure about this, but there is usually an exaggeration of the lips when people speak silently), "I've transcribed three of the tapes. I've been working in the bedroom because of the street noise and the kids. I'll get the transcripts for you." She left the room.

I had the feeling that Evie wanted to hand over the transcripts while Celia was busy in the kitchen, but, unhappily, they nearly collided at the entrance to the living room. Celia was carrying the pitcher and three clean glasses. Evie was carrying a thick manila envelope. They passed together through the doorway and then separated out to stand in isolated pools in different areas of the room. They stared at one another, and then Celia broke the tension by putting the pitcher and glasses on the coffee table and pouring out the drinks. She went to Evie and me with a drink for each with the helpless charm of a nine-year-old serving hors d'oeuvres at a grown-up party. She was, to me at least, utterly disarming. She picked up her own glass then and said, "Cheers."

"Cheers," I croaked. I took the barest sip from the rim of my glass, but I noticed Evie had taken a very healthy swig and didn't bat an eye. I was clearly outclassed by these ladies. I was outclassed in conver-

sation too. The ladies were conversing on that plane of
social intercourse that leaves men numb, long series of
apparently inconsequential observations that one feels
has underneath it the groundwork of a minefield. However cautiously I was sipping at my martini, I was
growing steadily more crocked and was following them
with only the barest comprehension until I noticed
Celia staring at me and obviously repeating herself:
"Joe? Are those the medical records you were talking
about?" She was referring to the manila envelope in
my lap.

"I guess so," I said woodenly.

I keep forgetting that other people do not have to
look at one another to hold a conversation, and so I
was a little surprised to see Evie, standing behind
Celia, say, "It has absolutely nothing to do with you
or the family history, Celia. This is strictly private . . ."
and see Celia's expression change while she was still
turned away from Evie. She was staring at the envelope.

"Mysteries," said Celia, "are never private." I was
not at all sure she had spoken aloud. Evie's expression
did not change from one of grim defiance. She had
been swigging her martini, and now she drained it. I
looked into mine and saw that it, too, was nearly
gone. It was time for me to leave. Celia, too, apparently had decided that the game was up. I saw her
make a remark about the Carlyle and assume all those
gestures and activities preliminary to good-bye. I was
a bit surprised that she was not staying in the apartment with Evie, but my curiosity was badly blunted. I
put my glass down carefully, tucked the heavy envelope under my arm, and stood up. In my mind, I had
rehearsed the words, *"Well, I must be going now,"* but
when I opened my mouth, I knew that nothing had
come out. Possibly my jaw worked, flapped rather
helplessly. I was unable to recognize anything but light
and dark, because tears were flooding my eyes. I did
not feel the sharpness of pain I had felt in the other
episodes because the gin had almost completely anes-
thetized me. I was panicked, however. I pressed the
envelope tightly into my armpit. Then, although I still
couldn't truly see, I was conscious of my voice work-

ing, saying, "I'm all right. I'm all right. It's just this
damned infection. Just get me into a cab and get me
home. OK? I'm all right. Don't worry. It's nothing
. . . nothing serious."

10

The cab ride home had its share of hallucinations too. The short day had been a crowded one, and I was well and truly sozzled, as well as half blind and wholly deaf. Because my eyes refused to clear, the city swept past me in patches of light and dark, gigantic images refracted in tears. The tears were purely automatic; there was pressure in my head but no pain. But the tears also closed me inside myself. I remained hardly aware of the person beside me, and instead questioned the images that kept rising up in my mind—the orange face of Heemstra, the saturnine face of Dr. Beaman, the astonishing face of Celia. They were hallucinatory, and I questioned them. Had Heemstra really showed up in my office this morning? Had Beaman really suggested that they might have to drill a hole in my skull? Was it really Celia sitting beside me now in the cab? Had I really gotten this hopelessly drunk on three martinis? Was I really holding a fragment of Gene Listing's mental history in a thick brown envelope in my lap?

Heemstra's fleshy face swam into the foreground—again, something totally unexpected and strange. He had been there in my office when I opened the door at ten o'clock in the morning. He had been talking to Edna, his big face topping not the clothes of a normal human being in a business office in New York, but a costume that seemed to be a cross between lounging pajamas and mechanics' coveralls. It was a nasty shock for a poor bastard like myself looking only for a cup of hot fresh coffee and the white, solicitous hand of Edna on my brow. They had both looked up at me with that expression that informs you that you are intruding. Intruding! In my own office!

He was wearing the kind of rig that I understand has become unisexually popular, but in the days before my time had been called by Winston Churchill a siren suit. Churchill had worn one pretty much throughout the second world war, explaining that it was handy to jump into when the air-raid sirens shrilled. Underneath it, I believe, he wore nothing, for I have always had the impression that Churchill entertained a bent for nudity. Apparently, it was always a simple matter of zipping in and out for Winnie.

Heemstra, too, gave the impression of being naked under the royal blue jump suit. An impressive amount of hairless chest shone forth from the unzippered V at the top. He was sitting on the corner of Edna's desk with an air of easily controlled gracefulness for so big a man. And, again, he gave the impression of considerable mass that was easily activated. He had a half smile on his face, and his blue eyes under the lashless lids showed a good deal more vitality than they had in Milgrim's office. Edna also had a half smile on her face. The two of them were obviously quite charmed with one another.

I tried to get up a welcoming half smile on my mug, but nothing worked for me. Before I could get out any kind of salutation, Edna seemed to chirp, "You've met Mr. Heemstra, Don Heemstra, haven't you?"

"Yes," I replied. I suppose that the syllable dropped like an anvil. The half smiles diminished. Edna picked up her end. "Don, Mr. Heemstra, has been telling me the most wonderful things about how to defend yourself and all."

"Stout legs and a sound wind," I observed, "are the best defense for all practical purposes." Somehow, I did not want to ask Edna to get me a cup of coffee at this moment. I had already given a very strong impression of being old, sick, and crabby. I went over and got it myself. Holding my cup, I said, "Why don't we take the show into my office, where I can sit down too." I banged into my office and lunged into the chair at the desk.

When the two of them came through the door, they both had that *Now-let's-be-patient-with-Joe* expression that I have learned to loathe. I said to Edna, "I'm not tracking terribly well this morning, so maybe you'd better get out your book and keep a record of all this." I smiled at Heemstra to indicate there was nothing abnormal in this procedure. He had been towering over me at the desk, but had the civility to lower himself into the golden oak chair across from me. Edna had gone back to pull her notebook from who knows what warren and then joined us, seated in the other chair. I sipped my coffee.

"Well, Mr. Heemstra," I said with what I thought was reasonable joviality, "what brings you here?"

I guess it was not all that jovial-sounding. Both he and Edna glanced at me sharply. He waved a thick orange hand. "Don," he said. "Please call me Don."

"All right then, Don," I repeated, "what brings you here?" As a matter of fact I was none too pleased with his showing up at my place of business because it sure as hell ripped open the gauzy illusion that I was counselor-at-law. If Heemstra was feeling smug about this revelation, however, he refused to show it. He said seriously, "Ralph was pretty upset with what you had to say the other day."

"Ralph—that's Dr. Milgrim?" Heemstra nodded. "Hadn't he heard that Gene was dead?"

"Yes. Certainly. Of course he had."

"Gene's company ask for their money back, did they?"

Heemstra relaxed in his chair and laughed. It was a marvelous display of teeth. He leaned forward, still smiling, and said, "That's just exactly what Ralph is so upset about."

"The money?" My eyebrows climbed.

"No—no." Heemstra waved me off. "The attitude. Your attitude. All that stuff about money, coercion. We don't coerce anybody." He was still smiling.

"I never said you did," I replied. "I said that Gene's company had coerced him."

"It was in his own interest, really." Heemstra urged this on me. "Gene was heading for trouble."

"He sure got there in a hell of a hurry."

"It was an accident, like being hit by a bus. As a matter of fact, very often the medical term is accident. Sometimes strokes are called ischemic accidents." Without being grim, he was nonetheless earnest. "Barring the accident," he said, "our program would have been the best thing in the world for Gene." He pleaded suddenly, holding up both his hands, "How do you think I feel about it? I was trying to work very carefully with Gene, to bring him on."

"But he had a heart attack," I objected.

"Not from anything we did, believe me," said Heemstra.

I finished my coffee, absently handed the mug to Edna—who, bless her, thoughtlessly put down her notebook and went off to get me another cup—pulled out a Lucky Strike, lighted it, took a deep drag, and regarded Heemstra through a cloud of blue smoke. Edna returned with the coffee, picked up her notebook, and was ready to go again.

"Are you feeling any better?" Heemstra asked me. It was not a phony question. He seemed genuinely solicitous.

"No," I answered. "I feel like hell. But I'm going to see my doctor at noon, so I guess I can hold out until then."

"That's good," Heemstra said abstractedly. Edna had not jotted down any of this, but with his next statement, she took up her shorthand again. "What we're really anxious to make clear to you—more to Mrs. Listing, actually—is that our program couldn't possibly have contributed to Gene's heart attack. If Gene hadn't been unlucky, the program would have done him a lot of good."

"But Gene didn't want anyone to do him any good," I complained. "He just wanted to be left alone."

"Sometimes people need a little nudge to get them on the right track," said Heemstra. "They just don't think about these things until somebody points them out." He had totally relaxed in the chair, not an easy thing to do. His expression was neither contentious nor zealous. I didn't think he was trying to sell me anything.

"I'm sure that Gene had always been aware of his options," I said.

"I don't know." His blue eyes fixed on the ceiling as he considered it. "This town is full of middle-aged men who go to the office every day, sit at their desk, drink black coffee, smoke cigarettes, and work like hell without moving their bodies at all. They're headed for trouble, and yet they live in the closed world of their jobs. I'm not sure that they consider the options. Sometimes they need help."

"Don't you think they ought to be allowed to reject it?"

"Sure," he said, "but they ought to know that they're rejecting the best advice of the whole health industry."

I blew out another gray-blue cumulus of smoke. "Right there, I think, is where you put your finger on it," I told him. "What you're referring to used to be called the medical profession."

He shifted uneasily in the chair and mumbled something about "doctors can't do it alone any more," but his blue eyes were distracted.

"Look," I said, "we could have this argument all week, but you got me at a bad time this morning. I appreciate your coming, but I still don't really know why you're here."

"I told you," he said earnestly, his big hands gripping the arms of the chair. "Ralph, Dr. Milgrim, is worried about your attitude. I mean, our entire business depends on helping people like Mr. Listing. The trouble with all this is that Gene Listing was a journalist. Journalists mean publicity. And with the attitude you've got and that he had, it could only mean bad publicity for us, particularly if you're thinking about a lawsuit. I mean, there aren't any grounds for a lawsuit at all, but that doesn't mean there couldn't be one."

He took his hands off the chair and clasped them in his lap. "Look," he said, "I don't own any part of

Execu-Trim. I'm just an employee—maybe a key employee, because I started out with the place, but I don't own any interest in it. On the other hand, I don't like people going around with the idea that I somehow killed a guy I was trying to help. And believe me," his eyes were piercing in his concentration now, "I did everything I could to help Gene.

"He was a difficult client," Heemstra continued, leaning back a little. "Probably the most difficult I ever had—not physically, but in his attitude. He was hostile, aggressive, and contemptuous. If I'd let him go ahead, he'd have burnt himself out in an afternoon. He would have almost literally killed himself. He took on the whole thing as a challenge to—to—" He searched for a word.

"To his dignity perhaps?" I asked him.

"His masculinity, personality—whatever," Heemstra waved it away.

"Let me give it to you straight," I said to Heemstra. "Nobody has mentioned anything like a lawsuit to me, and I have absolutely no interest, personal or financial, in seeing one mounted. I went over to your place simply to pick up any medical records you had on Gene so I could take them to a consultant. You people acted like I wanted the great ruby from the idol's eye. It's my business to get those records in the hands of a consultant one way or another, and that's what I'm going to do. That's what I'm being paid for." It was a long speech for me and it exhausted me. I slumped and put out my cigarette.

Heemstra put his hands up in the gesture of surrender, but he was smiling between them. "All right," he said. "That's all I wanted to know. That's all Ralph wants to know, and both of us regret any misunderstanding you may have taken away with you. You aren't going to have to worry about the records because I've brought copies of every single thing we have on Gene over here with me."

He stood up and went out to Edna's desk. He came back with a cheap plastic envelope of the kind they give away at conventions. It was thicker than I had expected. He dropped it on my desk. "There you are," he said. "That's everything, lab tests, EKG, medical history, physical examination, notes, and exercise records. The works. But remember, you promised to show this only to the proper medical authorities. This ain't confetti."

"I promised," I told him. "I meant it. And I thank you."

"Okay," he said. "That's that. So long." He smiled then and turned to Edna, saying something that I couldn't see. She smiled back and nodded. He disappeared through the doors in a fluid burst of energy.

"Interesting guy," I observed to Edna, my eyes gloatingly fixed on the plastic envelope. "I wish we knew more about him."

"Maybe we will," said Edna. "He's taking me to the movies tonight."

That was this morning. Now, as I sat in the bouncing capsule of a taxi making its tumblebug's progress through the late afternoon traffic, Edna's pensive smile hung briefly in my memory and then dissolved.

The cab jolted to a stop so suddenly that I almost fell off the seat. Were we at my place? I still couldn't see very well, but I fumbled toward the door handle. A small, cool hand laid itself over mine and gently tugged it away. Another hand was put on my chest, pushing me very gently back into my seat. Her perfume drifted up around my face. It seemed that we were only in a traffic jam of the well-known kind that has made the Lower East Side almost impenetrable. I sat back, relaxed, and closed my dripping eyes. Dr. Beaman's dark, disappointed face immediately swam up beneath the lids.

"You still have the pressure. You still have the pain."

"The pain comes and goes. Attacks. Not as many of them, but sometimes more severe."

"You took all the antibiotic."

"Every single pill. Finished up yesterday afternoon."

"I'm going to give you a different prescription, a different antibiotic."

"The lab show anything?"

"Inconclusive. Nothing I could go on."

"Those X rays show anything?"

"I didn't really expect them to. A shot in the dark. I wouldn't have taken them at all if I hadn't had earlier ones to match them up with. You've got a few loose bone chips in there. I wanted to see if they were displaced. Sometimes that tells us something."

"How long do you think this is going to last?"

"Obviously we can't let this go on much longer. I may have to open you up, have a look inside."

"Jesus Christ. I don't want that."

"I don't want that either. Wednesday morning I want to see you at eight o'clock, but not here, at the hospital."

"At Lenox?"

"No, at the Veterans' Administration."

"Are you kidding? I don't go to the VA. I've got a medical plan, as well you know, bought and paid for."

"You need the VA this time because there's a very great doctor there, and I want him to see you."

"I've already got a great doctor."

"Stop the bullshit. This man trained me before I went into ENT. He's an internist, but internal medicine doesn't say one-twentieth of what he is. I called him about your case. He's interested. He says if it's what he thinks it is, he hasn't seen one in maybe thirty years."

"He just wants a few laughs, huh?"

"Mind your manners when you see him. Don't get smart with him like you do with me or I'll hit you with a mallet. This man has seen everything, done everything."

"How'd he wind up at a bullring like the VA?"

"He'd retired, but the chief of medicine there wanted him aboard. The chief promised him his own laboratory to play in, so you can guess what kind of a reputation this man has. He, himself, has been chief of medicine at some of the greatest hospitals in the world. A great clinician, a great teacher."

"You'll pardon me if I wonder whether my poor little medical insurance plan is going to stand still for this consultation."

"I told you he was at the VA. It won't cost you a

dime. It won't cost them a dime. He just wants to look at you."

"For free?" I said scornfully, "He's no doctor."

"A lot you know about doctors."

"What's his name?"

"Dap. Israel Dap. Dr. Dap."

"Why should I see him?"

"Maybe he'll figure out a way we don't have to open you up. He hates surgery. To him, to lose a patient to a surgeon is like losing one to the grave. If a patient goes from him to surgery, he sobs his heart out."

"I'm on," I said.

"Be there. Eight o'clock."

I felt the cab slow down and pull to the curb and surmised that we had reached home at last. I got onto the sidewalk and was conscious of Celia beside me dealing with the driver. I didn't really need much vision to find my keys and let us in the street door, nor to find our way upstairs and into the big, dim front room. The girl in her multicolored, swirly dress, her white face, her brown hair, and the aura, unmistakable, of her perfume, seemed to be all about me without touching me, like a ghost. I was also aware, happily, that my eyes were beginning to clear. Being on home ground was a great comfort to me. I saw Celia walk into the depths of the room, giving the books and furnishings a quick, all-enveloping scan. Then she moved toward me, reaching for the package under my arm.

I pulled back and said, "Coffee. I need coffee. Don't worry. I could make it in my sleep. Sit down, why don't you, for a minute, while I put this away, and then we'll have some coffee."

I stumbled down the hallway toward the kitchen, but stopped off at my bedroom, where I put the thick envelope in the bottom drawer of my nightstand. Then I went into the kitchen where, with automatic movements I had so often practiced while semiconscious in the morning, I put coffee in the filter, and boiled the water. I got two mugs from the cabinet and brought the whole show back to the front room. By now, as if the activity had sharpened me, I could see fairly well, well enough to pour us both a mug. The first sip was excruciating, but the steam going down my pipes drove a lot of the mistiness away. When I was able to take my first full swallow, the effect seemed to restore me completely. I could see her face very clearly, camellia white, entrancing. She smiled and said, "What on earth is in that envelope? Uncut diamonds?"

"Just some papers of Gene's," I said, "that Evie wanted me to look at. It wouldn't have anything to do with your family history. Not anything you'd want to print, anyway."

Celia said with a triumphant look, "Your eyes have cleared!"

"Yes," I repeated stupidly. "My eyes have cleared." I stared vacantly at her as the whole day rushed back at me—the records from Heemstra, the transcripts from Evie, the nearing solution to my illness, the presence of this luminous girl. . . .

"Jesus Christ," I said to Celia. "I think I'm going to faint!"

11

But I didn't. No. What happened was much more surreal than a simple fainting fit, for which the prescribed description is, *"Everything went black."* No. No. Everything went white. It was very different. Everything went white except for a very small patch of darkness.

I had said, *"Jesus Christ, I think I'm going to faint."* I had been standing in front of my big easy chair, sipping my coffee, and Celia had been standing a few feet away from me. When I made my dramatic statement, she stepped up to me as if to catch my arm. But I sat down suddenly in the chair—*bump*, like that—and in so doing I spilled my coffee all over the front of her dress.

It did not scald her. She had made a step, so that her legs were apart, and the black coffee splashed over the middle of the lower part in the center of her dress. It took her an instant to realize what had happened, and after that instant there was another in which she seemed paralyzed by indecision. She looked down at the dress with its steaming ruin of a stain, looked directly at me with astonishing penetration, and then, in her eyes at least, appeared to make a decision.

She said directly and unmistakably to me, "Unzip me!" She whirled around and presented her back. I stood up, found the little catch at the nape of her neck, closed my fingers on the tiny tab of the zipper, and pulled. This accomplished, I fell back into the chair. She wheeled around, crossed her arms to grab opposite sides of the hem, and pulled the dress over her head. There was absolutely nothing underneath it but Celia Listing. It was, as I have mentioned, all white, snowy, dazzling white, except for a dark, razor-trimmed patch. I was, for an instant, snow blind. She whirled again and disappeared down the dim hallway toward the bathroom, a fluttering of white, like a moth escaping the light cone of a lampshade.

I sat there witlessly, wondering if I had really seen what I thought I had seen, and if I had felt what I thought I had felt. I am not ordinarily the fainting type. What had brought it on? I wondered. Was it simple shock—the straightforward realization that Beaman intended to drill a hole in my head? I preferred that to the alternative—to the idea that the pressure was now pushing in a new direction.

Celia came back into the room and moved around in front of me so I could see what she was saying. I began, "I'm—I'm terribly sorry. . . ."

But she said, "Not to worry. The dress is saved and is at this moment drying out in your shower stall."

Sorry, however, was not what I felt. Electrified was a lot more like it. I had expected her to find a robe, a shirt, even a towel, but she came back as naked as when she had left the room. She seemed to wear her nakedness as unselfconsciously as she had her dress. She was utterly composed. I felt the gentlemanly urge to say *"Can I get you a robe or something?"* But I did not say it. I believed that saying it would have made me out to be a fool.

Celia asked with a businesslike expression, "Are you feeling better?"

"Yes," I replied, and added, like your average maiden aunt of seventy, "I don't know what came over me."

"This hasn't happened before?"

"Christ, no!" I answered almost violently. "It must have something to do with this Goddamned ear infection."

She put on her owlish look again. "Ah, yes," she said wisely. "What's being done for it?"

"Day after tomorrow," I told her, "I see the big panjandrum. They're supposed to figure it all out on Wednesday."

"Then let's relax until Wednesday," said Celia.

Oh, how that idea appealed to me. I said to her, "You know, right now I'm as screwed up as I've ever been in my life. I'm still half drunk, half sober, overwhelmed by what they like to call events, and totally confused."

"Half drunk isn't bad," said Celia, "but half sober is dreadful. If you've got the makings, I'll whip up another batch of martinis."

"No!" I said explosively. She looked startled. "I mean," I amended, "that yes, I have the makings, but I'll do the honors. I'd better check out my wheels anyway. You wait here. If you hear a dull thud in the hallway, remember, it's only me."

She laughed—a lovely sight.

As I tromped down the hallway to the kitchen, where I keep my liquor (no fashionable wet bars in *this* apartment) her image remained in front of me. I kept thinking astoundedly to myself, her skin is as white and smooth as the silk of the dress she had just whipped off. But unlike the silk of the dress, she was alive, oh, so alive, and she was constructed with a symmetry that no designer could match and no artist even begin to render. Her breasts, for instance, seen from the front, were perfectly circular and punctuated with small, rosy nipples that bobbed just above the center. Her whiteness was contained in a roundness, a roundness of depth and volume and utterly perfect joinery so that her thighs touched together without any hint of fatness, and the dark *cache sexe* dipped to its disciplined point like an apostrophe. Above all this was a beautiful, witty, intelligent face that seemed to hold as many secrets as her body did. Why, I wondered, had I felt the urge to offer her a robe? Was I really embarrassed by her nakedness? I'd spent a little time in Japan before heading for Korea, and had had the chance to see nakedness in a different context. No, I hadn't been embarrassed by her nakedness, but by her beauty. I had felt an embarrassment in claiming to belong to the same species.

She had composed herself on the couch by the time I got back with the jug of martinis, glasses, and the cylindrical bottle of olives shoved in my back pocket. She had her feet tucked up under her and, in the late dimness of the apartment, seemed to glow out of the dusk. I set the drinking materials on the squat table in front of her and switched on the lamp. She looked up at me and said, "Do we really need a light?"

"If I'm going to understand anything you say, we do," I told her. "That is, if there is anything to say."

She laughed. "Oh, yes, there's plenty to say." Her laughter then turned into a rather sympathetic smile. She said, "Does my being naked bother you?"

"Not at all," I lied. It was a bad question and a foolish answer.

"I like being naked," she announced. "Clothes are a bore, and bikinis are obscene. I will never understand why people wear them."

I bent over to pour the drinks, and inhaled the dizzying scent of her perfume. I pulled up a chair, then, and sat at the table across from her. She lifted her glass to say "Cheers," and I hoisted mine, too, while watching the beautiful structure of her breast follow the ascent of her white, round arm.

"Cheers," I repeated. I sipped my milder, controllable martini, and said, "Let's talk."

"By all means," said Celia.

"I don't really know anything about you," I said. "Tell me more.

"An epic of triteness," said Celia. "I live at home in the family manse in Maryland. My father is Sam Listing, Gene's older brother—nine years older, in fact. My mother died while I was in convent school, shortly after the birth of my little sister, Anne. From convent, I went to Trinity College, history major, and thence to Georgetown University, the official family school, for postgraduate work in political science, and rounded off all this nonsense with a stretch of hard labor at London School of Economics."

"The family manse," I suggested, "is not a tract house in a development?"

She giggled over the rim of her glass. "How right you are," she said. "It's a huge, ugly old pile that wanders over half of Maryland. It is a bore and a penitentiary, and I, unhappily, because my mother died, have to officiate as chatelaine."

"After all that schooling," I complained, "that's it?"

"Well, not quite." She held out her glass for more, and as I poured it, I realized that I had finally got accustomed to her nakedness. It seemed now that she was simply wearing clothes of skin—her skin. "I do have a job and an office in Washington, where I perform the odd errand now and then."

"And just how odd are these errands?" I asked her.

"An endless round of shuffling papers," said Celia. "In our family either you're a housewife or you work for the government. I suppose I'm on some kind of career ladder, although I cannot quite see where the rungs are leading, nor do I honestly care all that much. However, Father would be inconsolable if I didn't have a career."

I dug out my cigarettes. Celia said, "May I have one?" I lighted both and after we'd blown out a cloud of smoke both of us said at once, *"Tell me about Gene."* We laughed and drained our drinks, exhausting the pitcher, and I went back to the kitchen for another round.

When we got resettled Celia said, "You first."

"There were so many odd things about Gene," I began. "I knew him only briefly, and part of that time was when he was in trouble, serious trouble. But I liked him, and even when he was impossible I sympathized with him. But he really was an exotic, at least to people like me. Let's start with one thing that jumps out at me. You say that traditionally the people in your family go to Georgetown, and yet Gene went to Johns Hopkins. Do I make too much of that?"

"Oh, no," she said. "You're very right. Gene's going to Johns Hopkins was regarded very much as we might have regarded the skeleton of a baby buried in the walls. It was unthinkable. Everyone recoiled."

"Well, was it just a gesture on Gene's part, a revolt? Or did he have any kind of serious purpose?"

"This is all ancient history to me," replied Celia, "and I have to construe. Knowing what I know of Gene, I would say he'd had a serious purpose, but a purpose that got lost somewhere. I don't know where or how. I know that his major, his passion, was Asian studies, and I know that Johns Hopkins was the place to be for all that. I must say that it seemed incredible to me that he stood up to the family that way."

"Yes," I agreed. "He seemed to be very good at standing up."

I sipped my tamed martini. "Did this lead," I asked her, "to a complete break with the family? Was it as serious as that?"

"That's hard to answer," replied Celia, setting down her drink. "It certainly wasn't a social break. I mean Gene and Brat and the kids used to come down for weekends. There was always plenty of room—God knows there is room. But there was, of course, a definite sense of estrangement between Gene and my father. My father kept up a kind of older brother's disappointment attitude with Gene, and I'm sure it was very wearing."

"Were there sparks? Big arguments?"

"Not really. They seemed to be past anything like that."

"Well, was there a sense of Gene's family being," I made quotation hooks with my fingers, "poor relations?"

"Only a little where Brat was concerned, I think. I don't believe it ever really occurred to Gene. After all, they had their rooms as a kind of permanent establishment there. Gene kept his pinks there."

"His pinks?"

"Yes. He belonged to the hunt club. It was all paid for by some codicil or other. Gene rode every weekend when they were down, and never missed a hunt. He loved riding, and he was a marvelous horseman."

Another lens dropped into place. Gene as a "marvelous horseman" explained a good deal that had been missing—the firm handshake and the good hands, not too often found among office workers. There was also his odd square stance that bespoke the good legs of a horseman. Celia was adding, "Really, we didn't see all that much of Gene when he was down, because he spent most of his time at the stables."

"The stables, meaning your own stables?"

"Yes. Gene had two hunters there, Flake and Haeckel."

"Heckle, as in heckling from the audience?"

"No. Haeckel. Aitch ay ee see kay ee el, after the biologist. Something about his having a gaseous vertebrae, but don't ask me to pursue it."

"All right," I said. "This is all news to me, and I'm trying to put it all together. Now, Gene and his family would come down on weekends. They rented a car?"

"Oh, no. Gene hated to drive. They always took the train down on Friday evening, and Ridge would pick them up at the station and bring them in."

"Ridge?"

"Jack Ridge. He drives and looks after the cars. He loves Gene and Gene's kids. There would always be a little tension between Ridge and Father on Fridays because Ridge would always work it out so that he could pick up Gene, no matter what my father's plans might be."

"An odd thing," I ruminated, "is that Evie, Brat, seems to be missing from the picture. Did she enjoy these weekends?"

"I think so," said Celia, who had drained her martini and proceeded to pour herself another, sans olive. "She didn't ride much with Gene, although she could ride. She never joined the hunt. She stayed pretty much in their rooms—Gene had staked out a sort of area surrounding his old room, so they had a sitting room and separate bedrooms for the kids—and I think she simply did what every mother of young kids would like to do of a weekend—relax. The kids were either with Gene at the stables or with Simpson."

"Simpson?"

"Bob Simpson, the groom. Or with Ridge. Or Hetty."

"Hetty?"

"Cook."

"Hetty Cook?"

"No. No. Hetty *the* cook. Anyway, Brat would spread herself out in their sitting room and relax, reading, writing letters, drinking bourbon. Mostly she just showed up for meals, or if we were having any sort of a do. I mean, it isn't that she didn't fulfill social obligations. She just relaxed as much as she could, which she had every right to do."

"This estrangement between Gene and your father . . ."

"My father regarded Gene as a traitor to the family, and thereby"—she pulled a long face and rolled her eyes—"a traitor to his class. Father couldn't understand what Gene was doing, and whatever my father doesn't understand he hates or fears."

"He hated Gene?"

"No, no. That's entirely the wrong impression. He hated what Gene was doing, living in that rather sordid apartment, working at that rather pointless job . . ."

"I thought you said your father insisted that everyone in the family have a job."

"Not a job—a career. There's a difference. Actually depending on one's salary for income makes it a job, which Father thinks is disgusting. Father offered to help Gene establish his own paper or magazine, if Gene was dedicated to that sort of thing. But Gene refused. He insisted on keeping that silly job and putting really tremendous effort into it—wasted effort, as Father saw it."

"What about you?" I asked. "Do you think it was wasted?"

"Oh, God," said Celia, holding out her glass, "you mustn't ask me to make judgments. I have absolutely no morals or ethics. I couldn't possibly give you an answer from my remote position without the aid of another martini."

I took her glass and the pitcher and trudged back to the kitchen. Obviously, she didn't have a hollow leg, but this girl, I decided, had a bladder as big as the Ritz and a brain that was absolutely impermeable to alcohol. My own brain had turned into Jell-O.

When I came back she was standing over at the table where she had dropped her little lizard purse, and was doing something to her nose. I set the pitcher and glasses down very carefully. "Nose candy?" I asked her. "This early? Before dinner and all?"

"Aitch," she said, holding her hand out. "Lovely, lovely. Care for some? Very good aitch, I guarantee."

"You snort it?" I asked stupidly, having seen her do exactly that.

She approached me with her wrists extended together as if in handcuffs. "You may, if you insist, Officer," she said solemnly, "inspect every inch of my body for telltale tracks of the needle."

"No kidding," I said, moving away from her. "Where the hell did you pick up a dumb stunt like that?"

"Something I picked up in London," she told me, moving to the cocktail pitcher, "along with my economics. Are you terribly, terribly shocked and all that?"

In fact I *was* terribly, terribly shocked. I was too used to seeing the hags around Tomkin's Square to associate heroin with anything this beautiful. "Of course not," I said falsely. "Every clown in the world is using that stuff now."

"Ah," she said, moving away, "the raspy voice of disapprobation. How I would miss it, were it not there. Like Cunard, disapproval is half the fun of getting there."

"Celia," I said, "no kidding—why?"

"Could you force yourself to believe," asked Celia, "that economics can be an extremely boring subject, and that heroin, along with the people who use it in London, can be extremely amusing?"

"I can force myself to believe almost anything," I answered, "but I have a little trouble with the idea that studying economics can turn you into a junkie."

"Are you about to eject me naked into the street?" asked Celia.

"Ah, balls," I said, sitting down. "It's none of my business what you stick up your nose."

"But only in my nose, remember that," said Celia.

"I don't have that sick fascination for needles. There isn't a mark on my skin, and, if I can help it, there never will be."

"If you can help it," I muttered.

"Take a good look," Celia displayed herself. "Do you think I would ruin a perfectly good skin like this?"

12

It was an invitation to touch, and touch I did—the pale softness of her shoulder, like the brushing of a butterfly's wing. But she whirled away from me, with her breasts swinging slightly ahead of her, and flashed a smile back over her shoulder. It certainly wasn't a rejection, nor was it coyness or cuteness. She stopped again, facing me, and sipped the drink, which she hadn't spilled. She said, "Now I must ask you questions, because if I don't come back with something to put in that bloody book, Father will kill me."

I said, "Celia, Evie's the one to give you all that. I don't really know anything."

"Brat has decided she hates me," said Celia. "And who am I to blame her?"

"I'll tell you whatever I can," I said. "But for Christ's sake sit down or you'll make me faint again."

"My question is very simple," said Celia. "What on earth was Gene working on before he died?"

"I don't know what Evie's told you so far," I began, "but the fact is that Gene was hardly working at all, which is one of the reasons he was off in orbit. He couldn't concentrate enough to get a story out. So, I guess he spent most of his work hours making notes and marking time."

"But notes on what?"

"Evie mentioned that he was following some kind of harebrained story about nightmares."

"But that doesn't," Celia objected, "have anything to do with what . . ."

"What he was supposed to be doing? No, it doesn't. But it figures, you know, that if you can't do your work, you'd go off into the wild blue yonder."

"This was all," asked Celia, "simply on the subject of nightmares? Medically? Poetically? Culturally?"

"Particular kinds of nightmares," I answered. "As I get it from Evie, having to do with Southeast Asians. It seems that some of those people die in their sleep—from nightmares."

"Yes," said Celia thoughtfully. "I've heard of that." She had composed herself again on the couch, and I had retired to my chair across from her. Her face, which had been laughing, had settled into an expression of direct intelligence. "I've heard it seems to be happening with certain Southeast Asian refugees over here.

"Why," she asked suddenly, sharply, "was he messing around in the greasy leftovers of that horrible war?"

"It might have been part of his aberration," I suggested.

"Not really likely." She appeared to have muttered the words. Then she said directly, "Surely he must have talked to Brat about it."

"They weren't really talking very much in any civilized way by then," I recalled. "And there's another thing. Evie was pretty sore at him for chasing the story. Her point was that he was slipping badly at the office, and yet he was fooling around with a story that couldn't possibly have anything to do with his work. She thought the whole thing as silly as hell and a complete waste of time."

"She might well have been very wrong," said Celia. "There may be medical aspects to it—even criminal."

"But Gene was a financial writer," I objected, "not medicine, not crime."

"It would be a wonderful world if we could separate finance from crime and medicine," Celia told me. She had bent one leg under the other on the couch, utterly composed, sipping her cocktail. "But, indeed, we can't.

These people dying of nightmares, I've heard of them. They're called the Hmuong, and they come from northern Laos. Northern Laos being, of course, part of the famous Golden Triangle, the great trading center of the lovely, lovely China White. I daresay the area is as inseparable from the opium trade as finance is from crime.

"*Now*," she gestured sharply, "the embarrassing burden of the opium trade is not the opium, which can be gotten rid of anywhere, but the proceeds from the sale of opium. Money is the *corpus delecti* in this particular kind of operation, and it must be buried, dissipated—laundered as it's sometimes called, and where else but in a bank, and what is a bank if not finance?"

"Well," I responded lamely, "I don't know about all that. I mean, of course I've heard about the banks in Miami and up in Boston and the coke dodge, but I also hear that's all being cleared up now. . . ."

"And no doubt moved to offshore banks," Celia observed, interrupting.

"Well, sure. Possibly. But that doesn't have anything to do with nightmares. I think you're stretching here. I think that what really happened was that Gene started having nightmares and simply latched on to a fragment of a story. I mean, a few Laotians die in their sleep when they come over here after all kinds of hardship. Sure, they'd be having trouble sleeping. It's a wonder they didn't all go nuts."

"It wasn't just a few Laotians," Celia objected. "I think the last count was seventy."

"Seventy?" The figure surprised me. "Seventy of those people died in their sleep? Are you sure?"

"It may be more by now, but seventy was the last number I saw somewhere. It sticks in the mind."

"Is it some kind of a virus or something? Something like AIDS?"

"No one has been able to establish a cause that I know of," said Celia. She had drained the pitcher again, and I was terrified that she would order another round from my kitchen. However, she seemed to be, at last, content. "Medical investigators, as far as I've heard, have come up with exactly nothing."

"Nobody dies of nothing," I said. A thought illuminated me. "These are perhaps the older people who got worn out during the trip?"

"No," said Celia. "They are mostly in their thirties and forties. And they are almost all men. And they are mostly men who had something to do with the armies that were surging to and fro in the area. Very, very few women, as I recollect."

"Armies?" I asked her. "Soldiers?"

"Private armies, mostly, controlled by warlords," she answered. "Surely you've read about this. Everyone has. Foot soldiers, mostly, who have died in their sleep. All very mysterious. No wonder Gene was looking into it."

"But it wasn't his business to look into it," I insisted.

"If it had anything to do with banks it was, wasn't it?" She had tilted her head and smiled up at me.

"What the hell has nightmares got to do with banks?"

"Apparently that is what Gene was trying to find out."

"Laos is a long way from Miami or Boston."

She smiled when she said it, to remove some of the sting. "Are you being purposely dense?" she asked me. "Banking is international. Banks can be formed anywhere. They have only one requirement—money—as a greengrocer requires vegetables. Surely you've heard, for instance, of the Nugan-Hand bank operation?"

"Yes," I admitted. "I've read about that."

"As who has not?" she inquired rhetorically. "A repository for funds is needed and so a bank is formed—not necessarily in Miami. When the jig is up, the principals die or disappear. And the bank turns out to be the usual mixture of illicit funds mixed with government funds. And all the money is traceable to the old bedpartners of warlords, drug dealers, and government hirelings or officials—very much the mixture as before."

"But you just said," I pointed out, "everybody in the world has read that story. It's old stuff, not something Gene would be tracking down."

"Whenever you have a story that plain and that

public," Celia assured me, "you are talking about a symptom, not the disease itself. Nugan-Hand was obviously only an angry red pimple on the subject's chin. There must be more. There must be much, much more."

I sat back and laughed. The laughter hurt my head. "You think these Laotian foot soldiers with funny dreams are bank officers in disguise?"

She smiled back and set her empty martini glass carefully on the table. It had been forgotten in her hand. Again, the fluidity of all those white curves had the effect of hypnotizing me briefly. I had to force myself to look at her face when she spoke.

"Of course I'm not saying that," she allowed. "They are no doubt what they are said to be, Laotian foot soldiers who fled Laos when they had the chance. But soldiers in whose army? A warlord's? The Royal Laotian Army? A secret army financed by God knows what agency from where?"

She settled back again to lecture me. "People tend to forget," she said, "that the most important thing about an army is not its equipment or its uniforms, if any. It's the payroll. Troops will struggle along with bad equipment and ragged or no uniforms at all, but the money must be there. The commitment must be kept. Payrolls are not wafted out of thin air. They have to come in recognizable, dependable currency. The currency must first have a base, a certifiable base, and then a mode of transmission. The money must first be gathered in a repository, a bank if you will, and then brought out to distribute among the men. Unless this is done with reasonable regularity, the men will desert or mutiny."

I thought about my paydays in the navy, in Korea, the gigantic importance they had assumed. I nodded at her encouragingly.

"There is another general misconception about armies," she said firmly, apparently needing no encouragement from me. "People tend to think of the soldiers as myrmidons—ignorant lumps of earth that manage to form either a target or a trigger finger. This is a dangerous misconception. Each soldier is a thinking, reasoning human being with a personal history, a family, a home, a community, all of which are very dear to him, or at least as dear as they are to anyone else. Nowhere is this more true than among the outlying villages of the so-called undeveloped countries, where one's village often comprises one's true ethnic identity—one's tribe.

"Now," she said, the lecture implacably continuing, "one thing that characterizes a tribe is the sharing of information—gossip. Outsiders might find a closed face and a blank stare, but fellow tribesmen, fellow villagers, tend to share gossip, and, I should think, lonely soldiers in some godforsaken, isolated outpost would tend to gossip more than anyone on earth.

"Payrolls must be delivered," she said, holding up a small white hand. "How are they delivered? By helicopter? By troop carrier? Landing strip? Parachute? All these modes require personnel and equipment, both of which are recognizable in the closed world of the Southeast Asian mess. Remember, please, what the foot soldier said to Henry the Fifth, 'If the cause be not good'—etcetera. 'When all those arms and legs shall join together at the latter day and cry out *"We died at such a place."*' So a helicopter or plane pilot is recognized delivering the swag. The equipment is recognized, and the gossip begins—'*Who is paying for this operation?*' It is reasonable that some banks or corporations would not be pleased to have it known that they are financing a drug operation. After all, International Telephone and Telegraph were not overjoyed to have it known that they proposed to send millions down to overthrow the elected government of Chile.

"So it may very well be," she concluded her lecture, "that someone saw something he wasn't supposed to see, or a glaring mistake was made, as they so often are in these operations. The information spread by grapevine to other soldiers, and from them to the relatives and friends of soldiers. And all these arms and legs are joining together at a latter day, capable of crying out in these United States, '*We saw such and such a thing at such and such a place.*' And someone may be harvesting those arms and legs before they truly join together."

I said, "My God, Celia, you're talking about seventy people . . ."

"Not a very large number in terms of warfare."

"Who simply died in their sleep without a mark on them."

"Purest conjecture on my part," she answered. "But you rather challenged me on why Gene could have been interested in the story."

"But you're talking as if these people could have been murdered. And nobody ever found anything."

"Stick pointing," she said with a brisk air of dismissing the subject.

"Stick pointing?"

"Surely you've read," she said impatiently, "that in certain societies the shaman will point a stick at some poor hopeless bastard and pronounce *'Thou must die!'* And sure enough the fellow will trot obediently off into the bush and waste away."

"That's heart of darkness country," I remonstrated. "It doesn't apply . . ."

"Does it not?" she interrupted. "Check the actuarial tables on men who have devoted their lives to a firm, a corporation, which, after all, is only another kind of primitive tribe, and see what happens to them after a gold watch has been pointed at them. Indeed, they crawl off into a trailer and waste away."

"Even at that," I insisted stubbornly, "these people are separated from their villages, their tribes. No shaman, no stick, and no environment that would support any kind of black magic crap like that."

"You are putting yourself on very false ground," said Celia, the naked schoolmarm. "And I can only suppose you're doing it for the sake of argument. Every immigrant or refugee brings his culture with him. You have many a voodoo rite in Manhattan performed by disenfranchised Haitians. The Rastafarians have not given up ganja or dreadlocks. The Black Hand, later called the Mafia, operated in the nineteenth century precisely because the Sicilian immigrants brought their culture with them. It is not impossible to believe that some Southeast Asian gangsters came over with the refugees and are merrily operating at the same old stand, only in a different hemisphere."

She leaned back and took a deep, eye-popping breath. "As I said, this is only the sheerest conjecture on my part, but I hope I demonstrate that Gene was not completely mad when he thought of investigating the story. Now, no matter what Gene scratched up, I'm sure that Father can turn it all into something that was just about to save Western civilization when Gene expired, and enter the whole silly business in the family book. Therefore, I must have Gene's file to bring back, and all will be well."

"File?" I asked stupidly. The gin had settled into stagnant pools and was dripping rivulets throughout my brain.

"No journalist would work on something like this without a file. There would be backup, interviews, notes, what have you. Particularly not Gene, who did, after all, in spite of a rather foolish way of life, have an orderly mind."

"There's no file that I know of."

"But you are looking around for Gene's things, aren't you? Rushing in where nieces fear to tread?"

"Well, I don't know," I hesitated. "I've got an appointment to see old Basket tomorrow. . . ."

"Old Basket?"

A smile managed to part the gin-glazed front of my face. "The new editor they've got there, who is said to wear peculiar pants."

She gave me a quick returning grin of appreciation. "Then you will get a chance to look at Gene's files?"

"I suppose so," I answered slowly. "Evie told Basket that I'm supposed to pick up Gene's belongings. I suppose that the files are part of them, or at least copies of files."

"Why copies?"

"Well, they might want to hang on to any work Gene did while he was on the payroll."

"But wouldn't this story be among his personal papers? I mean, after all, it wasn't an assignment, just something he was developing on his own.

"It would be much better for me," she said determinedly, "if you could get the original and to hell with the copies."

"I'll try," I said loosely, vacuously. "But don't expect too much. I'm not my usual ball of fire these days."

"Are you hurting now?" She shifted to reach out across the table, and put her soft, pale, mothlike hand against my cheek.

"No, I'm not hurting," I answered, dazed. "I'm afraid I'm not anything at all."

"We'll see about that," said Celia.

She undressed me, and we collapsed on the bed. The gin had taken its frightful toll. There was much technical maneuvering. Afterward, I felt like an exploded melon. We had spoken only very little, and what cries might have come out of us were, of course, silent to me. I remember only one thing she said to me, and that with a mischievous light in her eyes. "Tell me. Did you spill that coffee on me purposely to get me out of my dress?"

"No," I answered innocently.

"Oh." Her lips formed a moué, and the mischief went out of her eyes.

13

I had dropped off to sleep with the unconscious expectation that I would sleep long and deep. This was not the case, however, and I awoke before dawn with the girl a shadowy mound beside me, my mouth dry and my kidneys full. The gin had extracted every bit of juice from my body.

I tried not to groan as I eased myself out of bed. I did not want company. The machinery noise in my head was unbearable. My eyes seemed to open and close on jagged bits of volcanic rock. I found a robe and stumbled into the kitchen, where I set the coffee on the stove. I was hopelessly awake and saw no chance of returning to sleep. When the coffee was done, I crept back into the bedroom and took the packet of transcripts out of the drawer. I had a hope that they would divert me from the agony inside my head, which was the standard regulation hangover accompanied by a looming pressure and twinges deep inside that were not so much painful as the echo of pain.

It took two cups of coffee to get my eyes into focus. I had closed the bedroom door so that the famous coffee smell would not awaken Celia. I put a fresh pack of Luckies next to the stack of transcripts. I lifted up transcript #1 and pushed the stack to the far end of the table. I was in that mental state where we do not read so much as drink in the words, uncritically, unreflectively.

It turned out that the therapist's name was Kragmeyer, Paul Kragmeyer. His contributions were to be symbolized by a *K* and Gene Listing's with a *G*.

K: *What have you got there?*

G: *It's a tape recorder, don't you see?*

K: *What for?*

G: *To record words on tape, I'm told. At our last session you kept intoning, "Oh, if only you could hear yourself, Mr. Listing." So I've decided to record our sessions and listen at my leisure, picking up tiny clues, don't you see—deadness of affect, inappropriate response, and so on.*

K: *This is very unusual.*

G: *Do you object? That seems hardly fair. You make tapes of your clients, don't you, for your own amusement?*

K: (Sternly) *Not for my amusement, Mr. Listing.*

G: *Of course not. I apologize. Anyway, I shall now be able to hear myself . . . and you.*

K: *That sounds like a threat.*

G: *Not at all. I am the victim. You have the whip hand. I am the one required to reveal his shabby soul, his pocky hopes and dreams, his errors, his fatuity. You shall, on tape, of course, remain godlike.*

K: *Get something straight, Mr. Listing. You came to me to help you quit smoking.*

G: *You see? How valuable this is for both of us! You have already made two mistakes in nine words. First of all, I did not come to you. I was sent to you—at peril of my employment, i.e. my livelihood. Second, and this is something that you kept dodging around all through the last session, which I remember quite well without the aid of a tape recorder, thank you, and that is that I have already quit smoking. I had no difficulty in quitting smoking. My difficulty is quite other.*

K: (Eagerly) *And that is?*

G: *That in quitting smoking I have undergone an*

> *emotional and mental change that prevents me from doing my work and has made my personal life an absolute hell.*

K: (In a level, encouraging voice) *And what do you think I can do about this?*

G: *Help me to find a way to earn my living and return to normal personal relationships, or, as Freud put it, "Endure the ordinary miseries of life."*

K: *You've read some Freud then. That's good.*

G: *No, it is not, unfortunately. There is no way that I am going to fit into any Freudian system you may be constructing to deal with me. I want to talk about this now for a few moments to help prevent you from getting started on terribly the wrong lines, wasting our time and the company's money.*

K: *Time I can understand, but why should you worry about the company's money?*

G: *Because I must dance to whoever pays the piper, and I would like to keep this dance as short as possible.*

K: *I don't really understand what you mean by that.*

G: *I mean that with you I must dance on a rope festooned with hand grenades. I must reveal exactly enough to show that I am in earnest, and yet not so much that I will have my employers rolling on the floor with laughter or rigid with horror when you turn in your report to them.*

K: (Incensed) *I am certainly not going to turn in a report to your employers!*

G: *Nonsense. They're paying you, and as Georg Wilhelm Friedrich Hegel wisely observed, "Man is the slave of whose bread he eats." If they held a hundred-dollar bill above your nose you'd put your little paws in the air like a fox terrier in front of a biscuit.*

K: *That is the most outrageous . . .*

G: (Overriding) *I'm glad to see you're capable of outrage. You didn't demonstrate any when I laid my problem in front of you.*

*　　*　　*

The machinery noise was still grinding away, but it had taken on a sort of comical hitch to the rhythm of it, like a ruptured clock. I reached helplessly for my pack of Luckies. The black, steaming coffee flooded all the arid reaches of my gin-soaked body.

G: *I want to steer you away from Freud for very serious reasons. My childhood had nothing to do with middle-class Vienna. I never had a sister, and, oddly enough, my mother did not tromp around the house with her skirts hoisted up to her shoulders, so that I was not the hapless staring pupil of female deprivation. There were no toilet bowls full of blood or bloody rags strewn about for me to make any connection with the idea of emasculation. Indeed, I had no idea of what female genitalia really looked like until I was fifteen, at which time I found them, and do to this day, ineffably charming. I was not masturbated by my nurse to keep me quiet, Mrs. Clancy having quite other means at her disposal, poor old crone that she was. I was not seduced by the chauffeur, groom, butler, or neighbors, since we did not have neighbors willing to make the trip merely to seduce an ungainly boy like me. When I fantasized about sex at all in my youth the fantasies were so innocent they would bore both you and the company that hired you.*

K: (Heatedly) *I wish you would stop referring to . . .*

G: *Just listen to me for a while, won't you? After all, that's what you're being paid for. Now, as to the inutility of the Freudian canon in my case, I would like to point out that I was never exposed as a child to the primal thumpings and groanings that characterize the parental primal scene, since my parents lived in the west wing of the house, and I the east. Neither did I ever see or hear any of the service rising and falling together. I was a total innocent, and any knowledge or misconceptions I had concerning sex rose like Meno's from the purest propaedeutic in utero.*

K: *I think you ought to know that I'm not any kind of classical Freudian. I really don't know any therapist who is.*

G: *Well, that's a blessing, and I'll tell you why. Although I venerate Freud as an originator and systematologist, I will never quite forgive him for vulgarizing the Oedipal conflict.*

K: *Vulgar . . .*

But here Gene erupted on poor Kragmeyer a Vesuvian flow of scalding anathema that torched off and then buried in the cold ashes of contempt the whole disciplines of psychiatry, modern medicine, and the plastic, heuristic attitudes that public health has trained on normal modern life and death. Gene apparently believed that the aim of public health was to make life as deprived and miserable as possible and then extend that misery, by the extension of life, for as long as possible.

This was not my idea of light early morning entertainment reading. My eyes still felt the sting of gravel under the lids. My mouth again was totally dry, and unlikely to be moistened by the cigarette I stuck in my face and lighted. I sighed out a cloud of smoke and trudged to the stove to heat up another cup of coffee. I stood there watching it stupidly in my customary early morning trance with the spiky stubble scratching my palm as I rubbed my chin.

Was Gene Listing really and truly crazy? Had he gone nuts? Had he always talked like this? (Not to me, he hadn't.) I am not even an amateur psychologist, but I thought I could see the way Kragmeyer's mind must be heading. For at the end of his tirade, Gene was zeroing in on death.

The coffee had begun to spout during my reverie. Disgusting, black bitter brew, now rancid with oils. Exactly what I needed. I poured a cup full and slouched in my bathrobe back to the table.

K: (Very gently, sympathetically) *Do you think about death very often, Mr. Listing?*

G: *As much as any standard horse's ass. Although, I*

admit, I've been thinking about it a lot more recently.

K: *And why is that?*

G: *Why, for Christ's sake, because it's being poured in on me from every side, from doctors, employers, newspapers, gymnasts, well-meaning idiot friends—stop smoking, stop drinking, stop eating, stop sitting on your ass of an evening or thou shalt surely die. Almost everything you touch today reminds you that you're going to die, just as one of those bloody mechanical seat belt warning voices reminds you that you are probably doomed to have a horrible, disfiguring, or fatal accident if only you drive long enough. As if the threat of nuclear incineration hanging over us for forty years weren't enough, we have made a fad out of death. We are entranced with death. I am sick to death of it. Reminding a Catholic that he is going to die is like reminding a shoemaker to stick to his last. I have always been aware that one day I am going to die. Any Catholic is. It is branded on our foreheads; indeed, it is the meaning of life, or at least the conduct of life. I don't need some asshole in a white coat warning me daily that it is coming.*

K: (Primly) *I think the doctors are doing what they think is best for you.*

Here, the therapist's remark ignited another eruption that would have been comical if Gene hadn't been in such deadly, desperate earnest. He managed to excoriate nearly every trope and finding in modern medicine, and if doctors were, indeed, what Gene made them out to be, then hell would soon be overcrowded.

G: *Look at how they have hedged us around with death! Look at what is supposed to be killing us—all the constituents of normal modern life. Tobacco, alcohol, salt, refined sugar, coffee or any beverage with caffeine in it, butter, red meat, chicken fat, and on and on so that our lives are*

> *reduced to the idea of eating unlubricated spa-
> ghetti and running our balls off. How can you
> ask me why I am concerned with death when
> absolutely everything I have ever enjoyed is pointed
> out to be an agent of death!*

After that he took a sober look at the whole modern
mythology of self-destructive behavior, ending up with:

> G: *Did Freud have a death instinct? What Freud
> said was, "After all, this cigar may be only a
> cigar." The reasonable conclusion, I think, is
> that there is no death instinct, and there is no
> such thing as self-destructive behavior. People
> simply live as best they can, given their imperfec-
> tions, and so-called self-destructive behavior is
> only a symptom of their struggle to exist in a
> difficult world, an imperfect, dangerous, and
> deadly world. How could a person be without
> anxiety unless he had no concept of both the
> spiritual and physical dangers of the world? The
> only persons I have seen with that sort of bovine
> calm are like the missionaries described by Lévi-
> Strauss in* Tristes Tropiques, *people who feel that
> they have made a sealed pact with God and there-
> fore could perform any brutality, any cruelty,
> any outrage with perfect impunity. But God, of
> course, not in any religion, does not make little
> personal deals, and I think that anyone who be-
> lieves he has bargained with God has just shaken
> hands with the devil.*
> *Life is imperfection: And God is anxiety.*

The air in the kitchen was blue with the smoke of
Lucky Strikes. The acrid smell of burnt coffee penetrated the smoke, and along with it there was the
redolent cloud of last night's liquor. I stared glassily at
the typewritten page. And then I became aware of
another scent, the unmistakable perfume that was
loaded now with the odors of sweaty exercise and the
ascending musk of sexuality. I reached my arm blindly
behind me, no different from your ordinary Ringling
Brothers contortionist, and brought my palm up to

spread across the firmest, softest, smoothest bottom constructed on this earth. She bent to kiss the back of my neck, and when she straightened, her breast rubbed against the whiskery spikes of my jaw.

My empty cup was knocked off the table and smashed. I pushed away the transcript I had been reading and shoved the other stack to one side. I stood up and seized her, and thanked God for the sturdiness of my old-fashioned oak kitchen table.

14

"You must be feeling better, you look better," Edna said to me when I came into the office.

I was taken aback. When I had last seen myself knotting my tie in the mirror, I had looked like just one more botched job by Dr. Frankenstein.

"Well, I don't feel better," I announced portentously. "I feel like the Wrath of Christ. What makes you think I look better?" I scowled to dismiss any possibility that I felt better.

"It was just an expression on your face," offered Edna, cowed. "It was just a different expression, that's all."

I swallowed this information in silence and planted myself behind my desk, which could always be counted on to supply a certain smoke screen. A desk is a mask of authority or it is nothing, Goddamn it. Edna remained at her much smaller, nonauthoritarian desk in the anteroom, quite properly waiting until she was called upon.

In spite of the no doubt sappy expression I had been wearing when I entered—the product of some exertion in my kitchen—I did not really physically feel better. The pressure in my head was inexorable, like the weight of an unsecured cannon on a tilted deck. When things tilted the other way there would be a deep, mysterious twinge of pain, nonetheless unsettling for being blunted. It was no longer as sharp, as tearing as the earlier pain, but it was there, all right.

I had put myself in an awkward position. I wanted my morning cup of coffee, but I had already screwed things up so badly there was no way I could impose on Edna to bring it for me. A nice tradition was being ruined on the spot. I got up and went into her precinct with that high-shouldered air of hostility that is so hard to shake once it's assumed. I poured myself a cup of coffee, turned around, and looked at her.

"C'mon, Kid," I said to her woebegone face. "Grab yourself a cup of coffee and come in and put your feet up." I was ashamed of myself. I often am.

She came slowly into my office and perched tentatively on the oak chair at the desk's corner. Her face was hard to read, and the freshly drawn coffee rested forgotten in her hand. I had the feeling that even I, with my nasty behavior, had been forgotten, lost somewhere under the veil of pensiveness. I tried to think of something nice to say—never an easy task for me—and finally settled on an offering coupled with a wholly artificial smile: "How was the movie?"

"All right, I guess," said Edna.

This was not very promising. I plunged on with the same false grin. "What movie was it?"

"Something about outer space," she replied absently. "Little men with pointy ears—ray guns—you know."

"Uh, what's his name, your date, did he enjoy it?"

The pensive expression became genuinely troubled. "I guess so," she said. "It's very hard to know what he's thinking. He's very reserved."

"He is?" It struck me as a truly surprising revelation. "He seemed to be doing all right yesterday morning."

Her expression became even more troubled. "A different situation, I guess," she cogitated. "He's a lot quieter when you're alone with him." Her eyes evaded mine and gazed at one of the four dusty corners of the office. *Ah*, I thought, my heart sinking, *there's something serious going on here.* It also explained the contretemps of the morning grouch. Edna was quite used to my being impossible in the morning. It hadn't been like her to cave in the way she had.

I suggested kindly, "A lot of young guys clam up when they're alone with a girl. With some of them it never wears off, you know—shyness . . ."

"I didn't say he was shy," she interrupted, giving me the sense that I had stepped into forbidden territory. "I said he was reserved."

"You also said, or intimated, that you were alone together," I pointed out with somewhat less kindliness. "It's very difficult to be alone in a movie theater."

"Oh," she shrugged, "we went on from there."

"Aha!" I pounced, smiling, I hope, lubriciously. "And on to where did you go?"

"His place."

My God. Judging from Edna's expression it must have been some rat hole gouged out of a bridge abutment. "Nice place, was it?" I ventured, smiling encouragingly this time. Lubricity did not seem of the moment.

"Beautiful," Edna pronounced surprisingly. Her eyes widened, and for the first time in this encounter she looked at me directly. "Absolutely beautiful. I mean, I never really thought that a man could have an apartment so beautiful."

"Beautiful meaning," I probed, "lace curtains, antimaccassars on all the furniture, genuine oriental rugs freshly loomed in Terre Haute?"

"You don't have to get snotty," said Edna. "And if you do have to get snotty, why don't we just stop talking?"

"I apologize," I said. "I really do. I'm as touchy as hell this morning." In fact, I was nettled by Edna's judgment of another man's apartment. That is the curse of bachelorhood. Since my apartment suits me, I feel, quite naturally, that no one need look farther for the zenith of interior design. "Honestly," I asked Edna, "what kind of a place is it?"

"Well, it's modern without being flashy or horrible," she began slowly, "although he has some old furniture in it that really is old furniture, not those reproductions you see all the time. The place is what I guess you would call harmonious, you know, the rug, the furniture, the lighting—everything just fits together without looking phony or tried on. And he has paintings on the walls that look original, although I wouldn't know, and I didn't want to look stupid by asking."

"Paintings," I said, interested. "What kind of paintings?"

"Well, modern," she said, ruminating. "But not crazy modern. I mean everything was sort of recognizable." She thought for a few seconds. "Did you ever hear of a painter called David Hockney?" she asked me.

"Sure."

"Well, there was one very pretty painting, modern, with lots of light green in it with that name on it, and it looked to me to be original, although it might have been a hand copy. I don't know. But it looked to be an original painting."

I *was* jealous, Goddamn it. It all seemed to make my apartment sound like the back room of a cigar store. Also, Edna was terribly, rather helplessly taken with the idea of anyone actually owning an original painting. I got the feeling that Edna thought this was sort of illegal. I resolutely shoved my emotions to the side and said as gently as I knew how, "Let's see if I have the scenario. You go with him to this tastefully lighted, beautifully decorated apartment near . . . near?"

"Murray Hill," said Edna. "A nice, old-fashioned building."

"Near Murray Hill. Okay. The stereo is snapped on, and the low throb of music saturates the room. He brings out a bottle of wine he has saved for the occasion, uncorks it, and sets it aside to let it breathe. There are some canapés, an interesting cheese, say, a Tomme de Savoie? And possibly a couple of Anjou pears. You're nervous, so you knock off a raft of canapés and belt down the wine like there's no tomorrow. Right?"

"Boy," said Edna admiringly. "Talk about the fly on the wall!

"I, too, have lived in Arcadia," I quoted at her.

"Okay, now, I don't want to hear anything prurient, but obviously you both sat around and talked some. But then what?"

Again, she got that remote, almost vacant look on her face. "Nothing," she said.

"Nothing at all?"

"Nothing. Nothing at all."

I put my fingers together in a steeple and leaned back. Wise old Joe Binney. "Edna," I addressed her, "if this guy is gay, you could get hurt very badly. You must know that."

She shook her head impatiently, although her face still held the expression of remoteness. "No," she said, as if talking into space instead of to me, "no. I would have caught on if he was gay. It isn't that. I know."

I began, "Things have changed, Edna," but she threw me such a startled glance that I felt foolish—and old. Things had changed, indeed, in my lifetime, but not in hers, at least not in her dating years. Emptying the closet had done away with much of the deception that had made life into hell for many boys and girls. Possibly now there were different kinds of deceptions and different kinds of hells. But when Edna said *no,* I believed her.

Nonetheless, it made my basic irritability return. "So what's eating you then?" I asked her. "Just that you're sold on him, but you don't think he's sold on you? Why don't you give the guy a chance?"

I had expected her to flare up at this, but instead she slumped back in the chair, her lips fiercely compressed in thought. Finally, she struggled to come out with, "Yes. And I'll kill you if you laugh. Yes, I am sold on him. I don't think I've ever really felt this way about anybody before."

Therefore, I had been right. It was serious—Heartbreak Hotel—more serious than your everyday set of scorched knickers. Because there is absolutely nothing to be said in these cases, I sought to close down the conversation, foreseeing that almost anything I said would be wrong, offensive, or both. "Well, that's that,"

I concluded. "Now let's see what we have to shape up today with, shall we?" I moved to pick up some papers.

"What I feel," said Edna, still looking vaguely over my shoulder, as if I had not spoken at all, "is a kind of security with Don I've never felt with any other man. It's just a completely different feeling from what I've ever felt before, like I'd trusted him all my life."

I tried to fit this emotion in with the young man in the jump suit, and came up nowhere. He'd seemed amiable, competent, self-possessed and . . . well, that was all. On the other hand, I was not a panting young woman eternally searching for love in a heartless world. I sat back and waited.

"What he's like," Edna continued, "is like a big gentle bear. When he puts his hand under your elbow, it's like he could lift you right up off the sidewalk with one hand. And yet he's so gentle, so soft. His voice even" (she had me there as far as character analysis is concerned) "is deep, but it's soft and gentle, and—educated, cultured."

"The guy sounds interesting," I admitted, still wanting to bring the whole subject to a close. I actually picked up the papers and started shuffling them, although I didn't really know what they were: bills, both pro and con, probably.

"And he *is* well educated," she pursued her inexhaustible encomium. "I mean that apartment wasn't put together out of a guide book or *Playboy*. It is really in good taste."

"Edna," I said sternly, "good taste and education don't necessarily go together. I can introduce you to full professors who wear brown shoes with blue suits."

"But he really is educated," she protested. "He was going to be a doctor, he told me. He took pre-med and everything. And then something happened."

"He ran out of money," I predicted.

"That was part of it, I guess. But it was something else too. He was in the medical corps in Vietnam. That's where he got the idea he wanted to be a doctor, he said." I put the bills down and stared hopelessly at her. "But he said, too, he saw so much suffering that after he came back he wasn't sure he could stand to see people suffer anymore. I guess when I said he was so gentle, I also meant, maybe that he is so—so kind. Like he just can't bear to see anybody hurt, suffering."

"Well, if Gene is to be believed," I said with some asperity, "he didn't mind seeing those poor bastards suffer in the gym."

"Oh, that's not suffering." She dismissed it with a wave of her hand. "He laughs about that—those middle-aged guys running around with their bellies hanging out."

"It's suffering for them," I observed. "In fact, the whole thing about suffering these days is a little screwy, what with runners wanting to go through the wall and all that to prove, I guess, that they can stand pain. It's all like that *Man Called Horse* movie—nuts."

"He's not nuts!" Her face flashed. She hadn't been listening. She was wrapped in a monologue that brooked no interruption. "He's very, very well balanced, except, except, that he got hurt somewhere. I can tell."

"Hurt. You mean wounded?"

"No. Hurt inside. Scared. I can tell. Scared of emotions. Scared of being hurt again. Scared of—I think, I believe—a relationship." Her pretty face was screwed up tight as she worked it out. "He doesn't want to be hurt emotionally, and so he stays very cool."

"Very cool, such as afraid of girls?"

"No, *not* like that," she emphasized, tracking the conversation accurately this time. "I can always tell when they're afraid to touch you, I mean if you're a girl."

"Aha!," I zeroed in again. "Then, indeed, he touched something besides the marvelous support of your elbow. Flesh met flesh."

Her head jerked back and offered me a sneer. "Not in the way you're thinking."

I declined any indication of what I had been thinking.

"No," she said. "It was different. He was showing me some Tai Chi exercises and some of the moves in Aikido, you know, how to defend yourself."

"That makes him sound not quite the peace lover you were describing."

"Oh, you're so wrong, so wrong!" she exclaimed.

And, indeed, the memory—if only of this activity—brought a flame to her cheek. "Before we even started, he explained the philosophy of it to me. You know, it's just being calm, and quiet, and nonaggressive. It's using other people's aggression against them when you have to."

"Do unto others before they do it unto you," I suggested.

"No," she objected. "Not before. Not unless you absolutely have to. It's all a discipline. Mind and body. Perfectly calm. Relaxed." She looked at me appraisingly. "I'll bet," she said, rejecting unconsciously the entire philosophy, "that I could throw you over my shoulder."

"Sure you could," I agreed. "And shall I tell you why?"

"Because I've learned the moves," she asserted.

"No," I contradicted her. "It's because I wouldn't punch you in the nose first. You'd be surprised how a broken nose can dissolve all this mind and body crap."

"You think it's crap?" She looked at me contemptuously.

"No, I don't." I was contrite, having overstepped myself. "But I can't see making a religion out of Chinese back alley fighting. The truth is that anybody who thinks or trains at all has got an almost impossible edge over the average guy. Anybody who can actually think while he is fighting—can stand back and watch himself fight—is miles beyond ninety-nine percent of the men or women in this world. Do you know that about half the men in the average cocktail lounge actually cry when they fight, just like a high-school girl? If you take the surface emotion out of violence, you've got an entirely different ball game. Then different techniques are just a conflict of disciplines. Almost any discipline can win in the right situations."

"What he showed me is not about winning," she insisted. "It's about control. Like what you said about standing outside yourself and watching yourself. He does that. He said he's got this image, this image of himself, not just for Tai Chi, but for everything, his whole life, and he watches himself to make sure the image is right. It's all control, control."

I couldn't figure out what to do with my pacifistic tigress, who was talking about control, control, but was pretty obviously out of control. It appeared that she had been set up with all this moiling and toiling in the Tai Chi manner and then sent home in a cab. The complexities were beyond me, as is so much of the modern world. I pretty much resigned myself to letting her run down through the morning. On the other hand, I had one appointment and wanted to set up another. "Do you think," I asked pleasantly, "that we could control ourselves long enough to get through this morning's business?" She assented with a scowl.

We got through the bills and mail, answers to inquiries we'd sent out and inquiries to us. Two letters seemed promising as investigations, and I dictated the answers. Two other letters were more or less extraterrestrial, and so I had Edna reply that we didn't do that sort of thing.

When we had finished with all this, I said to her, "I have to be at *BusiNews* by eleven. But before I leave, I'd like you to see if you can set up a meeting with that shrink Gene was going to. His name is Paul Kragmeyer." I spelled it for her. "I don't think he's an M.D., but if you can't find him in the phone book, you can probably nail him through Execu-Trim, because they're the ones who referred Gene to him."

Edna flipped open the phone book, found the page, and ran a manicured fingernail down the row. She pinioned a name, held her fingernail there, and with her other hand picked up the phone and punched out the number. I stared at my calendar. I don't know why I don't like to watch people talk over the phone, but it creates a kind of unease, anxiety in me. I waited until I saw, out of the corner of my eye, Edna putting down the phone again. She produced a three-by-five card from somewhere and wrote down the name and number. This meant that she had succeeded right off the bat—a rarer occasion than you might think. "Okay," she said. "Two o'clock." I glanced at the address. It was in the east fifties, not too far from the offices of *BusiNews*.

I asked Edna, "What did he sound like?—I mean," I explained, "I've been reading transcripts where the guy hardly ever gets to say anything. Is he old, young? Foreign accent? Cold? Dry? Warm? Melting? Personality boy? How did he sound?"

"Muffled," said Edna.

"Muffled?" This had me stumped.

"Yes. Like he had his hand over the phone or something. He was hard to understand. His voice was slow. He didn't seem to speak clearly."

"Did he sound like he would be glad to see me?"

"Sort of," she answered judiciously. "I got that impression. Yes."

"All right." I rose from the desk, feeling that I had balanced the cannonball in my head. "I'll go see this guy Basket. Then I'll have lunch. Then I'll see Kragmeyer. There are things in that transcript, what I've read of it, that I don't really comprehend. I might get back to the office, and I might not. Don't worry about anything. Tomorrow morning, as you know, I'm off to the hospital to seek my fortune, so I don't know when I'll be in tomorrow." Edna was taking this all in on a superficial plane of her consciousness. She was still staring at the corner. I put my hand on the side of her beautiful neck. "Take it easy, Kid," I said. She put her hand on my hand and, reluctantly, I pulled my hand away and left.

15

BusiNews was sandwiched into two floors of one of the older buildings in the fifties off Madison Avenue. Around it new buildings spurted in the throes of construction, and huge trucks and derricks clogged the street to permit only the barest cursing sludge of traffic. I could feel the vibrations of the pile drivers chugging at yet another excavation, and I supposed with a certain smugness that the noise must be deafening for those who could hear.

Even in the small reception area on the fifteenth floor, I could feel the throb and tremor of the pile drivers working away at the stone base of Manhattan. It must, I thought, give everyone working at this location the inexorable boom of a hangover headache, whether they drank or not. Possibly the drinkers were the lucky ones. The young black receptionist did not seem to have the dull refuge of a hangover. Two hours into the workday she was showing signs of strain. Something about my appearance, and the intentness with which I must watch strangers talk, seemed to put her on edge. There was difficulty in establishing who I was and what I was there for. When the communication finally was complete, she put through the call to Basket's office.

A pleasant and competent-looking young woman in a summery dress came along to collect me. She led me through the editorial area, consisting of rows of carrels, little booths with no top to them, each emitting the sickly gray-green light of a video display terminal. I saw only the backs of the men and women hunched over their keyboards. It threw me back to the early days when I had worked in a bookkeeping department, which I had loathed, but which in retrospect seemed much more comfortable, gemütlich, than this sterile train of isolation booths. We passed a water cooler *cum* coffee station, and it was notable that there was no collection of idlers around it. *BusiNews* seemed as efficient as its name.

She led me into an office, far from impressive, which boasted only a steel desk with an expensive swivel chair behind it, a file cabinet in the corner, and a tubular chair in front of the desk, to which she directed me. "Mr. Basswell will be right with you," she said, and left me alone to contemplate my surroundings.

Unlike the drones in their little carrels, Mr. Basswell had a window behind his desk through which to view the world. The world through that window consisted of a new building mid-construction that seemed to have Venusian aspirations. The surface of his desk was very tidy—a communications-center-type telephone, an empty in-out tray, a file folder, and a memorandum from someone placed squarely in the center of the green blotting pad. The writing was, of course, upside-down from where I sat, but reading upside-down is one of the skills any investigator must cultivate (a-hem). The printed heading was promising because it did not state "From the Desk Of." Only the name, BILL MURCHISON, adorned it. The typewritten message read:

BASSWELL:
Might well have quit smoking in time.
Might even have got used to not smoking.
Never will get used to blowing smoke up somebody's ass.
I resign, effective today.
BILL

Naturally, I couldn't hear Basswell come in, and since my back was to the door, I wasn't aware of him till he swept past me and wheeled around behind his desk. The memo caught his attention, riveted it for the space of a few seconds, and then the blood rushed to his face. He picked up the note and tossed it into the top drawer of his desk. I gave him good marks for recovery. He took several deep breaths, and the blood faded from his cheeks. His expression remained serious, however, even menacing.

In fact, as we regarded one another warily, I recognized that there was an air of menace underlying the natural vitality—I suppose the word is dynamism—of his expression. He was a stocky, brown-haired man with blue eyes, in his late thirties. He had powerful shoulders and good forearms, which were revealed by the rolled-up sleeves of his blue oxford-cloth button-down shirt. The collar was open, and the rep tie hung at half mast. He was wearing light brown tweed trousers, which, sure enough, revealed the unseemly bulge that had prompted his nickname. Having thrown the memo into the drawer, he now seemed unsure as to what to do with his hands. They were held away from his sides as if yearning to grab something. He remained standing, rather looming over me.

"Let's see," he began, "you're here for . . ."

"Gene Listing," I answered. I felt, however, that he knew perfectly well what I was there for and was still recovering.

"What about Gene Listing?" The question seemed needlessly belligerent.

"Mrs. Listing, his wife, asked me to pick up whatever personal belongings he'd left in the office." I added, "I think she said she'd called you about it."

"Maybe she did." There was a definite scowl on his smooth, heavy face now. "I haven't got time for—for everything." He waved, contemptuously it seemed, toward the work area outside his office.

"I realize you're busy, of course," I offered mildly. "That's why I had my secretary make an appointment."

"You a lawyer?" His attention had been pricked by the word secretary.

"No," I hurried to disabuse him. "I'm a friend of

the family. I'm just trying to help out Evie—Mrs. Listing."

He seemed to regard this statement with even more suspicion. Was I a parasite?—a con man chasing after a widow who was lonely and distraught? Well, bullshit. He wasn't really serious, and he didn't really care. He was merely searching for leverage, an edge. That's what the perennial air of menace was all about. He was a competitor, perpetually seeking the edge over someone, anyone. I did not have to play this cheap and quirky game with him. I stood up very suddenly—his head jerked back—and I said forcefully, "If you'll show me Gene's office, I'll clear out his things and go."

"Like hell you will," said Basswell. "I'll show you the stuff you can take."

"I want all of his personal belongings," I retorted, emphasizing the *all*. I kept my face straight, but I was astounded. He had, in a minute's time, turned a rather sad and distasteful job requiring tact and circumspection into a personal confrontation. I wondered if this was his habitual manner, and I suspected with dread that it was.

"Come with me." It was an order, not an invitation.

I followed him down a line of five or six offices until we came to approximately the center of the long row of doors. Basswell opened this door to reveal an office approximately one quarter the size of his—little more than a cubbyhole. The window gave only a slightly different view of the construction across the street. The window, however, was the only thing the room had in common with Basswell's office. The desk was an ancient wooden contraption pushed up against the wall. A rickety table interposed an old standard Royal typewriter between the desk chair and the door. Much of the desk top was taken up with stacks of journals. The telephone was secreted among them. There was a bookcase behind the chair. Its shelves were crammed with heavily bound books, and its top groaned beneath towering stacks of journals. Shoved between the bookcase and the wall was an olive-green filing cabinet. Identifying cards had been inserted in each of the four drawers, but they had been rubbed into illegibility.

My heart sank under the sheer weight of all this material, and my mission looked foolish. There was no way I could lug this stuff out of here. It would take a van. But I also felt, for the first time, an understanding of how Gene had spent his hours. He had inserted himself daily, like a cam, in this paper and ink machine, and had performed his function of blending raw news with the information stacked here and the background intelligence he carried in his head. The close quarters gave the impression of someone mining information, the way coal is mined.

There was barely enough room for the two of us. Basswell said to me, "Sit down over there," shoving the desk chair up against the bookcase. I sat. He picked up the phone and punched a two-digit number, rapped out some instructions, and opened the top drawer of Gene's desk.

I couldn't begin to catalogue what came out of that drawer and the others, except that it all came under the heading of *junk*. In the forward section there were exhumed rubber bands, staples, boxes of wrong-size staples, Scotch tape, empty spools from which the Scotch tape had been stripped, ancient memorandums that had been thrown in the drawer, just as Basswell had done this morning, pleas for subscriptions, broken ballpoint pens, a shoe shine kit, countless menus from lunchrooms that had opened, thrived for a while, then failed. From the back compartment of the drawer came birthday cards from the kids, hand-drawn and colored in crayon, two clay ashtrays formed by fat fingers in kindergarten, a coffee cup with a broken handle decorated with the legend BIG DADDY, three color snapshots of Gene and Brat with the kids, apparently in Maryland, and a few scattered tissues from credit card receipts.

It was the ten-year accumulation of a working life. I wondered if Gene had ever thrown anything away. So far, however, there had not been the one thing constituting my main reason for being here. There was no packet of delicately scented envelopes tied up with a ribbon, no small leather address book with mysterious numbers and designations.

A girl came in carrying two flat-folded moving boxes. I took one and began assembling it. Basswell laid a command on her, and presently she returned with a huge, empty, cylindrical wastebasket. Much of what had been taken out of the drawers went directly into the wastebasket.

I nodded toward the bookcase. "Those books," I asked, "are they Gene's or the company's?"

"I'll check them out," said Basswell.

About half the books bore bookplates on the flyleaf—*ex libris Listing*. They were mostly histories of Asia, or studies of Asian politics. These I put into the open box. The others had apparently been purchased by the company—the flyleaf bearing the rubber stamp *BusiNews*. These were mostly financial studies, fraught with tables and charts of economic projections. I put them back in the case. Of the journals, only two had Gene's name on the mailing sticker—*Foreign Affairs* and *Journal of Asian Studies*. These I also stacked in the big box—it would have to be shipped. There didn't seem to be much in the way of personal papers to lay on top of them, although I carefully put in the clay ashtrays and the broken coffee mug along with the photographs.

"Well," said Basswell, straightening up, "I guess that's it."

I pointed to the big lower right-hand drawer of the desk. "I'd like to check out the desk file, if you don't mind," I told him.

"Those are all stories Gene was working on," said Basswell. "They're the property of *BusiNews*. They'll have to be followed up."

"It won't hurt to look," I suggested. "He might have stuck some personal stuff in there."

The suggestion was met with ill grace. He pulled open the drawer, which revealed a thicket of file folders, each with a heading or "slug" on the tab. Basswell bent over them and began leafing through them, nodding slightly as he recognized each slug. But when he had finished, he stiffened, still in his bent posture, and then stood up and glared at me. "Were you in here before you got to my office?" he demanded.

"Of course not." My patience was wearing very thin. "Your girl planted me in your office, where I waited for you. I didn't even know this was Gene's office. What the hell is all this?"

"There's something missing," he muttered. "Anyway, there's nothing personal in here."

I knew what was missing. I'd been reading the slugs over his shoulder as he thumbed through them. There was no nightmare file. There was no slug even suggesting the nightmare file.

We both turned to stare at the big four-drawer file case. Basswell intercepted my thoughts. "That's a backfile," he said. "It's only stories done in the past. Everyone in the place uses it. I guarantee there's nothing personal in there."

I stepped over rapidly and jerked open a drawer. It was crammed with ancient file folders. So were the other three. If anything was secreted in these drawers I would never find it. I closed them all. I did not want to make a federal case out of collecting a few of Gene's things. Also, it was true, a sadness and depression had settled over me as I regarded the personal effects of ten years' work stacked up in a cardboard box. I reached automatically for a cigarette. Basswell's eyes lit up.

"No smoking on the premises," he barked.

"Not even if we close the door?" I pleaded.

"Especially not if we close the door," he said firmly. "I don't allow anyone to smoke in my presence."

"How come you're so hipped on it?" I asked him mildly. "Were you a heavy smoker at one time?" Indeed, he seemed to have all the self-righteous indignation of a reformed drunk.

The question had an odd effect on him. It did not soften his features so much as glaze them. His eyes got a distant focus, and I realized that I had struck the PLAY button on a prerecorded melody. "I smoked when I was a kid," said the melody, "when it seemed that just about everybody smoked—before the warning, that is. And I came home on furlough because my father had had a heart attack. He had been a two-pack-a-day man, and, of course, he had to quit. My mother asked me if I wouldn't make it easier for him by not smoking myself. It was tough, of course, but I quit then and haven't smoked since."

I was speechless. This was the most blatant put-on I had ever been exposed to in my life. It was an insult. It was an almost word-for-word playback of the surgeon general's press conference. Did this idiot think he was the only man in the world who read the *Times?* I drew a deep breath and composed myself.

"And how is he?" I asked the editor.

"How is who?"

"Your father."

He gave me an astonished look. Apparently his recital had always been followed by a lengthy period of silence steeped in piety. He repeated, with his mouth in an *O* and his blue eyes still widened, "Who?"

"Your father," I answered, smiling. "Up and about now, is he? Jogging? Lifting weights?"

"My father is dead, of course," he said. I am deprived of gauging a tone of voice, but even his face had a hollow ring to it.

"It's a pity," I said, "that you went to all that trouble for nothing."

I thought he might take a swing at me. He struggled with himself, and I could see the conflict pass over his face in a series of waves. He managed to control himself. I knew he would. At this point there was something he wanted from me.

"Why don't we go back to my office," he said.

I was agreeable. I told him, "I'll send around a delivery service to pick up the box and deliver it to Mrs. Listing." He nodded with a taut arch of his neck.

He'd got better hold of himself by the time we were in his office. He may have been reassured by the neatness and simplicity of the place. He sat down behind the desk and gestured to the guest chair I had originally occupied. He leaned back, but again, did not know what to do with his hands. They remained awkwardly out toward the edges of his desk. "You an old friend of the family?" he asked me.

"Not too far back," I answered cautiously. "It's just that Evie needed somebody in a hurry, and I guess my name came up."

"But you know Mrs. Listing fairly well." It was a statement made for his own satisfaction.

"Reasonably well."

"I'd like you to do me a favor," said Basswell. This man was full of surprises. I couldn't think of any reason in the world why I should do him a favor. Nevertheless, he exuded self-assurance. "I'd like you to ask Mrs. Listing to look around the house and see if Gene didn't bring home a manila folder slugged *Nightmares*. It's a screwy slug, I know, but it's a story he was working on and we were counting on. It's going to leave a hole in the book if we don't get it."

"Really?" I asked in all innocence. "What's it about?"

"Some medical stuff, I guess. I really don't know too much about it. I only know that it's slotted."

"I'll ask her," I said doubtfully. It was kind of fun playing games with this much ingenuousness. "But I wouldn't sit up nights waiting if I were you."

He straightened up in his chair. "What does that mean?"

"It means that Mrs. Listing isn't too wild about this place or the people who run it," I told him. "She sort of sees you people as the main reason Gene died."

"Us?" He really was surprised. He sat up even straighter and put his palms flat on the desk. "Where in hell would she get a crazy idea like that?"

"It's not so crazy if you look at it her way," I said. "Gene worked here for ten years, perfectly happy, perfectly normal. A new regime comes in and changes all the ground rules. Gene gets the feeling that he's out on his ass. It's called stress. It kills people."

"What ground rules are you talking about?" Basswell asked me, wide-eyed. "It's the same book he always worked for."

"C'mon, Mr. Basswell," I encouraged him. "You've got a guy who spent his entire working life smoking cigarettes while he hammered a typewriter. Suddenly you tell him he can't smoke, at which point he finds out that he can't hit the typewriter, either. He suddenly feels he's on the skids. One thing follows another. His life turns into pure hell. Mrs. Listing holds you personally responsible for it."

"*Me?*" He was thunderstruck. He turned his palms up in piety. "Why would she blame me?"

"You're the one who put the binger on smoking, aren't you?"

"What a crazy idea," said Basswell. "I couldn't do a thing like that even if I wanted to. Senator Marston, the director of the company, is the one who laid down the rule. He doesn't permit smoking in any of his companies."

"Marston." I tasted the name. "Would that be Representative Marston of one of the House finance committees?"

"Senator Marston has many divergent interests." It was a statement out of a brochure. I took a shot at it.

"And where do you fit in with all these divergent interests?"

"What?"

"You. I mean, you suddenly come in from outside as part of the new broom. None of the people here, according to Gene, ever heard of you, knew anything about you, or cared for that matter. Suddenly you're the new editor. How come?"

"My association with Senator Marston goes back some twelve years," he said with a stiffly presented pride.

"What kind of association?"

"I was his aide for years. I've had extensive experience in public information services."

"You mean you're a flack?" It wasn't really a question.

At last he knew what to do with his hands. They gripped the edge of the desk almost convulsively. Possibly he was thinking of picking it up and hitting me with it. Then he stood up and took a deep breath. I rose too. "I guess that's all we've got to say to each other," he concluded, his face very tense. "Except one thing. Tell Mrs. Listing that the nightmare file is our property. We paid for it, and we want it."

"I'll tell her," I answered woodenly.

I had almost turned to go when I caught his jaw working again. "Another thing you can tell her," he said with a sneer that matched the contempt in his eyes, "is that her darling husband was definitely on the skids, and was on his way out anyway. Smoking had nothing to do with it."

"How's that?" I was astonished. "What was wrong?"

"What was wrong was Gene's smartass attitude. I would never tolerate anyone like that working for me."

"His attitude!"

"Mr. Know-it-all. Mr. Patronizing. Mr. Superior. Mr. Wonderful. I don't know how anybody ever put up with him."

"He seemed to get along all right before you arrived," I said. The glittering ghost of Gene stepped gently in and out of my thoughts.

"This organization was a stinking mess before Senator Marston took it over. No direction, no purpose, no vigor, no discipline."

"I don't think Gene signed up for the Marine Corps when he took the job," I said. "As a matter of fact, I distinctly remember Gene remarking that he thought the Marine Corps was full of shit." I watched his reaction. I knew it! My voluntary antagonist was an ex-gyrene. It was written all over him. I am an ex-sailor. We were mongoose and cobra.

"I would have expected a cheap remark like that out of a loser like him," said Basswell. "His smart mouth was what got him into trouble."

"His smart mouth was what put words on paper," I objected.

"Words on paper was what he was paid for," said Basswell. "Wising off at the director of the corporation is not."

"I can't believe Gene would insult anybody without provocation," I answered. "At least not until he went haywire."

Basswell said, "When the senator came here to give everyone the right orientation under his leadership, Gene could not, like anyone else, simply listen. Oh, no." Basswell's face twisted into an ugly parody of gentility. " *'If you don't mind, Mr. Congressman, would you please tell us what plans you've made for screening our raw information out of your investment portfolio?'* Can you imagine asking a question like that of the director of the company? There was absolute hell to pay."

I couldn't keep a slight smile from breaking on my lips. "And what did the congressman have to say?"

"Nothing to Gene. You can be sure of that. He simply picked up his papers and walked out. He was perfectly composed, but I've never seen him so embarrassed. He was furious. And he said only four words to me before he left: *'Get rid of him!'* I caught particular hell that night."

"So you fired Gene the next day?"

"Do you think I'm a fool? A replacement had to be developed. You can't replace ten years' experience overnight. But the replacement was developed, very satisfactorily. Nobody's irreplaceable. Gene knew he was on the way out, all right."

I took a very happy shot in the dark. "That replacement," I said. "His name wouldn't be Bill Murchison, would it?"

It had the desired effect. It wasn't until the man's face went white that I realized he had a lot of freckles.

16

The rueful, smiling ghost of Gene continued to slip in and out of my consciousness as I left the building and walked up Madison. Although I was walking slowly and carefully, the activity managed to joggle the cannonball, and I again became conscious of the pressure in my head and the machinery noise that also, like a ghost, weaves in and out of my consciousness.

I got entrained, as if by instinct, for Henry's. It was early for a drink, but I wanted some fortification before I went to see Kragmeyer, the psychotherapist. I also talked myself into the idea of ordering a ham on rye.

Henry's was so jammed that it seemed to crowd out the ghost of Gene. Nonetheless, I felt saddened and ill at ease. The meeting with Basket had explained a lot about Gene's behavior. How could anybody work with a son of a bitch like that and keep any remnant of human dignity? If Gene had been aware of his being on the way out—and Gene had never struck me as being insensitive—then a lot of his shock and anxiety at suddenly having the smoking prop kicked out from under him was explained. What needed further explanation was how far this shock and anxiety had gone— whether it had gone into a real depression. I remembered Gene's sad statement about smoking: *"I feel as if an old friend had died."* Had he been so depressed he considered suicide? Had he accomplished the kind of silent suicide that keeps insurance adjusters from the widow's door? I had found standing room at the end of the bar and chewed away thoughtfully at my ham sandwich. I limited my drinking to one bourbon and soda.

I was left with some time to kill, and so I ambled on, carefully balancing my cannonball. I wound up at a stylish little bar, nearly empty, not far from Kragmeyer's address. The drink was weak and the price was strong, but it gave me a chance to get off my feet.

I stared into my drink and "redefined my goals," as the businessmen like to say. If Gene *had* committed suicide, my job was to keep this fact away from Evie, and, indeed, from the insurance company. Evie would blame herself for it all, and that simply was not fair. Gene had been caught in something akin to the tulip craze of Holland or the dancing madness of the Middle Ages.

There are limited categories in which a man can die: natural causes, misadventure, suicide, or foul play. I knew that Evie harbored notions of foul play, but I saw this as a defense, a denial. She feared suicide, and could not admit to natural causes or misadventure. But here she had medicine on her side too. For all their breeziness about "It can happen to anybody," I didn't think that the doctors were wild about people dropping dead while engaged in a hygiene program under their supervision. Neither were they apt to cheer the idea that Gene had died of his medication (misadventure). Like it or not, they would come down with Evie on the idea of suicide or foul play. Foul play had been very far from my thoughts until I saw the hatred in young Basket's eyes. He hadn't hated the recent, impossible Gene, but the old, gentle, well-mannered Gene, a man I had liked very much. Was it possible that a number of people had hated Gene? It didn't seem possible. Basket was a special case. The arrow turned more toward self-destruction, the new Gene, the impossible Gene.

Had Gene been self-destructive all these years? The first indication I'd had of it was his remark to the congressman. On the surface, it seemed like a challenge, but I also could see, very easily, the old Gene asking this question as a simple request for instruction, a procedural question. Certainly the congressman should have been prepared for it, and the fact that he was not, as far as I was concerned, meant that he had, indeed, hoped for certain raw information that would help his investments. But the simple, straightforward question had put the skids under Gene, as well, very probably, as his manner of asking. Gene was not likely to be in awe of congressmen or, for that matter, directors of conglomerates. It appeared to me now that this is what had made Gene so valuable to his publication. The publication had changed, not Gene. He had not expected a simple, realistic question to ruin his career.

Then there was the matter of the nightmare file. From what Evie had told me, there was only one way that Basket could have discovered it, and that is by going through Gene's desk after hours. (I suppose this is any executive's privilege. But was it while poking through the clay ashtrays and crude birthday cards that he conceived his hatred for Gene? Corporation and family are natural antagonists, each pulling at the opposing arm of their common property.)

What, then, did Basket make of the nightmare file? Here was a story with no source, no assignment— something based on sheer initiative. Was initiative permitted in the new regime? If Evie was right, then *BusiNews* was not supposed to know about the story. How could it make a hole in the book, as Basket had said? How could a totally undeveloped story be slotted? Was it simply that they wanted every word that Gene had written on their time? It did not make a great deal of sense to me. Evie had said that the story was a nut case, but Celia had pointed out that it might well have to do with international finance, or at least the shady side of it. If Basket was interested, then Celia, apparently, was right.

Where had the file gone? Gene hadn't taken it home, that much was obvious. It wasn't anywhere in his office. (I'm sure Basket was thorough, if nothing else.) I thought about this, twirling my slowly subsiding drink. Where else could it be? It occurred to me,

then, that Gene had only one other cubbyhole to be
explored. He must have had a locker at Execu-Trim.
Had it been cleared out? There'd been no sign of gym
gear at his home or office. I decided I'd drop in on
Execu-Trim on my way back from Kragmeyer's. I also
decided I would charge Evie full rate for the day. I
finished my drink, balanced my cannonball, and left
for Kragmeyer's.

He practiced out of the same place he lived, in a
respectable older building that catered to profession-
als. There was no doorman, so I had to let my hand
rest on the doorknob for the vibration of the buzzer
after I'd rung. On the door of apartment 3D there was
a plastic sign that said ENTER. I let myself into a very
small waiting room containing three Danish chairs, a
corner table to match, and a disheartening supply of
People magazine. The sole ashtray was filled to overflowing with different kinds of cigarette butts. I assumed that Kragmeyer was busy with a patient or
client or whatever they call them now.

But the face that stuck out of the opening door did
not seem to be involved in consultation. It said, "You
Joe Binney?" Startled, I answered, "Yes," and got
up. I hadn't even had a chance to sample *People*.
"Come in," the face said. "Come in and look at this."
Before entering, however, I was riveted by the face
itself. It had a huge purpling bruise on the left side
that was spreading to swell the left eye and the left
side of the mouth. *Muffled*, I thought. *This is what
Edna meant.* The body below the face was clad in a
green cardigan over a white shirt open at the collar.
He was wearing faded blue jeans and moccasins, no
socks.

At first, the damage in the consulting room was not
all that apparent because he'd made an attempt to
straighten things up. It wasn't until I'd stepped into
the center of the room that I saw the cabinet behind
the small blond desk with its doors ripped off and the
thin shelving broken. Books and papers were stacked
on the floor, but they had the air of being hurriedly
assembled. Some of the smaller books had had their
bindings ripped off. I looked back at the bruise that

now seemed to dominate the young and rather vulnerable face of Paul Kragmeyer.

"Lucky me," he said. "Early this morning I walked in on him from the other door—the exit door." He nodded toward the other side of the room. "The guy was a Goddamned monster."

I nodded sympathetically. "He saw you leave, but he didn't see you come back, right?"

"Right. The exit door goes through the hall in my apartment, so the patients don't meet one another coming and going. I'd gone down for the morning paper and a few other things and I was down on the street before I realized I'd forgot my wallet and change. I came back in through the apartment. He'd come in through the entrance room. He'd already got whatever he wanted. He had it all in a barracks bag, the taping equipment, the tuner, everything. And all the cassettes he took, too, crazy bastard, notebooks that couldn't be any use to anybody." He stopped and his eyes flared with outrage. "Why'd he have to tear up my books? Throw my papers all over hell? Smash everything he could? Why didn't he just take what he could use and leave?"

"Can we sit down?" I asked. He gestured broadly to the comfortable chair he'd uprighted in front of his desk. I sat down and he assumed his no doubt accustomed position behind his frail-looking desk. I pushed it a step further. "Do you mind if I smoke?"

"Hell no," said Paul Kragmeyer. "Wait a minute. I'll get an ashtray." He went back into the waiting room and retrieved the big ashtray I'd noticed. He dumped its overflowing contents into the wastebasket. After I'd lighted my cigarette he looked at it and said, "Can I have one of those?" I laughed and put my pack on the desk. When he'd extracted one, I lighted it with my trusty Zippo.

"These break-in types are pretty infantile," I told him. "It's what doesn't appear in the family newspapers. Somehow, if you read the newspapers, you get the idea that these guys are cold, calculating, go-ahead types. Actually, most of them are panic-stricken half-wits who'd have trouble holding down a job as a doorstop. You're lucky he didn't shit on the floor. A lot of them do. It's all put down to malice, but the fact is they lose control of their bowels, their bladders. They become very literally infantile. That includes," I nodded toward his face, "striking out wildly, blindly, at anyone who discovers them. You could have been killed."

"I damned near was," said Kragmeyer. "I never saw it coming. He damned near broke my neck."

"Did you get a look at him? Could you identify him?"

"There was nothing to see. He had a stocking mask over his face, and he was wearing gloves. Dark pants, a dark jersey pullover with a hood like a parka. I don't even know if he was black or white."

"Still," I said, trying to be helpful, "it's an MO of a kind. He slipped the locks, right?" Kragmeyer nodded. "He didn't kick in the doors. So that's part of the MO too. They'll be on the lookout for him." It was scant comfort, but it was all I could offer, at least as far as any recourse went. There was, however, a lot more to it. I looked at his young, stricken face and gauged him to be just past thirty. It was an intelligent face, even with the bruise and the dismay that kept leaking out of his dark eyes. He hadn't tried to shave around the bruise, and so he had the beginnings of a black, wiry growth of beard that set off his pale complexion. The black whiskers went with his curly, undisciplined hair.

"Do psychotherapists ever take advice?" I asked him.

"All the time," he answered with an attempt at a smile.

"Okay. Are you married?" He shook his head gingerly in a negative.

"Then go out and get laid," I advised him. "You've been invaded, raped. Reestablish yourself right away. It's important. I don't care with whom or how it's done, but get yourself laid and get back in the real world. Get back in control of things. Does that make sense to you?"

He nodded. "Yes," he said. The monosyllable was followed by a long stream of cigarette smoke.

I decided to move on. "Do you mind if I ask you a couple of questions about Gene Listing?" It took him a moment to recall that Gene Listing was really the reason I'd come up. Then he made an open gesture with his hands and sank back in his chair. I judged that this was not a good moment to tell him I'd been reading the transcripts. I felt it might be just a bit too much for him to handle.

"What we're worried about," I began, "Mrs. Listing and I, is that Gene might have been so depressed that he attempted, succeeded, in committing suicide somehow. Does that seem possible to you?"

He sank back even farther in the chair, and his eyes became darker, duller. "That would be terrible," he said. "Is there any evidence that he killed himself?"

"Not yet," I said. "But Gene was very intelligent. Mrs. Listing has the suspicion that he might have done away with himself in a way that couldn't be traced. She doesn't think, nor do I, that he would have made the grand gesture that sort of accuses everybody else in the world."

"I didn't get any sense of impending suicide from Gene," the therapist said slowly. "If I had, I'd have tried to do something about it." His eyes were still troubled.

I ventured on, gingerly. "Did he ever talk about death?"

The gesture was at first dismissive, but then the hand crept up to touch the bruise. "Only abstractly," said Kragmeyer. "Philosophically, and by that I mean in terms of abstract philosophy. But not in terms of suicide."

I tried to hit a conversational tone. I said, "The trouble is that you only saw the new Gene, the troubled Gene. He wasn't like that at all before. Could you tell me what professional impression you got of him?"

Kragmeyer took another cigarette, lighted it with my Zippo, and studied the smoke. "Well, he was extremely hostile," the therapist said into the blue-gray cloud. "He might have been the most hostile patient I've ever had. He made it almost impossible for me to help him."

"Did he actually want help?"

"Oh, yes," answered Kragmeyer. "He needed help to quit smoking."

"I thought he had quit smoking. Was he backsliding? Was that it?"

"Oh, no. No. Not at all." Kragmeyer was quick to dispel the idea by waving his hand through the smoke.

"Then what was it he needed help in?"

"Well, of course, to adjust to having quit smoking." He considered what he had said. "It's sort of unusual. Backsliding is the major problem usually. People want sharing, you know, help in exerting willpower."

"But Gene already had enough willpower?"

"Too much for his own good," Kragmeyer said with a grimace stopping just short of the bruise. "He went about it all wrong. He had the wrong attitude."

"Ah." Now it was my turn to light up another cigarette. I asked cautiously, "Is there a right attitude about these things?"

"Of course there is. It's documented. In fact, the right attitude is everything. If you can modify the patient's attitude, the whole problem disappears."

"I'm really interested," I offered. "You say it's documented. Then there's a sort of description of the right attitude?"

I never know what my voice sounds like, of course, so I don't know what was in the tone that made him look up at me. Apparently he sensed yet another hostility. He considered his words before he spoke, and I sensed that the easy, conversational tone had been broken. "The right attitude," said Kragmeyer, "is an instinct for health and a trust and confidence in the world around you—a sense of being at one with the society you live in."

I swallowed this prescription mutely. Then I said, "But there was something in Gene that wouldn't let him accept this?"

"Something!" The eyes widened, squinting sharply at the edge of the injury. "He didn't trust anything, anyone. He wouldn't let me help him because he didn't trust even me. For instance"—he ground out his cigarette with exasperation—"when I arranged for a tranquilizer for him—really, the first step in calming him down—he said, 'I didn't quit smoking in order to become a prescription junkie.' "

"Arranged for?" I didn't understand.

"I can't write prescriptions myself. I don't have a medical degree. But I arranged it with Dr. Milgrim, who agreed, of course, that Gene could use an anxiolytic. But Gene wouldn't have it. He wouldn't accept it. He didn't trust me."

"Ah." I tried to compose my face into the semblance of sympathy.

"I suggested hypnotherapy, and Gene said, and I can quote this, 'I'm not going to let some moron who picked up a certificate in night school play around with my brains.' He'd heard about the Morton Prince scandal, you know."

"No, I don't know."

"Well, the Morton Prince Institute was one of the most prestigious of the hypnotherapy institutes, and it turned out that its director was a fraud. I mean, he'd been giving expert testimony in court, and all that, and it turned out his degrees were phony. It's very unfortunate that Gene knew about this, although, being a journalist, I suppose he had access to a lot of information, harmful information."

"I can see where it would be a problem."

Again, I caught the sharp look from him. He said, "Well, this mistrust extended—I hate to use technical terms about any of my patients who come up here—" he broke off, "but his mistrust extended to the entire world, it seemed. Almost a paranoia. He really did feel that people were working against him."

"Do you mean at his job?"

"Yes, yes," Kragmeyer said eagerly. "Particularly at his job."

"And you considered it abnormal?"

"To the extent that Gene carried it, of course it's abnormal—the feeling that things are somehow against you."

"In my racket," I told him, "people come up to my office and tell me that they think they're being followed by a tall guy who's wearing smoked glasses and a bottle-green overcoat. It always sounds a little nuts. But very often when I go out and look around, sure enough, there's the guy in the smoked glasses and bottle-green overcoat.''

He sat back with an expression of impatience on his face. "What on earth was there in Gene's job that could possibly hurt him?''

"Well, for one thing, they were getting rid of him.''

"Because he wasn't producing? He had an extreme reaction to that. I'm sure the company was giving him time to adjust.''

"No. They decided to get rid of him before the no-smoking ban went into effect. He made an innocent but unfortunate remark to the new owner, and the new owner said 'can him.' '' I stopped Kragmeyer's interruption. "They didn't just can him, of course, because they had to set up somebody to replace him. But they put the skids under him. I'm sure he realized that, although he probably didn't know why.''

Kragmeyer sighed. "These things happen,'' he said, "but the important thing is the patient's reaction, not the event itself.''

I stared at him. "So the important thing up here is not that some guy walked into your office and trashed it and put a welt up alongside your head, but your reaction to it, right?''

This annoyed him. He said, "Of course it's not the same. What happened up here was traumatic—in every sense of the word.''

"I think it's traumatic because it happened to you instead of to one of your patients. I also happen to think that it's plenty traumatic for a guy to be eased out of a job he's had for ten years, and at the same time to be forced into a view of life that he doesn't share at all. It's even more traumatic if he's told that he has heart trouble, and impossibly traumatic when the guy is fifty years old and can't see himself getting another job—too young for a pension and too old to start over.''

"With the hostile attitude that he had,'' Kragmeyer said, "I'm surprised that he ever got a job at all.''

There was a look of bitterness, even outrage, in his black, intelligent eyes.

"I repeat that you saw Gene only after he'd been beat up, so to speak. He wasn't like that at all before. Any more," I added with some satisfaction, "than you always had a purple bruise on your face."

He took the whole thing in ill humor. "Just what is it you want from me, Mr. Binney?"

"Just what I asked you. Is it your professional opinion that Gene Listing was ready to attempt suicide?"

Kragmeyer put his elbows on the desk and made a steeple of his fingers. "Probably not—for two reasons," he said. "First of all, Gene Listing was a Catholic, and in some ways, a serious Catholic. It would have taken an enormous amount to shove him into suicide. Secondly, although he was filled with rage, his rage was vented outwardly. What was turned against himself he seemed to be handling—at least as far as expressing it was concerned."

"Rage against himself?"

"He was terribly humiliated that quitting smoking had interfered with his ability to work. He simply refused to accept it. I kept telling him that he'd get over it in time and be all the better for it. But he kept butting his head against a wall, or a typewriter, rather."

"How long did you figure it would take him to get over it?"

Kragmeyer shrugged. "Six months—a year."

"Did you have any solutions as to how he was going to keep his job during this time?"

"Job! Job!" exclaimed Kragmeyer. He dismantled his steeple and spread his hands impatiently across the desk. "What's so important about a job?"

I looked at him. I was thunderstruck.

"Particularly when one has the family resources that Gene Listing had? I got the impression that his family is quite wealthy."

"What's that got to do with it?"

"Well," the therapist reasoned, "during the period of readjustment, I'm sure the family would have been able and willing to take over, to support him while he regained his—uh . . . equilibrium. All he had to do was go to them and explain the problem."

"Jesus Christ," I said. "You didn't counsel him to do this, did you?"

"Why not?" answered Kragmeyer, offended. "That's what families are for, for sharing, helpfulness. To be supportive. From what I gather, there was a lot of hate in that family, but there was a lot of love too."

"From what *I* gathered," I responded, thinking of Celia, "the whole family is cuckoo."

Nonetheless, I had got what I had come for. It was summing up time. "Your advice to Gene, so far as I can make it out," I said to Kragmeyer, "was to surrender up his way of life, his attitude toward life, surrender up his job, surrender up his independence, and go crawling back to a family he'd been financially independent of for something like twenty-five years. It sounds to me like you were asking him to give up his will, his character, his whole individuality—the whole thing that made up Gene Listing."

"But of course he had to give it up!" said Kragmeyer, startled that this idea should be challenged at all. "That's what therapy is: to persuade the patient to surrender harmful characteristics, harmful attitudes, until he reaches a peaceful compromise with himself and society."

I felt that there was nothing more I could get from him or give to him—except for one thing. "You've been very kind," I said, "to give me all this attention, and it's been a great help. Now there's something I can do for you. If you leave this office you've got here the way it is, it's going to turn into a regular God-damned racetrack for heist artists. I know a very good, very trustworthy locksmith who'll come over and fix up the joint for you at a very reasonable cost. OK?"

He nodded OK.

17

I carried my cannonball with a compensating tilt of my head as I set off by foot for Execu-Trim on the west side of Manhattan. My main reason for staying on foot was simply speed, because getting tangled in the guts of Rockefeller Center by vehicle has been known, by its interminable delays, to destroy a man's career. My career was not in danger, but I did want to bring the day's work to a speedy halt, and get home to my newfound girl. It was a nice day for walking, anyway, and cannonball or no cannonball, I felt I could use the air, dangerous and hydrocarbonated as it was. It would also give me a chance to reflect on what I had seen.

Bits and pieces nagged me. I was happy enough to be able to tell Evie that there was now a professional opinion that Gene had not attempted suicide, an opinion that I respected. However, this left us with the three other categories. One of these I privately struck down immediately—misadventure. No matter how drunk or crazy he might have been, I couldn't see Gene accidentally taking the wrong pill or the wrong number of pills. It is hard to fit the idea of misadventure to a man who has died in his sleep, even if it was a nightmare. That left natural causes and foul play. I was not very happy with either idea.

It struck me as I was passing the tourists at Radio City that Kragmeyer hadn't mentioned the nightmares. Certainly Gene must have complained of them to him.

If the nightmares were so terrible that they would make a man rise up and cry out in his sleep, certainly he would mention them to, of all people, a psychotherapist, wouldn't he? And the therapist, would he not explore these nightmares as an index to the psychical problems that had brought his patient into consultation? No doubt, I told myself, turning south on Seventh Avenue, something about the nightmares would turn up in the transcripts.

Foul play, the last category, was really an unthinkable category. It was the widow's last resort. How Evie wanted to be able to strike back at someone! How little I blamed her for it. How unfair the recent turn of events had been to her and, not least of all, to Gene. But foul play seemed as remote as misadventure, unless there was some crazy Goddamned voodoo mixed up with it—"stick pointing," as Celia called it. I couldn't believe that for the same reasons Kragmeyer couldn't believe suicide. Gene was a Catholic—a serious Catholic in some ways, Kragmeyer had said. Underneath everything, a certain logic, handed down from Thomas Aquinas, informed his sensibilities. Stick pointing at Gene would break the stick. I was sure of that.

I had gotten down into the bowels of the old hotel that housed Execu-Trim and was gazing at the brilliant pipes before I realized that I was sick—that the simple crosstown walk I'd made a million times before had exhausted me. My knees felt watery, and my hips ached. In fact, I seemed to ache all over. Somehow, I had never associated the pain and pressure in my head with actual sickness and weakness. It unnerved me. I put my hand up against the wall and rested.

So I was very grateful to see the orange face above the blue jump suit of Don Heemstra. It promised to save me all the trouble of going through God knows what procedures to get to Gene's locker. Heemstra came up to me, his expression very concerned, and put his hand under my elbow. I felt again what Edna had been talking about. There was a deep fluid strength to his support that bespoke gentleness and reassurance as well as power. "Are you all right?" he asked me.

"A little played out," I answered. "This Goddamned ear trouble is finally getting to me."

"Aren't they able to do anything for it?"

"Oh, yes," I replied. "Tomorrow's my big day. I'm off to the hospital to see some big poobah who's supposed to have all the answers. I guess I'll be spending the whole day at the hospital seeing if my hat's on straight."

I pushed myself erect then—even the presence of this guy made me feel better—and said to him, "I've just popped in to pick up the stuff in Gene's locker. I've been doing the rounds to pick up all his stuff."

"Wasn't that already sent to Mrs. Listing?"

"Not that I know of."

"Let's have a look then."

I accompanied him down the corridor and turned off with him to the locker room. As we were going through the door he said, "Edna's very worried about you."

"She worries too much. I'll be okay."

We plodded through the repellent murk of the locker room—a smell I've always hated. At the end of the long, narrow room, Heemstra unlocked a wooden wall cabinet and took a ring of keys from it. He singled out what was apparently a master key and we went to Gene's locker, one of a million olive-drab lockers exactly like it all over the world. When we opened the door there was nothing inside but a brand-new blue gym bag. I reached in and picked up the gym bag. Heemstra stopped me. "Would you mind," he asked, "if we took a look inside? I just want to make sure he doesn't have a hand grip or some other piece of equipment he was using. I'm accountable for all that."

I set the bag on a wooden dressing bench and pulled the zipper. Inside were a sweat suit, a clean jock strap, a pair of running shorts, a T-shirt, a barely used pair of running shoes, and a balled-up pair of sweat socks. I pulled all these articles out and set them on the bench. Heemstra stared at them and then looked inside the empty bag. "Well," he said. "That's that." He seemed puzzled. I put the stuff back in the bag and zipped it up. "Is there anything else I can help you with?" Heemstra asked me. His face hadn't lost the puzzled expression.

I shook my head. "I'm just going to get myself in a cab and go home and rest," I told him. A palpable lie. I was going home, all right, but I doubted that I'd get much rest. Not with Celia there.

Heemstra walked me through the lobby and got me into a cab. He waited until I had satisfactorily given the driver my address, then he closed the cab door and waved good-bye.

But by the time the cab had reached the end of the block, I had sat up sharply and unzipped the bag. I felt around for the rolled ball of socks, took them out, and pulled them apart. An amber plastic container fell out—I had felt it when I first reached into the bag in the locker room. The cab was too dark and too jouncy for me to read the label accurately. I loosened the childproof cap and poured some pills into my hand. They were yellow pills about the size of aspirins. I couldn't make out the printing that was stamped on them, but they looked to be professionally manufactured medication. I poured them back in the container and capped it. There was bigger game below. When I had reached into the bag, I'd felt a certain springiness on the bottom. I reached in, now, and lifted out the fabric-covered cardboard base of the bag. Underneath was a manila folder. The tab had been folded under. When I bent the tab back I saw the slug written on it: *Nightmares.*

I opened the folder and facing me was a page with a short list of unfamiliar names and notes. They were completely meaningless to me, and, in fact, they were nearly impossible to read in the cab. The pages comprising the rest of the file were blank. It was all hopeless here. I put everything back in the bag, settled back and relaxed. Nonetheless, I was a happy if sick and tired man.

She was dressed, by God, when I got home. I hardly recognized her with her clothes on. She was wearing a light green skirt of some soft, supple material with a million pleats in it that swirled and danced whenever she moved. On top was a rather diaphanous blouse that was buttoned quite low. There was nothing under the blouse, in the way of undertrappings, I mean. She held my face and kissed me. "You look tired," she said. "Sit down and put your feet up and I'll get you a drink."

"Make it bourbon and water," I croaked. "No more martinis for me!" I sank my frame into the easy chair and waited, feeling rather like Old King Cole. She brought in the drinks—bourbon and water for me, but the insistent martini for herself. "Where'd you get the clothes?" I asked her. I wondered hurriedly if another lady of times past had left a change of clothing somewhere in the recesses of my closets.

"I sent over to the Carlyle for my bag," said Celia. "They put it in a cab for me."

"You checked out?"

"Until you're well," said Celia. "Do you mind?"

"Jesus, no," I answered feelingly. I stared at her, stricken for a moment, and made a careful decision. It might not have been the same decision if I hadn't been sick and weak, but I took the flyer. "Anyway," I said to her, "I've got a present for you."

"A present?" She nodded toward the gym bag. "In there?"

"It's Gene's gym bag," I told her. "He made a false bottom in it and it's where he put the nightmare file. You can send it home to Daddy." I thought again for a moment. "After Evie sees it, of course."

"Can I look at it?"

"Sure," I said. "We'll both look at it."

I unzipped the bag, set aside the gym gear, and pulled out the manila folder. I opened it and stared at the top sheet again. In the clear light of my front room it seemed to make even less sense than it had in the cab. "I don't know what the hell all the excitement was about," I said. The top sheet bore the notes:

Vientiane
Pak Beng
Nam Tha
Ou Neua
Phong Saly
Nam Hou
Landseer Ltd.
Ergot? Ergotism?

See Bangutgut.

I asked Celia, "Does any of this mean anything to you?"

She was thinking. I had to crane my neck to see her speak because she would not lift her eyes from the paper. "Vientiane, of course," she said, "is the capital of Laos. Nam Hou, I believe, is a river in Laos. The other Asian names don't mean anything at all to me."

"What about Landseer Limited?"

"That," she said, slowly, thoughtfully, "rings a very tiny, remote bell. My hunch is that it's either a bank or a holding company in Southeast Asia, but that's only because it's listed with all those names. I could be very wrong."

"Ergot? Ergotism?"

"I haven't the slightest. Oh, I mean, of course, I know what ergot is. It's a mold or a yeast that grows on rye, and ergotism is the poisoning by ergot. It resembles the effects of LSD, but everybody knows that. Peasants in Europe used to get it from eating moldy rye bread. If I remember correctly, it gave the sensation of being on fire and caused hallucinations."

"Was it fatal, the poisoning?"

"I really don't know. We could look it up."

"Okay, what about bangutgut—see bangutgut?"

"Never heard of it," said Celia, shaking her head. "He's lost me there."

I sighed. "Gene was obviously putting together some kind of a story, but he had most of it in his head. Let me get the atlas," I said, standing up, "and we'll see what these other names amount to."

The atlas map of Laos showed that Pak Beng, Nam Tha, Ou Neua, and Phong Saly formed a rough isoceles triangle subtended by the Nam Hou River. It was the names of the little towns inside the triangle that caught our interest: Muong Yo, Muong Hai, Muong Sai, Muong Beng. Other villages with the prefix Muong were scattered to the south, but this seemed to be the heaviest concentration of them. "Muong," I said. "Hmuong. Those were the people with the nightmares, the refugees who were dying in their sleep. So it evidently does have something to do with nightmares."

Celia was troubled. "This isn't the sort of thing he was doing at all for that silly magazine," she said. "Why on earth did he go off on this tack?"

"I think I know now," I answered, "having had the resistible pleasure of meeting their new editor. Gene was on his way out. It really didn't have anything to do with smoking. He came up the rough side of the new owner, and they wanted to dump him. But they were holding on to him until they got somebody else primed for the job."

"That is a horrible situation," said Celia, "like being marooned."

"Yes," I said. "Well, I think Gene got the message and decided to do something on his own, something he could develop into a saleable article or a book. The funny thing is, it might not be typical of what the magazine publishes, but the new editor was very interested in it. He was sore as hell when he saw it wasn't in Gene's desk file. Why would he want what they would never print?"

"Bitchiness," Celia smiled. "It's not limited to women, you know."

"Nightmares, nightmares," I repeated. "I tell you what. I'll make a xerox of this sheet tomorrow and give it to you. I'll still have the original then to give to Evie."

"Nonsense," said Celia briskly. "I'll just copy it down now and hand it over to Father. He can make what he wants to of it." She went over to get her purse, the skirt bouncing entrancingly as she crossed the room in the slanted light, making me yearn to get my hands up under it. She came back and took a small gold pen from her purse, took a blank sheet of paper from the file and, using the atlas as a desk on the floor, began to copy down the notes on Gene's paper.

"Nightmares," I mused aloud while she was copying. "Did I tell you that I saw Gene's shrink today, and he never mentioned nightmares?" She shook her head, still intent on getting the strange names right. "I never saw any mention of it in the transcripts, either," I said. I looked at her then. "Have you been reading those transcripts by any chance?" She nodded her

head in assent. "Did you see any mention of nightmares?" She shook her head—*no*. "Are they still in
the kitchen?" *Yes*. "Did you tidy them up?" *Yes*. I
began to laugh—helplessly. She put down the final dot
to her copy, and she, too, began to laugh. She laid
herself back on the floor and opened her arms. "No,"
I said. "First—just for a little while—I want to scan
those transcripts for the word *nightmare*."

I went into the kitchen rather quickly lest all my
resolve be lost on the floor. The transcripts were or-
ganized into three neat piles on the kitchen table. I
fixed myself another bourbon and water—Celia had
made herself a pitcher of martinis and was not wanting
yet—and carefully balanced the three separated transcripts in one hand. With the other, I picked up my
drink and made my perilous journey back into the
front room. Celia had her tiny purse in her hand. She
was standing up and doing something with her nose. I
paused. It was old-fart time—the time for remonstrance,
warning, advice, recrimination—ultimately, possession.
Did I want to possess Celia? No, no, I mean truly
possess her in the sense of attempting responsibility
for her life? The decision was made while I stood
there stupidly with the drink in one hand and the
transcripts in the other—helpless, idiotic. No. I was
not up to it. She was glittering, beautiful, brilliant, and
mysterious. Taking responsibility for her would have
been like wearing the Kohinoor diamond on a thick
gold chain while cruising the Lower East Side at midnight. I am as full of self-delusion as any man, but
there was no way I could offer Celia Listing anything
at all. She was there to be loved for the instant, and I
made up my mind that that was how it would be.
What she put in her nose was not now and was never
going to be my business.

"How far did you get?" I asked her, setting the
transcripts awkwardly on the coffee table. I absorbed
a quarter of my drink before she answered.

"Halfway through the second one." She had closed
her purse and tossed it into a chair.

"Okay," I said. "You finish up the second one and
I'm going to scan number three."

But scanning the record of Gene's encounter with the shrink was easier said than done. In the carefully typed sentences, Gene recreated himself and rose from the page.

K: *I'd like to talk a little bit about your animosity toward doctors—medicine.*

G: *Oh, God. I have no animosity toward them. I simply don't want to be exposed to yet another product of the Charles Bovary school of podiatry.*

K: *Podiatry? You're having trouble with your feet?*

G: *Never mind. Skip it.*

K: *But . . .*

G: *On the other hand, neither do I like being exposed to the top-of-the-class types who managed to race down to the library from the lecture room and razor out the pages in the medical texts before their classmates could get there. I agree that it shows an initiative that is awe-inspiring, and I'm sure that they're terribly intelligent, energetic, ambitious, hard-working, and hard-driving. It's only that I don't think I want one of them around when I'm sick, helpless, and unable to defend myself.*

K: *Putting that aside, it seems that you object to the whole philosophy. I mean even the simple recommendation of healthful exercise.*

G: *Look here. I live in an apartment uptown, and my job is in an office midtown. It is a forty-five-minute vigorous walk between those two points. I make that walk every morning and every evening unless the weather is cataclysmic. I do that to keep my legs in shape because I ride every weekend that I possibly can.*

K: *You ride? Er, horses?*

G: *Horses—yes, the hounds being inadequate. I get all the exercise any sane doctor would recommend.*

K: *Yes, but smoking.*

G: *(Resignedly) Well—smoking. . .*

I glanced down at Celia, who had settled herself on the floor and was engrossed in her transcript. The skirt was spread out around her in a circle of green that was verdant and full of light. The dark hair cascaded over her shoulders and her back. The opening at her blouse revealed a breast which, except for the tart nipple at the end, was whiter than the gauze that enclosed it. Poor Kragmeyer. If he was having trouble with Gene, what would he have done with this radiant girl who was sticking heroin up her nose? She did not look up. I turned back to the transcript in my lap.

K: *You mention possession of self, but isn't it possible that if you possessed yourself you wouldn't be having this difficulty with quitting smoking?*

G: *But I didn't have any trouble quitting smoking! I quit on the dot!*

K: *(Hastily) With your job then.*

G: *My job! Let me tell you about my job. My job requires the utmost concentration.*

K: *Mr. Listing, I've taken the trouble to read a couple of issues of* BusiNews. *You'll pardon me if I say it doesn't seem to amount to much. Your job simply seems to be one of collecting information and putting words on paper.*

G: *My job consists of tap dancing on a tissue-paper drum. The sound, the rhythm has got to be there, but infinite caution has to be exercised that a toe doesn't poke through the drum head and produce a truth. Do you really think that the pap you read in* BusiNews *is the retailing of information? Do you actually think that the reportage you read in magazines, journals, newspapers is true? Are you crazy?*

K: *Of course I realize there is a style . . .*

G: *The style is to maintain a tacitly recognized fraudulence, to maintain a wonderworld of stalwart, right-thinking leaders of the world on whom our livelihood, our very existence depends. It isn't until there is an overwhelming catastrophe that the least semblance of a truth comes crashing through— undeniable, irrefutable. Then there is the oohing and ahing and the apologetic all-meant-for the-best tone that pervades the columns while the leaders float down in their golden parachutes. There isn't a hint in the columns anywhere that the leaders, that leadership itself is sick, mad, dangerous, destructive, and doomstruck.*

* * *

K: *But if you feel this way about what you are doing, how can you—*

G: *How can I go on doing it? Well, we owe it all to Mary Shelley, don't we? Out of the corpse of my youth I created the monster that I am. The self that I possess—or don't possess, as you have pointed out—is, like the self of everyone I know, a construction. When everything that was young in me collapsed, I raised the phoenix which is myself today. This is the self that confronts you. No doubt it is your mission to sweep aside my phoenix and reach into the charred bones of my childhood. I assure you this is fruitless. You cannot reassemble them. They are ashes.*

Out of the ashes of my youth I constructed me. When I was putting these bones together I decided to make a man, which is to say someone who would reproduce himself and accept responsibility for what he had reproduced. That meant taking a wife, and that meant supporting the wife and the children by the sweat of my face. This is the biblical condemnation, and I find nothing unjust in it. Supporting them meant taking a job, and taking a job meant giving up a certain amount of my substance to labor, although not my entire mind, and certainly not my soul.

Anyway, with this new-constructed me I went off to find a wife, and in Stuttgart I found Brat. Do I love Brat? Oh, yes. Oh, God, yes, I love Brat. Because she was not only Brat, whom I loved on sight, she kept tightening the nuts and bolts in my newly constructed self. And my children, Nick and Claire, I loved from the minute they were pulled out of Brat's belly. Does this make me out to be a fool?

So this is the simple-minded, articulated construction you have in front of you. And this is the construction that applied for the job, got it, and labored at it for ten years. I had jobs before, of course, jobs that came and went. But this was the first job that promised that mysterious thing called a career.

And so I was committed. Do I resent it? Not at all. But was I myself? The self beloved of philoso-

*phers? No. Not that either. But let me mention
something about philosophers—Kierkegaard and
Sartre, for example. Many of them crawled out of
the cauldron of life. They were not about to be
boiled for the cannibal's feast. Many of them remained outside that circle in the dust where one
goes in to grapple with the ghost of physical life
itself. By remaining outside that circle they lost to
some extent their authority to speak.*

*The one philosopher who recognized this per-
sonal problem, I think, was Kant, not in what he
wrote but what he said when he was near death.
You know, he died in the same room he'd slept in
all his life, in Koenigsberg. When he was dying this
tiny, frail man was in his huge bed in the icy room
and a delegation came to pay their respects. In his
nightgown and cap, Kant levered himself out of bed
and tottered across the icy floor. The burghers were
horrified. "Oh, please, Herr Doktor Kant, do not
trouble yourself," and so forth. "No, no," said
Kant, stretching out his translucent hands to them.
"I have not lost my humanity."*

*And that really is what I want to be able to say
when I have to walk across the freezing floor—"I
have not lost my humanity."*

I had had about all I could take for the day. I hadn't
come across any sign of the word *nightmares* or even
the mention of dreams. Celia, now flipping nervously
through the remaining pages of her stack, showed no
signs of it either. She felt my eyes upon her, looked up
and smiled. However, it was a sad, reflective smile.
"Poor Gene," she said. "And poor K. *K*?" She raised
her eyebrows.

"Kragmeyer."

"Poor Kragmeyer. He got the full-bodied Listing
assault, all right. I can just hear Gene." She thumbed
back a few sheets and with a sweetly reasonable expression on her face she read: *"But why did you quit
smoking so precipitately, Mr. Listing?"*

Her face then assumed a choleric frown. Her pretty
eyes tried to glare. *"Do you expect me to temporize*

with some cheap scoundrel about my personal regimen because he happens to have seized control of a company?" She collapsed, laughing helplessly. "Oh, God," she said. "I don't think there's another person in the English-speaking world who uses the word *scoundrel.*

"But you're right," she said, sitting up then. "There's no mention of the word *nightmare.* Not in this packet, anyway."

Hunger had begun to gnaw at my vitals, and I decided to make use of Celia's ears—no, not to eat them, although they were marvelous for nibbling at—but for the telephone. "Can you eat Chinese?" I asked her.

"I'm as omnivorous as a cockroach."

I went to my desk and pulled out a flyer with a menu from one of the take-out Chinese restaurants in the neighborhood. "How about you pick up the phone and order some grub sent up?" I asked her. "It'll be a thrill for me because it's something I can never do for myself."

Celia scanned the menu, went to the phone, and obliged. From the length of the phone call, I suspected that she had gone into some detail. I wouldn't have been surprised if she'd been ordering in Cantonese.

The meal arrived in all its plenitude and with heartening promptness. We fell upon it in the kitchen, and when we had finished I knocked off the dishes while Celia reflectively picked her pearly whites.

I knew how sick I was when I realized that just washing the dishes had exhausted me. I dropped heavily into the kitchen chair and sighed. "Poor baby," said Celia, touching my cheek. "You look gray."

I put a palm on my thatch. "My hair is turning?" I asked, alarmed.

"No. Your face, silly. You look very tired."

"I'm getting old," I said, disheartened.

"The Chinese know how to do more than cook," said Celia. "Do you know how the Chinese emperors managed to live to those terribly advanced old ages?" When I shook my bemused head she explained, "By sleeping with their faces pressed between a maiden's legs." She smiled encouragingly.

"Damned clever, those Chinese," I said, getting up and following her swirling skirt into the bedroom.

18

I was surprised to see Beaman standing out in front when my cab pulled up to the doors of the VA hospital. He signaled wildly for me to stay put and, cupping his hands, yelled something to the cabbie, who slumped back in resignation. I remained where I was, suspended in puzzlement, with Gene's blue gym bag next to me on the seat. I'd taken out the gym gear and loaded it with all the material I'd collected in Evie's behalf, the medical records Heemstra had given me, the nightmare file, the transcripts, which I was returning to Evie, and even the little amber container of medication. I intended to take it all up to Evie after I had finished with the hospital.

Beaman had popped back into the lobby and then emerged with a portly, white-haired old duck who walked up to the cab with that purposeful dignity that was the mark of a personage in years gone by, but now has all but disappeared. I got out and held the door open for him.

"Doctor Dap," said Beaman, "this is the patient, Joe Binney. Joe, this is Doctor Dap, the consultant I was telling you about." The old, heavy face, which was just about on a level with mine, was decorated with thick white eyebrows under which two very piercing blue eyes shone forth. Dr. Dap seized my hand with his right and put his left hand on my elbow as we pumped up and down. His grip was strong and his left hand, I sensed immediately, was gauging my muscle tone and guessing my weight. He smiled heartily, revealing a set of strong yellowing teeth that reminded me of Teddy Roosevelt.

"Delighted," the old man said, enunciating very clearly. "Delighted to meet you, Mr. Binney." The old Dutchman had on a dark suit with some indefinable pattern that had sunk back into the threads. His white shirt was ancient and his tie seemed to outwit a common hazard, being more or less the color of gravy. I was momentarily nonplussed, not only by the presence of the two doctors outside the hospital, but by the fact that the strong, simple handshake and the firm, reassuring grip on my elbow had almost instantly made me feel better. Out of my confusion, I cracked wise, perhaps stupidly.

"I know the VA is hard up," I said, "but I didn't expect to be examined out in the street." Beaman shot me a thunderous scowl, but Dr. Dap shook with laughter.

"Ah, no, Mr. Binney," he said. "We have at our disposal something much better than that. I've arranged to have you looked at through an NMR, a nuclear magnetic resonator." Beaman glared at me to make sure that I was suitably impressed, but I didn't know what in the hell Dap was talking about. Dap seized my arm again. "Get in, get in," he urged me. "I will sit up in front as befits my huge behind. Dr. Beaman will explain what we are up to."

Seated next to me in the cab, Beaman said, "Because Dr. Dap happens to know the chief of medicine at the Clinic, we've been invited to use the new NMR they just got in. It's ideal for visualizing the problem you've got with your ear." He prevented me from interrupting. I could see that he was on his best behavior, and I felt a strong suggestion emanating from him that I should be on mine. "The NMR visualizes interiors, like the X ray, except that it uses a powerful magnetic field crossed with radio waves. The interaction of these two forces on the tissue, which actually affects the protons in the atoms of the tissue, produces an image of the tissue we want to look at. One of the

main advantages is that there is no interference of
bone in the image, because bone doesn't react the
same way. It seems almost to disappear completely.
This means your skull won't interfere with what we're
looking for. We are very lucky to have this opportunity."

We might be lucky, I thought, but it also sounded
like it was going to cost an arm and a leg. "Does my
medical plan cover this, do you know?" I asked.

Dr. Dap turned around to face me. "Don't worry
about cost," he told me. "Adelstein's doing this as a
favor to me, as well he might. I've been very curious."

This scared me even more. "Is my case that serious?"

"I was curious about the machine, the NMR." Dr.
Dap smiled. "I haven't had a chance to see one in
operation. Your case is ideal. I like to keep up." He
turned back and looked out the windshield.

After we arrived it was an odd experience for me to
walk into a hospital without being asked a lot of questions, filling out forms, waiting endlessly on a maple
bench. I simply followed the two doctors as they
tromped along with the air of studs who are very sure
of their turf. We went down various corridors that
joined and intersected and joined again in a seemingly
endless maze. Later I learned that the magnet in the
NMR is so powerful that the machine has to be isolated from the other equipment in the building.

When we got to the NMR, Dap and Beaman stepped
up to a white-coated doctor, a tall, spare, middle-aged
man in heavy-framed glasses. After the greetings they
began a vigorous discussion with him, to which, of
course, I was not privy. I stood in the background,
feeling rather forlorn for the first time, holding the
blue gym bag and looking distractedly around.

After they'd finished talking about what to do with
my head, the sandy-haired stringbean came over to
take me by the arm. What followed then was a kind of
nonviolent medical mugging. I was relieved of my
watch and wallet, since the magnet would have stopped
my clock and wiped out the magnetic numbers on my
credit cards. They also took my keys and any spare
change I had. I jibbed at giving them the gym bag,

however, and looked for Beaman. I beckoned him over. "Take this and hold on to it," I instructed him. "I don't want it misplaced."

But Dr. Dap got interested, perhaps in my concern. He said, "You brought your pajamas and shaving things?"

"No," I told him. "This stuff in the bag is the records of a client of mine—an ex-client. He died in his sleep and I've gone around to pick up his medical records."

"Ah," said Dr. Dap. He smiled a blank, heartening smile at me, but I saw his sharp blue eyes return to the bag.

The host doctor took me by the arm then, and we all went into the room where the big machine resided. It was a huge, round, white-enameled affair with an opening in it that had the look of an isolation chamber, or perhaps a massive iron lung. In front of the opening was a gurney that apparently slid directly into the machine. The strangest looking thing about the whole outfit was a brass bell fixed to the side of it. A long string hung down from the bell.

"Some people get claustrophobic and upset," the skinny specialist told me. "The procedure can take anywhere from a half hour to an hour, so we let every patient hang on to the string, and if he feels something is really going wrong, he can ring the bell." He smiled grimly. "We don't encourage it," he added.

While Beaman and Dap stood around oohing and ahing at the machine, an attendant eased me onto the gurney and adjusted a clamp to hold my head still. This was very much as they had done in the infancy of photography, I thought, clamping you down for the tintype. I looked at the three doctors from the viewpoint of my toes as the attendant placed the end of the string in my hand.

The gurney was slid into the maw of the machine. I am not really claustrophobic, but since I have no hearing I always feel a bit uneasy when my line of sight is cut off. I told myself sternly to relax. After all, this was no different from having a picture taken, but relaxing came hard to me. The minutes followed one another like hanging drops of molasses. I gave up trying to gauge time. Finally, I closed my eyes and simply put myself into suspended animation. Thoughts, fantasies, and images passed like high clouds over my brain. I discouraged them. I tried to regulate my breathing and finally fell into something like a semitrance.

The gurney was pulled out at last, and I saw the technician through the gunsight of my toes. He released my head, took back the string, and helped me off the gurney. Through the window in the control room, I could see Beaman and Dap staring at a series of monitor screens. The specialist was twiddling some dials. The doctors looked very happy with the results, but I felt a little sick to my stomach. On the screens were various versions of my brain. Finally, another attendant came out and handed Dr. Dap some eight-by-ten glossies. He studied them sharply, handed them to Beaman, who nodded, and then they slid the pictures into an envelope. I had been forgotten. The three doctors were congratulating one another.

When they came out of the control room, Dap immediately came over to me and seized me by the arm. He seemed to have the habit of laying hands on people. "This has been a splendid success," he told me. "We now have information that is extremely valuable, all but confirmation of our diagnosis." Again, I got the hearty, approving smile from him, as if I had just done something brilliant.

After I'd collected my wristwatch, gym bag, and other belongings, we were out of there and back into a cab in a matter of minutes. Time, it appeared, was not to be wasted with a machine as expensive as that. When we got back to the VA, I tagged along after Beaman and Dap on the way up to Dap's office. There, Dap changed into a white coat, and the simple change of costume multiplied his authority by a power of ten.

I was invited to go into a small examining room and remove my shirt. A nurse took my temperature and blood pressure, and then Dap and Beaman came in. "Would you mind very much if I examined you, Mr. Binney?" Dap inquired with deceptive mildness. I made the only appropriate response. He donned a stetho-scope—a really ancient-looking affair—and remarked to Beaman, who was watching intently, "This isn't really a bad room for auscultation. It's away from the traffic noises and the admissions area. Not too much outside noise, but regrettably, some." He then put the tube up against my chest and began to listen. He listened in more spots on my chest than I knew I had. He then asked me to lie back on the examining table and pulled his stool over closer to it. "I am sitting," he told Beaman, "not because I am tired, but because it is the proper posture for palpation. It takes the weight off the feet and also the pressure off the fingers. It is rapidly," he added, "becoming a lost art.

He began to explore, then, the area around my ear, the throat, the cheek, up under the eyes. The touch was so light it was like being brushed by a butterfly's wing, yet every move of his fingers seemed precise, assured. When he was finished he examined my ears with an otoscope, and his touch was even lighter than Dr. Beaman's, which is something. Then he looked into my throat with a flashlight. Finished, he again gave me that approving smile. He said, "I'm going to take just a little drop of blood from your earlobe," and before I'd had time to think about it, reached up with a gizmo and gave me a little sting on the ear. He caught the blood on a glass slide.

Beaman said, "Shall I send that down to the lab?"

"As old as I am," replied Dr. Dap, "I am still capable of doing a white blood cell count." He lum-bered to his feet and left the room. Beaman followed him out. Before stepping out the door, however, Beaman told me to put on my shirt and wait for them in Dap's office.

Sitting in Dap's office, I was left alone with my thoughts—not something I've ever appreciated. I opened Gene's bag and rooted around for one of the tran-scripts. Scanning the transcript that Celia had read would, if nothing else, help pass the time. The tran-scripts were in the bottom, so I set the other stuff to one side: the medical records that Heemstra had oblig-ingly brought over, the nightmare file, and the bottle of medication. I sifted the three transcripts and had just opened #2 when Beaman and Dap came into the office. I set the transcript back on the corner of Dap's desk with the other material.

Dap sat behind his desk while Beaman lounged against the wall. Both were smiling. "Mr. Binney," said Dap. "We believe that Dr. Beaman's diagnosis has been confirmed. Your ear infection has developed into petrositis. What we had been looking for was to see if it threatened to become something called Gradenigo's syndrome, an abcess that grows from the inner ear to the brain."

I tried to follow this as best I could, but in fact, I was rigid with fear.

Dap continued, "We wanted the very best visualization we could get because the geometry of your inner ear is atypical, owing to the results of your wound. We were worried that Gradenigo's syndrome could develop without showing typical symptomatology until it was very far advanced. Had this been the case, surgery would have been mandatory."

"But, but," I faltered, "the antibiotics . . ."

"The spongy bone of your inner ear is not well supplied with blood or lymphatics," Dap went on imperturbably. "Which means that the antibiotics carried through these channels did not have much opportunity to work against the infection. Secondly, although we were unable to get a satisfactory culture, we know that these infections are usually caused by either streptococcus or staphylococcus. Both of these organisms are prone to developing highly resistant strains—resistant to antibiotic therapy, I mean. Dr. Beaman quite properly started you on what should have been an effective antibiotic, and when that didn't seem to work, he began another. The latter may have had some effect, but not enough in our estimation. We are afraid that more resistance is developing."

My throat was very dry. I said, "So you're going to have to open up my skull anyway?"

"No, no." Dr. Dap shook his head as if this were the most repulsive idea imaginable. "If you truly had Gradenigo's syndrome this far advanced, you would not be sitting here. You would have severe diplopia—double vision—and possibly a frank meningitis—inflammation of the covering of the brain. No. We believe we can arrest it now. Cure it, without surgery; without invasion, in fact, except for an intramuscular injection."

I had become exhausted following his lips, even though he spoke slowly, clearly, and expressively. He looked at me closely, sympathetically. He said, "Really, Mr. Binney, you must not worry about this. I know that it has been quite painful, very disturbing. The pain has come from irritation of the sixth facial nerve and the trigeminal nerve, both of which are exquisitely sensitive. The pressure has come from the abcess itself, quite relatively small, I assure you, but nonetheless a space-occupying lesion where there is little space. But now we are going to cure that."

I couldn't help it. I challenged him. "What makes you think so?"

It was immediately obvious that Dr. Dap loved being challenged. He gave me his best Teddy Roosevelt grin. "Because, Mr. Binney," he said, "we happen to have an antibiotic, a new antibiotic, that is extremely effective against these organisms, including those that have become resistant. It is still an investigative drug, but we have permission to use it on stubborn infections like yours. Let me advise you that we use it sparingly, because the cost, believe it or not, is one hundred dollars per dose."

"Jesus Christ," I said reverently. Then I brightened. "This means I can get my shot, give you the hundred bucks, and take off?"

I got another flash of the big yellow teeth. "Not quite," he said. "Your white blood count is quite high, over forty thousand, with a pronounced shift to the left. This means you are still fighting the infection. We think it would be wiser if you simply stayed here where I can take care of you for the next twenty-four hours. In other words, we would like to give you an injection now and check the results in twenty-four hours. Fair enough?"

My heart sank. I hate hospitals. However, there was something in the old Dutchman's expression that suggested that if I tried to leave he would slam me down on the deck. I caved in. "Somebody's going to have to call my secretary and tell her," I mumbled piteously.

They got me back into the examining room, where I changed into one of those damned backless gowns. Dap administered the miracle injection, up high on the shoulder, and then provided me with a bathrobe, to hide my posterior nakedness, and a set of paper slippers. Beaman bade me a fond farewell and took off. Dap very graciously said to me, "I'll see you to your room. It's quite near, on this floor."

"If you don't mind," I answered, "I'd like to have Gene's bag back. I left it in your office."

We went back in, and I started putting the transcripts in the bottom of the bag. Dap picked up the medical record, rather helplessly, I thought, like a junkie reaching for a fix. "You say this fellow, Mr. Listing, died in his sleep?" I nodded. Dap seemed to sense what was in the record. He asked me, "Do you mind if I look?" I most certainly did not mind. What he had sensed under his fingertips was the long EKG of the stress test, which was folded into a packet. Dap took the long narrow strip and laid it out on his desk.

I cleared my throat. "They told Gene the EKG showed there was something wrong with his heart," I said. "Some kind of irregularity."

He turned and looked at me. He had put on gold-rimmed glasses, but his sharp blue eyes burned through them. "Did they indeed," said Dr. Dap. He turned back to look at the strip and went over it with agonizing slowness and concentration. Finally, he turned to me again. "There is an irregularity, of course," he said. "Come take a look." I shuffled over in my paper sandals and stared at the incomprehensible squiggles. "An ectopic beat," said Dr. Dap, "almost directly at the beginning of the test." His finger jumped along the squiggles. "Here, here, here, and so on."

"Then they were right?"

"Oh, no. These ectopic beats are ventricular extra systoles. They are purely and simply the product of anxiety. This man was nervous—a real emotional conflict—possibly about taking the test. There is no organic problem at all revealed in this tracing."

He took off the gold-rimmed glasses and looked at me sternly. "On the evidence we have here," he told me, "unless this man killed himself either deliberately or inadvertently, I would have to say he was murdered."

19

I followed his lips, tracing out the word *murdered,* and suddenly felt very weak. I sat down suddenly in the chair next to me. Dr. Dap reached over quickly and put his hand on my shoulder. "Are you all right?" he asked me.

"Yes, yes," I answered. "I'm OK. It's been a busy morning for me. I guess this whole thing about my ear just got to me. Now, it's all just sinking in. To tell you the truth, I thought I had cancer."

Dap pulled up a chair and sat down across from me. He tilted his head to one side and smiled sadly at me. "You were more afraid of a tumor than an infection?"

"Who wouldn't be?"

"Let me tell you, Mr. Binney, a brain tumor here," and he touched the side of my head, "can often be cut out with no one the worse for it. A brain abcess, on the other hand, for instance, one beginning with an ulceration here," he pointed to where his nose met the valley of his upper lip, "can kill you as surely as a bullet fired through the brain. Because we have antibiotics does not mean that we can be contemptuous of infection." He patted my knee. "Relax," he advised me. "We have found out what your trouble is. We will cure it."

I looked at Dr. Dap and wondered if I could unload. He was totally relaxed, sitting opposite me, his head tilted and his blue eyes absorbed in my troubles.

He was the first doctor I had spoken to in many years who did not give me the impression that he was a few minutes late on his way to catching the Concorde. It was a feeling of incredible luxury. I asked him, "Were you serious about the possibility of murder?"

Dr. Dap said, "I spoke hastily, perhaps foolishly. But I must admit, Mr. Binney, that on the evidence of that electrocardiogram, there is nothing to indicate any problem at all with the man's heart. If he was alarmed over the ectopic beat—it feels like an extra thump, you know—then it should simply have been explained to him. But there is surely nothing organically wrong."

I already knew enough to stay away from absolutes, so I chose my words carefully. "Then it is unlikely that his heart would have done nip-ups and killed him in his sleep?"

"Very unlikely," said Dr. Dap.

"I'm going to have to think about this," I told him.

"Let us get you settled in your room," he suggested, "and then I wonder if you couldn't oblige me by letting me look at all this material. Perhaps a little later in the day I might have some useful information."

"I'd be grateful," I responded. "I'd be very grateful."

Dr. Dap stood up and began assembling the papers that went into Gene's bag. He stopped, however, and picked up the little amber medicine bottle. He put on his gold-rimmed glasses and read the label carefully. Then he opened the cap and poured a few tablets into his palm. He stared at them, frowning. He put the tablets back in the bottle, capped it, and put it in the pocket of his white coat.

"Let's leave these papers where they are," he said, "and get you into bed where you belong." For the first time that morning, I saw that his mind was on something other than my case.

He got me settled in bed, pulled a chair over, and sat down. "Now, Mr. Binney," he said, "I am going to be watching your white blood cell count very carefully for the next twenty four hours. Because of this I want you to rest, and to relax, because both exercise and stress—anxiety—can raise the count." He glanced at his watch. "I have about ten minutes before I have to go on rounds. I would like you to tell me about this case you have."

I told him all about Gene, the job, the smoking ban, the nightmares, and the nightmare file. When I had finished it seemed that someone had lifted a safe off my chest.

Dr. Dap pursed his lips. "First the nightmares," he offered. "If this is the medicine Mr. Listing was taking," he patted the pocket of his coat, "then the nightmares might very well have been merely a side effect. The label says that this medicine is propranolol, and nightmares are a very well-known side effect of propranolol. We shall see.

"The job insecurity," he continued, "that sort of silent, ambiguous insecurity is deadly—one of the most stressful situations there can be. I am not surprised that his blood pressure rose, and that propranolol was prescribed for it. It is often the drug of choice in a situation like that. However, the mere fact that they prescribed it—I assume responsibly—means that his lungs were in reasonably good condition. Propranolol cannot be prescribed for patients with bronchial problems such as bronchitis or asthma. The next conclusion, therefore, is that there was no clinical reason for Mr. Listing to stop smoking. The sudden, arbitrary ban on smoking might very well have added to his stress. It is unlikely, however, that stress alone would have killed a normally healthy middle-aged man. After rounds I want to sit down and look over the material very carefully. Then I'll come in and tell you what I think."

"While you're at it," I pressed him, "would you look at the nightmare file and see if you can make any sense of it? It's really only a few words on a sheet of paper, with a lot of blank sheets underneath it.

"I suppose it proves what he was complaining of when he quit smoking," I mused, "He could get ideas, but he couldn't concentrate enough to organize them into anything workable. On the other hand, there's something in that file that got his editor all steamed up, and I can't figure out what the hell it could be."

"I'll take a look," Dr. Dap promised. "Now, you must rest. In a few hours someone will take another small blood sample, and then late this evening we'll give you another injection. All right?" He rose to go.

"Wait," I asked him. "Will you have someone make two phone calls for me?"

"Certainly." He took out a pen and a small notepad.

I gave him the phone numbers of both my office and my apartment. "Just have them tell whoever answers where I am, that I'm okay, and that I'll be out tomorrow morning. Can that be done?"

"Consider it done," said Dr. Dap. He put a hand on my forehead. "Go to sleep," said Dr. Dap.

And the odd thing is, I did go to sleep. I felt that I had somehow transferred an enormous load of responsibility from my shoulders to the broad if sagging shoulders of the old Dutchman, and that he had walked away with this load as if it were a feather.

I was awakened by a nurse bearing a tray upon which were not food and drink, but a shiny little gizmo and some glass appurtenances. She took a drop of blood from my finger this time, not from my ear, caught the blood on a glass slide, and was about to depart. "Wait a minute," I growled, still trying to clear sleep from my eyes. "Am I allowed to smoke in here?"

She registered a severe disapproval. "If you must," she said.

"What do I use for an ashtray?"

"That's up to you," snapped the nurse, and she bore her bloody sliver of glass into the hallway.

I got out of bed, put on my robe, found my Luckies in my shirt pocket and my Zippo in my pants pocket. There were some paper cups in the bathroom. I put an inch of water in one of them and made that do for an ashtray. I sat down in the room's single chair, put the makeshift ashtray on the window ledge, and wondered why a nurse should believe it was her duty to make someone feel guilty or miserable. I exhaled a cloud of rich blue smoke and decided that I was not going to feel guilty or miserable. I felt curiously at peace, although there was a terrible question gathering itself, like a snake coiling to strike, at the bottom of my mind.

Was Gene murdered? Could he have been? Who was there in the apartment to do it except Evie and the kids? An intruder sneaking in at the middle of the night and then departing unheard, unseen? A day earlier these questions would have had me jumping out of my skull. Today, sitting in this neutral hospital room with the afternoon sunlight streaming through the window and the cigarette smoke drifting above me with its familiar comforting smell, the questions arranged themselves meekly before me with no more emotional import than the choice of dishes in a cafeteria. However he had managed it, Dr. Dap had done his work well. I truly felt relaxed and at ease for the first time in a week. I sensed—hell, I *believed* that the old Dutchman actually meant to help me, that he was not an antagonist, that he was on my side, and that his weight on my side was considerable.

Long shadows were growing from the base of the building outside my window by the time Dr. Dap reappeared. He looked at me, smiled his sad smile, and said, "Would you mind getting back into bed?"

"But I feel fine," I objected.

"Be that as it may," said Dr. Dap, "I want to sit in your chair."

I jumped up and got in bed. He pulled the chair over to the side of the bed and sat down heavily. While I had been sleeping and staring emptily out the window, Dr. Dap had been working. It showed. He looked even older. Fatigue had made marks around his eyes and in his cheeks. He reached inside his white coat and took out a cigar, which he ceremoniously prepared and lighted. "I would offer you one," he said, "but I carry only one at a time." I acknowledged the graciousness with a smile and a nod.

The cigar put some lift back in his cheeks and made his eyes look younger. "First thing of all," he said through the fragrant smoke, "what do you intend to do with the contents of that bag?"

"Take them to Mrs. Listing tomorrow morning."

"Could I impose upon you, do you think, to leave

them with me for another day? I have looked over the
medical records and the nightmare file, as you call it.
As a matter of fact, I've brought that piece of paper
with me." He patted his pocket. "And I've also looked
into one of the transcripts. Very interesting. I'd appreciate the opportunity to read the transcripts fully before I turn back the material."

"I have no objection at all," I replied. "And I'm
certain that Mrs. Listing would be delighted to have a
disinterested opinion."

"Disinterested, yes." He smiled. "But certainly not
uninterested.

"I think first we should talk about the nightmare
file," he began, pulling the folded paper from the
pocket of his coat. "A very, very interesting conjecture on Mr. Listing's part, if I interpret what he has
put down here correctly." He unfolded the paper, put
on his gold-rimmed glasses, and stared at it. "Vientiane and the place names that follow it are, of course,
Laotian, and I suppose they all have to do with the
nightmare deaths you tell me he was investigating."
Dr. Dap took a huge inhalation from his cigar, blew a
speculative cloud into the air, admired the tip, and
returned to the paper. "Landseer Limited means absolutely nothing to me, except, of course, it must be some
kind of business organization. It is the last two lines
that throw a little illumination for me: *Ergot, ergotism,*
then *See Bangutgut.*"

"Bangutgut," I interrupted eagerly. "Do you know
what that means?"

"Bangutgut is an illness very much like that described among the Southeast Asian refugees—death
by nightmare—except that it occurs in the Philippines.
The most important thing about it in this context is
that it is associated with the consumption of large
amounts of rice—that is, feasts where large amounts
of rice have been eaten by the patient. Another interesting thing in this locality is that the Philippines has
been noted for occurences of *amok,* that is, Moro
natives running wildly through the village as if possessed, in the grip of a hallucination, which, after all,
is a kind of waking nightmare. Once begun, these

unfortunate victims were virtually unstoppable. They would kill or break down anything in their path."

"But what has rice got to do . . ." I began. Dap sharply waved my comments aside with a lordly gesture of his cigar.

"Mr. Listing saw the association, and also saw that it hinged on something that was not put down on this paper. It is an astute clinical remark written by Charles Dickens in his story *A Christmas Carol*. When Scrooge sees Marley's ghost in a dream, he says, you will remember, that Marley's ghost may be nothing more than a bit of underdone potato. The effect of digestion on dreams is famous in folklore, but relatively ignored by theorists. We cannot afford to ignore it here."

The old bastard was enjoying himself hugely in my mystification. He inhaled again, and the smoke punctuated his words in aromatic puffs. "You do not see the link yet, Mr. Binney?"

"It may be," I answered, "that some of my brains have leaked out of my ear, but right now, no, I don't see any link."

"The link is in what Mr. Listing was striving after with the words *ergot, ergotism*. Ergot grew as a mold on spoiled rye, and when it was ingested caused hallucinatory behavior, very much as lysergic acid does in modern-day drug abuse. Now, obviously, these Asian populations were not cramming themselves with rye bread, but they were, you notice, eating large amounts of another grain, rice.

"Now, rice not only has an important, almost mystical distinction in Asia, but also a social one that is of extreme importance. Any Asian who can afford it eats the white, hulled, polished rice. The brown, unpolished rice, with its hull intact or clinging, is left for the poor. The irony of this, of course, is that the brown rice is far more nutritious and supplies many vitamins and minerals lacking in the polished form. However, the reason brown rice is rejected whenever possible is that the husk is also the provenance of weevils, other insects or pests, molds, yeasts, blights, what have you. Rice is stored best in its polished state.

"So far as I know," he continued more slowly,

staring off into some private library in his frontal lobes, "the etiology of bangutgut has not yet been discovered, or at least verified. I think that what Mr. Listing may have been aiming at was that in a large feast of rice, polished or not, *some* hulling would have been included with the bulk—some chaff with the grain, as it were. In these bits of hullings, probably dissolved in the cooking, there may have been the residue of yeast or molds that grew during the period of storage—microscopic spores—that eventually proved just as deadly, just as hallucinogenic as ergot. The fact that it occurs after large feasts points to this."

"You think the refugees went nuts from eating rice?" I asked him bluntly.

The cigar stopped midway to his mouth. He stared at me for perhaps five seconds. "No, I do not, Mr. Binney," he said. The cigar completed its dignified arc, and he took a consolatory drag.

"I am sure that the rice the refugees eat is a standard American variety, polished and put in boxes or bags like everyone else's. It remains, even here, a relatively cheap substantial food, or staple. I'm sure they're not importing it from Asia. However," he said, his face curling in a satisfied grin, "there is one substance which the refugees are known to import and ingest from their homeland. Can you guess what it is?"

"No," I said. "I can't."

"Opium," said Dr. Dap.

"I'll be Goddamned."

"I was talking to a fellow from the Centers for Disease Control in Atlanta—you know, they're very interested in all this—at a meeting, and he told me there's a lot of trouble with the refugees getting opium from Laos. They have an attitude toward it much different from ours. They look upon it very much as we look upon taking a cocktail, and they're having to adjust to the American attitude. Their friends and relatives keep sending them fairly large packets of raw opium—and sometimes these are discovered, and sometimes they're not."

"Have the nightmare deaths been connected with opium?"

"Not that I've heard of. But on the other hand, these refugees understand that smoking opium over here is forbidden, and they would not be apt to mention whether or not any of the victims were smoking it. Indeed, no one but the victim might actually know whether or not he had smoked opium. Of course, they all deny it."

"With something that serious, don't you think they'd level with the police?"

"No," said Dap thoughtfully, "I don't. I'll tell you a story." He drew on his cigar and admired the firm white ash at the end. "When they were investigating the disease Kuru in a remote tribe that had remained more or less at the level of Stone-Age culture in New Guinea, they found out that it was caused by a slow virus, that is, a virus that takes many years to produce symptoms. The symptoms of Kuru are frightful, a wasting away, loss of nervous and muscular control, convulsions and inappropriate laughter, giggling. It is a terrifying disease and was the major cause of death in this tribe. It is linked to scrapie in sheep, but, of course, much more horrible in human beings. What puzzled the investigators was how this disease was transmitted. They couldn't figure it out. Actually, one had to ingest, to eat or absorb the virus in order to be infected. There was an exhaustive inquiry into the eating habits of the islanders, not excluding cannibalism. Cannibalism was stoutly denied, and the investigators could find none of the familiar indications of cannibalism—the warrior tradition, captives, what have you. They were about to pack up and go home, completely frustrated. Finally, it came out, however. In this group of Stone-Age people, there was a religious tradition of cannibalism. They ate the brains of their forebears right after death as a sign of respect and continuity. This was only about twenty years ago, mind you. It's all been forbidden now, and I suppose that the incidence of Kuru has dropped. But I tell you this only to show that people tend to keep things to themselves and are reluctant to give officialdom their confidence. Who can blame them? These people have already been victimized many times over. They are not likely to tell authorities that they are breaking the law. Who knows what might happen then?"

Cannibalism, opium, nightmares, spoiled rice, inappropriate laughter—I said to Dr. Dap, "I'm hooked, but I'm lost."

"I believe," answered Dr. Dap, "that your client, Mr. Listing, saw opium, raw opium shipped from Asia, as the most common, most likely vector for the nightmare deaths. Opium, particularly in the ancient form these people have traditionally used, is quite famous for producing dreams, dreams that were most often described as happy and peaceful, heavenly, as it were. What comes across here is the vividness of these dreams, the famous opium dreams. However, we must ask, where is the threshold that separates a vivid, beautiful dream from a vivid, terrifying nightmare? Further, we must ask, what kind of dreams might be produced by adulterated opium?"

"Adulterated?" This made me sit up.

"The raw opium shipped to these refugees, I'm told, is often naively disguised, wrapped in bedsheets or some ordinary material. I am simply wondering; what else might it be wrapped in—rice paper, possibly? What other substances might be somehow secreted in the raw opium that is sent halfway around the world? Indeed, could microscopic particles of some toxic substance be stuck into it—some yeast, some mold, some spore?"

"But if they smoke it," I objected, "wouldn't the fire in the pipe kill this stuff?"

"It is not necessarily the organism that is dangerous," Dap told me after a puff on his cigar. "It is the toxin, which is, after all, a chemical secreted by the organism, which is dangerous—incredibly dangerous. The toxin secreted by botulinum, for instance, the exotoxin of botulinum type A is so deadly that seven ounces is sufficient to kill the entire population of the world. A microgram, which is one-thirty-millionth of an ounce, is sufficient to kill two hundred thousand white mice. Toxins may very well survive the heat of the opium pipe and pass into the bloodstream through the tissues of the mouth or lungs."

"Have they found anything like that in the autopsies?"

"Not that I know of," Dap responded. "But you must understand that we are conjecturing about an unknown substance possibly introduced by means not admitted to. The very words *unknown substance* are enough to give a pathologist nightmares himself. What should he test for? Where should he look when all the familiar and known channels are exhausted? It could take many years—endless tests. It might never be discovered."

He sat up suddenly and looked at me sternly. "You understand this is purest conjecture," he said, "and not to be quoted. It is actually conjecture founded upon conjecture, a very shaky structure, indeed. But I am going to pursue it—the possibility of contaminated opium. That is why I want to hold on to the transcripts. I want to see if Mr. Listing dropped another clue somewhere."

"This toxic substance," I mused, "gave these people nightmares and then stopped their hearts. Either that or the nightmares themselves stopped their hearts. Does that sound reasonable to you?"

"Can a man die of fright?" Dr. Dap considered it. "Even in his dreams? An interesting question. Let's change the nomenclature just a bit. Can a man die of shock—emotional shock? Oh, yes, most certainly."

"Then those must have been some nightmares."

"Ah, I have been thinking about that. What is it that could come in a dream so terrible, so frightening, that a man could die of it? Two things come to mind here, one linked to the folklore of Southeast Asia, and at the same time linked to very real, quite brilliant neurological studies."

He puffed away for a while before continuing. "It is impossible," he said at last, "to be trained in the Netherlands, where I was trained, without learning something of Southeast Asian lore. Dutch holdings in that area were considerable, and many young Dutch doctors were sent to Jakarta and beyond to begin their practice. At any rate, one thing I learned was that in

Southeast Asian folklore—and, indeed, in many others —there is a very distinct duality of soul and body. One of the great primitive fears of the world is that the soul may somehow leave the living body. When this happens, they believe, the soul is unable to return. It is expelled, in other words. And so the body dies, is dead. That is the folklore.

"Now the curious thing," he continued, settling even further into his chair, "is that about twenty-five years ago, a very great neurophysiologist and brain surgeon, Wilder Penfield, conducted some experiments directly on the living human brain."

I sat up sharply. "Jesus Christ," I said. I reached for a cigarette and lighted it. Dr. Dap moved the makeshift ashtray closer and knocked some of his cigar ash into it.

He waved the cigar at me. "Relax," he said. "No one was hurt. This wasn't mad scientist or concentration-camp stuff. Dr. Penfield's subjects had to undergo brain surgery for one reason or another, usually for focal epilepsy. While the brain was uncovered, under local anesthesia—you know, oddly enough, the brain itself is incapable of feeling—these patients felt no discomfort, although the tops of their skulls had been removed. Indeed, it is unlikely that they knew that their brains were exposed. With these patients, Dr. Penfield did his great work in mapping the brain. I won't go into it, but you might, yourself, want to read this marvelous work sometime. He applied tiny electrodes to discrete areas in the brain, the cortex, the hippocampus, and recorded the reaction of the patient.

"You understand, this was done with exquisite precision. It amounted, I think, to stimulating, or 'firing,' as they call it, one nerve cell at a time. He would fire the nerve cell, and the patient, who was wide awake, would express his sensations. When one nerve cell was fired, for instance, the patient would say something like: *'Everybody is yelling. Something dreadful is going to happen.'* When another was fired, he would say: *'I feel as though I were standing up and falling over toward the floor.'* Or, *'People are getting smaller and moving away.'*

"And then, with one nerve cell, Dr. Penfield got a response that, when I read it, made the hair stand up on the back of my neck. The nerve cell was fired and the patient said: *'Oh, God! I am leaving my body!'* Remarkable, no?"

I stared at him helplessly, my cigarette forgotten in my hand. "This is true?" I asked him softly.

"It is true, I assure you," said the old man. "Part of a very great scientific enterprise. What fascinates me about it, other than its inherent drama, is that the other responses were linked to memory—the yelling of a family quarrel, the memory of standing unsteadily and falling down, as infants and children must do endlessly, the memory of people leaving, getting smaller, moving away, leaving one alone—all these are stored memories. But—*'I am leaving my body'* is surely a sensation that has been stored for the future, for death." He smiled comfortingly at me and took a deep drag on his cigar.

"I am not trying to spook you," he said. "I believe that there is a very rational, very physical explanation to this response. I believe it is a reflex akin to that of the so-called 'playing possum.' Have you ever actually seen an oppossum who fakes death when he has been attacked?" I shook my head. "Well, I have," said Dr. Dap. "It is amazing. My Labrador seized a possum one time out in the country, and the animal simply flattened out—dead. The dog dropped it in disgust and went off to other things. In a few minutes, the possum simply got up and strolled away. Now, the remarkable thing I observed in this was that to all intents and purposes the possum seemed really to be dead—the possum soul had left the possum body. Metabolism had all but stopped. So I have come to supposing that there may be a vestigial brain cell in most if not all mammals—certainly all mammals who may be preyed upon, as the human most certainly was, and still is to some extent—a brain mechanism that both mimics and prepares us for death. It is, perhaps, a brain mechanism for shock. Death, after all, is breakdown, disorganization. The nerve cells may fire randomly—thus: *'I saw my whole life pass before my eyes.'* And thus: *'I had left my body and was looking back at it.'* These are experiences quoted from persons who have been very near death or even pronounced clinically dead. Now do you see what I am driving at?''

"Perhaps," I replied. "Perhaps." In truth, I was mesmerized. There was something hypnotic about the old man weaving his hypothesis with the glowing tip of his cigar. The air of the room had become a thick blue haze.

"So very possibly we are talking about a mechanism that both protects us from death, in the very useful case of playing possum—not so very different, after all, from fainting—and at the same time prepares us to accept death when it arrives—simply to step away from our bodies, possibly our last glimmering of life.

"Very well," he sat up straight, as if he, too, were fighting off the spell. "We have here patients who may have been smoking the old form of opium, which creates a cortical irritation resolved in dreams usually interpreted as pleasant, even heavenly. But if the opium is contaminated with a toxic substance, this cortical irritation becomes completely incoherent. Nightmares are formed by the random, inexplicable firing of nerve cells. One of the nerve cells says to the patient, *'You are leaving your body. You have stepped outside your body. The soul has left your body never to return.'*

"Because of his culture, his religion, the emotional shock is so great that his heart begins to beat wildly, insanely, arrhythmically, like a pump that has lost its prime. It flails on empty air, stuttering, stammering without force or purchase—what we call fibrillation—the panic-stricken heart beating wildly but out of synchronization, unable to pump blood to the brain or other vital tissues. He undergoes cardiovascular collapse, and indeed he dies. The soul truly has left the body. He has died of shock, of fright, in his sleep."

The old doctor stood up and stretched himself. The tip of his cigar shone fiery against the darkening window. "If you have just a few more minutes, Dr. Dap," I begged him, "could you answer a couple of questions for me? Not about myself, but about Gene Listing?"

"If I can." He smiled down at me.

"First of all, since you're up, would you please light the lamp for us? It's getting hard to see you talk."

Dr. Dap obliged me, and bright light flooded the room, making the window darker, nearly opaque. "From what I've told you," I began, "from what you've seen, what do you make of the case of Gene Listing?"

"As to his death," Dap said slowly, reflectively, "I would need much more information. As to the events leading up to his death, I can only say it is extremely regrettable. Mr. Listing was caught up in the conflict between two great systems of medicine. Everyone knows about the school of Hippocrates, but few people realize there was a rival school, the Cnidian, named after the city in which it flourished on the coast of Asia Minor. These two schools of medicine have gone through history like a sine wave, now one in ascendancy, cresting, now the other. It was my hope that in my lifetime Hippocratic medicine would crest again, but I am afraid it is not to be. The difference between the two is that the Hippocratic school concentrated on the individual patient; the Cnidian concentrated upon the stored learning of its philosophy, the so-called Cnidian Maxims, or Cnidian Sentences. The patient was measured against these rules and was handed his Cnidian Sentence. He was judged.

"Now, it seems to me we are using statistics very much like the Cnidian Sentences. Even for a physician to use these statistics, any number of which are quite problematical, to intervene in the personal life of a patient is quite a serious undertaking. For laymen, mere businessmen, to do it is unthinkable.

"As to Mr. Listing's death, there is a tendency to say of someone who died in his sleep that he has died a so-called natural death. But what is natural about it? Dr. Merrill Mitler at the Scripps Clinic is pursuing this question, along with others. Even ten years ago, Littler, Honour, and Sleight were publishing electrocardiograms of patients during sleep. Some of them experienced attacks of angina pectoris brought on by the exertion and fright of dreams." The old man raised his palms upward in a question. "Who among us has led a life so devoid of experience that he has never awakened from a nightmare with his heart pounding? In a sick man that pounding could be fatal."

He finally came to light in the chair again and sat down heavily with a visible sigh. "But your client, your friend, Mr. Listing, so far as I can make out, was not a sick man. Neither," he added, "did he seem to be pursued by a guilt that would punish him in his sleep."

I said to Dr. Dap, "You make me very glad that I went down to Gene's office and went through his things. There was nothing incriminating there. He was as clean as a baby's breath."

"I'm glad to hear it," said Dr. Dap, "because if you are correct, it removes one more area of speculation."

The cigar had guttered, finally. Dr. Dap stared at the tiny brown shred in his fingers, heaved an immense sigh, and dropped it into the paper cup. He stood up. "I must go now," he said. "But first let me see your hand."

Puzzled, I held out my hand to him, and in the blink of an eye he had extracted a drop of blood from the fingertip. He smiled at me. "You will soon be served the usual inedible dinner," he said. "It is a way we have of discouraging people from getting sick. Later on this evening someone will give you another injection of antibiotic, and will also take another blood sample. You will sleep. Tomorrow morning we will take another blood sample and then you can be discharged. All right? But be sure to rest. Don't worry about things. We will cure you, and I will help you with your case. So, from now until morning I want you only to relax and sleep. Sleep the sleep of the just."

He left, and events followed as he had predicted. Most surprising of all, I did relax. I did sleep. When I awoke in the morning I felt refreshed, although weak. Dr. Dap came in early and took another blood sample from my finger. Fifteen minutes later he was back in my room to tell me that I had responded very well. He handed me a bottle of antibiotic tablets with stern instructions to take all of them according to the label. I thanked him before I left, but I could see that he was busy. Although he was gracious, as usual, he was on his way through the door almost before I could get the words out. I was cured.

The nurse with him, however, handed me a note folded over. Edna had called the night before. It said, "Evie wants to see you right away. Get well darned quick."

Evie, I decided, could come later. I ambushed a cab in front of the hospital and headed for home. When I opened the door, I could see that Celia was out of her clothes again. A welcoming committee of one? She was sitting asleep, an ivory figurine at the end of the couch. I began to tiptoe across the room, and then the odor assailed me. Celia wasn't asleep. She was dead.

20

I became an automaton.

Behind the tin forehead and photoelectric eyes a small red demon raged and stamped and shrieked out, *"No! No! No! No! No!"*

Everything I registered and did became mechanical, as if my eyes were receiving electronic signals and my fingers the extensions of a robotic arm.

On the couch next to her hand, lying palm up, was the empty unfolded packet of her kicky China White. I picked up the hand, very, very cold to the touch, as cold as marble by moonlight, and dropped it. She had been dead for quite a while, perhaps even when the phone call from the hospital, unanswered, had gone ringing, ringing through the apartment, with my lamps flashing on and off to indicate the noise, which, now, neither she nor I could hear. Her head was thrown back, her mouth slightly open, relaxed. From one corner of it a pastel pink worm of vomit had worked its way toward her chin. She hadn't thrown up very much. She had strangled on it. Celia's brown eyes, glazed with the bemusement of death, stared at the corner of the ceiling. I put my fingers out and closed her sightlessness, registering with surprise I suppose a robot wouldn't feel, how hard and unyielding the eyeballs were.

I stepped back and looked at her. A patch of hardened blood had stained the inside of her thighs. *"Pos-*

sibly the beginning of menses," my mechanical mind said to me. *"And possibly not."*

Quote: "Do you want to inspect every inch of my body?" she had asked me, glowing white, incandescent. This time my eye, inhuman, a mechanical lens, inspected all I could see without moving her body. That was for the police and the ME.

Finally, I went to the phone and sat in front of it. I was reluctant to make the call because people are not truly dead until one pronounces them dead. I knew that once I made the call my mechanical man would begin to shudder and crack. The gears would grind to a halt, the wiring would smoke and burn. The lenses would begin to flicker and flash, repeating their images over and over.

I punched out the number of my office and watched the little red light on the phone react to the buzzing of the distant bell. When the lapse between glows indicated that the phone had been picked up, I said, "Edna? Just signal me *OK,* so I know it's you." The red light flashed a reassuring, - - -/ -.-/.

I said, "Listen, Edna. Celia Listing, Gene Listing's niece, is in my apartment, and she is dead. Don't try to answer. Two things you have to do. Call the police and give them my address. Tell them what's happened, and that I'll be waiting here. Next, call Evie Listing and tell her what's happened. I'm sure she'll want to call Celia's father. I really can't tell you much more about it, except that I think she died here yesterday—and I guess she OD'd."

The light flashed the code letters: *R U O K*.

"Yes," I answered into the mouthpiece. "I'm OK. The doctor seems to think I'm all cleared up. It's all over but the shouting. I'm going to hang up now. Make those calls, and I'll wait here for the cops."

The police, too, have their way of keeping you out of the real world. When they come up into your house, they occupy the whole thing. They change it. They exhaust the oxygen. They change the room. It is no longer your house. It is theater.

And they are theater—unreal, improbable—acting out roles invented less than two hundred years ago.

They, too, are robots, operating on a punched-out program that can tell, like a robot, left from right, but not right from wrong. The law isn't programmed that way. The law can tell legal from illegal—most of the time—but that's about all. The enforcement arm is even more limited. Its cybernetics steers between two stars—*A pain in the ass-No problem.*

I decided to be a pain in the ass. The two cops from Homicide were standard issue, one in his late thirties, one in his early thirties. They were well dressed, as befitted their income. They had trouble accepting the fact that I was deaf. It took a while to make this clear to them. The younger, shorter one balked a bit at using my Code-Com telephone, afraid that it might explode or shriek imprecations at him. At last he buckled down and made the necessary calls. I had identified myself, showing them my PI license, and then, standing in the middle of my own front room, which was no longer my own front room, I gave them as professionally as I could the plain recital of events. When I was finished I caught the attention of the taller, older man long enough to tell him that I had additional information. "Before she's moved," I said, "there are some things I think you ought to know." I might even have sounded like a robot. I don't know. My suggestion was greeted as a random noise in the street. I realized that I had paraphrased that most unwelcome of modern phrases: *We have a problem.*

After the other functionaries had arrived, I coaxed the two Homicide men into the kitchen and seated them at my table. While I busied myself with making coffee, I said to them, "It's not my business to interfere with your investigation, but I think there are a couple of things you ought to know for your own protection." I had turned briefly from the stove to look at them, and saw them both bristle at the word *protection*. It was not to be helped. I nodded toward the hallway to my living room. "That girl's old man," I told them, "is a high roller in Washington—State Department, National Security Council, something like that. This guy, his name is Samuel Listing, by the way, has not only got government clout, he's got enough money to rent the Trump Tower for an afternoon card game if he wants to. I'm telling you this," I emphasized with a nod, "so you'll know to make square corners when you put this thing to bed."

Their names were Gier and Rosenbloom. Rosenbloom was the older, taller, skinnier one. Gier appeared to scoff while Rosenbloom continued to listen. Gier said, "So this turns a straight OD into a federal case?" Rosenbloom looked at him across the table, and Gier stopped talking.

I set out milk and sugar, in case they used it, and set the mugs of coffee on the table. I was surprised to see how my hands shook. They both looked at me sharply, but said nothing about it. My robot was beginning to tremble and squeak. I sat down at the table and rested my arms to keep my hands from shaking. I said to them, "I think there might be a couple of rocks in the OD theory. For one thing, when the residue in that packet is examined, you'll find out that it's China White."

Gier said, "Are you a supplier?"

"No," I told him levelly. "I am not a supplier. To the best of my knowledge, the young lady either brought the stuff over from London or has a source in Washington, D.C., which is probably not available to your investigation."

Gier insisted, "But you knew she had it? Used it?"

"Yes," I replied. "I was trying to persuade her to turn herself in for rehabilitation, give up her career, and sign herself into an institution, but unfortunately I was forced to go to the hospital before I could complete this task." Our eyes locked.

Rosenbloom broke in. He touched my arm to call my attention away from Gier. "If that stuff really is China White, the McCoy," he said, "it's no wonder she OD'd."

"No," I answered. "That's the paradox. Apparently, China White was what she had been turned on with over in London in the first place. If she was going to have a reaction to it, that's when she should have had it. At this point it doesn't make sense."

"Maybe she shot up," said Rosenbloom, showing even as he said it that he didn't believe it.

I shook my head. "No string, no works, and no visible marks on her body that I could see. Also, she told me she had a thing about needles."

"Something made her puke," said Rosenbloom, emphasizing it with a slight nod of his head.

"That," I said gratefully, "is the problem. And that is why," I continued, "I think that when she is taken out of here you ought to take the couch cushion underneath her along with you. The urine and feces in it might be a help, but there's something else." I put my hands palm down on the table. "The blood between her legs," I said, "could possibly have come from menstruation, but if it was active bleeding, then it had to occur while she was alive. I have trouble believing that she just sat here menstruating on the couch. I think the cushion ought to be tested for semen and pubic hairs."

"You think you were long-cocked?" asked Gier.

I put my hands down between my knees and squeezed them together. "It is a possibility," I said. "But most importantly it would mean that she was not alone yesterday. It would mean that someone was here just before she died, or when she died."

I brought my right hand up then to make a stop sign. I didn't want another comment from Gier, however brilliant. "We also have a kind of stopper on the time of death," I told them. "Yesterday at the hospital I asked them to call here and tell Celia that I'd be staying overnight. I don't know if she answered the call. But you can trace the call and find out. If she answered, then she was alive at that time. If not, there's a possibility she was already dead." Gier started to say something, but Rosenbloom shut him down. "If you call the secretary of Dr. Israel Dap at this number," I said, taking the little slip from my wallet, "she can tell you what time the call was made, and whether anybody answered." Rosenbloom took out his notebook and copied down the number.

He asked me, "Anything else you think we ought to

know?" There was a dry, rather cynical expression on his face.

"You probably noticed," I said, "that there were slight bruises and little abrasions on her wrists. I don't think they were there the last time I saw her."

"Which was when?"

"Early yesterday morning."

Gier said, "You think her new playmate was playing games with her?"

He had touched my shoulder to get me to look at him while he made the remark. I swung my gaze back to Rosenbloom and kept it fixed there.

"Look," I said to him, "I'm trying very hard not to make a fool of myself. I don't know why your partner is trying to goad me, but it really won't help us get on with things. The Mutt and Jeff operation doesn't serve any useful purpose here."

Rosenbloom had a saturnine complexion to go with his hawk's nose. However, I could see the blood flushing up under it. He said, "I'll decide what's useful here."

Gier wanted to get back some lost ground. He touched my shoulder again and said to me, "How come you had to go to the hospital?"

"I had an earache," I answered. Gier rolled his eyes up into his head and smiled. "This is a Veterans Hospital?" he asked.

"Yes," I said. "I'm one of those malingering welfare bums you keep hearing about who haunt the Veterans Hospitals for a free meal and a place to bunk."

"It was a very convenient place to be," said Gier.

"So was wherever you happened to be."

"I wasn't sleeping with her."

"Do you sleep with anything at all?" I asked him. This time he flushed, and it was not a rewarding sight. Then I asked Rosenbloom, "Am I supposed to sit here and match wits with this midget?"

Gier said, "That does it. We can take you down as a material witness."

"Before you fuck up everything," I told him, "call

Bekin or Lange down on Centre Street. It's all right with me. I'd just as soon be there as here."

Rosenbloom turned his head slightly and said two words to Gier. I couldn't really see what they were, but they could have been "Lay off."

We all sat there staring at each other for a while. I asked them if they would like some more coffee. They said no. I asked them if they would like a drink. They said it was too early. Finally, Rosenbloom asked Gier to go into the front room and see how things were getting on. After he had left, Rosenbloom asked me, "What do you think happened?"

"I think she was raped and murdered," I said.

"Any idea why?"

"No," I answered. "Not really." Rosenbloom continued to stare at me. I continued to keep my mouth shut.

"All right," said Rosenbloom. "We'll get back to you."

"Let me give you my office number," I said. "I can't answer an ordinary phone, and you'll have to work through my secretary." I gave him our office number and he wrote it down.

Gier came back in. "I told them to take the cushion," he said.

Rosenbloom stood up. "We'll be in touch," he told me. I stayed in the kitchen while they let themselves out.

In fact I stayed there quite a while, debating whether I should reach for the bottle of whiskey in my kitchen cabinet. I decided against it. The machinery was roaring in my head, and I still felt the weight of the cannonball, which had by no means disappeared. Finally, I nerved myself to going back into the front room to see if I could reclaim it.

It still seemed changed to me, and the couch, with its end cushion missing, looked wounded. I stared all around me for a while, and then I went downstairs to the furniture store. Salvador, the owner, was standing by the front of the store, looking out the window. He had been watching all the police activity. He greeted me with sympathetic wariness. I told him, "Somebody

died on my couch last night, and I want to get rid of
it." He nodded with speechless understanding. I went
down the row of garish couches he was retailing and
picked out a dark brown number with gold thread
running through it. I gave him the keys to my place.
"I'd appreciate it if you'd deliver this right away," I
said. "And take the old couch out and throw it away. I
don't ever want to see it again." He nodded and
placed a hand on my shoulder. "I'm going to go down
and get something to eat," I said. "It would be worth
a lot to me if the whole thing was done before I got
back."

"Right away," said Salvador.

I walked westerly, more or less toward City Hall,
until I came across a modern, unfamiliar, characterless
luncheonette. The walls were covered with plastic.
The furnishings were plastic. The waitress was plastic.
I had plastic scrambled eggs, toast, and coffee. My
mind was as blank as the food. I chomped away until
it was eaten, swilled down the coffee, left a tip, paid
the bill at the register by the door, and began the
blind, deaf, senseless walk back to my apartment.

I retrieved my keys from Salvador. He was trying to
tell me something, but I simply shook my head and
pushed past him. My first sight of the front room
showed me the corner of the new couch. Salvador had
done his job. The second step brought me into view of
someone sitting at the other end of it. It was Evie, and
she was holding a gun in her lap. The gun was pointed
at me.

21

When I had absorbed what I was looking at and was finally able to speak, I said, "For Christ's sake, Evie, put that gun away." I remained rooted at the door.

She, too, seemed to be operating on a circuit of delayed reactions. Her eyes widened as she stared at me, and the gun remained braced in her lap and pointing at me. At last she lowered it to her hip and left it on the seat of the couch as she stood up. She came over to me and grabbed my hands. "Joe," she said, "Joe. I'm so frightened. They've hurt Nicky."

"Easy," I answered, leading her back to the couch. "Who hurt Nick?"

"They broke into the apartment while Claire and I were downstairs at the Gaylords'. Nick was studying in his room. I guess they didn't know he was there. He heard the noise and came out, and they hit him, hurt him. They hurt his neck. They don't—I mean, at the hospital—they don't know if it's broken."

She would not let go of my hands. "Sit down, sit down, Evie," I urged her, pushing her down on the couch. "First things first." I gently freed my hands and picked up the gun. It was a nickel-plated Beretta automatic, .25-caliber. I checked the safety on it and saw that it was in firing position. I thumbed it back. "Put this back in your purse," I told her, "and don't go around waving it at everybody."

"I know how to use it," Evie said solemnly. "My

father taught me. And I'll kill the son of a bitch that hurt Nick." She put the gun reluctantly in her purse.

"Just make sure you're pointing it at the right guy when you do it," I admonished her.

She looked contrite. "I didn't know who was coming through the door," she said. "I mean—Celia . . ."

I was suddenly alert, cold, interested. "What about Celia?" I asked her sharply.

"When your Secretary called and said Celia was dead, she told me you thought she'd taken an overdose. I know Celia. Never, never would that happen. If Celia is dead, she was killed. Nicky was almost killed. Gene is dead. And I'm frightened—so frightened." Her face screwed up, and she commenced to cry.

I pulled up a chair facing the new, ugly couch and sat in it. I patted her hand. "It so happens that I agree with you," I told her. "But let's get a grip on things. First of all, exactly when was the break-in at your place?"

"Last night about nine o'clock. Claire and I had gone down to the Gaylords' for a late supper. They've been awfully nice. Nick said he'd already eaten, and had to cram for a biology test. We came back at about nine-thirty. The door to the apartment was open, so we knew there was something wrong. When we came in the place was terrible. Everything was torn apart and topsy-turvy, and Nick was lying on the floor. He was unconscious. I thought he was dead." She twisted her hands together. "His face was pale, and his head was at a funny angle. Claire wanted to pick him up—to hug him—but I knew we shouldn't touch him except, except, of course, I felt the side of his throat to see if he was still alive. But I kept Claire from moving him. I called the police and told them to bring the ambulance."

"Has Nick regained consciousness?"

"Oh, yes. He came around while they were strapping him into the stretcher."

"Could he talk?"

"We didn't want him to. I just kept telling him that everything was all right. He was very upset, ashamed that they'd got away."

"You keep saying *they*," I observed. "Was it two of them? A gang?"

She shook her head. "It's just a way of speaking," she said. "You know—somebody out there. Actually, I guess, there was only one."

"Ah," I said. "Did Nick see him well enough to give a description?"

"I guess there wasn't much to see," she answered. "The man was wearing a stocking mask. Nick remembered that he had gloves on and dark clothes. A dark jacket or something with a hood."

"And he tore up everything in the place?"

"Just about. As if he was crazy. The electric typewriter I had in the bedroom, the one I rented, he threw that out the window. It crashed in the little alley where they keep the garbage cans."

"What did he take?"

"The cassettes, the cassette player, all the manuscripts of the last three transcripts, my jewelry box, anything small enough to carry, I guess."

I looked away from her and stared at the wall. "Ah, shit." I said. I heaved an enormous sigh.

Evie saw beyond the simple exclamation. "What's the matter?" she asked. "Why do you look like that?"

I rubbed my face. "Maybe you'd have been better off hiring somebody else," I told her bitterly. "Somebody who wasn't sick, somebody who was competent."

She reached out and took my hand comfortingly. She had enough left for that. "C'mon, Joe," she said.

"All right," I said. "Somebody is looking for something, and isn't too worried about how he finds it. There was a break-in at Kragmeyer's, Gene's therapist, that was a carbon copy of yours. Same MO, same description, same recklessness, same violence. All that trashing—your typewriter out the window, for instance —that's all part of the game, I think, a clumsy game. But somebody's looking for something."

We both remained perfectly still for a moment, staring into the short space of the air between us. Finally, I said, "When I was in the hospital Edna left a note that you wanted to see me urgently. That was before the break-in, wasn't it?"

She sat up straight, her eyes alert. "Yes," she said. "There was something I wanted to ask you, something I'm not sure I understand." The diversion was beneficial to her. She clasped her hands over her knees and concentrated on what she was about to say. "The bank statement came in, and I had to handle it this time. Usually, Gene did it, balanced the checkbooks. It never really mattered. I mean, there were no big secrets. We both always knew what was there. But this month when it came in and I started going over the canceled checks, there were a lot of them made out to Cash that seemed, well, a little excessive. They amounted to about two hundred dollars a week. So I went back and looked at the month before, and it was the same thing. We can't really afford an expense like that. It's very unusual that Gene would be cashing checks like that."

"Well," I began, "Gene was drinking quite a bit. At certain bars, here in New York, this can get very expensive."

"Two hundred a week?" asked Evie, "In bar bills?"

I thought about it. "What about weekends?" I asked her. "Did he go out on weekends over the last couple of months, or did he stay home?"

"He stayed home," answered Evie. "We didn't go down to Maryland. He stayed home and it was hell on earth. You couldn't live with him. He was drunk all the time."

"But from a bottle at home?"

"Yes. Martinis. Martinis that were more or less straight gin."

I nodded. The Listing family seemed to have a penchant for busthead deadly drinks. "All right," I said, "that means the two hundred dollars was spread over five days, or evenings, which amounts to forty dollars a night. Can a man spend forty dollars of an evening in your average Manhattan bar? Very easily."

"But every night for two months?" asked Evie, troubled.

It troubled me too. "That's pretty tough," I admitted. "In the best bars, drinks go for about four dollars a smash. That would come to ten drinks, or eight drinks if you subtract the tip. Laying on that kind of load every evening is pretty hard work. In a lot of bars," I added, "drinks would be either three or two dollars. That makes the intake astronomical. But there's something else you have to figure."

"What?"

"Drunks don't spend most of their money in saloons, unless they're good time Charlies, buying drinks for the house. Where the real money gets spent is after the guy is loaded, probably thrown out of the bar. Then it's taking a cab somewhere to buy a steak, pissing away money, making mistakes in change, handing out ten-dollar bills for ones, that kind of thing. Of course, the real money, for real drunks, gets spent in sanitariums while they're drying out."

Evie said sharply, "Gene never went to a sanitarium."

"I know," I answered softly. "I know."

"And," she added, "there was always money in the budget for Gene to stop off for a drink when he wanted to. That was already provided for. This was additional."

"All right," I said. "It's a little bit out of line. I'll check around."

"Joe," she said, staring into my eyes, "Tell me honestly. Was there another woman?"

I took her hand and shook my head. "Never," I told her. I thought of Gene's desk at *BusiNews*. "I would have seen the signals." My heart was seized with pity. "Evie," I asked her, "didn't Gene talk to you at all?"

"Almost never. Oh," her face brightened. "There was one time when he was just bursting—over that stupid story, of all things. He called me up from some place, probably a saloon. He talked in such a rush I could hardly understand him, but I remember he said, 'I've got the line on that son of a bitch, and when I get the story out, we'll blow him out of the water.'

"He had to talk to someone," she said desolately, "and I guess I was the only one who would listen." She heaved a sigh then that was almost a sob. "I don't know why I should worry about another woman so much," she said. "Maybe another woman could have helped him."

I said, "The only thing that could have helped Gene

was people leaving him the hell alone in the first place."

"Oh, Joe," said Evie. "I feel so lonely."

"Stop that," I told her. "You've got Nicky to worry about, and Claire. Claire must feel like she's been dropped off in outer space. Where is she, anyway?"

"She's in school right now," Evie answered. "And when she comes home, she's supposed to go to the Gaylords'. I don't want anybody to go up to that apartment."

"Anybody," I repeated. "Including yourself?"

"Yes," she said. "I'm terrified. It isn't my home anymore. Where can we go?"

What flashed instantly into my head was *Maryland,* but I held my tongue. I thought about it very carefully, and then I said, "I suppose whoever broke in got what he came for, and really ought not to be back. But there is no way I can assure you of that or guarantee it."

We both gave ourselves a moment to think. Then I said, "If you wanted someplace to go where you were sure it was safe, where would you go?"

There was another lengthy pause. She seemed to be gathering courage to speak. At last she said, "I know it would be a terrible imposition on you, but could we possibly stay here until we know what's going on?"

"It wouldn't be an imposition at all," I said quickly. "But I'm not so sure it's a good idea."

Evie gave me a brief, hurt, knowing smile.

"Look," I said. "In the first place, how did you get in here while I was out?"

"Some men were bringing a couch up, and I asked them where your apartment was, and they let me in."

"All right," I said. "So it wasn't like getting into Fort Knox, was it?" She pursed her lips and looked thoughtful. "More importantly," I continued, "we're pretty well agreed that somebody got in here after Celia." Identifying what had happened to Celia gave us both a shock. We both sat speechless for a moment. Then I said, "If you want my professional advice, I think the best place for you and Claire right now is in a good hotel under an assumed name. I doubt that it

would have to be for more than a week. Tell the
people at school that you and Claire have to go out of
town to settle the estate." She began to protest, but I
held up my hand to stop her. "It so happens that I'm
in thick with the house dick of a very decent old
midtown hotel. I can get you registered there under
any name you want, and I'll ask him to keep an eye
out for you. How does that sound?"

She smiled sadly. "Claire would love it."

I got out my address book and had Evie call Jack
Bell at the Park Towers. When she connected with
him, I began the monologue that is necessary to my
condition, and told him that Evie would be signing in
with her daughter under the name of Mallory and to
have the bills sent to me. I said that Evie would ask
for him when she arrived there and that he could
oversee the registration. Then I handed the phone
back to Evie. She spoke briefly into the mouthpiece
and appeared to confirm the arrangement. When she
turned to me, however, her face was still troubled.
"You really think this is best?" she asked me.

"Yes," I answered, "and I'll tell you why. Do you
see that little light flashing over the door?" She looked
up, startled. She hadn't noticed the light over the door
or the lamp that was flashing in the corner. "That's my
doorbell," I told her. "Do you have any idea of who it
could be?" She shook her head, solemn, frightened.
"Neither do I," I said. "I'm sure as hell not expecting
anybody." I put my hand out, palm up. "Let me have
that gun in your purse."

She dug out the little automatic and handed it to
me. I snapped the safety off and held the gun in my
coat pocket as I pressed the buzzer at the door. I kept
my hand on the gun as I peered down the stairs of my
hallway. It wasn't until I saw the tall detective,
Rosenbloom, that I relaxed my grip. I smiled reassuringly at Evie. "It's OK," I told her. "It's just one
of the detectives who was here earlier."

My reassurance died, however, with my first clear
look at Rosenbloom's face as he came through the
door. His mouth was a hard slit, his dark cheeks were

sucked in to emphasize the high, unyielding bones of his face, and his black eyes had points of fury in them.

"All right," he said, closing the door behind him. "No more dum-dum. Who did you call when I left?"

I was not only astonished, I was frightened. I longed to reach for the slight weight of the automatic in my pocket, but wisely kept my hands to my sides. "I don't know what you're talking about," I said.

"Somebody called somebody," he insisted. He was trembling with rage. "Somebody is jerking me around. If it's you, you can forget your license. You can forget everything. Because if it's you, I'll get you."

"Look," I said, holding out my hands in placation. "I haven't got the least idea what you're talking about. The only call I made was to my secretary, and that was before you got here. In fact, that's the only way you knew anything had happened. My secretary called you. If you'll let me know what's going on, maybe I can tell you something. What happened?"

"What happened," said Rosenbloom with a furious accusing stare at me, "is that this whole Goddamned case has disappeared into thin air. The ME never got his hands on her. The body was taken to the airport, where there was a plane waiting for it. It's gone—shit, the whole record of it is gone. I'm supposed to keep my mouth shut. It never happened."

Evie stepped up to look at him, rather disapprovingly, I thought. "Perhaps I can explain," she said.

"Who are you?" he demanded.

"I am Evalina Listing, the aunt of the woman who died."

"So?"

"I called Celia's father in Washington and told him. It is the correct thing to do. Her father, Samuel Listing, is what they call well-connected in the Federal Government. It's possible that he arranged for this, uh, special treatment."

"I never heard of him," said the detective with a scowl.

"Samuel Listing would be very pleased to hear that," returned Evie placidly. "At any rate, he's perfectly capable of arranging something like this, and of making it stick. I don't say I approve. I only say it's possible. I think the only place you'll find out what's happened is in Washington, and I don't think you'll have much luck."

The detective's thin, dark face fought with rage and frustration. He wheeled abruptly away from Evie's composed presence and pointed a long bony finger at me. "You watch your fucking step, Binney," he said to me. And then he was gone. I watched him go, observing that he was so blinded in his wrath he hadn't noticed the new couch.

I glanced at Evie to see if she had felt any shock at the bad language. Her face showed no sign of it. In fact, she said, "Oh, shit!" displaying her own access to bad language. "This is absolutely typical of Sam. He has to show that he's in control, no matter what."

"Do you think that's all it is?" I asked her, shaken, "Just to show that he's in control?"

"Part of it, at least," she answered, her face going rigid and cold. "He wouldn't want anything as undisciplined as the law messing around in his family affairs." She paused, and then a look almost of shock appeared on her face. "My God," she said. "I almost forgot to tell you. When I called Sam he asked me to tell you that he wants to see you today, and . . ."

"Forget it," I interrupted her. "I'm not flying down to Washington."

"No, no," said Evie. "He's coming here."

"Here?" I must have sounded as dismayed as I felt. "Jesus Christ. I don't want to see anybody."

"You'll see him," Evie predicted. "When Sam wants to see somebody, he sees them. And that includes the president. He asked me—he told me—" she amended, "to see to it that you stayed put, here in your apartment, until he could get here this afternoon."

"Oh, I'll stay put, all right," I told her. "I'm not going anywhere. But," and with this question I hoped to ward off the sense of doom that was enclosing me, "did he tell you what he wanted to see me about? I mean, is it just curiosity?"

Evie looked at me almost sadly and shook her head. "It wouldn't be curiosity," she said. "If it was that, he'd send somebody down and get a report. Sam doesn't believe in much, but he does believe in reports. No. He wants something from you—something personal. That's the only reason he'd come up here."

I reflected on this for a moment, then I reached in my pocket, took out the little gun, thumbed back the catch, and handed it to her. "Here's your gun," I told her. "Better you have it than me. If he's coming down here to get what I think he is, I might just possibly shoot the son of a bitch myself."

"What is it he wants?"

"I'm not going to tell you now because I think you've got worries enough. I'll tell you this, though. He's not going to get it."

"If he wants it, he'll get it," said Evie with a sad look of foreknowledge.

"Not from me he won't."

"Brave words," said Evie. She stood up, came over, and kissed me on the cheek. "Take care of yourself," she said. "I'm going to go back and pack now. I'll have somebody come up to the apartment with me— the janitor, the Gaylords—somebody."

"Atta girl," I said. I saw her out and watched her go down the stairs. I felt too tired and shaky to go down with her. When the bottom door had closed, I went back to sit in the easy chair and pondered whether I wanted a drink. It seemed that I did not. I simply sat there. After awhile my robot started to rattle and shake; the wires commenced to smoke and burn.

22

In the bottom cages of my mind there paced and prowled the essential question of whether I would have a drink—whether I would start drinking. My ear had begun to hurt again, and I realized that in its shrinking, the abcess in my skull would retreat across the same territory it had invaded, inflamed nerves that glowed with pain as it approached. The machinery noise that is part of my deafness had mounted to a crescendo of noise that filled my head like the roar of an anchor chain rattling down the hawse pipe. I did not fix a drink. I sat immobilized—in quiet shock—a metal construction with electric eyes.

The red light flashed, and my circuits blinked. Samuel Listing, father to Celia, brother to Eugene, had arrived. It would not do simply to push a buzzer for a personage. I prepared myself to go downstairs to the outer door to meet him.

When I opened the downstairs door I was greeted by blackness. A Maloney stretch limousine seemed to extend the length of the entire block. Salvador and a few of his minions were standing in front of the store gaping at the long car as if it had just arrived from Mars. The blackness was intersected by the chauffeur, who was standing at the lip of the stoop below me. He was certainly not the kindly old retainer of whom Celia had spoken so warmly. He was your standard-issue government agency thug, the gun holstered carelessly under the coat of his gray worsted suit. He said, "You Joe Binney?"

"Yes."

"Mr. Listing wants to talk to you." His brown eyes, I saw, were capable of two expressions—death and scorn. There was death in them as he spoke.

"Sure," I said. "Tell him to come on upstairs." I turned away, but the government hand shot out and seized me by the arm. I turned back to look at him. "Wait here," he said.

I rested patiently at the threshold while the chauffeur went back to open the door of the limousine. I looked at Sal and saw his eyes widen at the flash of burled walnut, fur rugs, a fur lap robe, gleaming leather upholstery, and the requisite telephone system and television set, which were documented by the antennae jutting from the trunk. They make steam locomotives, I reflected, which cost less than this car must have cost. Samuel Listing stepped out, bald, glittering in his pinstripe blue suit and tastefully striped foulard tie. When he smiled at me his teeth glittered, too, as did his eyes. The chauffeur stepped up to me and said, "Is the door at the top open?"

"It's wide open," I told him. "Step right in."

He went up first. Samuel Listing followed him, two steps behind, and I, feeling rather forlorn and dispossessed, brought up the rear. The chauffeur went quickly through my apartment, his coat unbuttoned, while Listing and I waited in the front room. When he returned, he buttoned his coat. "That will be all, Jones," Listing told him. "Thank you." The chauffeur adjusted his coat and prepared to leave. His eyes looked at me again, this time with their other expression, scorn.

So we, the two of us, were left alone in the big room. He seemed momentarily to be suffering from something entirely uncharacteristic—unease, displacement. He looked all around him, and I realized that he was searching for a platform, a position of power. My big room does not offer this convenience. There is no hearth, no fireplace, no mantel over which to drape one's arm. Books resolutely line the walls. The furniture is scattered. There is no center. Why should I need one? At last he seized on the last resort and headed toward the windows looking over the street. This would put his back to the light and make his face difficult to read. But it doesn't work that way in my apartment. Falling through layers of smog, soot, and dirt that are the atmosphere of Manhattan, light breaks its spine before it ever reaches my windowpanes. There is no dazzle. As he took up his position by the windows, I smiled at him and switched on a lamp. Its yellow glow revealed every line in his face. He frowned.

I said to him, "Can I get you something? Coffee? A drink?"

"A drink would be nice," said Samuel Listing.

I took a shot in the dark. "Martini?"

His face brightened. "Oh, yes. A martini would be very nice." But then it clouded again, and I realized that he was wondering what *kind* of a martini would be served.

Well, the glasses were not chilled. That couldn't be helped. I left him alone to ruminate over my quarters while I fetched out the extra bottle of Tanqueray's and carefully made the busthead martini of which Celia had been so fond. I put the two glasses and the pitcher on the tray and carried it all back into the front room. He was pretty much where I had left him, in front of the windows, but the pinkness in his cheeks and the beaming expression told me that he had been prowling and had hastened back at the sound of my footsteps.

I served him the drink and took one myself. The martini, deadly in its concentration, was as limpid as brook water. Still, he looked into the glass with dubiety. I wondered if he might ask Jones to come up and taste it first. He took a sip, and there was a fleeting expression of appreciation as he recognized the provenance. This, however, was replaced by a very slightly rueful grimace. It was not, not quite, the perfect martini. He took another sip and set the glass on the windowsill.

He gestured, taking in the room with a wave of his hand. "This is where Celia died." It appeared to be neither a question nor a statement.

"Yes," I answered. "It happened while I was in the hospital. I came back and found her here."

"That," he said, "must have been very distressing."

I looked at him. It was very hard to connect him with Gene, although there was the same attention to manners, courtesy, and presence. Where Gene had been rather softened around the contours, this man was angular. He was slim and sharp, with a lantern jaw that balanced the oval plate of his skull. His complexion was somewhat liverish (he was, after all, ten years older than Gene had been, I reminded myself), and the yellowness set off the absolute whiteness of his shirt collar, whose gleam indicated the attention of a dedicated laundress. The suit was bespoke. The material had a depth and richness to it that suggested infrequent wear—that suggested, in fact, that Samuel Listing had many, many such suits that were dismissed from his wardrobe when the nap began to lose the richness of its texture. I thought briefly of the ancient suits that Gene had worn.

"It was a shock," I replied finally. "In fact, I think I'm still feeling it—the shock." I had sat down facing him with my martini next to me. I picked it up to take a sip and tried to control the very slight trembling of my hand. The trembling did not go unnoticed.

"You and my daughter," he said. "You had—er—plans, did you?"

"No," I told him quickly. "No. Not at all. I met Celia over at Evie's apartment just after Gene had died. I was sick. I've had an inner ear infection that's been difficult to clear up. That's why I was in the hospital. Celia, very kindly, offered to come over here and take care of me. I needed taking care of. And she was marvelous. But no—we had no plans."

"You've been helping Evie," said Samuel Listing.

"Yes. She's had a hard time—is still having a hard time accepting the idea of Gene's death. I have a lot of sympathy for her. It does seem unlikely that he'd keel over right after he came under a doctor's care and took up the so-called healthy life. But he was having a hell of a hard time adjusting to it, the new regime at work. I'm just trying to help Evie sort things out."

"What kind of things?"

"The possibility of suicide or foul play."

"Jesus Christ," said Samuel Listing. "Is that what she's thinking?"

"She simply can't see how he would have died in his sleep the way he did, or appeared to do—in a nightmare."

"People do," he observed. "Although I've never known Gene to have nightmares."

"They began after he started the new regime—quitting smoking and all. He took it very hard."

For the first time he showed some emotion. "The job," he said. "That stupid, Goddamned job. Why didn't he just up and quit?" He lifted his martini from the windowsill and took a healthy swig.

"He had ten years invested in it," I answered. "The investment of time, effort, and discipline seemed to mean a great deal to him. I confess, though," I held up my hand here, "I'm a hell of a long way from understanding Gene or his motives about anything at all." I paused and thought about it. "Way back when," I said, "something obviously happened to Gene. Something made a radical change in his life that sent him around the world and finally into that job. He never told me really what it was. Do you know?"

"Oh, there was a crisis, all right, at least what he chose to think of as a crisis." Samuel Listing stared off above my head into the center space of the room. Then he looked back to me and studied me for a long time before he decided to continue. He drank the last of his martini. I rose with the pitcher to pour him another, and went back to the chair.

He took a deep breath and began. "When Gene was at Johns Hopkins for his graduate work, for his doctorate, he was doing brilliantly, and his whole life was laid out before him. Everything was absolutely perfectly set for a marvelous career in the foreign service. I had alerted everyone. I was terribly proud, and kept telling them—'Wait till you see what's coming along. My kid brother is going to absolutely eclipse me.' I should have been jealous. Very possibly I was. But the sheer radiance of what looked like Gene's future made everything else look petty and stupid. I was just terribly, terribly proud.

"I wouldn't shut up about him. Finally, the people I was working for gave me a proposition to tender him. As you know, at that period Johns Hopkins' Asian Department was under something of a cloud. There was a lot of business about Owen Lattimore, who was at Johns Hopkins then, and there were other Asian experts at Harvard and elsewhere whose careers were being examined very carefully. There was, you'll remember, a terrible congressional storm about having 'lost' China. Well, the people I was working for felt very much under fire, and they sort of wanted a better grip on things, which Gene was in a position to provide. They wanted Gene to draw up personal dossiers on everyone he was associated with in the Asian Department at Johns Hopkins. It would have been a magnificent entrée to the foreign service. It would have put him miles ahead of anyone entering at that time." Samuel Listing paused there to take a startlingly deep draft of his drink.

I waited to let him swallow it before asking the necessary question. "And how did Gene react to that?"

"Like a virgin being assaulted in the ladies' room at the Astor. I will never ever forget it, nor will I ever, ever understand it. He was simply being asked to do a straightforward job that would have given him an immense leg up in the service. His reaction was incomprehensible to me—to all of us. He didn't ever really reply to me. He didn't say anything. He simply turned white—as white as paper. We were in my office at the time. I had called him in, thinking I was offering him a marvelous present. Well, he just turned very white, and did a kind of about-face and marched out, marched out without so much as a by your leave. The next day he left Johns Hopkins. He never turned in his dissertation, which I happen to know was just about finished and was brilliant. He simply threw all that away. Seized some money that had been left to him, money which, in my estimation, should never have been touched, and set off across the world. Utterly irresponsible.

Utterly unpredictable. I simply will never understand it."

I stared at him. Finally, I said, "You're kidding me, aren't you? About not understanding it?"

"I assure you I am not kidding." His lips grimaced around the last word.

"You were asking a young man to be a spy, to spy on his teachers and his friends, literally to tell tales out of school. I'm surprised he didn't hit you."

"But he was slated to go into service, don't you see?" objected Mr. Listing. "What the hell are a few professors and a pack of students compared to that? He muffed the very beginning of what should have been a brilliant career."

"Perhaps he wanted to be his own man," I suggested.

"Don't talk absolute rubbish. How was he his own man sitting for years in a ratty little office working for a sick joke of a publication, and finally being pushed around by people like—like—" he paused with a wary look in his eyes, and sipped from his glass.

"Why don't you finish?" I asked him. "You mean by people like Senator Marston, don't you?"

Now Listing regarded me suspiciously over the rim of his glass for what is known as a pregnant pause. Finally, he said, "Senator Marston. Yes."

"Something puzzles me," I said. "Why is he called senator when he is really a representative, a congressman?"

"He was a senator for years in his state's legislature." Listing waved his glass. "These people tend to cling to the higher ledge."

There was a dividend left in the pitcher. I didn't want it. I got up and poured it into Listing's glass. He appeared not to notice.

"Of course," he said, "I didn't come down here to talk about Gene, but about Celia. I wanted to see where she died." His eyes had the marble quality that is seen in the busts of Roman dignitaries.

"She died over there," I nodded toward the couch. "I had my secretary, who I can get through to by special telephone, call the police and then call Evie, who, I suppose, called you."

"Yes," he nodded. "She did."

"The police," I said cautiously, "questioned me for about an hour. But one of them came back later. He was very upset that the whole thing had been pretty much taken out of his hands."

Listing took a careful sip from his glass. "The police often have big mouths and itchy palms," he said. "I didn't want official photographs of my daughter turning up in the *Enquirer* or *True Detective*—à la Lenny Bruce."

"You know," I began conversationally, "I believe she was murdered."

"That is a possibility," said Samuel Listing. "If that is the case, it will be taken care of."

The statement was as firm as the closing of a vault. It left me nothing to say except to ask a question. "Why are you here?"

He said, "Celia was putting together some of Gene's things and was supposed to send me a report. I never got it. It must be here."

"The police and I both went over this place very carefully," I said. "There was nothing like that here. She must have mailed it to you."

"She wouldn't have mailed it," he objected. "She would have sent it by courier. I checked. She hadn't given anything to the courier."

"She would have used a government courier to send you something to paste in the family album?"

"It was very important to us. It's an old tradition."

I waited a while before speaking. Then I said to him, "How many of these martinis would it take, do you think, for you to cut out the bullshit?"

He stiffened. Even the nap on his suit seemed to become erectile.

I pursued it. I said, "Shall I make another batch?"

"Please do."

I made them sloppily, returned, and poured one for each of us. I said, "Is it all right if I talk for a little bit?"

"By all means."

"The New York Police," I said, "are quite powerful in their own right. And since New York is even more of a center of international relations than Washington is, they aren't exactly naive where government diplomacy is concerned. There is no way you could have extracted a case as important as Celia's from them unless Celia had been actively working as a government agent with the highest priorities. All right. Let's accept that. She was using the occasion of her uncle's death to pursue something very important to the government. Now, let's just step back a bit. Gene had been thrown for a loss by the takeover. He was upset and he said something foolish to Senator Marston while Marston was addressing the troops. Marston immediately decided that Gene had to go. I got this from Basket himself . . ."

"Basket?"

"The editor of that rag. Basswell is his proper name."

"Ah."

"Basket got his wind up and started prying into Gene's files. He came across something called the nightmare file, and what he saw there made him soil his knickers and run off to Marston with," I hooked my fingers into quotes, " 'important information.' My question is: What was the news?"

"You've seen the file?"

"Yes, I have."

"I haven't," he admitted. "The editor should have made copies, but he didn't. I presume the whole file is in Celia's report. But I don't have the report."

"But why was Celia sent to make the report in the first place?"

"Clearly, Gene was investigating things that had nothing to do with the publication he was working for."

"That's because he was on the skids and had to use some initiative to save himself."

"Be that as it may, he had no business poking around the structures of Southeast Asia, particularly around the Thailand border, which, right now, is one of the most sensitive spots, diplomatically speaking, on earth. If Gene went blundering in, he could cause enormous trouble for some extremely delicate negotiations that are being carefully—exquisitely—pursued.

"I shouldn't have said 'blundering,' " he corrected himself. "Gene didn't blunder. Therefore he was infinitely more dangerous than your typical errant journalist. We had no handle at all on Gene, ever, to shut him up. The nightmare file simply cannot fall into the wrong hands. It could do incalculable damage. We really must have that file, and when I say, 'that file,' I mean all possible copies of it."

"Senator Marston is an elected representative, not a functionary," I said, noticing Mr. Listing stiffen at the word *functionary*. "Why should he be concerned with these negotiations? Why should Basket have been concerned?"

"Representative Marston," said Listing, "is the chairman of a very powerful House committee, whose decisions directly affect the Pentagon and other important agencies. Men in his position are well informed. Furthermore, they are listened to—carefully. More than that, they wield enormous power—power that works in a parochial sense. It gets things done, benefits for their constituents, jobs, pork barrels, military contracts, military bases. For instance, Marston's predecessor on that committee was once told that if any more military installations were established in his state, the state would tip over and slide into the Atlantic Ocean. When Marston speaks, the government listens. It has to. Something in the file alarmed him."

"What could alarm him?"

Listing glared at me. "Exactly what I've just told you," he said impatiently. His cheeks reddened. "That someone unauthorized was poking around the area where Vietnam, Cambodia, and Laos all come together on the borders of Thailand. The—the—"

"Golden Triangle?" I suggested helpfully.

"Oh, for God's sake." He stamped impatiently. "You're not going to drag up all that cheap muck, are you?"

I sipped my martini. I said, "The United States Government has been nipple deep in shit, skag, H, horse, heroin, whatever you want to call it, for a long time now. Everyone knows that. Everyone knows that the government made deals with warlords and independent drug dealers who had clout one way or another. It was the expeditious thing to do. It greased a lot of wheels financially, not to mention a lot of palms. I suggest that Senator Marston was standing around somewhere with his little tin cup catching some of the drippings."

"Senator Marston has never set foot in Southeast Asia."

"You don't have to live in Texas to invest in an oil company," I observed. "Certainly Marston has been in a position to know where money could be made over there, and certainly his friends at the Pentagon or Langley could arrange things for him."

"You have a vivid if deformed imagination."

"My twisted imagination suggests to me," I replied, "that Marston had money in an offshore bank that was laundering cash for heroin dealers in Southeast Asia."

There was an expression of sneering derision on his face. "And I suppose you know the name of the bank?"

"Yes," I said. "I do."

"And what is it?"

"Ask Senator Marston. I'm sure as hell not telling you."

He watched my face very carefully. "I already know, of course," he said. "You're talking about the Landseer Bank, aren't you?" I kept my face absolutely immobile. I, too, have played poker.

I said, "Senator Marston has jammed the zipper on his weenie. I know he's a big-time flag waver, but nobody loves a pusher."

Listing picked up his glass from the windowsill and stared at it thoughtfully. He took a generous sip. He extruded his lower lip as a demonstration of reflection. His features softened. His eyes mellowed. Because I am deaf, I cannot, of course, hear changes of tone, but even through my deafness I could hear the sweet drone of violins playing softly in the background. He smiled at me, rather shyly, I thought, over the rim of his glass, which he held expertly, tirelessly.

"Joe," he said, "I think we've gotten off on very much the wrong foot for very obvious reasons. We've both had a terrible shock, and added to that is the natural hostility we might feel toward one another over Celia. I think we ought to try to brush that aside for now, and, when I go away, each of us can grieve in private."

He finished his martini, and I automatically rose to pour him another. I was being entertained in a very grand style.

"Of course I've prowled around here," he said, "and I've scanned your shelves. You are obviously a very intelligent, sensitive man. It isn't everyone who reads Karl Popper. I realize that you have run your own agency as a one-man operation for years. I can't tell you how much I admire that, how much I wish I saw that kind of guts around me, working for me, with me."

He sipped at his martini. I watched and waited.

"Let me put this as gently as possible," he began. "If you are willing to show the least sign of willingness to cooperate, there could be some very challenging and lucrative assignments from my shop. Initiative and guts are not in so great a supply as you might imagine. I can immediately think of five or six things you could do for us, and all of them are very well funded." He took another sip and stared at me.

It is very curious that I was not feeling what I was drinking. I gulped at my glass rather than sipping. I suppose Listing was right, that we were both in shock and circling one another like stray dogs. I cannot hear myself, but when I replied to him, I do not think my speech was thick or slurred. I said, "Thank you very much for your offer, but I must respectfully decline. At this time, I am not really ready to join a mutual masturbation society. But that is beside the point." His hand tightened on the stem of the glass. I hoped he wouldn't break it. "I can't accept your offer because I simply don't believe it. In fact, I can't really believe anything at all you say because you don't really have any validity as a man." I smiled at him sympathetically. "You can't give your word as a gentleman, etcetera, because you don't have a word. Your word is made up somewhere else and handed down to you, and that's the word or the line you have to pursue. So," I took my final gulp, "this makes you into an interesting figure of logic. You are a Cretan. 'All Cretans are liars, said the man from Crete.' Well, are they, or aren't they? There's no way to know. There's no way to test the validity of what you say. You're somebody's creature. You are a Cretan—spelled with an *a*.

"The other thing"—I put up my hand to stop him—"is that it is bad enough for a man to use his daughter's life to further his career, but for him to use her corpse is really unforgivable."

He said, "I want that story and I need it. And you will hand it over promptly, or there will be very severe consequences."

I replied, "I'll hand it over promptly, but not to you. The report belongs to Evie with the rest of Gene's effects. I'm going to turn it over to her."

He was thunderstruck. He said, "Brat? That silly bitch? What on earth could she do with it?"

"It might have some monetary value. Perhaps you could find some challenging and lucrative assignments for her. Or she might want to dicker with Senator Marston himself. Maybe she'd like to see him crawl around on the floor for it, the way, I'm told, some junkies have to perform for their ration."

Any emotion he might have had, feigned or real, had departed his face. He said somberly, "You are an extremely foolish man, and I regret having wasted my time with you. You're really not worth a conversation. There's nothing for anyone to do now except step on you." He gathered himself with a shrug and began to move toward the door.

"One thing," I stopped him. "When Gene turned you down all those years ago you must have panicked. You must have run a check to see if he was in league with anyone dangerous to you. Did you come up with anything?"

Listing's face was a cold mask. "Not a thing," he said. "Not a hint. Not a breath. As clean as a whistle. Damn him. Goddamn him."

I followed him down the stairs and saw him out.

23

The letter was stuck under the ball of Edna's Selectric.
I read it three times before I absorbed it. It said:

> Dear Joe:
> The following is written under dictation.
> "If you want to see your secretary, Edna Purvis,
> alive and in one piece, you will follow these in-
> structions carefully. Within 72 hours (it is now 5
> o'clock, Tuesday afternoon) you will deliver to
> the place specified below all papers you have ac-
> quired from the Eugene Listing story file. The
> time allotted is generous so that you may gather
> them from wherever you have secreted them, and
> also to permit you to locate the place of rendezvous.
> You will bring the story file to the junction of
> Pennsylvania State Highway 119 and County Road
> 23. Turn right on 23 and drive one mile. This will
> bring you to the edge of Pennmere Lake. In the
> middle of Pennmere Lake you will see an island
> with a white house on it. This is the place of
> rendezvous. A rowboat will be tied up nearby on
> the shore. Row out to the island and declare your-
> self. When the papers are delivered, you and your
> secretary may depart in the rowboat.
> Be advised that if anyone is alerted, and that if
> there is any sign of activity, all that will be found

*on this island is the dead and badly abused body
of your secretary."*
I have to go with him now.

> Love
> Edna

I had already used up sixteen of the seventy-two
hours, but, of course, they would have known that. It
was now nine o'clock Wednesday morning. I had until
five o'clock Friday afternoon. I shook my head, not in
despair, but to clear it. They had almost, but not quite,
caught me at my lowest. The codeine had just about
worn off.

I had been very glad to see the back of Samuel
Listing departing my doorstep, and had not waited to
see the stately limousine pull away. But toiling back up
the stairs, I had become aware of the pain assailing my
inner ear with the persistence of an electric drill. It
blotted out even the roaring in my head. It was worse
than anything I had felt before. By the time I stood in
the center of my front room, I was unmanned—frantic.
I got out the bottle of codeine, and in the unconscious
habit of a longtime aspirin user, simply took two of
them instead of the one very powerful tablet prescribed.
I sat down heavily on the new couch. I was unable to
reflect on what had just passed with my visitor. I was
unable to think. I gritted my teeth and endured. Presently, the codeine did what it was supposed to do. The
pain dulled. I stretched out and fell asleep.

Not the wisest combination, martinis and codeine.
Do the comatose dream? It was only the shuddering
remembrance of the dreams that convinced me that I
had not been in a coma. My unconsciousness had lasted
from approximately four in the afternoon until eight the
following morning. While Edna was being kidnapped I
was dead to the world.

There was one faint ray of encouragement to all this.
I was not worried about obtaining the papers they wanted.
When I had awakened and staggered off the couch I
had looked out my kitchen back window while the
coffee brewed and noticed a fine rain falling from a

dirty sky. A sense of urgency fought its way through, and before I really understood what I was doing, I bolted from the kitchen, ran downstairs and out the back into the little courtyard behind Sal's store. The old couch, now missing two of its cushions, was right where they had dumped it. It was in the lee of the rain and not much moisture had got to it. I plunged my hand deep into its guts, and, sure enough, I was greeted by the touch of a heavy envelope. The address on it said only: *Samuel Listing. By Courier.* Wise Celia! She must have thrust it deep into the couch at the first sound of an intruder.

So I had the papers they wanted. I had read them over, and they didn't contain much that Celia and I hadn't discussed when we were doping it out. Somebody, I thought, was going to be in that odd suspension between relief and disappointment. There was nothing actionable in the report itself, except, I suppose, that Celia knew very well that her father would read between the lines.

I put a hand on the envelope in my breast pocket for reassurance and sank into Edna's chair.

Sitting in Edna's chair (so much less comfortable than mine) and putting myself in her place dissipated some of my reassurance. What my mind had been circling dully was finally grasped. Relieved or disappointed though they might be, there was no way this party was going to let Edna and me off that stupid island alive. There was an ominous note of absolute certainty in the letter that Edna had typed. The envelope in my pocket would buy us a little time, with luck, but not our lives. At best it would buy us only an easy death. I got up out of the uncomfortable chair and went into my own office.

I extracted a road map of Pennsylvania from the assortment I keep in my lower desk drawer and looked for a Lake Pennmere in the *Parks and Recreational Areas* list. Nothing. Then I looked in the list of cities and towns. There were a Penndel, a Penn Hills, and a Pennline, but then it jumped to Penn Run. No Pennmere. Wearily, beginning with a quadrant in the northeast section of the state, I began to search for a

small box denoting State Highway 119. For once, I
was in luck. The highway started up near the northern
border and ran down past Honesdale and farther south
just east of the Poconos. I scanned it quickly for lakes,
but although many small lakes dotted its course, none
of them was called Pennmere. I went back to the top
and began to check each and every junction. None of
them was labeled 23. I needed a better map.

And why not, I wondered, get the best map of all,
an insurance map? I was about to sing out to Edna to
call Hubie Bannister, and then checked myself at the
thought of her empty chair. It was a sickening little
drop, like landing on your heel when you've mis-
judged a curb. There were not to be any convenient
phone calls. I was now strictly on my own. I missed
her terribly, and the missing of her threw a protective
cloak over the rage that was gathering in me.

Hubie Bannister was a claims clerk at Trident Insurance. Trident was a very powerful old-line outfit whose
name I could never figure out, but I always suspected
it meant only that they could always find three ways to
screw you. Hubie, who was now thirty-five, had started
with them as a map clerk—one of the lads who hauled
out the huge books of carefully detailed maps that
registered each house on a given block, spotted the
fire hydrants, and also spotted various characteristics
of the neighborhood population. These map books are
crucial to the art of red-lining, which is now forbidden
by law, but which also had great effect on the compo-
sition of our cities.

Such things were beyond Hubie. He was a small,
pale, blond man with washed-out blue eyes and a
permanent stoop to his shoulders. The eyes, magnified
by thick glasses, were all-embracing. He had been raised
in a Colorado mining town and had a background of
poverty far beyond anything I had ever known. I had
learned all this during a lunch I'd treated him to after
concluding a successful investigation for Trident and
receiving my check. Hubie had helped me with the
investigation by rapidly extracting those huge, heavy
books from their shelves and detailing information
otherwise unobtainable. "If I just stick with it," he

had told me over the tablecloth, enchanted with the sumptuous meal, "in ten years I could be making as much as twenty-five thousand a year." I did not mention the size of the check in my pocket.

I jammed the road map into my coat pocket and left, locking the door carefully behind me. I took a cab down to Beaver Street, which is where Trident hung its sign, went into the dark-paneled reception room, and asked for Mr. Hubert Bannister. Was he expecting me? No, he was not expecting me.

I am never quite prepared for the pallor of Hubie, carp's belly white. I don't think, really, that a ray of sun has ever touched him. It didn't affect his smile, however, which was broad, sunny, and conspiratorial.

"Joe," he said. "Great to see you!" The pale blue eyes picked up some voltage. "Another case?" He must have whispered it because he looked quickly at the grim, gray-haired receptionist, who apparently wouldn't have cared if Hubie Bannister had suddenly screamed *"Fire!"*

"Yes," I answered, "but not for Trident. I need some help, Hubie, and I'm hoping you can give it to me."

"Anything I can do, Joe."

"I'm trying to get a line on a skip," I told him. "The guy seems to have gone to Pennsylvania. Is there somewhere we can talk?"

"Sure. Come on and sit down over here." He led me to a settee at the other end of the room, away from the receptionist, who had, in any case, remained oblivious.

I pulled the map out of my pocket. "I found out that this skip is supposed to be holed up in a house somewhere around Pennmere Lake, which is at the junction of State Highway One-nineteen and County Road Twenty-three. Now, here's Highway One-nineteen," I traced it with a forefinger, "but there's no County Road Twenty-three on this map and no sign of a Pennmere Lake. I was hoping that you could haul out one of those big map books and find it for me."

Hubie shook his head. "We don't have any Pennsylvania books here," he said. "That's all handled by

Philadelphia." My spirits sank. I must have looked far
more depressed than could have been occasioned by
trouble with a skip. Hubie put his hand on my arm.
"Tell you what, though," he said. "I can call a guy in
the Philly office and he can look it up." I not only
brightened, I glowed. "Give me the map," commanded
Hubie, "and wait here." He took the map and went
into the main offices, where, I know, he had a desk in
a long row of similar desks for similar clerks. I was left
alone with my thoughts and the granitic countenance
of the receptionist.

And where did these thoughts lead me? Into confusion. Samuel Listing was undeniably a powerhouse,
but it was startling—paralyzing, in fact—that he could
have left my apartment, climbed into his well-furnished
limousine, and set in motion anything so elaborate as
the plan I was faced with. Had he simply settled
himself into the rich leather, picked up the phone and
muttered, "Proceed with Plan B"? It was the kind of
thing you might see at the movies, but were such
things possible? Had he worked it all out beforehand?
And the thought of what might have gone beforehand
made me bite my lip. Had he muttered not "Plan B,"
but "Plan C"? If he was that anxious to get the file,
had he sent up to my apartment some black-bag man
or one of the polished, plausible operators who wink
in and out of government service, who had come upon
Celia inadvertently and, not knowing who she was,
not listening, not really caring, killed her to keep her
mouth shut? The government, after all, has copiously
demonstrated its capacity for monumental fuck-ups, as
well as its frequent bouts of blind, murderous rage.
Was Samuel Listing, after that, capable of visiting
me—to see where Celia died—and blindly pursuing a
mission so footless as saving the reputation of a nasty
little prick like Senator Marston? These were shadowy
depths to look at, depths that made me take a very
deep breath and release it in a sigh.

I had thrown back my head to think things through
a little further, but then I saw Hubie coming back into
the reception room. He had put on his coat and straightened his tie. He had decided to appear more business-

like under the gaze of the receptionist. There was something infinitely touching about Hubie's donned air of seriousness, his desire to live up to the paneling that surrounded us. He sat down next to me, looking very grave.

He showed me the map and said, "I got it located for you, all right. A strange place, weird. I don't know how you're going to find anybody down there." He had drawn a line perpendicular to State Highway 119 and labeled it County Road 23. The road went a mile west and then curved north. West of the curve, Hubie had drawn a fairly large circle and labeled it LAKE PENNMERE.

"This lake, Lake Pennmere," Hubie explained, "isn't a real lake. I mean it's what they call a manmade lake, and from what Arky told me, it's more of a swamp than a lake, although it gets pretty deep in places."

I must have looked totally confused as I stared at the map. "What happened," Hubie continued when I looked up at him, "is this. Fifteen, twenty years ago they were going to put in a dam and the government went out and bought up all the houses on the property, which was considerable. A lot of people were evicted from houses their families had owned for over a hundred years. There was a lot of hell raised about it. The environmentalists got in on it, and everything was slowed down for a year or so. Nobody was allowed to go back to his house, and pretty soon squatters moved in and took over a lot of property. The government people got scared the whole thing was going down the drain, so they started preliminary work, even though the permits hadn't been granted. The permits were never granted, and the whole idea started to slide. The government went in there and chased the squatters out and then they tore down all the houses so the place wouldn't become a kind of shantytown, you know? Arky said it had been a real beautiful place originally. Well, with the preliminary work, they opened a channel that ran into a valley that had a knob with a big white house on it right in the middle. That valley is now Lake Pennmere, the knob is an island, and the big white house is the only one left standing. It was too much trouble for them to tear it down. It's deserted, of course. Nobody could live there. So they're just waiting for it to fall apart. Nobody much uses the county road, and you can't see the house from the highway, so I guess, out of sight, out of mind. But I don't know how you're going to find anybody hiding out down there."

I put my hand on his arm. "Hubie," I said, "I don't know how to thank you, but, believe me, I'll think of a way. Write your home address on this map." He jotted it down. "This means a hell of a lot to me," I told him. "It's an important case, very, very important. And if I win out, I'll owe it all to you." Hubie glowed. "Take care of yourself," I told him—and I meant it. I felt that he was going to spend his life wriggling on one of Trident's prongs. "I'll let you know how everything comes out."

As soon as I got back to the office, I wrote out a check for a hundred dollars to Hubie and put it in the mail. It was no time to be a piker.

24

By the time I was writing out the check for Hubie, all speculation had stopped. Except to take the measure of the enemy, there was no point in my wondering who had kidnapped Edna. The problem was how to get her back.

Almost absentmindedly, I had unlocked the drawer in my desk, taken out the .38, checked it, and stuck it in my belt. This was part of my measurement of the enemy. I also decided to accept the idea that I would be under some kind of surveillance. I took out the map that Hubie had marked up and stared at it.

Hubie's scrawled circle indicated the location of Pennmere Lake but gave no hint as to its size or shape. He hadn't bothered to draw in the island, which was presumably in the center, but I did this now and contemplated it. The fact that it was an island gave me some notion of scale. The lake, after all, could not be simply a moat surrounding the house. It constituted a reasonable body of water—negotiable by rowboat, not by wading or even a quick swim. I looked at the scale of the map, measured a mile on Road 23, and pondered. No other roads appeared to the west. The lake could be miles across. A simple sense of proportion told me that the distance from shore to the island must be something over a mile, roughly two thousand yards.

I began to make a checklist of things I would need. I knew I could get a topographical map of the area, but there didn't really seem to be time for that. It would all have to be done by reconnoitering. I finished my checklist and closed up shop. Before locking the door, I took a last look around. I didn't really know if I would see it again.

I hailed a cab and gave him the address of a car rental agency. I had decided not to use the old Buick, partly because of its untrustworthiness, but also because it would be too easily spotted groaning its way out of the parking lot. I rented a nice anonymous gray Ford and parked it a block away from my apartment, one street east of mine. I went to the corner bus stop and took a bus about fifteen blocks north. Then I took another cab back to my front door. There was nothing terribly fancy about all this, but I thought it was probably effective. Above all, I wanted to be seen entering my front door.

But when I got upstairs, I paused, opened the door carefully, and unbuttoned my suitcoat. I went through the apartment exactly the way Listing's chauffeur had gone through it. There were no surprises.

I went to my spare room at the back and opened the commodious closet there. I put my checklist on the bed and began to lay out my gear by the numbers. When it was all there, I checked out each and every piece of it. It all still seemed to be in good working order. I began to pack it then, and no matter how I rearranged things it made a heavy, awkward bundle. There was no help for this. Besides, while someone may have seen me enter the building, it was not my intention that anyone should see me leave with the bundle. I left it all there on the bed and went into my regular bedroom. I took out the Colt Python from its keepsafe next to my bed and checked it out carefully. I took a spare box of cartridges from my night table. I was equipped, I suppose, to start a small war, but for all I knew, that was what I was entering.

Getting all my gear together and checking it out had taken me close to two hours. The remainder of the day loomed ahead. There was nothing to do now but wait. I decided that I would have two drinks, no more, and then try to sleep. I also reminded myself that I should eat something. I got a steak out of the freezer and set it out to thaw.

My two bourbon and sodas (I had decided that I would never drink another martini) lasted me a long, long time. As I sipped them, I tried to imagine different configurations of the lake, the road, the landscape, and for each I tried to plan a contingency. When the second drink was finished, I had stored these configurations and contingencies in my head, and hoped that I would have the brains and guts to act quickly and decisively on each of them. I tossed a potato in the oven, made a salad with lots of carrot in it while the potato was baking, and broiled my steak. When I was finished eating I cleaned up meticulously. During cleanup, I sensed, as I had at the office, that I might be saying farewell. I set up the coffee for quick brewing when I awoke, and went to bed. It was only late afternoon, but I felt exhausted. I intended to be up at four in the morning.

The unhappy fact is that I was up at two in the morning after hours of churning restlessly in bed in a kind of semiconsciousness. There were no dreams because I hadn't sunk deep enough into sleep to sustain one. I stumbled out of bed finally, feeling anything but rested, and made my pot of coffee. I drank it all, black, and made another. I smoked and stared at my map and at my conjectures. I checked out my awkward bundle again, went over the checklist, and examined the Colt. Finally, I put on an old pair of slacks, good walking shoes, and an old sports shirt topped with my Windbreaker. Four-thirty finally rolled around. I picked up my bundle and left. Before I left, however, I armed a few booby traps in the apartment. If they wanted to come back here and play games, it would cost them. With the bundle on my back, I said so long to the apartment and locked it up.

When I got downstairs I went out the back and into the courtyard instead of out the front door, on whose activity I hoped any nightwatchers were concentrating. My penlight gave me enough of a beam to pick my way to the back wall, leading me carefully around the rain-soaked couch on which Celia had died. I upended a discarded crate and stood on it to hoist myself and my bundle over the wall. This put me in a narrow gravel parking lot that occupied a strip of ground between two buildings. From there I was able to go directly to the street, where my car was parked only two doors down. I had left the trunk unlocked. I opened it and slung my bundle inside. I eased the car away from the curb without bothering to warm up the engine (my old Buick would have required at least five minutes to keep it from stalling). I drove very slowly and leisurely out of the neighborhood and down toward the Holland Tunnel.

There are plenty of big, broad interstate highways rushing westward out of New York, but I chose a state highway because there were infinitely more access roads off which I could escape if I had to. There was also the probability that there would be less traffic and that anyone tailing me would be more exposed. After crossing the Pulaski Skyway, I picked out my route and settled down for an hour's drive. There didn't seem to be any headlights hanging on behind me. Traffic was thin, and all of it seemed to go past my careful 55 mph or turn off behind me. As dawn rose, I began to look for the turnoff that would lead me to Benny Pintchick's Bait Shop.

Benny had started out with a tiny bait shack in the days when things were a lot wilder in the industrial wilderness of New Jersey. As suburbs encroached, Benny expanded, addition by addition, until now he represented a complete sporting goods and camping equipment emporium. One thing, however, had not changed. He still opened before dawn to serve the serious fisherman. I pulled my car around to the back and went in to talk to Benny. He was a small, hard, nut-brown man with black glittering eyes that nothing could startle. He listened to me, nodded, and together we went out to service my gear and make some crucial adjustments.

Leaving Benny's, I continued away from the highway and found an all-night diner. I had a substantial breakfast with yet more coffee and several cigarettes. There was a local newspaper, which I read, as always, slowly and carefully, paying particular attention to the classified ads. Patrons, who were undeniably working men, came and went without even a curious glance at me.

When I emerged the day was full and seemed fair enough, although clouds appeared to be building up in the west. The cars parked at the diner were pickup trucks, commercial vehicles, or, finally, an ancient station wagon crammed with fishing tackle. It didn't seem that any of them would be trailing me. Neither did any car heave into sight of my rearview mirror and stay there for any distance.

My chosen route brought me, perhaps unfortunately, quite close to the junction of 119 and 23, so that I wasn't given much time to familiarize myself with the area before I had arrived. I had swung off the highway, turning south, and within fifteen minutes I had passed the junction. At least I assumed that it was the junction. There didn't seem to be a sign. I continued south without slowing down—I did not want to be seen loitering—until I crossed the next junction, one that was marked. This made it certain that I had, after all, passed 23. I continued on until I found a gas station where I pretended to check my tires and made use of the can. Coming out, I asked the nearly catatonic attendant whether there was a lunchroom farther down the road. He allowed that there might be one two or three miles down, although he wasn't sure if it was open.

I wanted to find a place where I could sit and think, because what I had seen on the swift journey past the junction had sunk my heart. My drive down 119 for most of the way had alternated small pleasant towns with fat, rolling farm country. As I had approached 23, however, the land rose in steeply ascending woodland on the eastern side of the highway, but on the western side showed a decaying slope that had rapidly degenerated into a swamp. The swamp itself was a cemetery of dead trees that stretched their skeletal branches to the cloudy sky. In all my contingency plans I'd held out the hope that I could somehow sneak up unseen to the edge of the lake. But the swamp, which obviously stretched for a mile between the highway and the lake, offered very little cover. Anyone seen floundering through it would be a target either for a rescue mission if seen from the highway, or a bullet if seen from the lake.

The lunchroom was there, a forlorn little clapboard affair that had apparently been at one time a genuine restaurant. The faded sign above it read THE COTTAGE. The waitress was also the proprietor, and I had the feeling that this establishment had a staff of one. There was no lunch counter, per se, only a few tables and chairs. There was the smell of fresh-made doughnuts in the air, so I ordered coffee and doughnuts. The lady who ran the place was a heavy-set woman with white hair and a sweet face whose eyes had a stunned expression. She had a characteristic fatal to entrepreneurs; she was shy with strangers. I did not impose myself upon her. I did not particularly care to be remembered. She left me at the table to myself.

I munched my doughnut with its powdered sugar coating (delicious and as light as air), sipped my coffee, and tried to reconstruct my brief passage down 119. I needed some way of reconnoitering without being plainly visible myself. I had no desire to cruise back and forth along the highway, which was bound to raise attention, and I felt that I could drive down the county road past the lake's edge only once. While I had been driving south most of my attention had been focused on the stark features of the agonized trees that had struggled with the swamp and lost. Now, I tried to remember what had been on the right-hand side. Most of it had flashed by as a wall of greenery rising abruptly from the road. It was possible that I could climb that wall, well protected by the live trees in full foliage, and get some sort of glimpse through the swamp below. The problem was that I had no place to put the car. A car left stranded on the shoulder of the highway would be sure to invite inspection, from the state troopers if no one else. I forced myself to review again and again the section of road I had passed. *Had* there been some sort of structure there on the green, eastern side—a house, a cabin, a roadhouse? Maybe I was kidding myself, I thought, but there was a vague image of a log-cabin sort of structure nearly hidden by trees at the side of the road. I decided to risk being noticed. I cleared my throat and asked the lady carefully, "Didn't there used to be a roadhouse somewhere along here? I kind of remember years ago . . ." I let it trail off.

"Oh, it's still there." She nodded northward. "The Dell—three or four miles up the road. Jake's still hanging on, but there isn't much anybody can do nowadays."

I nodded sympathetically and hid my excitement. A roadhouse meant parking space, and yet there hadn't been any parking space in front that I could remember. That meant the parking lot would be in the back, which was precisely what I needed. I finished my doughnuts and coffee, paid my bill, and restrained myself from leaving an overly generous tip. I didn't want to be that well remembered.

Driving back, I tried to maintain a speed fast enough not to be noticeable but slow enough to give me a chance to spot the roadhouse nestled in the trees. Even at that, I very nearly passed it, and had to brake sharply to swing in and then back up to the driveway leading around to the back. Was he open? There were the usual beer signs in the window, but none of them was lighted. However, there was a light on over the bar, which I could see through the front window. I tried the door and stepped gratefully inside.

The interior was the typical compromise between rusticity and poverty. At one time, I reckoned, there had been an effort to gain the appearance of a "lodge." Now, however, the cheap, varnished paneling had swelled and split. The floor sagged alarmingly. The bar did not seem to have been polished for years. The rickety tables tilted in sympathy with the sag of the floor. When the proprietor emerged from the room behind the bar, I saw at least one reason why the place had pretty much gone to hell. His milky blue eyes were nearly blind. It was obvious that he could see me, but he had a tentative way of feeling his way around things that made me realize he could not iden-

tify smaller objects in the area. I sat at the bar and
ordered a Miller's. He opened the cooler and carefully
reached into the Miller's section. I could see him identify the bottle by the shape of it. I put two dollars on
the bar. He took one of them but didn't give me any
change. He did not seem inclined to talk, for which I
was grateful. My voice is a dead giveaway. I did not
want him to remember me at all, and I doubted that
he would notice the dull gray car parked near the
building in the back. Unless he went outside, he couldn't
see it at all, because none of the back windows looked
over it. Jake (who else could it be?) retired to his back
room, leaving me to my thoughts, which were happier
than they had been. I finished my Miller's and left,
banging the door severely behind me so he would
know I had departed.

So, a little luck had begun to run my way. I opened
the trunk of the car and took out my old binoculars (a
friend of mine had once complained that he could get
the same effect by looking through a pair of Coke
bottles). Never mind. They were mine and I loved
them; I also know how to focus them. I slung the
binoculars around my neck and shoved a small notebook in my jacket pocket. I was a birdwatcher. When
I looked across the highway to the swamp-killed stand
of dead trees, the only birds I could summon up in my
mind were vultures. Nonetheless, the greenery rising
behind me seemed to be a reasonable habitation for
birds (about which I know nothing).

I faded into the woods and began to climb. It was
obvious that others had taken the route behind the
roadhouse—newly made lovers out for a midnight frolic,
no doubt—because a pathway soon asserted itself. The
path wound a leisurely progress upward. The trees,
which had seemed to present a solid wall from below,
had given themselves plenty of space. It was the foliage that made the woods look thick. In a little while I
reached a leveling-off along an outbreak of schist running horizontally along the brow of the hill.

I sat down and began to focus my glasses. From my
elevation here I was well above the tops of the trees in
the swamp, but the azimuth from my vantage to the

lake collided with the branches. At this point I couldn't
distinguish between the swamp and the lake. I began
to move horizontally along the brow, stopping every
few yards for another line of sight. After about the
tenth move, I swept my glasses across the tops of the
dead trees and then paused. Had I seen a flash of
white? Could it have been a bird's wing? I braced
myself to hold the glasses steady, and began another
slow sweep of the area. The first sweep showed me
nothing new, but I lowered the glasses slightly and
tried another. Again, there was the flash of white as
my glasses wove among the branches. I held steady
then. It was the barest patch of white, but it certainly
was no natural part of a swamp or lake. I needed more
elevation. I looked up the sheer wall of schist rising
for some ten feet upward behind me and took a bearing on my line of sight. There didn't seem to be any
kind of dependable marker above me, so I took off my
Windbreaker, made a ball of it, and flung it up to the
top of the ledge. It took me four tries before the
damned thing finally caught on a sapling. Then I went
back to the path and climbed the safe easy route to the
top of the ledge. I am no mountaineer.

Even after I had located my jacket and reestab-
lished my bearings, it took me three or four sweeps to
locate the house. However, in a lucky opening between two swamp trees, I was able to see nearly half
of it at an angle that included the portico and the side.
It had once been, I could see, a quite beautiful house,
nearly square, topped by a mansard roof. The portico
was supported by classic pillars. It had once gleamed
white, but the miasma drifting up from the lake had
peeled the paint so that the house was badly splotched
with gray. It was, unmistakably, a ruin. The windows
in view had been boarded up. I couldn't see too much
of the island itself, but what was visible was wild with
high weeds, and sloped sharply downward. I kept my
glasses fixed on it, hoping for a sign of some kind of
life, even a dog. I remained fixed, praying that an idle
villain would stroll into view, but there was absolutely
no sign of life. No smoke from a cooking fire, nothing.
It was as still as death. I swept my glasses across the

entire area, raising them and lowering them, and realized, unhappily, that the dead trees extended out into the lake. Its separation from the swamp was only a matter of depth. The water, like that of the swamp, would be black and forbidding. The county road, I realized with dismay, could be little more than a causeway dividing the various depths of the swamp.

There was little for me to do now but watch and wait. It was getting close to noon, and the doughnuts had worn off. I cursed my own stupidity for not bringing a couple of sandwiches, because the unaccustomed exercise and sharp fresh air had awakened a gnawing hunger in me. Nonetheless, I had no intention of returning to the highway. I was safe here, unseen, and, even if seen, I was only a mere happy birdwatcher. I tried to think of some kinds of birds I might have spotted to make up a story. Sadly enough, the only kind of bird I could think of was the prothonotary warbler. I decided that if anyone should brace me, I would go into my deaf dummy act. If that someone was threatening, I had my heavy Colt Python tucked in my pants. It was heavy, awkward, and a bore, but it was also, certainly, a sheet anchor toward continued existence.

I settled down grumpily, sweeping the house and patch of island every few minutes for a sign of life. Nothing. I would not be able to go back down until the sun had begun to sink. I wanted to traverse the county road in twilight, not, certainly not in the dark. But twilight came late these days. I prepared myself for a hungry vigil.

25

The day passed with agonizing slowness, punctuated only by pangs of hunger and curses at my own stupidity for not bringing food along. My glasses swept back and forth across the tiny corner of island and every inch of the house exposed to my view. I found myself muttering, "C'mon, you sons of bitches, show me something." The only things that moved were the shadows as the day lengthened. My mouth kept watering at the thought of the morning doughnuts until it began to dry of thirst. I hadn't brought any water, either.

The hunger, the thirst, and the frustration at craning endlessly to skip among the dead trees with my glasses annoyed and irritated me, giving my senses an edge that was constantly honed as the day wore on. But the edge made me aware of something else too—an absence—an absence like the surprised feeling you would get in walking against a high wind that has suddenly dropped. The pain and pressure in my head were entirely gone! There was no trace left of anything like them. I had been sick with the abcess for so long that the normality itself seemed strange. But when I recognized what had happened, I got up and stamped around in a little circle, a little celebration, a tiny victory dance. The normality extended all the way through my body. I raised my arms shoulder high and flexed my biceps. I did a quick couple of squats to test

my knees. Everything responded as it should, as it had
before this sickness had come upon me. I was well.

The new sense of well-being exhausted my patience
and made further waiting on this unrewarding hill
almost unendurable. At last, earlier than I had planned,
I threw in the towel. I returned to the roadhouse and
looked through the window. It was as empty as it had
been in the morning. I went in, and when Jake ambled
out of his shadowy back room I ordered a Miller's,
two hard-boiled eggs from the bowl in the back of the
bar, two bags of peanuts, and two packs of Blind
Robins. Jake set the feast in front of me. I asked him,
"Anybody in here today asking for me? I was supposed to meet some guys around here but they never
showed up."

"Naw," he said. "Couple of motorcycle punks come
by and played the slot machine. Never said nothing to
me."

I cracked my eggs and devoured them. I scoffed
down the peanuts and the Blind Robins and had another Miller's. Then I prepared to leave.

"Screw 'em," I said to Jake. "Anybody comes around
looking for me now, tell 'em you never saw anybody.
OK? The hell with them."

I left an extra five on the bar separate from the ones.
When I left and turned to look back, I could see him
holding it up under the light very close to his eyes.

This time I warmed up the car engine, not because
it needed it, but because I wanted to review my cam-
paign before I started off. When I had it set in my
mind, I pulled out of the driveway and headed for
County Road 23. I swung into the road at a good clip
and maintained a speed that was probably too fast for
the loose gravel surface. When I reached the edge of
the lake, I took a fast and furious look at the whole
house perched on its island. In the gathering twilight,
the old paint appeared to gleam, but no light showed
itself from the inside. In my quick glimpse of the
building it seemed to me that all the windows were
heavily boarded, upstairs and down. The narrow road,
which was more of a built-up ridge separating the
swamp from the lake, curved north and took me quickly

away from my view of the house. I followed it north until it began to enter onto solid ground again. There was a widening in the road, where I turned the car around and crept back until I was about a mile from the lake's edge. Here, too, there was a slight widening in the road, where a shoulder had been built out into the swamp. I pulled the car under a dead tree and looked at the sky. Clouds were accumulating, which was very much to my advantage. There should not be much of a moon. I took my package out of the trunk. It would be another hour before total darkness fell.

I opened my bundle and rolled out the equipment, putting the Colt quite close to hand in case I should be interrupted. I got into my wet suit, but left the flippers behind because they would have been nothing more than a hindrance on the tangled bottom of that lake. The tanks were still matte black, unreflective, and I couldn't see any bright spots where the paint might have worn. I adjusted the hood and tested the mask. Then I put the Colt and all my other equipment, except the compass, in my broad, tight waterproof belt. The oilskin packet I secreted elsewhere.

I slipped down over into the swamp side of the causeway and felt my thin sneakers sink into an ooze that didn't seem much better than quicksand. Nonetheless, the height of the road screened me from the sightline of the lake. It was now dark enough that any car driving along would be using headlights, and any walker, most probably, a flashlight. I reminded myself to look for any light bouncing off the denuded trunks of the trees. The swamp was about waist deep where it followed the causeway, so I could easily duck down into the water out of sight—blackness in blackness. I kept a good grip on my compass. It would not do to lose it.

The one-mile journey seemed endless, and was tiring beyond belief. Each step I took sank me ankle deep in muck. Each step meant pulling my foot out of a vacuum, and then, inevitably, tripping over a root or the rotten remnant of a vine that snaked along the bottom. It was almost completely dark when I reached the bend in the road. The house, which I was able to

Jack Livingston

see as I raised myself cautiously to peep over the
causeway, was only a faint, vague blob in the distance.
It was, however, enough for me to sight on the compass. I shielded the compass with my hand, flicked on
the little light in the waterproof box, and took a bearing on the house. The bearing was east by south—
fairly easy to follow. Without it, I might have gone
wandering in circles forever on the bottom of the
black lake. Once on the bottom, except for the compass, I would be not only deaf but blind. I waited
another half hour for every vestige of light to die out
of the land and sky. Then I slithered across the road
and eased myself into the lake. I slipped the mask on,
adjusted the valve, and submerged.

For a while I had to crawl along the bottom as a
baby crawls across the floor because I did not want to
risk my hood's breaking the surface and catching an
errant moonbeam (clouds part and let the moon
through, invariably at the worst possible moment). I
had never been spooked under water before, but there
was a real horror in sinking my hands into the dead
ooze, the muck, the rotting corpse of what had once
been pasture. I bumped blindly into the stumps of
trees and the trunks of trees that had not yet fallen,
but remained standing like corpses buried upright.
There wasn't much detritus in the lake. I closed my
hand only once or twice on what felt like a beer can.
My feeling was that people did not care to come here
to recreate. It wasn't until I felt that I was in a reasonable depth, say ten feet, that I dared to light my
compass. I set my course and decided to leave my
compass lighted. For one thing, if it slipped out of my
hands into this black subaqueous world, I would have
no chance at all of finding it. I turned my head to look
above me. The light did not seem to penetrate much
beyond my face.

The journey across that mucky bottom was horribly
slow. I couldn't swim with any confidence because I
never knew when I would bang into a stump or, worse,
catch myself on a snag and rip my suit. I couldn't walk
upright on the bottom because the journey through
the swamp had taught me that I would be hopelessly

exhausted by the time I reached the house. I traveled along the way I suppose a lobster must travel, slowly, sullenly, blindly. I kept my eyes fastened on the tiny dot of light held out in front of me and followed the pip lying just below the cardinal arrow of east.

I have never been in an isolation tank, but I can't imagine that it is any more disorienting than the bottom of Lake Pennmere. The blackness, except for the point of light, was absolute. While there were things to touch—the bottom, the slimy trunks of the slowly rotting trees—these were primordial sensations that seemed to have no relationship to anything in what is happily known as normal life. The pinpoint of light was comforting, but it was also hypnotic. I had to force myself, again and again, to make sure I was following the pip and hadn't begun to circle slowly through the muck in an endless circle, as the caddis worm is seen to do on the rim of a glass.

It was close to an hour in this black, ugly suspension before I began to realize that I was bumping into more and more trees and touching more hard, discrete objects on the bottom. I began to sense the rising of the lake's floor, and then it ascended suddenly to the edge of the island. I put my hand out and touched grass that was moistened only by the evening dew. I switched off the light on my compass and gingerly raised my head above water.

I had been very wise not to trust the clouds. They were passing rapidly overhead and dispersing. The moon, while not clearly in sight, had penetrated the thinnest of them and cast a gray light on the island. It picked out the decaying paint of the house and showed me that I had drifted south and was facing the portico dead on. I crawled back, crabwise, into the lake, and made my way farther south for about ten minutes. When I surfaced again I was looking at an angle the opposite of which I had watched all day with my glasses. It was impossible to see detail. The house shimmered with the shifting of moon shadows in the gray, intermittent light. Again, there was not the feeblest spark of light to be seen coming from it anywhere. It was intensely secret.

What few moon shadows existed were still on my side of the house, although I would have to hurry to take advantage of them. I crawled a bit farther south to get in the lee of a broad shadow cast both by the house and a gigantic surviving oak. I lay perfectly still at the edge of the water, first to make sure that my eyes had adjusted, and secondly to let the water run off my suit. Wet rubber gleams. Slowly and cautiously I detached my mask and unstrapped my tanks. Automatically I separated the mask from the tanks and set it aside. I set the tanks standing upright so that the valves would not foul with mud. This was all automatic —everything neatly disassembled, as I had been taught.

After a moment's thought I put the heavy awkward Colt in my fist and left the combat knife stuck in the back of my belt. There would be time to change over if I spotted a lookout. Knives have the inestimable advantage of absolute silence if they are used correctly— cutting the renal artery, plunged directly into the solar plexus, or stabbed into the carotid plexus—but they're not good for fending off a sudden, direct attack. The gun it would be. I remained prone, the Colt held in front of me, and began to inch through the broad shadow up toward the house.

It was a worm's progress, and once I had reached the foundations of the house, I heaved a sigh of relief. I was no longer totally exposed. I was in very deep darkness, and was looking out over the relatively light slope of wild grass going down to the lake. A lookout who was not hugging the house could be spotted before he saw me. Since the windows were boarded up securely, and I had no intention of presenting myself at either the front door or the back, I had decided much earlier that my only hope was to find some entrance to the basement. I began to creep slowly along the foundation, stopping to run my hand over the old stone blocks that had grown slimy with moss. There was no sign of a basement window. I continued on to the corner and then began my blind inspection of the back of the house, which was as unknown to me as the backside of the moon used to be. When I turned the corner I rested for a moment to look out over the back area. It presented no silhouettes, no shadows with familiar shapes. I continued my block-by-stone-block fingertip inspection. I reckoned that I had gone about halfway across the back of the house before I was rewarded. I bumped into something solid directly in front of me and put out a cautious hand. It was a fairly large triangular structure, apparently made of wood. I put my seeking fingers on top of it and recognized the shape and feel of a hasp hinge. It was an old-fashioned cyclone cellar door, of the kind kids used to slide down in prehistoric eras. I raised up high enough to feel across where the two doors joined in the center and found a padlock holding them together. I decided to let the padlock lie, and instead I paid attention to the hinges. My suspicion was that the wood around the hinges was probably rotten and that the screws would come out without too much noise. If I tried to open the doors from the center, the shriek of the rusty hinges would certainly give me away. I shifted the Colt to my left hand and awkwardly worked the hinges loose with my knife. I was right about the wood; they came out easily. I put the knife back in my belt and slowly raised the side of the door. Feet first, I slithered in through the crack and found my footing on what must have been stone steps leading downward.

I was again in blackness, as black as the bottom of the lake, with no comforting pinpoint of light to guide me. Standing on the dirt floor of the cellar (I had reached down and touched it with my hand) I was deprived even of the gray light of the hidden moon. I stood stock-still and used my only other sense. I sniffed. There was a wild and musty smell of fruit and vegetables long since dead—it had been a proper farmhouse storage cellar—but no acrid smell of human sweat or foulness of breath. There was a great urge in me to take out my penlight, but I knew the indulgence could be fatal. The trick here was to move with such glacial slowness that the faintest bump would be cushioned. I held the Colt near my belly (the crack of metal against stone would have rung like a fire alarm), held out my left hand, and began to grope with infinite stealth away from the steps and toward where the wall must be. After inching myself across the dark space, my hand encountered something I took to be a wooden shelf that was thick with dust. On top of it were glass bottles, some of them broken, although I kept my touch so light that nothing could cut me. These were the jellies, jams, and preserves that had been left behind, now covered with wild molds. I kept my touch as light as a surgeon's as I followed the edge of the shelf to the corner. At the corner I waved my left hand slowly—an insect's antenna—and it encountered the rough wooden side of the cellar stairs. I followed the slope to the foot of the stairs, and with infinite caution began to ascend them.

All doors have a crack at the bottom. I figured that the inside door to the cellar should open onto the kitchen, a farm kitchen, which should be fairly large and commodious. My instinct was that if there was a gathering here, it would be in the kitchen, where food and coffee were available. I felt for the bottom crack of the door at the top of the stairs and tried to peer through it. There was nothing. Blackness. I had assumed that the door would be hooked or bolted from the other side, but when I very slowly turned the cold knob, the door swung open. I waited. More utter blackness. I stepped across the threshold, and suddenly there were lights, not lights from the room, but lights inside my head—a burst of rocketry. I had been slammed at the hinge of my jaw just underneath the ear. My head felt that it was being torn from my neck. There was a white-hot lightning spasm of pain down my shoulder, and then nothingness.

26

Had I muttered aloud? I hope not, although I may never know. It seems to me now that I had been muttering, *"Celia, Celia,"* although, of course, I can't hear myself, and what I thought were words, a name, might have been nothing more than semiconscious grunts.

But apparently I had thought that, like a Chinese emperor, I was awakening in Celia's lap. I had only two senses operating then, olfactory and tactile, and neither fully awake. But as I regained consciousness, I was aware of a powerful odor of womanhood, wild, and piercingly sexual. As I shifted my head—very, very slightly, because the pain shot with electric immediacy through my neck to my shoulder, I became aware that my cheek rested on the naked thighs of a woman, and that my forehead was pressed against her soft belly. My ear was nestled in the springy wire of pubic hair. I raised my head slowly, and my cheek touched a naked breast. Astonished, I guiltily jerked it back. However, I was still unable really to move, nor did I have any desire to. I became aware that my hands were manacled behind me.

In time, I became aware of an odd sort of pressure on my arm. Although it was intermittent, I wasn't really able to sense anything through the tough rubber of my suit. A soft hand shifted to my cheek, and the unmistakable message was tapped out:

. - . / . . - / - - - / . . -
R U O K

It was a question that needed no question mark, sent by a messenger who needed no signature. It was Edna, who had often tapped out this message between the office and my apartment on the Code-Com phone. It was Edna whose naked body cradled me.

I began to sit up sharply, saying, "Edna!" when her hand clamped over my mouth. Her fingers tapped out "Be quiet."

I managed to get my mouth up next to her ear and tried to whisper. It can be done, even though I can't gauge the volume. "Edna," I whispered, "are you all right?" It was utterly black in the room, but wherever I moved my face it seemed to rest finally on the soft, yielding flesh of Edna. There was an immensity to her, as if her naked and vulnerable flesh had stretched magically to occupy every bit of space in the small, black universe of the room.

Her fingers tapped out against my cheek, "He raped me."

Three words—two letters first word, five letters second word, two letters third word. I absorbed them like bullets, and it took me a moment to absorb them all. In that moment, however, Edna began to shake, and I could feel the sobs bursting out of her. I shifted so that I could put my face up against hers. The tears came down against my cheek.

After she subsided I got my lips up against her ear, brushing the hair away with my nose, and whispered, "Who?"

She tapped out the name on my cheek.

This rolled me back on my haunches, and I very nearly fell, but managed to catch myself awkwardly with my manacled hands. The name signified a conspiracy far beyond anything I had considered. It indicated an immense network stretching everywhere. It seemed impossible to link the name with long black limousines, offshore banks, and manufactured dreams.

I regained myself and got carefully onto my knees next to her. "Edna," I whispered, "there's a slit pocket on the left upper sleeve of this suit. Unless he found them, the keys to the cuffs should be at the bottom. They're hard to get out, so be careful, and be sure you don't drop 'em."

"OK," she tapped.

I felt her long, slim fingers dig into the pocket on my arm, and I asked her, "Is it there?"

"OK" was tapped out on my cheek. The long hair fell over my face.

"For Christ's sake," I whispered, "be careful."

There was an interminable wait while she carefully and no doubt silently positioned herself around at my back and blindly groped her way down to my manacled wrists. It seemed to take her forever to find the tiny keyhole to the cuff and get the key seated correctly. Finally, though, I felt it spring open. I brought my hand in front of me. "Now give me the key," I demanded. I opened the other one myself. Then I put my two free hands on her face, held it, and kissed her.

Given this new start, there were answers I needed, and a rapid conversation performed in whispers and tappings sprang up between Edna and me. We were on the second floor of the house. She was sure that the door was barred, and there was no way we could broach it silently. There was no furniture in the room at all—nothing I could use as a weapon. It was true, I thought, that the cuffs themselves might make an excellent set of brass knuckles, but I sensed that I needed a little more advantage than that. No: Edna had no idea what time it was, whether it was day or night. One thing she did know, however: There was a boat— here on the island. She had seen it—knew where it was pulled up on the steeply sloping grass shore. It was a boat with a motor, an outboard motor. This was not all laboriously spelled out against my cheek. She had tapped out *boat*, and then I had whispered the appropriate questions, to which she had tapped out *yes*, or *no*. So there was the possibility of making a run for it, however desperate, if only we could get out of the room, away and to the boat.

I began to crawl, hoping to find a wall, and moved, I hope, as silently as a spider. I reached a wall and began to explore it with my fingers. The plaster was damp, rotting damp. When I raised my hand some-what I reached a windowsill, and feeling above it, discovered that the windows had been boarded on the inside as well as the outside. There was no way of getting them off without making a racket. I reconsid-ered. As I thought, I let my hands wander over the plaster, which had a morbid feel to it, like everything else I had touched since the moment I had first sunk my feet into that black ugly swamp. I ran my thumb-nail along the plaster wall and noticed that my nail made an easy groove in it. I flicked a piece of it away.

I turned around then and tried to crawl directly back to Edna. I put one hand out in front of me and finally located her. Her flesh was cold. I whispered to her, "I want you to follow me absolutely silently. Keep one hand on my ankle. When I stop, you stop." We arranged ourselves in tandem, and she followed me back to the wall.

"Edna," I whispered, "this plaster is rotten. I think the whole house is rotting away. I think I can pull enough plaster and lathing away to get at the siding. If I can push out a few boards of siding, we can get out of here."

"The main trouble," I whispered, "is noise. I don't want to make any noise. So I want you to keep one hand on my shoulder, and if I make any noise, squeeze it. You understand?"

Tapped out: *OK*.

I set to work with my fingers then, digging them into the rotten plaster. Edna stopped me with a tapped-out question: *Smell*.

"Horsehair," I whispered. "They used to mix it with the plaster." The plaster came away in fairly large chunks, and soon I was able to feel the lathing under-neath, thicker and rougher than they use today. I followed along until I reached a stud, which I could feel through a space in the lathing. I continued in the same direction until I reached the next stud, about twenty-four inches away. I measured the distance from the line I had gouged to the floor with my extended hands, and judged it to be about eighteen inches. It would be space enough for us to wiggle through. The

rest of the plaster came off pretty easily. A lot of it
had already bulged away from the lathing with accumu-
lated moisture, and the lathing itself was dank and
slimy to the touch.

When the space was cleared from stud to stud, I
tried to pull one of the laths away from its nailhold on
the stud. No soap. I couldn't get enough purchase with
my hands. I sent Edna back, then, to locate the handcuffs, and waited an eternity until she arrived and put
them in my hand. She seized my shoulder again with a
reassuring pat. Using the long, serrated tongue of one
of the cuffs, I managed to make a small but effective
pry bar. At the first sensation of the wood's giving, I
felt a panicky squeeze on my shoulder. I went back to
work more cautiously. In time (too much, too much
time) I managed to free all of the lathing in the eighteen-
inch area. I moved slowly, crabwise, back to the other
stud and repeated the same laborious process.

Now the risk arrived. Only three of the laths had
butt-ended on the stud. The others ran on further, but
if I chased them down we would have been forever.
There was nothing for me to do but seize them midway between the two studs and break them. I broke
off the butt-ended ones first and was happy to notice
that Edna had not needed to grab my shoulder. When
I broke the first one in the middle, however, she did
grab my shoulder, and I eased off a bit. I couldn't tell,
of course, if there was the sharp crack you usually get
with breaking wood, but I felt that the dampness and
rot of the wood pretty much muffled the sound.

At last I had them all broken off and cleared away.
I felt through the open space and my hand rested on
the rough interior of the siding. I went back to work
with my handcuff lever, prying the siding away from
the exterior face of the studs. Fresh air began to seep
into the room. It was as welcome as an angel's breath.

Apparently I hadn't made much noise loosening the
siding, but I knew it would be impossible to force the
siding off without some kind of clatter. I whispered to
Edna, "I want you to turn around and make a back I
can brace myself against. I'm going to force this siding
off with my feet. Understand? The minute there's

enough space, I'm going out and dropping. I want you to come immediately after. Hang by your fingers and drop feet first. I'll catch you. OK?"

Tapped out: *OK*.

Two strips of siding were butt-ended, and so I pushed them loose first. I was eager to see if it was day or night, and the opening revealed a dawn that was rapidly approaching daylight. A rush of cool air entered the room, and with it the first light the room had seen in many hours. I glanced at Edna's back and smiled. The chill had given her gooseflesh. "Remember now," I said. "When I go, you go." She nodded. I hoped she meant it. There was no way I was going to yell, *"Geronimo!"*

I braced myself against Edna then and pushed mightily, first at one stud and then the other. The siding gave, but did not fall. I changed position and told Edna to turn around and get ready. Then I pushed the siding the remaining distance with my hands. The pieces fell to the ground, and I hoped beyond hope that when I jumped I would not land on an upended nail.

But jump I did, and luck held with me. I pushed myself out the opening feet first, clung to the edge for a second, and let go. When I hit I bent my knees and rolled away. But I scrambled back quickly because two naked legs were waving in the air above me. Edna, too, backed out, although with a little more caution and trouble than I had, until she was suspended from the opening. Then she let go—an act of faith. I caught her as I had promised, and we both fell down and rolled onto the grass. For an instant she clung to me, her eyes tightly closed, but I pulled her back to the lee of the house, where there was less chance of being seen, and motioned for her to keep low.

"Which way is the boat?" I asked her.

It was not an easy question. She was totally disoriented, and probably had not seen as much of the exterior of the house as I had. I said, "We're at the back of the house now. Did you come in the front?" She nodded. "OK," I said. "Just try to visualize coming in the front, and tell me which side the boat is on.

We don't want to have to cross the front of the house if we can help it." Edna took her time, thought about it, and gestured toward the southern exposure of the house. This surprised me because it was the direction of my approach, and yet I hadn't seen a boat. On the other hand, my attention had been fixed on the house.

"OK," I told her. "Keep low, stay close to the house, and when you see me break for the boat, you break with me, understand? Run as fast as you can, but keep low. Try to make as small a target as possible, and zigzag when you run." I stopped to think what I was saying. I stopped to think of Edna's naked body riddled with bullets. "I'm not being fair," I told her. "Would you rather just give up? If you would, I'll give up with you. No prejudice. I didn't come here to get you killed."

Edna put her head back and looked at the dawning sky and then looked at me. "No," she said. "We'd die anyway. I know that. I'd rather have it happen like this." I hugged her for a moment and held her next to me. When I let her go we began a kind of duckwalk along the back of the house.

I signaled her to stop when we reached the corner, and took a careful look at the steeply sloping southern part of the island. I couldn't see anything resembling a boat, but then, I couldn't see the edge of the lake, either. I asked her, "You're sure it's on this side?"

She looked then as if she were going to cry. "Oh, God, Joe," she said. "I think so . . . I think so . . . but . . ."

"Screw it," I said. "We'll make the run. If we get across all right, we've got the shoreline to hide in. Remember, keep low. Run like hell, and zigzag like crazy. Are you set? Go!"

We burst out from the side of the house, and I dashed in the prescribed manner, hunched over and cutting back and forth in erratic bursts. About halfway to the edge I turned quickly to look for Edna, and what I saw broke my heart. She was running full upright in the typical knock-kneed girl's run, her arms held out to her sides to hold her balance and her body shaking, bouncing and jiggling. Her head was thrown back, her eyes nearly closed. Her red-gold hair streamed in the wind, and her white skin drank the pale light of the dawn. *"Down!"* I shrieked silently at her. *"For Christ's sake, Edna, down!"* But she was utterly heedless, and I realized that when she had burst from the side of the house she had consigned herself to God and expected to die. She didn't believe that crouching low and zigging and zagging would truly save her, and what finally broke my heart was that I didn't really believe it either. I lay prone in the high grass and waited for her. When she arrived I leaped up and seized her arm, and we ran together, a double target— doomed idiots.

But we did make it. We got to the sharp drop that falls to the water's edge and rolled over together again in the grass. Again, we lay still for a moment, hugging one another.

When I got to my knees I saw the boat. It was only a few yards from where I had crawled ashore. My tanks were still there, still upright where I had left them. The boat had, as Edna had promised, an outboard motor cocked over the transom. Next to the outboard motor sat a large blond man in a blue jump suit. He had what looked like a small black metal box in his hands.

27

Edna had remained curled in the grass, where her whole upper body heaved and jerked with sobs and gasps. She stood up, finally, and very slowly turned in my direction. Then she saw the boat and the man in the blue jump suit. What must have been a scream escaped her. Instantly, she threw protective hands across her breasts and pudendum. She would have turned and hobbled away, I think, if I hadn't caught her by the shoulder. "Don't run," I told her. "Don't give him an excuse."

The small black box he was holding had a pipe jutting out of the end. I finally identified it as an Ingram MAC 10 machine pistol. It froze me. The MAC 10 spits out twelve hundred rounds a minute, and those rounds can be forty-five-caliber slugs. It is an army you can put in a briefcase.

When I got over the shock of recognizing what I was facing I loosened my grip on Edna's shoulder and led her over to a smooth grassy spot not far from the boat. "Sit down," I told her. She sat with her knees pulled up and her arms clasped around her calves. She buried her face, then, so that nothing showed but a mound of pale trembling flesh with red-gold hair spilling over it.

"Hello, Don," I said. "Want to talk it over?"

He smiled at me, a frightening smile because it looked so innocent and even jovial in that clear, strong, orange-tinted face. He had opened my waterproof holding belt and stretched it out near the boat. On it lay all the possessions I had brought with me except the handcuffs. My gun was there, the extra box of cartridges, my knife, my Zippo lighter, and two packs of Lucky Strikes.

He maintained his smile, but there was a vague look of disbelief in his eyes. "The papers," he said, "you didn't bring them?"

"Sure I did," I answered quickly. "I brought them. Definitely."

The MAC 10 had been held rather listlessly, but now he tilted it toward my midriff. "Where are they?"

"Somewhere on this island," I said. "That's a promise."

"I'll find them." The MAC 10 was firmed up.

"Maybe, maybe not," I said. "Why waste all that time when I'll let you have them for the price of a little conversation?"

I went over and sat down by the tanks and my discarded regulator. I was some distance from Edna. She would not raise her head to look at either of us.

"That's reasonable," said Don Heemstra.

"Do you mind if I smoke?" I asked him.

A thin line of contempt chased itself across his lips. He tossed a pack of Luckies to me. I opened them and put one in my mouth.

"Light?"

He lobbed the Zippo over to me. He was wary, but amused. With the MAC 10 at his disposal he was, quite correctly, supremely confident. After I had lighted up, he said, "Let's get on with it."

"Why did you kill Celia?"

"Who's that?"

"The lady in my apartment."

He shrugged. "She was there. I was pretty sure you were at the hospital. I didn't expect anybody to be there."

"You raped her."

He made a little self-forgiving moué. "I got excited," he said. "Can you blame me? She was naked. And then she put up a fight—I mean, just over my being there. She was trying to put me away. It was a hell of a surprise. She was a trained pro, obviously. She damned near caught me napping. I had to tie her up."

"You tied her up and then you raped her."

"Sure."

"How did you kill her?"

"Injection."

"Heroin?"

"No. Ouabain."

"What the hell is that? I never heard of it."

"A glycoside, like digitalis. There was the off chance you might be there when I arrived, in which case I thought I'd have to give you a jolt."

"Funny I didn't see any needle marks on her."

"They don't show up so well in mucous membrane," said Don Heemstra.

I tried to repress a shudder and didn't make it. "How come you didn't toss my place?" I asked him. "That's what you came for, wasn't it?"

"Your burglar alarm," he answered. "Somehow she triggered the damned thing. The lamps started flashing on and off. I had to get out."

That had been the phone call from the hospital, I thought sadly. "This ouabain stuff," I said, "that what you used to kill Gene Listing with?"

"No, no." He shook his head and looked stern. I was being prepared for a lecture. "There was no way I could have possibly given Gene an injection. I would have had to get him alone and under control. There was no way he was going to let me do that. No. I had to give him a digitoxin, orally."

"How did you do that?" My eyes had widened. I was startled.

"They upped his prescription to eighty milligrams, so I switched his pills."

"That's right," I said, "I keep forgetting you were a medic."

"I was more than that," he said, frowning. "I should have been a doctor."

I stared at him.

He got defensive. "OK," he said. "It got pretty clear I wasn't going to be a doctor. Never mind why.

But I thought, 'Goddamn it, I'll be something.' " He gestured with the MAC 10; I froze. "So I signed up for the medics and went to Nam. I was going to save lives."

He leaned back a little and looked at the sky before he looked back at me. "First time I went out," he said, "you know what I caught? A guy hits a trip wire. Stupid bastard. Caught him right midstride. Blew both legs to stumps. Cleaned off his balls, everything."

Heemstra's chest began to heave. The MAC 10 trembled. "So I ran up there. *'Gee whizz, fella, don't take on so. I'm gonna fix you right up.'* Huh! This guy was screaming noises I never heard before. He was saying things I never heard said. I shook and shook, and dropped everything all over hell and couldn't do anything right, if there *was* anything to do right. And so I tried to shut him up. I mean, I couldn't stand it. Nobody could stand that. I tried to talk to him, but it was like talking into a hurricane. And so I put my hand over his mouth to shut him up. But, of course, I put my hand over his mouth like this . . ." He demonstrated, his hand clamped over his mouth with his nostrils choked in the joint of his thumb and forefinger. "And I was holding him like that and watching his face. And the light went out of his eyes. And he stopped."

"You Burked him," I said. "You took pre-med? You know what I mean."

"Yeah," said Heemstra. "I guess I did. But what was interesting was watching the light go out of his eyes. I can't explain it. It's like a sunset."

"You got to like that, did you?" I asked him. "Watching the lights go out?"

"Yeah," he said, looking rather dreamy, "I guess I did."

I tried to keep my voice very conversational. "You're as crazy as hell," I said. "You know that, don't you? Did you try to get any help when you came back?"

"Help," he laughed. "Sure, I went to a shrink. *I think I'm nuts. Do something for me. Let me tell you what happened in Nam.*"

" 'I don't want to hear that,' says the shrink. 'Tell

me about your childhood.' The verdict was that I had a poor self-image. So now I'm improving my self-image. He's right. It works."

But something was troubling me. "I don't see," I said, "how you managed to switch pills on Gene."

"Gene kept his prescription in three bottles so he'd always have one. He kept one at home, one at the office, and one at the gym. Trouble with him was he kept carrying the bottles around in his pockets, so eventually all three of them wound up at the gym one time or another."

"How could you know which was which?"

"I could always tell the original pills from the ones I made up myself. In a little while Gene was just playing Russian roulette without knowing it." He thought over what he had said. "I'm surprised he lasted as long as he did."

I said, "I don't understand how he died in his sleep."

"Digitoxin is pretty slow-acting. Not like ouabain. He must have taken it just before he hit the sack."

I lighted another cigarette and let the vision of Gene waking in terror fade from my eyes. Finally I asked him, "Why did you rape Edna?"

Again, he shrugged and gave a little, slightly defensive grimace. "She's a woman," he said. "What else are they good for?"

"But why rape?"

"Bullshit," said Don Heemstra. "I don't have to explain myself to you. Where's the papers?"

"All right," I answered. I held my hands out in front of me with the fingers spread. "I'm going to have to reach into these rubber jeans to get them, understand? I'm not reaching for a weapon. I don't want to get greased just because you're jumpy."

"I'm not jumpy," said Heemstra. "Get the papers."

I eased onto one hip and reached down to the back of my thigh, where I had placed the oilskin envelope. It hadn't made much of a bulge there. In fact, Celia's report was not terribly lengthy. I extracted the envelope and tossed it over to Heemstra. He smiled a very bright, healthy smile at me. Things were working out. But once he began to read, the smile changed to a frown, and when he had gone through all the pages, he stared at me with his eyes glowing. "What is this shit?" he said. "This isn't what I want."

Now it was my turn to frown, and time for my eyes to pop. "What do you mean?" I said. I could feel the breath whistling in my throat. "That's all there is."

"In a pig's ass that's all there is," said Heemstra. The MAC 10 now was trained directly on me. "Where's the stuff about me?"

"I swear to Christ," I said, "there was nothing about you. Why should there be anything about you?"

I cannot hear a shout, but I can see it. The face colors—a deeper tint of orange in Heemstra's case— the cords stand out on the neck. "Because he was going to blow it!" shouted Heemstra. "You son of a bitch! Don't play games with me!"

"Blow what?" I asked stupidly. "You mean blow your cover? Is that what you mean?"

He continued to shout, his face getting redder. Edna looked up in fear and astonishment. "He was going to blow the game! The whole setup. He had a file on me. I know it. I heard him say it."

I told Heemstra, "I honestly and truly don't know what you're talking about. If there's a file, that's it."

"I heard him on the phone," shouted Heemstra. "He didn't know I was there. He was calling from the locker room and he didn't see me. Not then, he didn't. He said over the phone, 'I've got the line on that son of a bitch, and when I get the story out, we'll blow him out of the water.' "

"What line would he have on you?"

The redness seeped out of Heemstra's foce, and it became rigid, cold. He said, "I'm going to tell you once. I know you know it—don't fuck me around. But I'm going to tell you, and then you're going to give me that file, or I'm going to kill you and her inch by inch."

"Tell me. Honest to Christ, I don't understand, but tell me."

"Listing was paying me two hundred a week."

I was dumbfounded. "For what?"

"So I wouldn't send the EKG report to his company. When we told him about the EKG he almost went crazy—like some of the other guys. It's always, 'Jesus Christ, don't tell my boss. Don't tell my company. If they hear my heart is bad, my career is over. Please don't tell them. I'll do anything.' "

"And did they do anything?"

"Two hundred a week. That was the price. No more, no less. It was just about what any of them could write off, one way or another."

"How many?"

"Five besides Gene. All carefully chosen. I'm not a fool."

"So you were blackmailing these guys to keep the results of the physical from their company. Is that right?"

"Call it what you want," said Heemstra. "I call it my image-improvement program. I followed the shrink's orders. I've improved myself, my image. I'm near perfect now. But it takes money too. It means living well. You can't live on what I make pushing those slobs around the track."

"And they all go on paying without a word?" I asked in wonderment.

"One guy killed himself, the son of a bitch. I went to a lot of trouble setting him up, and then he blows his brains out. But the others came through—come through—like clockwork. No problem."

"But Gene . . ." I began.

"I made a mistake on him," Heemstra interrupted. "I sized him up to be like the others, soft, scared. But he turned out to be different. He was soft, all right. He was a mess. But he wasn't scared. It was just his way of talking. Even then, when I told him what it would cost him, he settled right down and looked at me. And I don't like being looked at that way—like he was looking through to the back of my skull. I knew I had made a mistake. He didn't bitch about the money. He didn't change the way he acted at all. He gave me the money the way you pay your subway fare, like putting it in a turnstile. All the others pissed and moaned and kept telling me this couldn't go on—although they all knew it would keep going on. But not Listing. He'd even smile when he was giving me the money. I didn't like his attitude. His application said he was an editor. What the hell is an editor? Nothing. But then, when I heard him on the phone, I realized he could make a news story out of this. That changed everything."

He repeated himself then, his blue eyes staring. "I didn't like his attitude."

"All right," I said. "I've got it."

"You've got the file."

"There was no file," I said. "You were mistaken about the whole thing."

"There was a file!" He must have roared. Edna jumped.

"Listen to me," I pleaded. "Just listen to me for a moment. What you heard Gene talking about over the phone was another file—the file you just read. It was a different story completely. He was talking to his wife. But it had nothing to do with you. I've read"—I put up my hand—"every bit that Gene left behind, and there was absolutely no mention of anything like that."

"There was a file," he insisted. The blood had left his face again, leaving it more yellow than orange.

"I'm not saying that Gene wouldn't have got around to you sooner or later. He was going to have to quit the job anyway, or be fired. But he was onto something much more important than you and your lousy two hundred a week. He could handle you, for a while at least. And that's why he smiled."

Sweat was collecting on the yellowing face. It began to run from his temples down the sides of his cheeks. "There was a file," he said. "I know it. I heard it. There was a file and you've got it, you son of a bitch. You've got it in that rubber suit. Take it off. Take off that suit." The MAC 10 was trembling.

It was slow work getting it off. I got the top off and then dropped the suspenders to the entry-waist pants, unzipped the ankles, and peeled them off. This left me in my jockey shorts. For some idiotic reason, I felt much more vulnerable to the MAC 10.

"Take off the shorts."

"How could I hide anything . . ."

"Take 'em off!"

Numb with outrage, I removed my jockey shorts and threw them on the suit. Edna had jerked upright at the thunder of Heemstra's voice, and her startled glance took me in. I felt as I must have looked, like a shaved ape. The whole surface of my body burned with rage and humiliation.

"Bring that stuff over here and drop it at my feet."

"Fuck it," I said. "I'm a dead man anyway. You want the stuff, you pick it up."

I sat down. I picked up my cigarettes and put one in my mouth. I picked up my lighter and draped one arm over the tanks. It was, perhaps, a brave show, but my hand trembled violently putting the cigarette in my mouth and I had to grip the lighter hard to keep it from shaking even more.

I flicked the lighter and looked away from Heemstra. He wasn't going to see the light go out of *my* eyes. He remained standing rigidly, and then I saw his shadow moving toward the suit. I gripped the valve on the tank with all my strength. When he bent over to pick up the suit I moved the lighter toward my cigarette, but continued its path toward the tank. The valve cracked open and a long blue jet of flame shot into Heemstra's face. I suppose he shrieked. His mouth was certainly wide open. As he spun away, the MAC 10 jumped in his hand and riddled the boat. I pivoted on my heel and kicked him behind the jaw. When he fell back I saw black flesh bubbling on his nose.

I dived for the MAC 10, and when I had it securely, I went over to the fallen tank and turned off the valve. Unfortunately, it had set fire to the suit, and there was nothing I could do about that except let it burn and pour its black cloud of smoke into the air. Heemstra lay on the ground with both hands on his face, writhing, possibly moaning. "Stand up," I told him. I put a few rounds next to his ear to convince him. He stood up shakily, his hands still covering his face. "Take that suit off," I told him. He shook his head violently.

"Take it off," I demanded, "or I'll shoot your toes off." It seemed to be the perfect argument. He unbuckled and unzipped and stood before us in all his orange glory. "Carotinemia," I said to Edna. "No wonder the son of a bitch can see in the dark. He must eat more carrots than a rabbit.

"Start walking backward," I ordered him. He began to step gingerly backward, one hand held over his nose and the other held out for balance. When I had stepped over the jump suit I said, "Stop," and he stopped. Then I said to Edna, "OK, Kid. There's your new wardrobe. Put it on." I did not take my eyes off Heemstra, but I felt Edna brush up against me as she picked up the jump suit.

I got him situated between three shadeless saplings. I had him lie supine and cuffed his hands. I told him to lie perfectly still while Edna went to fetch the painter from the boat and also my knife. I tied his cuffed hands to one sapling and his feet to the other two. It all looked pretty secure to me.

"The boat's useless," I told Edna, who nodded agreement, having seen the nearly shredded bottom of the transom. "I'll have to swim over to get help." She nodded again. Edna could not swim.

We both looked down at Heemstra. There was no doubt his nose was hurting. His eyes were running with tears. "You're not going to have any more nose," I told him happily. "It's all burnt off." Edna looked away.

"Don't take your eyes off this son of a bitch while I'm gone," I told her. "Sit over here in the shade and keep this gun trained on him. If he makes any funny moves, open him up."

She had rolled up the arms and legs of the suit, but it still fitted her like a barrel. I moved her over into the shade, well within range, and showed her how to operate the MAC 10, and how to prop it on her knees so it remained steady.

It took me about an hour and a half to get back there with the troopers. When we arrived Edna was still sitting in the spot I had left her, and the MAC 10 was still propped steadily on her knees. However, her eyes were wide and blank, almost to the point of hypnosis. Her face was white and expressionless.

The orange-colored man stretched out under the

trees was raving, and saliva flecked his chin. His long, thick muscles bulged as he pulled at the bonds. The sun had gone high enough to burn him, and the mild breeze of summer had played hell with his masculinity. His huge, orange erection jutted with outrage to a careless sky.

28

"What I don't understand," said Dr. Dap, "is this long blue flame you speak of from your breathing tank. An explosion I can understand. It's possible that the oxygen could explode with an orange flash. But you would have gone up, too, would you not? A controlled spurt of fire, blue in color, that defeats me."

"The answer is," I said smiling, "that my right-hand tank wasn't filled with oxygen."

"Nitrogen then?" asked Dr. Dap. "I know you sometimes mix oxygen with nitrogen. But nitrogen would only have smothered the flame."

"No, no," I laughed. "I knew I wouldn't need nitrogen, because I was pretty sure I wouldn't be going below thirty feet. You don't need a nitrogen mix above that. What happened was that I used only one tank for breathing. I had Benny fill up the other one with propane, ordinary picnic barbecue propane, under a little more pressure than usual. Then we put a torch nozzle on it, instead of a regulator valve. What I had there was a kind of flame thrower, or even a bomb, if I wanted a bomb."

"I see," said Dr. Dap. Edna was silent. We were sitting in Dr. Dap's office at the hospital. I had gone there for a final check on my ear (which was fine), and Edna had come down with me because Edna could no longer bear to be alone in the office.

"I didn't really know what I was going to find," I explained. "I was very confused. Edna's note in the typewriter said *'I have to go with him now.'* So I knew that only one man had pulled the snatch. On the other hand, it was hard for me to believe that only one man was setting up something this elaborate."

"A maniac," said Edna. Her face was still pale. She moved her lips very little when she spoke. Dr. Dap glanced at her covertly, as he had been doing more or less since we arrived.

"Yes," I agreed, "but I didn't expect to find a maniac. I guess I expected to find some kind of a crowd of government agents tripping over one another. I thought I needed something that could sweep a number of people, or blow down the side of a house, if necessary. We changed that nozzle a little bit, Benny and I.

"What I don't understand," I said to Dr. Dap, "is how this nut managed to switch pills on Gene. Do they look alike?"

"No, not at all," said Dr. Dap. "But when you showed me Mr. Listing's medication, those tablets didn't look right to me. Educated instinct is all. They just didn't look right. So I analyzed them. What Mr. Listing was given was something called Delanoside, which is hydrolyzed from a preparation of the leaves of *Digitalis lanate*. A sustaining dose of this drug is somewhere between one and one and a half milligrams. What Mr. Listing was given were tablets containing eighty milligrams, made up to look like eighty milligrams of propranolol.

"Apparently this fellow Heemstra—how I regret that it is a Dutch name!—cast a mold of the propranolol tablet, made a paste of the Delanoside preparation, and with a little vegetable coloring prepared a supply of counterfeits, which he put into Mr. Listing's bottles."

"Eighty times the dose!" I said. "It should have killed him like a stroke of lightning!"

"Not necessarily," Dr. Dap answered. "Bioavailability is a very tricky thing and often depends on the individual. The coating Heemstra used may have impeded the onset of the drug. Peak activity with Delanoside is usually reached within one to two hours, but it may have been longer. He may have taken his medication just before he lay down to sleep."

"And woke with what?" I asked, "a nightmare?"

"That, of course, is impossible to say. If the drug had acted merely to slow and regulate the heart, he might not have awakened at all. His heart merely would have stopped—cardiac arrest. But since he did waken, I believe that it slowed down first, and then, as so often happens, rebounded, went into ventricular fibrillation."

"A waking nightmare," I said. "He knew he was dying, knew he had been poisoned. That's why he made that cry."

"Very possibly," said Dr. Dap.

Edna must have cried out then, because Dr. Dap looked sharply at her. I swiveled around to see what she was saying. She was saying, "How horrible, how horrible to think of him, Don, sitting there, in his apartment, that lovely apartment, making those pills—to kill somebody with." I don't know what her voice sounded like, of course, but her face was curiously expressionless, masklike, and her green eyes were glassy.

Dr. Dap looked at her with sober sympathy. "Yes," he agreed, "it is horrible. Because this must have taken him quite a while to prepare, fixing the mold, getting the color just right, patiently, patiently working to trim and polish the finished product. Sixty of them, finally. Sixty little tablets. Endless patience." He shuddered.

"Monomania," I said, "an unfortunate by-product of his new self-image. Perfection in all things. Megalomania too. Whatever he was doing was important because he was doing it, Don Heemstra was doing it. That's why he couldn't believe me when I told him there was no file on him, that Gene wasn't doing a story on him. He couldn't believe he wasn't of primary importance. His scheme, his lousy little blackmailing plot was the whole universe to him. He didn't know that Gene was simply going to quit—when the time was ripe, that is."

"He seemed so nice, so gentle, so sweet," said Edna, still with the fixed stare. "And then I wanted to kill him." She was not looking at Dr. Dap, or at me, either. She was speaking to some abstract point of space in front of her. "I wanted to kill him. Even worse," she said, still staring straight ahead, "I wanted to shoot his thing off. I thought about shooting his thing off, and then putting bullet holes in his belly, his chest. I could see them, how they would look, the bullet holes. It was almost like I had already done it."

Dr. Dap reached out and put his hand over hers. "But you didn't do it. Remember that. You didn't do it. I suppose no one would have blamed you if you had. Indeed, you could have fixed an alibi. But you didn't do it."

Edna still did not look at him. "But I thought it," she said. "And it was almost like I had actually done it. I feel a lot as if I had actually done it—shot his thing off, and then killed him."

"But you didn't," Dr. Dap insisted, his kind face troubled.

His voice, apparently, was to Edna merely something that came out of the air, like a spirit message. She did not look at him or me. "But I feel as if I did—as if it happened. I can see it. I keep seeing it. I keep hearing him while he was stretched out there—talking to me softly, coaxing, soft and sweet, and then pleading, pleading and crying, and then raving—terrible, terrible things, and then screaming—'*Stop looking at me! Stop looking at me!*' He couldn't stand that I was looking at him. And he called me all kinds of names, horrible, horrible names, and curses. And all the time I was staring at him and thinking about shooting him—bullet after bullet . . ."

She paused and her shoulders shook. "Why," she asked, "did he rape me? Why did he have to go and rape me like that, when he could have—he could have . . ." Suddenly, she became aware of Dr. Dap and me. She blushed violently and turned her face away from both of us.

"Control, Edna," I said as softly as I could. "He needed control. It was part of the whole thing. He needed a kind of stillness in the center of things—a stillness like death—helplessness. He wanted people under control, helpless, bound, or dead." I noticed that she had withdrawn her hand from under Dr. Dap's. She kept her face turned away and wept inconsolably. Neither of us attempted to touch her again. Dr. Dap placed a box of tissues at the edge of the desk next to her.

A little pile of them grew in her lap, and then she was still, although she kept her eyes fixed on the floor. I said finally to Dr. Dap, "Have you gotten any further with that—what was it called?—bangutgut? You know, the nightmare deaths that Gene was working on?"

"Good heavens," said Dr. Dap. "You mustn't expect results on anything so tenuous this quickly. As I told you, it was pure speculation, conjecture on my part—merely something to look into. I have written to some old friends of mine in the Netherlands, and I wrote also to a very, very old party, nearly as ancient as myself, in Peking. I was there for a while, you know, during the Second World War, before I came to America. Naturally, I had to veil the questions somewhat in my letter. Governments seem to take an unseemly interest in these things.

"At any rate," he said, smiling, "I wouldn't sit up nights near a telephone waiting for results on a thing like this. It will probably be months before I get even a preliminary reply, and certainly years before all this is thrashed out. Meanwhile, I will keep looking into things on my own. There is a good deal of research being done, but no one seems to have reached a noteworthy conclusion."

I mused, "I wonder if Gene did."

"I would doubt that," said Dr. Dap. "His note on bangutgut showed which way he was heading, but I seriously doubt that he could have solved this by himself."

I stood up then. "I guess that's it," I said. I looked down at Edna, who seemed not to have noticed. "If you'll give me Gene's papers," I said to Dr. Dap, "I'll take them back to Mrs. Listing." He had the transcripts piled on his desk along with the other stuff. He handed the pile to me and I put it all in my briefcase. I looked again at Edna. "Edna?" I queried softly.

She stood up and bade farewell to Dr. Dap, but when I took her arm to usher her out, she drew it slowly away from me.

29

"I'm resigning," announced Edna.

"I don't blame you," I answered.

I was not surprised at Edna's decision. I'd been expecting it. What surprised me was that she chose a moment when someone else was in the office. I suppose it served as a buffer for her.

Evie had come into the office that morning—and not by accident. I had sent Evie a postcard asking her to come in, and she had dropped by on the pretext of settling her bill, the bill that had so outraged Edna. Now Edna toted it up perfunctorily and turned it over to Evie without a qualm. Evie examined it and wrote out a check. It was after Edna had received the check from Evie that she made her announcement.

I had coaxed Evie over because I had been terribly worried about Edna. She refused any professional counseling, but she moved about her life in a kind of glacial despair. Her smiles and gestures were mechanical. She did not seem to be able to bear my touching her, and she kept considerably more space between us than she had in the past.

So I said to her, "I don't blame you, but may I make a suggestion?" Her lips firmed up in a defense against any possible suggestion. "Why don't you just take a few months off—full pay. Take a trip. Stay home and read—anything. I'll get a temporary."

Although she had kept an unusual distance between

us in the office, neither could she bear to be completely alone in the office. When she arrived in the morning her face bore the telltale marks of sleepless nights.

"I don't want to travel," said Edna. "I don't want to stay home and read."

"Have you thought of anything you might possibly want?"

"I've been thinking I'll probably go back to Wilkes-Barre."

This shocked me into silence. Finally, I stammered, "You don't mean you'd give up your apartment!"

"Yes," said Edna. "The hell with it."

The shock reverberated in me. Edna had a very nice apartment at, of all places, Long Island City, only a few minutes' subway ride from Manhattan. The place was spacious, clean, airy, and rent controlled. It had been decorated slowly, carefully, and lovingly. It was a gem, a crown jewel, over which she had fought savagely as artists moved into the area and rents began to soar. So far, Edna had kept the landlord from the door and was prepared to keep him at bay well into the next century. I said, "I can't believe you'd give up a place like that. Give up your independence."

Edna said, "I hate it. I don't want to live there anymore."

Evie had been watching her. She said, "Has something changed in the neighborhood? The building?"

"No," said Edna. She had had me endorse the check, had made out a deposit slip, put it in the printed bank envelope, and set it in the mail basket. Now she sat down in the remaining chair facing Evie and me. "I can't stand being alone anymore," she said. "I hear noises at night, or even during the day. And I'm afraid. You can't live in New York if you're afraid."

Although the check was a sizable one, Evie was by no means a loser in the deal. Proof that Gene had been murdered (a confession, and a rather nutty one at that, from Heemstra, plus the evidence of the counterfeit pills) had invoked the double indemnity clause on Gene's insurance. There was also the matter of a sizable lawsuit against Execu-Trim, who in Evie's, as well as my own, opinion, should be put out of business. Evie said to her, "Don't just jump right out of your nest. Give things a little time to heal."

"I can't stay there," Edna repeated. "I can't stay in this office."

"I'll get a temporary to come in just to keep you company," I offered.

"Oh, it isn't just that."

"Heemstra's not coming back, you know," I said softly.

"Oh, it's not just him." Edna looked at me, and her green eyes filled. "It's you."

"Me!" I was self-righteously shocked. "What did I do?"

Evie cut in, saying, "I had a call from Basket yesterday."

"What?" My jaw was still hanging with injured innocence. Edna was looking into her lap. Evie repeated what she had said, and I realized that she had changed the subject purposely. I went along. "What the hell did he want?"

"Senator Marston wants to have lunch with me. Private-dining-room-style lunch. Should I go?"

"By all means. You can probably rack him up for a bundle. Make a deal for a lot of money. Stick to it. It's the only thing he understands."

"I don't want his money."

"Put it away for the kids." I thought about it for a moment. "But it's probably irrelevant, isn't it? I mean, the kids will get money from Gene's family, won't they?"

"Not necessarily," answered Evie. "Not unless there's some clause or codicil I don't know about. You're right. If I take some money from Marston, I can put it in trust for the kids."

I shook my head. "I still don't really understand Gene," I said. "It's all very well about his independence, but he was sort of robbing the kids, too, wasn't he?"

"It all depends," answered Evie with a soft look on her face. "He wasn't robbing them of himself."

Edna looked up from her lap. She said to me, "It's not anything you did."

"What?" I was caught off base again.

Edna repeated, "It's not anything you did. It's just what happened."

I said sadly, "Heestra made you hate all men? You can't live that way, Edna."

"No, no," said Edna. "What Don did was like covering me with slime. It makes me so I want to crawl out of my skin. But that's not it. I'm going back to Wilkes-Barre."

"No, you're not," said Evie. "You're coming home with me. I need somebody too."

"But what is it that happened?" I insisted.

Edna drew herself up in the chair and stared at me with a remote sadness, and then looked away again. She said into the air, "It's just that I got destroyed as a person. I mean, you were there with me in the dark when I was nothing more than a horrible smelly animal. And then we were out in the open in the daylight, and I was stark naked, and I didn't care. I didn't care then because I was sure I was going to die. That we were both going to die. But I care now. Now that we've lived. I care now that you've seen me the way no man should see me, running naked like an animal, like I wasn't a human being at all. How could you think of me as anything except an animal?" She began to weep.

I said, "For Christ's sake, Edna. You saw me naked, too, didn't you? Do you think I'm proud of it? Helpless? Trapped? Do you think I wasn't humiliated?"

"People shouldn't see each other like that," said Edna, weeping.

"What is it that either one of you think you saw?" interrupted Evie. "Both of you naked, humiliated. What is it that either of you was looking at except a human being?"

30

Edna did go to Wilkes-Barre—and stayed there for two weeks.

I learned of Edna's return to New York through a laboriously typed memo put on my desk by the girl from the temporary service. The memo said:

Ms. Listening callyou up and she sAYED that Enna Permis have cime back into town and is going sty with Ms. Listening. Ms. Listening sayed plase dont call her up or visit or anything. She sayed Enna Permis will call you in her own good time.

Sincerely yours,
Marsha

Dear, sweet Marsha: so terribly sincere. So temporary. So welcome in departure.

My next hint of Edna's disposition came a week later in the form of another memo dropped on my desk by the succeeding temporary "girl."

Some broad with a name like Listerine called up about somebody named Emma Purviance (the old movie star?) She's coming over here this afternoon—Listerine, I mean, not the old movie star. Do you want to hide or what?

Kevin

Yes, Kevin really is a girl—biologically a girl—with a very authoritative bosom. The trouble is that the bosom is clad in jungle fatigues—*cams* I think they're called at the local army and navy store. Her desk (Edna's desk) was stacked with issues of *Soldier of Fortune* magazines, another periodical called *Assault Weapons*, and still another called *Exotic Weapons*. Kevin had bucked for this job over at the agency and, terrified, they'd let her have it. After she greeted my astounded face with a grip that welded several of my fingers together, she informed me that she had been looking for an action-oriented job, by which she meant, presumably, one that produced oceans of blood. She was disappointed that my walls were not hung with an armory of MAC 10s, Uzis, hand grenades, and other murderous paraphernalia. Apparently these things come in Cracker Jack boxes now. Yes. Her name really is Kevin—Kevin McElroy. She made me yearn for the days when "cam," as applied to girls, meant camisoles instead of camouflage. She lent sweetness only to the blessed word *temporary*.

At lunchtime I sent Kevin back home to her bunker for the day so as to spare Evie's sensibilities.

Evie's sensibilities were not all that much in evidence when she appeared at my office door. She was dressed better than I had ever seen her dressed before—in a gray suit of the kind that is advertised for job-hunting. It turned out, however, that she was not job-hunting at all. She was merely dressed for the street, for shopping. Her face, too, was more carefully made up than I had been used to. The makeup almost managed to hide the marks and lines of grief and strain. Her hair, which had had the occasional streak of gray, now had only the occasional streak of brown. I kissed her on the cheek and sat her down in the only comfortable chair in the office—mine. We sat and stared at one another wordlessly for a short interval. I saw what the suit and the careful makeup were all about. Evie was being very, very careful not to fall into a depression. Good girl. I supposed that at this moment her apartment was cleaner and neater than it had ever been. She was right to do so. But, still, the struggle showed.

Nicky and Claire were fine, she informed me—well, if not fine, at least as well as could be expected, at least not moping, at least not wildly rebellious or sullenly acquiescent. Life, it seemed, simply went on.

Not entirely without incident, however. She had gone, after all, to the much heralded private-dining-room lunch with Marston. (Had the suit been bought for that gala event? I wondered.) And Marston, what was he like?

"Very gallant," said Evie. "So full of old-world courtesy and easy charm that you would not immediately guess that he is a miserable old son of a bitch."

"The charm," I asked her, "did it break down? Did he reveal his true colors, so to speak?"

"Only at the end," she answered. "And then not really. It wasn't all that dramatic."

"Were you allowed to smoke? In his presence? In the private dining room and all?"

"Oh, God, yes. I must have done away with a whole pack of cigarettes in the afternoon. And Senator Marston, by the way, smokes excellent Havana cigars. He lit up a big one over the brandy."

"So it was all brandy and cigars, was it?"

"Well, sort of. He asked me right away, I mean as soon as we were seated, if I'd brought the file with me, and I assured him I had. He pretty much relaxed after that, once he knew I had it with me. And we had lunch. A very good, very expensive lunch. It was during the brandy and cigars that we started the deal, or at least what he thought was a deal."

"And it wasn't? You didn't make a deal with him?"

"Not the one that he was counting on. No."

"What happened?"

"Once I'd told him I had the file with me, I saw that his eyes kept darting around as if the file was some immense portfolio that should be in a briefcase. After he'd lighted up his cigar, he made me a straight offer. He said he'd give me five thousand dollars in cash, here and now, right over the table for it. I'm afraid I laughed in his face."

"Good for you."

"The price ascended in fives, although he made it clear that he wasn't carrying that much in cash. When he got up to twenty-five thousand he stopped and declared he'd have to see the file before he went any farther. I told him, 'You don't have to go any farther.' "

"You settled for twenty-five? That's not bad."

"I settled for zero," said Evie.

I stared at her.

"Well"—she clasped her hands defensively on her knees in the big leather chair—"I think it was the brandy and cigars that did it. Here was this congressman who was at heart a drug pusher puffing away on his fat cigar and getting redder and redder in the face as the price went up. It happens to be a terrible defect in my character that I cannot loathe somebody without also pitying him. I don't ask you to understand that."

I shook my head wordlessly.

"And as it went on, the more I pitied him, the more I loathed him. There's that too. And finally I saw that if I really made a deal with him for whatever amount of money I would be, figuratively, in bed with him. There would be complicity. We would be partners in crime. Blackmail is a crime too. And what I was doing was blackmailing a drug dealer. Did I want the money that much? Not really. Did I want it for my children that much? Not really. So what was the point of all of it? It was to make a deal, a deal where I would drive the hardest bargain I could and he would come away feeling he'd got value for money. It would be a kind of satisfaction for us both. The sexual connotations are unmistakable. I didn't want it. I didn't really need it that much. If I did, things might have been different.

"So I took it out of my purse where it had been folded, the file, and I handed it to him and said, 'Let's stop all this nonsense. It disgusts me. Here. You can have it, and you're welcome to it.'

"He was terribly unhappy. First, he wouldn't believe that this was all of it. But after I'd convinced him that it was, he was still unhappy because while he had the file he didn't have me. There was no complicity. There was no deal, no sale. Since he hadn't bought it, he didn't really own it. He was terribly dissatisfied, but I felt much better about the whole thing. I felt I was really free of the nightmare file, and that was of enormous value to me."

I didn't really know what to reply to all this. It didn't seem that my judgment was called for. I did, however, become acutely aware of the hard oak client's chair I was sitting in, and this led me to wonder how I ever managed to keep any clients at all. I said to Evie, "If you'll open the top drawer of my desk you'll find a pack of Luckies. Will you give me one?"

I took a cigarette from the pack she'd tossed across the desk, lighted it, stood up, and arched my back. I contented myself with leaning against the wall by the door. "Edna," I said to Evie, "how is she?"

"Well, of course," began Evie, leaning back in the big swivel chair and looking at me very soberly, "that's why I came here. About Edna."

"Is she all right?"

"Physically, you mean? Yes. She's fine."

"I'm glad to hear it," I answered. "But I meant more than that, of course."

"More than that is not so easy to explain."

"I was hoping," I said, "that the trip to Wilkes-Barre might have done her some good."

"Yes and no," said Evie. She rummaged in her purse and found a pack of lengthy, low-tar, feminine cigarettes. She lighted one of them with Gene's small gold lighter before I could get across the room with my Zippo. She blew a cloud of smoke into the air and said, "From what Edna has told me—and she is not all that forthcoming—she went back to Wilkes-Barre to test the waters. When people are away, you know, they tend to idealize their families. Apparently the confrontation for Edna after all this time was something of a shock. I think she wanted to talk to her mother about what had happened, but after a couple of days of soaking up the general atmosphere she sensed that it was not something she could very easily discuss. The reigning philosophy seemed to be that women who get raped have pretty much gotten what they deserved. Decent women live in small white houses in Wilkes-Barre and join the Gold Star Mothers' Bowling League. She called me up from her family's place and asked me if the offer to stay at our apartment was still open. It was a terribly secretive call on her part—after midnight. Fortunately, I hadn't yet gone to bed. Of course, I welcomed her with open arms. She's a fine girl, and even as moody and miserable as she is, she's a joy to have around."

"Yes, she is," I agreed morosely. "Then, she's given up her apartment, has she?"

"No," said Evie. "She hasn't."

I heaved a huge sigh of relief.

"She goes over there every few days—Nick goes with her—to pick up her mail, including the salary checks you've sent her, and to look things over. She's very good for Nick. He's hopelessly in love with her, of course. Nick has some reestablishing to do himself, and Edna's been a tremendous help."

"Evie," I broke in. "Is she going to come back?"

"Back here?" Evie considered it. "It's asking a hell of a lot of her, don't you think?" There was a long pause while both of us thought about it. "There's no way I can tell you," said Evie, not unsympathetically. "All I can say is that when she has come to terms with what happened in that horrible place she'll be able to come to terms with you."

I went through three more temporaries. One was a captive princess, one was a religious fanatic, and one was the reincarnation of Mother Bloor. Finally, there arrived a paragon of the secretary's art. She was a divorced woman in her early forties whose boss had married her when she was very young and then dumped her for a stewardess. It took her about a week to get my correspondence in order, a little longer to get my finances straight. In a month's time she had the joint running like the well-known well-oiled machine. It seemed that I had settled down to operating a business more solid and more efficient than I ever had before.

I can't really see the front door from my share of the office, and, of course, I don't hear any introductory buzzing or irritable raps. But from my desk I saw the shadow of the door swinging open and then the shadow of a person quite obviously feminine against the wall. There seemed to be a lengthy colloquy while the door remained open. Then the shadow stepped inside—I wasn't expecting any visitors that day—and the shadow of the door swung shut. The shadow crossed the room and materialized at the door to my office.

"Hello," said Edna. "May I come in?"